Ace Books by Greg Cox
(Based on DC Comics Series)

INFINITE CRISIS
52
COUNTDOWN
FINAL CRISIS

52

GREG COX

BASED ON THE DC COMICS SERIES

ACE BOOKS, NEW YORK

THE BERKLEY PUBLISHING GROUP
Published by the Penguin Group
Penguin Group (USA) Inc.
375 Hudson Street, New York, New York 10014, USA
Penguin Group (Canada), 90 Eglinton Avenue East, Suite 700, Toronto, Ontario M4P 2Y3, Canada
(a division of Pearson Penguin Canada Inc.)
Penguin Books Ltd., 80 Strand, London WC2R 0RL, England
Penguin Group Ireland, 25 St. Stephen's Green, Dublin 2, Ireland (a division of Penguin Books Ltd.)
Penguin Group (Australia), 250 Camberwell Road, Camberwell, Victoria 3124, Australia
(a division of Pearson Australia Group Pty. Ltd.)
Penguin Books India Pvt. Ltd., 11 Community Centre, Panchsheel Park, New Delhi—110 017, India
Penguin Group (NZ), 67 Apollo Drive, Rosedale, North Shore 0632, New Zealand
(a division of Pearson New Zealand Ltd.)
Penguin Books (South Africa) (Pty.) Ltd., 24 Sturdee Avenue, Rosebank, Johannesburg 2196,
South Africa

Penguin Books Ltd., Registered Offices: 80 Strand, London WC2R 0RL, England

This is a work of fiction. Names, characters, places, and incidents either are the product of the author's imagination or are used fictitiously, and any resemblance to actual persons, living or dead, business establishments, events, or locales is entirely coincidental. The publisher does not have any control over and does not assume any responsibility for author or third-party websites or their content.

52

An Ace Book / published by arrangement with DC Comics

PRINTING HISTORY
Ace trade paperback edition / July 2007
Ace mass-market edition / February 2011

Copyright © 2007 by DC Comics.
52 and all related names, characters, and elements are trademarks of DC Comics © 2011. All rights reserved.
Cover art by JG Jones and Alex Sinclair.
Cover design by Georg Brewer.
Interior text design by Tiffany Estreicher.

ISBN: 978-0-441-01984-7

ACE
Ace Books are published by The Berkley Publishing Group,
a division of Penguin Group (USA) Inc.,
375 Hudson Street, New York, New York 10014.
ACE and the "A" design are trademarks of Penguin Group (USA) Inc.

Visit DC Comics online at www.dccomics.com or at keyword DC Comics on America Online.

PRINTED IN THE UNITED STATES OF AMERICA

10 9 8 7 6 5 4 3 2 1

ACKNOWLEDGMENTS

FIRST, a confession: in order to boil down a *fifty-two*-issue comic book series into one cohesive novel, I had to be merciless when it came to cutting out characters and subplots. I hope no one will be offended if their favorite scenes and heroes didn't make it into the novel; those missing elements are still alive and well in the original comic books that served as the basis for this book. And if you haven't read *52* in comic book form yet, you owe it to yourself to check it out. Trust me, there's a lot more where this came from.

Needless to say, I have to thank all the talented writers, artists, and editors who worked on the original comics, including Geoff Johns, Grant Morrison, Greg Rucka, Mark Waid, Keith Giffen, JG Jones, Alex Sinclair, Stephen Wacker, Michael Siglain, Harvey Richards, Jann Jones, and Jeanine Schaefer. They gave me a wealth of material to crib from, as well as let me pick their brains regarding upcoming issues.

I also have to thank my editors, John Morgan at DC Comics and Ginjer Buchanan at Ace Books, for working closely with me on this project. And my agents, Russell Galen and Ann Behar, for handling the legal arrangements.

52 (the comic book) attracted an extraordinary amount of attention from the fan community, and I took full advantage of the many comprehensive reviews and analyses of the series at such websites as absorbascon.blogspot.com, wizarduniverse .com, newsarama.com, comicsbulletin.com, wikipedia.org, and 52-pickup.blogspot.com. These sites were particularly useful when it came to elucidating various esoteric bits of DC Comics lore ("So who are all those guys at the mob summit anyway?").

I also need to thank my parents for letting me borrow their computer for a time, as well as Captain Blue Hen Comics in Newark, Delaware, and Action City Comics in Federal Way, Washington, for keeping me well supplied in comics and graphic novels.

Finally, as always, I counted on the support of Karen, Alex, Church, Henry, Sophie, and Lyla. The house, and my life, wouldn't be the same without them.

This novel was adapted from the *52* comic series, originally published in fifty-two weekly issues by DC Comics, from May 2006 to May 2007. The series was created by the following people:

EDITORS
Michael Siglain
Stephen Wacker

**ASSISTANT &
ASSOCIATE EDITORS**
Jann Jones
Harvey Richards
Jeanine Schaeffer

WRITERS
Geoff Johns
Grant Morrison
Greg Rucka
Mark Waid

COVER ARTISTS
JG Jones
Alex Sinclair

ART BREAKDOWNS
Keith Giffen

PENCILLERS
Eddy Barrows
Chris Batista
Joe Bennett
Giuseppe Camuncoli
Tom Derenick
Dale Eaglesham
Jamal Igle
Phil Jimenez
Drew Johnson
Justiniano
Ken Lashley
Mike McKone
Shawn Moll
Todd Nauck
Patrick Olliffe
Joe Prado
Darick Robertson
Andy Smith

INKERS
Marlo Alquiza
Mariah Benes
Keith Champagne
Drew Geraci
Dan Green
Jack Jadson
Ruy Jose
Dan Jurgens
Andy Lanning
Jay Leisten
Dave Meikis
Nelson
Tom Nguyen
Jimmy Palmiotti
Rodney Ramos
Norm Rapmund
Darick Robertson
Prentis Rollins
Lorenzo Ruggiero
Ray Snyder
Rob Stull
Art Thibert
Walden Wong

PROLOGUE.

CRISIS: AFTERMATH
Tears, Tributes, and Unanswered Questions
by Lois Lane
Daily Planet

METROPOLIS—Twenty-four hours after the Crisis that nearly tore this city, and many others, apart, the rebuilding has begun. But many questions remain unresolved about the actual nature of the catastrophe, as well as what happens next.

What is known definitely is that, after several days of seemingly random attacks and disasters, the so-called "Infinite Crisis" culminated in a titanic battle between the Secret Society of Super-Villains and nearly every one of Earth's costumed defenders. Rex Mason, better known as Metamorpho the Element Man, recalls: "The short of it is that, after years of hitting and running, all the super-villains—and I mean *all* of them—teamed up and declared all-out war on the white hats. Picked us off in twos and threes before mounting an assault the likes of which, by all rights, should have ripped this planet in half."

The resulting battle left much of Metropolis in ruins and cost the lives of many heroes, including Superboy, the Freedom Fighters, a number of former Teen Titans, and several others. A memorial service is scheduled to take place in Centennial Park at 4:30 P.M. Saturday. The Justice League of America and many other surviving heroes are expected to attend.

Yet as the world breathes a collective sigh of relief and slowly gets back to normal, one question remains on the lips of many concerned citizens: Where are Superman, Batman, and Wonder Woman?

The three heroes, perhaps the most iconic of all, were last seen leading the battle against the Society, but have not been glimpsed since. In the absence of any official explanation, speculation is rampant that "the Big Three" are injured, dead, or perhaps just taking some time off after saving the entire planet once more. Rumors and unconfirmed sightings abound.

Those close to the missing heroes are not worried, however. An anonymous (but highly reliable) source points out that many less famous heroes, including various members of the Justice League, the original Justice Society, and the Teen Titans, are ready to pick up the slack until their celebrated comrades return. "Things are in good hands," the source insists.

This much is certain: A world without Superman, Batman, and Wonder Woman is not necessarily a world without heroes.

Lois read the article one more time, ran it through the spell-checker, then fired it off to Perry White for his approval. *Not a bad piece,* she thought, *if I do say so myself.* Hopefully, it would serve to reassure a worried public and cut down on the wild rumors—just as Clark intended.

Sitting at her desk in the *Planet* bullpen, she wondered what her readers would think if they knew that her anonymous source was none other than Superman himself. Part of her wished she could reveal the full story behind the Man of Steel's absence, but she and Clark had both agreed it would not be wise to publicize the fact that he had temporarily lost his powers in the wake of the Crisis. That would be like waving a red flag in front of Intergang and Superman's other enemies. *Best to keep that info to ourselves.*

Likewise, she had to keep quiet about what was going on

with Batman and Wonder Woman these days. Only a handful of people knew that Batman, whose suspicious and paranoid nature had helped precipitate the Crisis, had decided that he needed to retrain himself from the ground up in order to achieve a healthier mental balance; he was also concentrating on rebuilding his strained relationship with his two young protégés, Nightwing and Robin. Lois hoped that Bruce Wayne succeeded in getting his head on straight; although Superman considered Batman a friend, she had never quite warmed to the Dark Knight, who had always struck her as somewhat grim and aloof. Then again, all heroes suffered in comparison to Superman, at least as far as she was concerned.

He's my husband, she thought. *I'm entitled to be biased.*

Wonder Woman was also taking a mental health break. After going through a number of traumatic events during the Crisis, including the loss of her native Paradise Island, Diana was attempting to get back in touch with her humanity by living as a mortal woman for a time. Lois wondered how the formidable Amazon princess was coping with her new secret identity. Rumor had it she had even taken to wearing glasses like Clark!

And why not? Lois thought. *Lord knows those glasses fooled me for years.*

Lois called up her article and read the last couple paragraphs again. "Things are in good hands," Clark had insisted, yet, if she was honest with herself, Lois had to admit that his forced sabbatical gave her the occasional flicker of anxiety. Sure, there were plenty of other heroes out there, but could anyone really replace Superman? Especially with the Flash and Captain Marvel and assorted other heroes also out of commission?

Deep down inside, Lois wasn't so sure. . . .

WEEK 1.

METROPOLIS.

IT was a sunny spring day in the City of Tomorrow. Uptown in a fashionable shopping district, people were taking advantage of their lunch breaks to enjoy the beautiful weather. A sidewalk hot dog stand was doing brisk business, while other citizens lunched at outdoor cafes. Schuster Avenue was crowded with buses, taxis, and private vehicles. Horns honked impatiently every time the lights changed. Speeding bicycle messengers risked life and limb to deliver their parcels in record time. Pedestrians window-shopped as they went about their afternoons. Pet owners walked their dogs. An elevated monorail zipped by overhead. A blue sky showed above the skyscrapers.

"LOOK! UP IN THE SKY!"

An amplified electronic voice, booming from high above the avenue, demanded attention. Pedestrians lifted their heads, while curious drivers stuck their heads out of the windows of their cars to see where the voice was coming from. Tourists and natives alike stared at the sky, hoping to catch a glimpse of Metropolis's most famous citizen. Eager eyes searched for a flapping red cape or bright red S. Was Superman back in action?

But instead of the Man of Steel, someone else was soaring through the sky. An heroic figure in a bright blue and gold uniform flew (sans cape) above the busy street. Translucent yellow goggles partially concealed the man's face, beneath a head of wavy blond hair. A brilliant white smile gleamed in the sunlight. A handful of corporate logos adorned his uniform, rather in the manner of a NASCAR driver. His well-toned arms held a dazed super-villain high above his head. Mammoth, of the Fearsome Five, to be exact. A shiny golden ovoid, about the size of a football, hovered in the air nearby.

"BOOSTER GOLD, LADIES AND GENTLEMEN!" the sphere announced like a carnival barker. "HE'S FROM THE FUTURE!" The robot's breezy tone belied the electronic nature of its voice. "HOW COOL IS THAT?" He zipped about in the sky, taking care to maintain a safe distance from the villain's thrashing limbs. "AND EVEN THOUGH BOOSTER'S WAY TOO MODEST TO SAY IT, I'M NOT ASHAMED TO SPEAK UP AND TELL YOU THAT THIS MAN IS THE FRESH NEW FACE OF SUPER-HEROICS."

You tell them, Skeets, Booster thought. *Who needs a press agent when I have my own cybernetic sidekick hyping me full-time?*

"What the hell is all this, ya flamin' gala?" Mammoth griped in a thick Australian accent. A red-haired bruiser in a studded black costume, the superpowered strongman had frequently clashed with Superman in the past. His gruff voice held both anger and confusion as Booster carried him even higher into the air. "What are ya pickin' on me for? I didn't even know I was gonna nick those diamonds 'til I did it. Spur o' the moment!" Hundreds of feet below, an upscale jewelry shop needed a new front window. "How'd ya get up on me so quick?"

"Call it an inside tip," Booster said with a smirk, enjoying a private joke. *This jerk's history . . . in more ways than one.*

Skeets continued to work the crowd: "BOYS, GIRLS, AND POTENTIAL CORPORATE SPONSORS! IF THE DAY NEEDS SAVING, BOOSTER'S YOUR GUY!" Not for the first time, Booster was glad that he had "borrowed" the levitating robot from that museum before traveling backward in time to this primitive era. Skeets had a real talent for promotion, among many other useful abilities. "IN AN UNCERTAIN WORLD, IT'S GOOD TO KNOW THERE ARE STILL SOME THINGS YOU CAN ALWAYS RELY ON."

Twenty-fifth-century technology, built into the fabric of his uniform, enhanced Booster's strength while also providing him with a protective force field. Plus, he could fly.

Unlike Mammoth.

Taking full advantage of the suit's capabilities, Booster hurled the yowling villain down at an empty intersection below. Mammoth smashed like a meteor into the asphalt, giving the transportation department a massive new pothole to worry about. A cloud of powdered pavement rose above the newly formed crater before settling back down onto the unconscious brute. The nearest civilians fled the intersection in a panic, but the majority of the onlookers reacted with cheers and applause. Dozens of digital cameras and cell phones captured the scene for posterity. Admiring eyes gazed upward at the triumphant hero. Basking in the attention, Booster felt like Superman himself.

This is more like it! he thought. Relocating to the past to become an old-fashioned super hero was the smartest thing he had ever done. Here in the twenty-first century, he wasn't Michael Jon Carter, disgraced professional athlete, anymore. He was Booster Gold, superpowered idol and celebrity. And soon to be one of history's most famous heroes. *Not to mention one of the richest . . .*

TV news vans were already arriving on the scene, so Booster began to dramatically descend toward the crater below. Mammoth was flat on his back amidst the pulverized blacktop, covered by a layer of dust and debris. A groan escaped the big lummox's lips. He wasn't going to be giving anyone a hard time anytime soon.

Skeets zipped over and whispered in Booster's ear. "ѕɪʀ—"

"I see it," Booster assured the robot. He had already spotted the adorable little girl standing near the front of the crowd below. No more than five years old maybe, the moppet was sporting a Wonder Woman T-shirt, star-spangled shorts, and a worried expression. A plastic tiara crowned the girl's curly red hair. "Photo op deluxe."

The kid's eyes grew wide as he dropped smartly to earth

before her. Kneeling, he flashed a smile at the girl (and the cameras) and mussed her hair. "Hey there, little lady. What's up?"

"My brother said Wonder Woman was dead," the child said, fighting back tears. Booster belatedly noticed an eight-year-old boy standing behind the girl, looking a tad sheepish. A Batman T-shirt suggested that he preferred the Dark Knight to the Amazon princess. "He said she was gone and she's never coming back."

"Is that right?" Booster looked sternly at the brother, while making a mental note to look into licensing his own line of T-shirts and plastic goggles. "Well, I've seen the future and I happen to know that Wonder Woman's fine. They're all fine." He rose to his feet. "Now step aside, kids."

A single bound carried him to the center of the crater, where he planted a foot atop Mammoth's beefy chest, like a big game hunter posing with a trophy. Digital cameras whirred all around him. The TV news crews shoved their way through the crowd to get live footage of Booster's triumph. With any luck, he'd be the top story on the evening news as well.

"TERRIFIC TAKEDOWN, SIR!" Skeets congratulated him, loud enough for all to hear. "YOU'RE A REAL PRO."

"Thank Mammoth here," Booster quipped. "He's the one who kept it from being a dull afternoon." He yawned theatrically. "Nothing to see here, folks. Just doing my job." He casually produced a can of Soder Cola from a pouch on his costume, making sure that the label was facing the cameras. "Now, if you'll just excuse me, sometimes even super heroes get thirsty."

Let's hear it for product placement. He drained the can in one gulp, then lobbed it into a curbside wastebasket. Sirens heralded the arrival of the Metropolis Special Crimes Unit, showing up to take Mammoth into custody. Booster was more than happy to let the S.C.U. handle the cleanup and paperwork; why waste his time on such less-than-glamorous duties? Waving at the cheering crowd, he took off into the sky. Skeets cruised alongside him.

"Did you see the look on Mammoth's face when I blitzed

him?" Booster crowed to the robot. Sometimes his old quarter-back skills came in handy. "I knew what he was going to pull before he did!"

"TECHNICALLY, SIR," Skeets pointed out, **"I'M THE ONE HOLDING ALL THE HISTORICAL DATA FROM THIS ERA."** Unlike Booster, the robot's shiny metallic housing boasted no corporate logos or trademarks. A panel of optical sensors served as his face. Tiny propulsion units orbited the sphere. **"I CAN'T EVEN GET YOU TO READ THE FILES."**

"And that's why we make such a good team." The wind whipped through Booster's blond hair as he soared above the city. "A couple of refugees from the twenty-fifth century come back to the Heroic Age, armed only with future weaponry, charm . . . and every news headline for the next half millennium."

He glanced back over his shoulder. "I wish I could have told that little girl back there what tomorrow is. My big day." He grinned in anticipation. "I may have flunked twenty-first-century history—"

"AMONG YOUR MANY ACCOMPLISHMENTS, SIR."

"But even I know that tomorrow is *the* defining moment of the new century, and I'm gonna be a part of it. The speech on Hope and Unity that Superman delivers will be taught in civics classes for the next five hundred years. And that photo of him, Batman, and Wonder Woman as they announce the new-and-improved Justice League? Jimmy Olsen gets a Howitzer for it."

"PULITZER, SIR."

"Whatever." Booster was not going to let the robot's nit-picking kill his buzz. "The dawn of this century's JLA. And they're going to ask me to join, aren't they?"

And why shouldn't they? he thought. His knowledge of future events had proven incredibly useful to Batman and the others during the recent Crisis. *The good guys couldn't have won without me.*

"C'mon, you can tell me," he urged the robot.

"I ALREADY HAVE, SIR."

"So tell me again. Make me smile." He couldn't hear about his destined good fortune enough. "Skeets, being a member of the greatest Justice League ever . . . Let's work out how much my sponsors will pay for *that* kind of placement!"

"FIRST THINGS FIRST, SIR," Skeets said. "MY REC-ORDS SHOW THAT THERE IS A SHIPYARD DISASTER ACROSS TOWN THAT YOU'RE DUE TO STOP IN EX-ACTLY SEVEN MINUTES." Booster veered west toward the harbor. "HEROES MUST BE PUNCTUAL . . . IF NOTH-ING ELSE."

They jetted past an enormous billboard that showed a smiling Booster holding up a frosty bottle of Lit Beer. The Lit logo was emblazoned on the upper right corner of his tunic, across from the fruity trademark of The Banana Co.; Soder Cola was advertised on his left shoulder, but there was still plenty of room on his uniform for even more corporate sponsors. The various logos were momentarily blurred by speed as Booster and Skeets rushed to star in yet another heroic headline.

The future looked bright.

GOTHAM CITY.

THE name of the tavern was 52 Pickup. Renee Montoya had decided it was her favorite bar. At least until tomorrow night.

Finding the right watering hole was tricky these days. Cop bars were out because she wasn't on the job anymore. The last thing she needed was the scornful or, worse, pitying glances of her former colleagues in the Gotham City Police Department. She could too easily imagine them whispering about her when they thought she wasn't listening. "See Montoya over there. Used to be a pretty good detective once upon a time, before her partner got killed and her life went into the toilet."

Screw that, she thought.

The gay bars were no good either. She might run into Daria, and no way was she ready for that just yet. It had only been three months since her ex had moved out, not that Renee blamed her. *Not after the way I messed things up.*

52 Pickup would have to do for now. Dim lighting helped to hide the cigarette burns on the bar counter and the scuffed tile floor. A neon sign advertised Lit Beer. A pool table and dartboard offered potential amusements to the largely blue-collar clientele. Yuppies and singles-bar habitués were mercifully absent; this was a place for serious drinkers who just wanted to get plastered as quickly and inexpensively as possible. The smoky atmosphere smelled of tobacco. A jukebox sat neglected in one corner, an Out of Order sign taped to its unlit exterior. Spilled drinks and stale beer nuts littered the floor. Let's face it: The place was a dive, but the booze was cold and nobody cared who she used to be.

Works for me, she thought.

Renee sat at the bar. An Hispanic woman in her thirties, she had on a black leather jacket, like the one Al Pacino wore in *Serpico,* a red T-shirt, and jeans. Her dark brown hair was tied up in the back. An empty bottle of tequila sat on the counter in front of her, next to an overflowing ashtray. She had a glass in one hand and a cigarette in the other. Smoking in public places was technically illegal in Gotham, but nobody in the tavern seemed too worried about that. The G.C.P.D. usually had bigger things to worry about . . . and so did the Bat.

If he was still alive.

Seated to her left, a drunk white dude was going on about the insanity that had passed for current events lately. "Listen," he said to no one in particular. A cheap vinyl jacket proclaimed his allegiance to the Gotham Wildcats. "I'm a Gothamite born and bred. I've seen it all, right? Earthquakes, plagues, and poison in the reservoir." Renee wasn't sure, but she thought his name was Kevin. "And I swear, even I thought it was the end of the world last night."

"It was," Montoya muttered. She lit herself a fresh cigarette.

"What, you find yourself with an empty bottle?" the bartender quipped.

"Funny guy," she replied. He sure had her pegged already. She waved the tequila bottle in his face. The last few drops sloshed around the worm. "Keep 'em coming."

The bartender, a stocky guy with bushy sideburns and a receding hairline, hesitated. "Uh, you might want to slow down there."

"Or you could pour faster." She shrugged her shoulders. *If I wanted somebody to keep me from drinking too much, I would have never driven Daria away. . . .*

The drunk dude (Kevin?) laughed at her suggestion. "That's a good one!" He clinked his own glass against hers. Bleary eyes looked her over. "I like your style."

Was this bozo actually hitting on her? Boy, was he ever barking up the wrong tree.

"So, you hear about this big memorial service in Metropolis this weekend?" he persisted, slurring his words. "If the roads are open . . . you wanna, y'know, go?"

A memorial service. The humor in the situation evaporated as Renee suddenly remembered standing over the grave of her partner. Detective Crispus Allen had been a good cop and a good friend. The fact that his killer was still walking the streets made the tequila in her mouth taste like turpentine.

"No, thanks," she mumbled, staring bleakly into her cup. She massaged her forehead in anticipation of the hangover to come. "I've had my share of funerals lately. . . ."

SHIRUTA.

BLACK Adam seldom allowed his feet to touch the ground. He was above that.

At the moment, he hovered over forty feet in the air above the capital city of his nation, the proud Middle Eastern kingdom of Kahndaq. A powerfully built Arab man, he wore a tight black uniform that contrasted sharply with his golden boots, belt, and wristbands. Sleek black hair met in a widow's peak above his brows. The golden thunderbolt emblazoned upon his chest matched that worn by Captain Marvel. His godlike powers, given to him millennia ago by the wizard Shazam, matched Marvel's as well, making him one of Earth's mightiest mortals. He had been Shazam's original champion, before he had rebelled against the wizard's foolish restrictions. It was then that Mighty Adam had first become known as Black Adam. Confident in his own righteousness, he bore the cognomen with pride.

So let it be written, he thought. *And may the world tremble.*

The people of Kahndaq—his people—thronged the sprawling courtyard below. By the thousands they filled the open plaza before the magnificent palace that Black Adam had inherited when he had deposed and executed the despot who had formerly ruled this land. The pellucid waters of a reflecting pool mirrored the palace's graceful domes and arches. Mosaic tiles, adorning almost every centimeter of the palace, created elaborate geometric designs. The Kahndaqi flag flapped triumphantly atop golden spires. The flag displayed three interlocking golden pyramids against a black background. The national anthem played over loudspeakers.

Black Adam's heart swelled with patriotism. He had been born in Kahndaq, over three thousand years ago. Indeed, the capital city was named after his beloved wife, lost to him so many lonely centuries ago, and the three triangles on the flag represented the immortal souls of Shiruta and his two sons, Gon and Hurut. The brutal death of Shiruta and his family had first taught him that evil had to be rooted out swiftly and severely. Recent events had only reinforced that painful lesson.

With a wave of his hand, he ordered the music silenced. His people looked up at him expectantly. Like the rest of the world, they had suffered much during the Crisis, but Kahndaq endured, in no small part because of the decisive role Black Adam had played in the final battle. He had fought beside Superman and the other heroes in Metropolis, laying waste to the treacherous Secret Society of Super-Villains. Thanks to him, several villains would no longer trouble the world.

Which was as it should be.

"Friends and countrymen," he addressed the crowd in Arabic. His deep voice required no artificial amplification. "In my attempt to protect our homeland, I turned my back on the rest of the world. And we were all the worse for it." Indeed, the entire planet had been stricken by catastrophic storms and earthquakes due to one madman's attempt to remake the universe. "I witnessed the true evil that lives within so many, and I realized that Kahndaq must teach the rest of the world how to deal with that evil. Ours is a glorious mission. I will be your ambassador of justice, and I shall lead the world by example." He crossed his arms atop his chest. "May the gods be with us . . . because they will not stand a chance against us."

The crowd cheered enthusiastically, save for one dissenting voice in the middle of the mob. The man's angry words were all but lost in the deafening uproar, but Black Adam's keen senses detected the disturbance at once. His dark eyes zoomed in on the insolent one.

"You are no messenger, Black Adam!" the man shouted, shaking his fist. The madness of the true fanatic gleamed in his wild eyes. "You and all of Kahndaq are heretics poisoned by lies." He yanked open his worn khaki jacket, exposing a belt of crude explosives strapped to his waist. "My people reject your wis—"

Perfect, Black Adam thought. *I could not have asked for a better example.*

With the speed of Heru, known to the infidels as Horus, he dived down and effortlessly plucked the would-be suicide bomber from the crowd. He yanked the explosive belt from the man's body and hurled it into the sky, where the fiendish device detonated harmlessly over twenty thousand feet above the palace. The explosion was barely visible to the crowd below.

"—dom," the bomber gulped, as he suddenly found himself held aloft above the gaping mob. Black Adam showed him more mercy than he deserved.

He ripped the man's right arm from its socket.

The severed limb splashed down into the reflecting pool,

turning the azure waters crimson. Bright arterial blood spurted from the bomber's shoulder. He shrieked in agony.

The West had its own heroes, of course, such as the so-called Justice League, but they too often lacked the will to do what must be done. Their sentimental and juvenile "morality" rendered them unfit to truly protect the world from the dangers ahead. Black Adam did not intend to make the same mistake.

"You have *three* more chances," he informed the prisoner, "to tell me who sent you."

FAWCETT CITY.

DR. Thaddeus Bodog Sivana watched Black Adam dismember the terrorist on the flickering screen of a modified RCA television set. The archetypal mad scientist, he peered at the TV through the thick, Coke-bottle lenses of his glasses. Acid burns and chemical stains marked his rumpled white lab coat. His bald dome gleamed beneath the fluorescent lights of his secret laboratory. His scrawny body was hunched in front of the screen. The television's old-fashioned rabbit ears antennae picked up bootleg signals from orbiting spy satellites.

"Bah, this is no fun to watch," Sivana muttered to himself. "Where's Captain Marvel?" Bored with the televised carnage, he leaned forward and changed the channel to the daily news. "Black Adam is much too serious for me." Although they shared a common enemy in the Big Red Cheese, Sivana had always considered the ancient Egyptian superman insufferably pompous—and a living anachronism to boot. "And now he thinks he can 'change' the world." The mad doctor cackled at the very notion. "Ha! Magic doesn't change the world. Science does!"

Heaving himself up from a rickety rocking chair, Sivana walked across his laboratory, which was cluttered with the detritus of countless diabolical experiments and inventions. A killer robot gathered dust in one corner of the converted basement, next to rusty cans of atomic rocket fuel. Cobwebs shrouded a bulky shrinking-ray projector that Sivana meant to get around to repairing one of these days. Vacuum tubes, spark plugs, 3-D glasses, wrenches, screwdrivers, microscopes, and a brand-new protein resequencer were strewn across the disorganized shelves and counters. Blueprints for time machines and electrodynamic death traps were taped to the walls above the various work spaces. Sparks leaped between a pair of upright electrodes. Beakers and test tubes bubbled over with devilish concoctions. Rotating reels of magnetic tape chugged noisily inside a genuine 1957 super-computer. A miniature flying saucer was suspended from the ceiling. The stuffy air smelled of ozone and Suspendium.

Sivana gravitated to a shelf at the rear of the lab. A clear plastic cylinder, about the size of a Quaker Oats container, glowed atop the shelf, its contents bathed in unearthly blue radiation by a lamp installed in its lid. Sivana flashed a buck-toothed grin as he affectionately patted the vertical cylinder. "Science *always* trumps magic. Isn't that right, my little friend?"

A tiny green caterpillar, no more than three inches long, wriggled inside the tube. Bulbous yellow eyes peered back at Sivana through the transparent plastic. Tiny forelegs waved in protest. A miniature microphone was strapped to the larva's thorax. Brownish red splotches ran along its back, so that it bore a distinct resemblance to the species *Papilio polyxenes*. Twin antennae twitched atop its head.

But before the wormlike creature could respond, the basement doors were thrown off their hinges by a powerful blow. A corner of one door clipped Sivana in the head, knocking him to the ground. His glasses clattered across the floor.

A pair of looming figures entered the lab. "Doctor Sivana?" a guttural voice inquired.

"Wh-what?" Rising to his knees, the dazed scientist groped for his lost glasses. He squinted myopically at the intruders, but all he could see were the blurry outlines of two towering male forms. He got a vague impression that one of the invaders was covered in fur, the other in scales. One thing was for sure:

Neither of them was Captain Marvel. "Wh-who are you? What do you want?"

His fingers closed on his glasses just as a shaggy hand grabbed onto his right shoulder, yanking him to his feet. Reptilian claws sank into his other shoulder.

"You," an inhuman voice growled.

Safe inside its protective cylinder, the caterpillar watched silently as two monstrous beast-men dragged Sivana from his lab. Its antennae twitched excitedly for a few moments, then settled down as it became obvious that the mad doctor was not coming back anytime soon. The tiny invertebrate turned its attention to the television set, which continued to blare in the background.

"Gathering since early morning, thousands are expected to show up for the memorial service, scheduled to take place in Metropolis later today. . . ."

The caterpillar watched the broadcast with interest.

METROPOLIS.

A gigantic bronze statue of Superman, an American eagle poised upon his wrist, dominated the open plaza at the center of Centennial Park. Dozens of super heroes were gathered in the plaza, ready to take part in the solemn memorial service being held this afternoon. Costumed heroes enjoyed VIP status, while photographers and TV crews swarmed the sidelines. A few of the more enterprising journalists, including Lois Lane and Jimmy Olsen, braved the throng of heroes, collecting interviews and photos. Police barricades held back hundreds of ordinary citizens who had come to show their support and gratitude for the extraordinary men and women responsible for ending the Crisis, and to honor the memory of those who had fallen in battle. Handmade signs proclaimed THANK YOU!, JLA FOREVER!, and similar sentiments. Cheers greeted the arrival of each new hero.

Booster Gold savored the applause as he touched down amidst the other heroes. *Pretty good turnout,* he observed, checking out the impressive assemblage of costumed champions. Looking around, he spotted Martian Manhunter, Zatanna, Green Arrow, Black Canary, S.T.R.I.P.E., Stargirl, Blue Devil, Ragman, Nightmaster, Enchantress, Power Girl, Black Lightning, Gypsy, Vixen, Plastic Man, Geo-Force, Aquaman, the Ray, Bulleteer, Hourman, Wildcat, Mister Terrific, Tasmanian Devil, Doctor Mid-Nite, Katana, Jakeem Thunder, Metamorpho, Mister Miracle, Nightwing, the Doom Patrol, the Teen Titans, various members of the Green Lantern Corps, and a few heroes he didn't even recognize. Firehawk came flying down from the sky, her glowing wings ablaze. Huntress swung onto the scene. Metamorpho gave Booster a friendly wave, but seemed to be busy chatting up the buxom new Bulleteer. *Just as well,* Booster thought. He was too excited to make small talk right now. Not when it was almost time to make history instead.

"SUPERMAN, BATMAN, AND WONDER WOMAN ARE DUE TO BEGIN IN LESS THAN A MINUTE, SIR." As ever, Skeets hovered above his shoulder. "I'D SUGGEST WORKING YOUR WAY TO THE STAGE."

Booster spotted a podium set up in the shadow of the looming Superman statue. As he navigated through the crowd, he overheard snatches of conversation.

"Assume Superman's going to deliver the eulogy," the Flash said.

"Oh yeah, he has to," Black Lightning agreed. "Who else?"

A green-skinned teenager looked about in confusion. "So, where are Superman, Batman, and Wonder Woman?"

"They'll be here, kid," Booster assured Beast Boy. "Just relax."

He took a position near the front of the crowd, facing the vacant podium. The absence of the Big Three did not concern him. Knowing Superman, he was probably putting out a raging forest fire in Brazil or something, nothing that would keep him from showing up on time for the ceremony. Batman and Wonder Woman were bound to arrive at the last minute as well. He had no doubt that all three heroes would be here shortly. History said so.

"FOUR SECONDS TO THE BIG MOMENT, SIR,"
Skeets alerted him. Booster checked his hair, using Robotman's
polished exterior as a mirror. Skeets counted down the seconds.
"THREE. TWO . . ."

"One," Booster said. "Ta-daaa!"

Nothing happened. The podium remained unoccupied. Superman, not to mention Batman and Wonder Woman, were
nowhere to be seen.

Huh? Booster looked around anxiously. He spun around,
searching the crowd for that world-famous red S. His eyes worriedly scanned the sky.

His initial outburst, and odd behavior, caught the attention
of the heroes standing nearby. "What's he doing?" Metamorpho
asked. The Element Man's body was a jumble of multicolored
ores and minerals. "Announcing himself?"

Firehawk shot Booster a disgusted look. "He would."

Booster was too flummoxed to even register the flaming
heroine's dig, let alone take offense at her contemptuous tone.
He turned to Skeets for answers. "Where are they?"

"THEY SHOU1010001 BE HERE, SIR." Static distorted the floating robot's voice. **"THE TIME—"**

"Is 4:32!" Booster yelped. More heroes took notice of his
increasingly agitated state. Elasti-Girl and Robotman backed
away from him, looking uncomfortable. Aquaman scowled at
Booster's unseemly conduct. "And I don't see them anywhere!"

J'onn J'onzz, the Martian Manhunter, tried to intervene.
The beetle-browed green humanoid, whom Booster had known
for years, was a respected pillar of the super-hero community. His deep, sonorous voice conveyed a sense of gravity.
"Booster, a little decorum, please . . . ?"

But good manners were the last thing on Booster's mind.
"No! You don't understand, J'onn!" he protested. Ignoring the
concerned stares of his fellow heroes, he shouted at his robot
instead. "Skeets, check the historical records again!"

**"I'M PROCESSING THEM AT TERABYTES A PICO01-
1000SECOND, SIR."** Another glitch in his voice indicated
that something was seriously amiss. Usually, you couldn't shut

the chatty robot up. "THEY ALL INDICOO11OTE A 4:30 APPEARANCE."

"4:35 and counting, Skeets!" Booster's goggles projected an internal chronometer before his eyes. "Your clock is off!"

This was a disaster. Of all times for the stupid robot to come down with a computer virus or something! A cold sweat broke out beneath Booster's uniform as he saw his glorious future slipping away. . . .

"ATOMIC TIME, SIR!" The levitating robot began to spin erratically. The gleaming orb listed to the right. "SOMETHING'S WROOO11ONG! SOM11OTHING'S WROOOO—"

Skeets' voice devolved into a burst of incoherent static. Sparks flashed around the robot's invisible antigravity field. Electricity crackled loudly as Skeets shorted out before Booster's eyes. The robot crashed to the pavement, clanging against the scuffed stone tiles. Coruscating energy briefly flashed across the golden surface of the sphere.

"Skeets!"

By now, everyone in the plaza was aware of the disturbance. Huntress, Negative Man, and several other heroes shushed him. He could tell from their expressions that most of them thought that he was acting crazy or disrespectful or both. Power Girl, never the most even-tempered of heroines, looked like she wanted to knock his block off, but was being held back by Hourman and Wildcat. Klarion the Witchboy tsked in disapproval. Doctor Mid-Nite's pet owl hooted indignantly.

"Booster, will you settle down?" J'onn said.

"No! You don't understand! Where are they?" He was ranting like a lunatic now, but he didn't care. All that mattered was that history was going wrong. "Where the hell are they?"

J'onn spoke to him in a soothing tone. "Where are who, Booster?"

"I'm talking about Superman and Batman, you extraterrestrial chucklehead! And Wonder Woman!" He yelled hysterically at the imposing green alien. J'onn was a telepath, but he generally refrained from reading his comrades' minds.

Booster tried to explain just how bad things were. "The future depends on them! I know, I've seen it!"

Attracted by the commotion, a photographer ran forward, holding a camera. Booster spotted the newcomer out of the corner of his eye. He recognized the man's red hair, freckles, and trademark bow tie. "Jimmy Olsen?" He lunged toward the startled photographer. "Take the picture!"

"Booster!" J'onn shouted in alarm.

"Take the picture, Olsen!" Booster demanded, heedless of the Martian's cry. This was his last chance to make things right. Maybe, he reasoned desperately, the Big Three had arrived while he was busy arguing with Skeets and J'onn. Maybe they were at the podium right now, just like they were supposed to be. "They're here!" he shouted at Olsen, afraid to glance back at the podium for fear of what he might see. "They have to be here!" Grabbing onto Olsen's camera, he yanked the lens toward the podium behind him. His fingers searched for the camera's shutter release button, trying to force the frightened photographer to take the shot. "This is your Howitzer!"

"Great H'ronmeer!" J'onn exclaimed, invoking an ancient Martian deity. His elastic arms stretched out and wrapped around Booster. Alien muscles, whose strength rivaled that of Superman himself, pulled Booster away from Olsen. The contested-over camera slipped from both men's fingers. Booster's eyes widened in horror as the historically crucial camera broke to pieces against the pavement. Panicking, he fought to free himself from J'onn's powerful grip. Metamorpho and Geo-Force hurried over to help restrain Booster, who was completely out of control. "Hold him!" J'onn ordered his allies. The rest of the heroes looked ready to step in if necessary. Hal Jordan's power ring flashed ominously. Green Arrow fitted a tranquilizer arrow to his bow.

What's the matter with these people? Booster thought in frustration. *Don't they realize how important this is?* He thrashed frantically against J'onn and the others. *I have to fix things before the future changes forever!*

"Booster!" a new voice called out. A figure cautiously approached the fracas from one side. Booster caught a glimpse of a civilian in a powder blue business suit. "They're not coming! They're-*ngggh*!"

Flailing wildly, Booster accidentally elbowed the poor guy in the nose. *Oops!* The clumsy mishap briefly startled him out of his frenzied state. He stopped struggling long enough to find out who exactly he had just clobbered. *Sorry about that, pal.*

He saw a mild-mannered reporter wearing a pair of horn-rimmed glasses. A press pass, pinned to the lapel of his blazer, identified him as working for the *Daily Planet*, the same newspaper Jimmy Olsen was employed by. Booster suddenly remembered that the reporter had been trying to tell him something right before their collision.

"What do you mean they're not coming?" he asked angrily. "How the hell do you know?"

"I just know," Clark Kent said. A trickle of blood flowed from his nose. Oddly enough, he didn't seem too upset that Booster had just walloped him by mistake. If anything, he looked more worried about Booster. "And I'm sorry."

Tell me about it, Booster thought. J'onn and the others let go of him as he gradually quieted down. He realized glumly that there was nothing he could do here.

The future—his future—was screwed.

WEEK 2.

GOTHAM CITY.

THE loft looked like it hadn't been cleaned in weeks, mainly because it hadn't. Unwashed dishes were piled in the sink. Fast-food containers, crumpled beer cans, and empty liquor bottles covered nearly every inch of counter space. Dirty laundry carpeted the floor. An open cardboard box, advertising Nachie's Gotham-Style Pizza, occupied the small table in front of the sofa. Roaches fed on the few remaining slices. The only illumination came from the city lights shining through the window curtains. The stuffy atmosphere was badly in need of air freshener. A trail of discarded clothing led to the king-sized bed at the far end of the loft.

Renee was oblivious to the general squalor as she dozed in the bed, entangled with a fetching young blonde she had picked up earlier tonight. Sweaty, disordered sheets hinted at the strenuous activity that had left both women spent and momentarily at peace. The blonde was curled up against Renee, breathing softly as she slumbered contentedly in the ex-cop's arms. Renee thought her name was Carla.

Or maybe Carol.

Renee was only half awake when a man's shadow fell over the bed. A gloved hand lifted a plain white bra from the floor, the faint noise causing her to stir uneasily. Shadows cloaked the figure as he stepped closer to the bed. A voice asked quietly, "Who are you?"

What the hell? It belatedly dawned on Renee that a stranger was standing at the foot of her bed. Her eyes snapped open and she reached across the startled blonde to grab the semiautomatic pistol resting on top of the nightstand. Twisting around, she sat up and fired two rounds at the intruder. Gunshots blared inside the loft. The blonde screamed in terror.

The flash of the muzzle, as well as the lights from outside, revealed a startling sight: a man with no face. Smooth pink skin covered the intruder's face from his hairline to his chin. Only two shallow indentations existed where his eyes should have been. A bump gave a vague suggestion of a nose. There was no mouth at all, just an unbroken expanse of flesh.

For a second, Renee thought that maybe her eyes were playing tricks on her, but then she heard the blonde cry out in fear. "Ohmigod, he doesn't have a face!"

Her shots hit him directly in the chest. In contrast to his bizarre countenance, the man's attire was unremarkable. Renee caught a glimpse of a suit and tie beneath a rumpled brown trench coat as the intruder tumbled backward. Her bra flew from his fingers, and he seemed to fall to the floor, dropping out of her line of vision. She listened for the sound of a body smacking against the woodwork, but heard nothing except the terrified young woman beside her.

"Ohmigod! Ohmigod!" the blonde kept shrieking. She grabbed onto Renee, getting in the way. "Where was his fac—?"

"Shut up!" Renee snapped. Breaking free from the other woman's panicky embrace, she scrambled out of the bed. Years of training and experience asserted themselves as she assumed the high-ready position, gripping the gun in both hands. Circling around the bed, she expected to find the intruder stretched out on the floor.

But all she found was the fallen bra.

"Wh-where'd he go?" the blonde asked, clutching a sheet to her chest. She sounded just as bewildered as Renee, and a whole lot more frightened. "You shot him, right? You . . . you hit him?"

Less concerned with modesty, Renee moved about the apartment, searching for their uninvited visitor. Goose bumps tingled upon her bare skin. She was fully awake now, with enough adrenaline flowing through her veins to power most of Gotham. A digital alarm clock informed her that it was 4:30 in the morning. Her pistol was raised and ready.

"Do you see him?" the blonde asked anxiously. "Did you get him?" She huddled fearfully on the bed, hiding behind the thin sheet as if it could actually protect her. "What do we do now? Do we call the cops?"

Renee tuned her out. Given the small size of her apartment, it took her only a few minutes to determine that the intruder was nowhere in the loft. It seemed impossible, but somehow he had escaped unobserved. Kind of like the way Batman always disappeared into the shadows when he was no longer needed.

But that wasn't the Bat, she thought. Nor did the faceless stranger fit the description of the Joker, the Riddler, or any of the other grotesque lunatics that infested Gotham. *Just what we need,* she thought sourly. *Another freak.* During her years on the force, Renee had encountered just about every one of Gotham's costumed lunatics—hell, she had even been stalked by Two-Face for a while—but this one was new to her. *First, Two-Face. Now, No-Face.* She shook her head in disgust. *Why me?*

As her eyes gradually adjusted to the gloom, she spotted an unfamiliar piece of paper sticking out from beneath the flung bra. Holding on tightly to the pistol with her right hand, she knelt down and picked up the paper. An empty whisky bottle lay on the floor nearby.

"What is it, Renee?" the blonde called out. What exactly was her name again? "C'mon, Renee! You're freaking me out."

The loose slip of paper appeared to have been torn out of a pocket-sized notebook. Renee stood up and stepped toward the window to get a better look at the handwritten message scrawled upon the slip:

520 Kane Street

?

The question mark was at least twice the size of the address above it.

That's the Riddler's trademark, she recalled, thinking like a cop. But this didn't feel like one of Eddie Nigma's usual word games. Besides, the last time she checked, the Riddler had a face. . . .

"Renee?" The blonde sounded a little less panicked, but desperately wanted to be told that everything was all right now. She crawled across the bed toward Renee, the sheet wrapped tightly around her. Renee doubted that this particular blonde would ever set foot in her apartment again, let alone her bed. "Uhm, hello . . . ?"

The former detective had other things on her mind right now. She stared at the puzzling note, examining it as if it were evidence at a crime scene, which she supposed it was. But who was the intruder and what was he after?

"Put some clothes on," she told the blonde.

METROPOLIS.

A large bronze globe spun atop the Daily Planet Building as Booster Gold zoomed past it into the sky. Photographers on the rooftop snapped shots of his heroic ascent. He hoped they managed to get his good side.

"HURRY, SIR!" Skeets urged him. The compact robot was up and running again, looking none the worse for wear despite his temporary crash at the disrupted memorial service. "THERE'S A FALLING JETLINER COMING IN FROM THE NORTH!"

"Are you sure about this?" Booster asked. He couldn't help recalling how Skeets had gone haywire before.

"ABSOLUTELY, SIR. LAST WEEK WAS A GLITCH, I ASSURE YOU. MY SELF-REPAIR PROGRAMS HAVE AL-READY ELIMINATED THE PROBLEM." Certainly the robot's voice sounded back to normal. "NOW THAT I HAVE

SUCCESSFULLY REBOOTED MYSELF, I CAN STATE
CONCLUSIVELY THAT THIS IS A JOB FOR BOOSTER
GOLD!"

Booster hoped so. "Okay, I'm on it."

He let the robot guide him over thirty thousand feet into the air. A field of fleecy white clouds billowed beneath him. A clear blue sky spread out above. Booster looked to the north, yet saw nothing but empty air and sunlight. A powerful head-wind blew against his face. There was no sign of any imminent aeronautic disaster.

"Are you positive this is the right place?"

His confidence in Skeets' predictions had been shaken by the Big Three's no-show at the memorial service. A week later, Superman, Batman, and Wonder Woman remained MIA.

What else might history have gotten wrong?

"THE JET'S FLIGHT PATH IS A MATTER OF HIS-
TORICAL RECORD," Skeets insisted. "YOU'RE POSI-
TIONED PERFECTLY. IMPACT—"

The wind roared in Booster's ears, so that he had to strain to hear what the robot was saying. "Speak up!" he shouted. "I can't hear you over the wind!"

Skeets turned up the volume. "IMPACT IN FIVE SEC-
ONDS, SIR! YOUR FORCE DAMPERS ARE FULLY
CHARGED! BRACE YOURSELF!"

"For what?" Booster squinted into the wind, grateful for the goggles protecting his eyes. He assumed a stationary position in the sky. He held out his arms in front of him, as though to catch a beach ball. He still couldn't see anything amiss. "You said north, right?"

All at once, the wind shifted and the smell of burning jet fuel flooded his nostrils. A gigantic shadow blotted out the sun. *What in the world . . . ?* He almost had a heart attack as, without warning, a burning 747 came barreling out of the sky behind him. Narrowly missing him and Skeets, the rushing jetliner flew over Booster, less than a yard above his head. The back draft generated by the plane nearly sucked him in. Skeets beeped in surprise.

"Oh God . . ."

The jumbo jet was plunging toward Metropolis at a horrifying speed. Thick black smoke gushed from both wings. Flames erupted from the burning engines. No loud thrumming came from the dead turbines. A whistling wind carried the smell of gasoline.

Choking on the fumes, Booster dived after the plane. Force-field projectors in his gauntlets locked onto the jet's wings in a desperate attempt to slow its breakneck descent. The effort was intense; only the future tech in his uniform kept his arms from being yanked from their sockets. It was like trying to drag a rocket back with your bare hands.

"God . . ."

Skeets darted beneath the undercarriage of the plummeting 747. A metallic probe extended from inside the robot, making contact with the plane's aluminum alloy skin. Twenty-fifth-century technology allowed Skeets to establish a cybernetic link with the jet's internal circuitry. An override command persuaded the plane to lower its landing gear.

His work done, Skeets withdrew his probe and scooted out of the way.

Good job, Booster thought. But would the robot's assistance make any difference in the end? Bits and pieces of the plane flew off the disintegrating wings. Loose flaps and panels went spiraling off into the sky behind it. Burning debris pelted Booster, bouncing off his protective force field and body armor, as he chased after the endangered aircraft. Terrified faces were pressed against the windows, staring aghast at the flames. Booster's mouth went dry. There had to be at least three hundred passengers aboard.

The plane tore through the cloud cover, shredding the damp mist. Metropolis Airport came into view below. The sprawling complex seemed to grow larger by the second as the jet rocketed toward the ground like a missile. Booster's headpiece picked up the frantic transmissions coming from the cockpit of the plane:

"Mayday! Mayday! Metropolis Tower, we have experienced a major instrumentation malfunction! Enact Emergency Landing Protocol 2X-2L!"

Booster had no idea what that protocol involved, but he doubted that it would do any good. At the angle the jet was descending, a fiery crash seemed inevitable—unless he did something about it in the next few seconds. Putting on a final burst of speed, he caught up with the blazing plane and came up beneath it. He pressed his palms against the fuselage and pushed upward with all his might. Energy flashed and crackled around his body as he pushed his suit's technology to its limits. Repulsive thrusters fought a losing battle against gravity.

An empty runway came rushing up at him. *Need to keep the nose up,* he realized. *Just a few moments more.* He gritted his teeth, refusing to give up. *I can do this.* The heat from the burning engines drenched him in sweat. *I'm Booster Gold, dammit!*

The flaming 747 hit the tarmac at high speed. The tail section scraped against the asphalt as the plane skidded down the runway, throwing off a rooster tail of white-hot sparks. Scarred metal screeched in protest. Staring down at the runway, only a few feet below him, Booster prayed that the jumbo jet would hold together.

C'mon, he thought. *Superman could do this with his eyes closed.*

Finally, just when Booster thought the plane was a goner, the jet squealed to a halt only fifty yards from the end of the runway. Fire trucks, ambulances, and other emergency vehicles came racing onto the scene. An inflatable slide sprouted from the side of the plane. Trembling passengers slid to safety. There appeared to be no casualties.

Booster let out a massive sigh of relief. Shaking, he flew out from beneath the jet and landed several yards away from the rescue operation. Exhausted, he collapsed onto the tarmac. He was sweaty and breathing hard. His heart was still racing.

That was a close one.

A news crew came running toward him. Booster realized that they must have been on hand to cover the crash. "Booster! Channel Seven News." A female reporter, whose name Booster couldn't recall, thrust a microphone in his face. "Can we get a quote?"

Rising to his feet, he waved the news crew back. Despite the opportunity for publicity, he wasn't quite up to providing a choice sound bite just yet. "Right with you, folks!" he promised, mustering a cocky smile. "Just give me a moment to . . . reflect on our luck."

"SIR!" Skeets zipped down from the sky. "IT WASN'T LUCK—"

"No kidding!" he snapped at the robot. Stepping away from the news team, he lowered his voice so as not to be overheard. "'North'? What the hell was that?" Skeets' faulty directions had nearly gotten them all killed. "You're still fragged!"

"NOT TO WORRY, SIR," Skeets declared. "MY APOLO-GIES. MERELY ONE LAST RESIDUAL GLITCH IN MY SELF-CORRECTING PROGRAMMING." The metal probe had receded back inside the robot. His polished casing appeared completely seamless. "EVERYTHING'S IN ORDER NOW."

Booster looked over at the jet, now liberally coated with flame-retardant foam. The passengers and crew had made it to the ground safely, but he was all too aware that things could have easily turned out very different. Hell, a few more feet and he would have been splattered all over the nose of the plane. He glared at Skeets.

"You'd better be right about that!"

GOTHAM CITY.

MYSTERY solved, Renee thought.

520 Kane Street turned out to be an abandoned building down by the waterfront, in a bad part of town. A thick layer of dust and soot smeared the front windows. The entrance was boarded up. The nondescript structure offered little indication of its function, but she guessed that it used to be a warehouse, or maybe a shipping office. In any event, it was nothing but a potential firetrap now. A sign posted above the door read, Private Property—Keep Out!

The neighborhood around the building wasn't much more hospitable. A solitary streetlamp created a small oasis of light amidst the nocturnal darkness. Renee's car, a beaten-up old sedan, was parked across the street, which she seemed to have all to herself. There was nobody else around, not even a few homeless vagrants. Waves lapped monotonously against the dilapidated pier to her right. A salty breeze blew litter past her ankles. Cardboard boxes and rusty trash cans were piled against the building. Greasy puddles filled the potholes in the pavement. Rats scurried in the shadows. Renee glanced up at the sky. It was odd not to see the Bat-Signal shining overhead. She wondered if the commissioner knew what had become of the Dark Knight. *Not that it's any of my business anymore.*

She used her sleeve to wipe some of the soot away from a filthy window. Scowling, she peered through the glass, but saw nothing out of the ordinary. Just murky shadows and cobwebs. From what she could see, the place had been empty for a long time.

Fine, she thought. *Curiosity satisfied.* She had wasted enough time checking out the address on the slip. The mother of all hangovers had kept her from driving down here earlier, but apparently she needn't have bothered. So much for playing detective on her own; it was time to get back to the serious business of drinking herself into oblivion. She briefly flirted with the idea of tracking down the blonde from the night before, but figured that ship had sailed. Chances were, Carla would rather go straight than hook up with her again. Renee took one last look at the abandoned building. Why would anyone bother to slip her this address?

"Kind of a dump, isn't it?"

A voice spoke up behind her, accompanied by a faint chemical odor. Renee spun around to find the faceless stranger emerging from a column of thick blue smoke. The swirling fumes briefly took the form of a question mark, before the breeze blew them away. Her jaw dropped in surprise.

"Son of a b—!" She hastily drew her pistol from beneath her jacket. Before she could take aim, however, the stranger grabbed onto her wrist and shoulder. Gloved fingers expertly twisted the gun from her grip. Some sort of fancy jujitsu move flipped her into the nearby trash cans, knocking them over. Metal lids clattered onto the pavement as she crashed to the ground. Rotting garbage spilled on the asphalt beside her. "Uhh!" she grunted, wincing from the impact. That was going to leave a bruise.

"Do you shoot everyone you meet," the stranger asked, "or is this a personal thing?" He loomed over her, holding on to her pistol. The glare of the streetlamp revealed a head of light brown hair above his blank countenance. He seemed to be wearing the same suit and trench coat as before. Renee fully expected to be gunned down with her own pistol, but the stranger casually dropped the gun's magazine into his other hand. The act did little to quell Renee's anger at being ambushed like this.

"Who the hell are you?" she demanded.

"I asked you first." He lobbed the emptied gun back to her.

She caught the pistol, then scrambled to her feet amidst the strewn trash. A greasy fast-food wrapper clung to her jeans. "I shot you," she insisted. "I know I shot you."

"Are you sure?" He opened his coat, showing her the bullet holes in his lapel.

Renee squeezed the grip of her pistol. Even though she knew it was empty, the feel of the gun in her hand was reassuring. Her memory replayed those frantic moments in the loft when she had fired at the intruder. Was it possible that he had somehow managed to dodge the bullets via some tricky kung fu move? "Pretty sure."

"So you are a detective after all." Even though he didn't have a mouth, she could practically hear him grinning. *Smug bastard.*

She frowned at his assertion. "No, I'm not. I've got a new job. It's called being a drunk."

He sounded dubious. "Do I judge you by what you say or by what you do, Renee?"

"How do you know my name?" she asked suspiciously. *What is it about me that keeps attracting these freaks? And how come it's never Catwoman that comes slinking into my life?*

"I'm hiring you. Two hundred dollars a day plus expenses." He reached beneath his coat and extracted a thick roll of bills, bound together by a rubber band. He shoved the roll in Renee's free hand. "First three weeks, paid in advance."

She blinked in surprise, completely taken aback by this unexpected development. She flicked through the bills, seeing plenty of crisp green hundreds. Benjamin Franklin smiled up at her. *What the hell?* she thought, trying to make sense of it all. *This guy breaks into my home, nearly gets himself killed, just to offer me a job?*

"Don't judge the building by how it looks," he advised her. "Judge it by how it's used and by who uses it. . . ."

Her nose caught a whiff of that same chemical odor. Opaque blue fumes began to rise from the stranger's clothing. Renee had seen Batman exit under the cover of a smoke screen too many times not to realize what was happening. Especially after the stranger's disappearing act in her apartment the night before.

"What? Wait!" She lunged forward, trying to stop the faceless mystery man from vanishing again, but her hands grabbed onto nothing but a dense blue mist. "I still have questions!"

She could forget about getting any answers, though. The stranger was gone once more, leaving behind a column of smoke in the shape of a question mark. The puzzling symbol fit her mood perfectly. She contemplated the roll of banknotes in her hand.

What was that all about?

WEEK 3.

SHIRUTA.

A marble statue of a beautiful woman and two smiling children dominated Black Adam's private sanctum. Clad in the garments of ancient Egypt, where he had fought on behalf of Pharaoh Ramses II, they occupied a position of honor within the spacious chamber, posed before an open balcony that looked out over the entire city. Massive stone columns, engraved with intricate arabesques, supported the ceiling. An imposing mahogany desk rested in one corner, beneath a large framed map of the world. Potted ferns and palm trees brought a touch of nature to the grandiose decor.

His arms clasped behind his back, Adam grimly contemplated the statue of his murdered family. Even after three thousand years, the pain of their loss still gnawed at his soul, spurring him on in his sacred crusade to stamp out evil wherever he found it. The sun set behind the statue, briefly granting the figures a radiant halo. Adam wondered if Shiruta's spirit still waited for him in the Land of the Dead, or if she had given up on him millennia ago.

Time weighed heavily upon him. Plans were in motion, but there was little for him to do at the present. A long, lonely evening awaited him.

"Black Adam." A servant addressed him from behind. "You have visitors."

He turned to find the aged servant, his head bowed in respect, escorting three unfamiliar personages into his presence. Two men, both wearing Western-style business suits, flanked a dark-haired young woman whose body was clothed in a shapeless violet gown. A blindfold was fastened over the maiden's eyes and her arms were tied behind her back. Black Adam did not find it remarkable that his guards had permitted the strangers to venture all the way to his office. Indestructible as he was, he required little protection . . . as past assassins had learned to their regret.

"Who are they?" he asked the servant in Arabic.

"We're friends," answered one of the men, a stocky fellow whose insincere smile reminded Adam of an unscrupulous camel merchant. A dark mustache and beard failed to conceal his greasy complexion. He held a black metal case before him, while his companion held on to the woman by her shoulders. The speaker's accent betrayed his American origins.

"You speak Arabic," Adam observed.

"I'm not just brawn," the man declared. His phony smile stretched even wider. "The name's Rough House. This is Noose."

The other man was tall and lanky, with sandy red hair and a smirking expression. "It's a pleasure, your highness."

"I am not a king," Adam clarified. He considered himself Kahndaq's champion, not its monarch. He regarded the men warily, his arms crossed atop his chest.

"Regardless," Rough House declared, "we've come here to offer you gifts." He opened the metal case, revealing a quantity of gold ingots. "Two million in African gold." He nodded at Noose, who pushed the barefoot woman forward. "And the most beautiful virgin in all of Egypt." An odious leer exposed his vile character. "Guaranteed."

Adam contemplated the pair's offerings. "May I ask why you have brought me these 'gifts'?"

"To congratulate you on the opening of your embassy in Metropolis," Rough House explained. Adam was scheduled to attend the opening later this week. "And to say hello on behalf of our employers. Intergang."

I see, Adam thought. Intergang was an American crime syndicate that was well-known for applying advanced technology to the practice of organized crime. Although he had never personally dealt with Intergang before, he was more than familiar with their infamous reputation. Then again, he recalled, he himself had often been unfairly maligned by the Western press. It seemed unlikely, but perhaps the notorious syndicate had also been misrepresented? He resolved to hear the men out before rendering judgment.

"The world is still recovering from the Crisis," Rough House continued. "My bosses are hoping to take advantage of that. We're already essentially running Bialya, as you may be aware."

"Perhaps," Adam allowed. Bialya, Kahndaq's neighbor to the south, was a rogue nation that been ruled by a succession of military strongmen for several decades now. Adam had heard rumors that a foreign crime syndicate was pulling the strings of Bialya's latest puppet ruler, one Colonel Harjvati. Apparently, those rumors were well-founded. "Go on."

"Now we're looking to expand," Rough House said. "And Kahndaq is essentially the bridge between Africa and the Middle East."

Noose expanded on his accomplice's spiel. "There are a lot of people willing to pay truckloads for the kind of weapons Intergang can supply. Thanagarian. Apokoliptian."

Black Adam caught the references to two warlike alien civilizations. Apparently, Intergang's tentacles extended beyond the boundaries of Earth's solar system. The thought of such weapons falling into the wrong hands gave him pause.

"We're more than willing to cut you in on the action," Rough House offered, "in exchange for, what shall we call it? Safe passage?"

Noose must have let his grip on the young woman relax, for she suddenly twisted free of his grasp and lashed out at her captors. "Let me go, monsters!" she shouted defiantly. Her unshod foot kicked Noose in the shins even as she rammed her slender shoulder into Rough House. Adam admired her spirit. Clearly, she was unwilling to be traded like chattel.

"Hey!" Noose reacted in surprise. He grabbed for the girl, his face contorted by anger. The genesis of his nickname became clear as his flexible fingers stretched like vines around the maiden's throat. Struggling to free herself once more, she gasped for breath. "Dammit, hold still! Hold still, you stupid—"

"Noose!" Rough House said sharply. "Don't damage his gift." He glowered at the other man until Noose ceased throttling the squirming girl. The lanky gangster retracted his fingers, and held on to the girl by her chin and hair, clearly intent on making sure that she didn't get loose again. Satisfied, Rough House turned back toward Adam. He acted as though the brief disturbance was not worth mentioning. "So. What do you say?"

Black Adam scowled. *I have seen enough,* he decided.

Without warning, he reached out and pulped Noose's head like a balloon filled with red gelatin. Blood and brains splattered the pristine marble floor. Rough House looked on in horror.

"I say no."

METROPOLIS.

THE cocktail party took place in a lavish penthouse suite overlooking Centennial Park. Stylishly dressed men and women sipped champagne, mingled, and networked throughout the suite. Picture windows offered a spectacular view of the city at night. Thirsty guests flocked to the free bar.

"To the future, Mr. Gold!" a dapper young CEO toasted Booster. Crystal champagne flutes clinked together. "And to the stock options that will make you a billionaire once we go public."

Sounds good to me, Booster thought. He had just signed a potentially lucrative endorsement contract with Akteon-Holt, an up-and-coming new pharmaceuticals company. The party was to celebrate his new relationship with the firm. The company's logo was already in place upon his uniform. He smiled in anticipation of depositing a sizable payment into his bank account. Last week's jet rescue had raised his price significantly.

"I'm curious," Leonard Akteon asked. "What made you so

certain that a relatively small company like mine was worth your time?"

"Skeets," Booster admitted, gesturing toward the robot floating nearby. "I was on the lookout for a new sponsor, and he recommended you as a man on the rise." In fact, according to Skeets, Akteon-Holt was destined to become one of the economic powerhouses of the twenty-first century. *And I'm getting in on the ground floor!*

"Shame," a new voice broke into the conversation. A trio of men in dark suits and sunglasses barged through the crowd toward Booster and the startled CEO. "Mr. Leonard Akteon?" The leader intruder flashed a badge. "Agent Rogers, Secret Service." A second agent held out a warrant. "You're under arrest for securities fraud."

"What!" Akteon almost choked on his champagne. "There . . . there must be some mistake . . . !"

"Yeah, yours," Agent Rogers snarled. "The SEC has had you under investigation for some time now. Their case is open and shut." His men clamped a pair of handcuffs onto the businessman's wrists and began to escort him toward the door. Stunned partygoers, including Booster, looked on in dismay. "So much for 'Akteon-Holt.' Hope you didn't spend too much on letterhead." Rogers sneered at the dumbfounded guests witnessing the perp walk. "Party's over."

Booster watched numbly as Akteon disappeared through the exit, taking billions of imaginary profits with him. He wheeled around to confront Skeets.

"You . . . you . . . !"

The robot seemed equally taken aback by what had just occurred. "SIR, I . . . I DON'T . . . THAT WASN'T SUPPOSED TO HAPPEN!" At least Skeets wasn't having a complete breakdown, complete with sparks and static, like he had at the memorial service. "PERHAPS I AM MALFUNCTIONING. SHALL I ATTEMPT A TOTAL REBOOT?"

"No," Booster decided. That hadn't worked before. "I want you to find someone for me." He stepped out onto the balcony outside the penthouse and launched himself into the air. Agent

Rogers was right; the party was over. "Get me everything you can on the current whereabouts of a man called Hunter."

I should have done this before, he thought. *The first time history went wrong.*

"Rip Hunter."

METROPOLIS.

THE brownstone had once housed the Themysciran Embassy, before the Amazons of Paradise Island withdrew from this plane of existence, leaving only Wonder Woman behind. Now the Kahndaqi flag flew above the building, as the crowd outside waited for Black Adam to make his promised appearance. Police officers had set up wooden barricades to keep back the mob of reporters and demonstrators swarming the scene. Picketers held aloft signs protesting Black Adam's illegal takeover of Kahndaq, as well as scores of alleged human rights violations. Other demonstrators attempted to remind the media of Black Adam's frequent clashes with Earth's true heroes, both before and after he became a de facto head of state. REMEMBER THE FREEDOM FIGHTERS! one handmade banner implored; rumor had it Black Adam had taken part in the grisly massacre of an American super-hero team early on in the Crisis. FREE KAHNDAQ! another sign demanded. BLACK ADAM IS A WEAPON OF MASS DESTRUCTION!

Lois Lane was among the reporters covering the embassy's opening. She dictated some background material into her handheld tape recorder:

"One of the most controversial individuals in the world today, Black Adam claims to have lived and ruled Kahndaq during the Nineteenth Dynasty as the historical figure Teth-Adam. Scholars and Middle Eastern leaders dispute these assertions and have called Black Adam a 'pretender' and 'one of today's greatest evils.'"

She hit Stop on the recorder, then played back what she had dictated to make sure it had recorded properly. Satisfied with the sound quality, she put away the device and went back to mingling with her fellow reporters, who were busily speculating about Black Adam's motives and intentions. No one was quite sure what to expect today, including Lois.

"Heard rumors from D.C.," Vicki Vale of the *Gotham Gazette* was saying, "that he's about to open up his country to super-villains. Anyone wanted for a crime gets a free pass."

Lois was skeptical. "Why would he do that? From what I know, he doesn't want anything to do with them."

"Well then, what does he want, Lois?" asked Steve Lombard of WGBS-TV.

Flashbulbs suddenly went off all around them. The protestors booed and chanted louder. Lois looked up at the balcony overlooking the embassy's front door. "I think he's about to tell us."

Black Adam floated above the balcony, defying gravity as easily as Clark usually could. He gazed down at the people below, his inscrutable expression giving little hint as to what he had in mind. His muscular arms were crossed atop his chest.

"Thank you all for coming." He spoke English with a slight Middle Eastern accent. "Over the last year, I have dedicated myself exclusively to the people of Kahndaq." He paused dramatically. "That ends today."

Uh-oh, Lois thought. *I don't like the sound of that.* According to Clark, Black Adam had all of Captain Marvel's powers and none of the Captain's innate decency and restraint. *That's a dangerous combination, especially these days.*

"The world has celebrated the aversion of disaster," Black Adam declared. "They have praised the heroes who stood up to save them. Superman, Batman, and Wonder Woman. But where are they now?"

Lois scowled. *Don't go writing my man off just yet,* she thought. *Superman will be back before you know it.*

Or so she hoped.

"I hope to gather allies. Brothers-in-arms who will deliver messages to everyone out there looking to take advantage of the heroes' absence."

He glanced down at the balcony, and Lois belatedly realized

that Black Adam was not alone. A stocky man in a business suit stood upon the balcony, looking apprehensively up at Black Adam. It took Lois a second to recognize the sweaty individual as Rough House, one of Intergang's superpowered enforcers. Was Black Adam in cahoots with Intergang? If so, that was serious bad news for the rest of the world. Talk about an unholy alliance!

Then again, Rough House didn't look too comfortable up on the balcony. He tugged nervously at his collar. Perspiration beaded on his forehead. He looked like he wanted to bolt from the balcony, but was afraid of provoking Black Adam. He swallowed hard as the floating superman continued to address the world. His eyes darted from side to side, as if searching desperately for an escape route.

"The first message is simple," Black Adam said. "People like this man don't deserve to live."

"What?" Rough House's eyes went wide with panic. He backed away fearfully, holding up his hands. "Wait, your highness! Please!"

Black Adam paid no heed to the hoodlum's pleas. Swooping down from on high, he plucked Rough House from the balcony . . . and ripped the man in two. Blood spattered Lois and the other reporters as the severed halves of the dead man's body rained down onto the sidewalk in front of the embassy. Crimson gore sprayed over the signs of the protestors, mocking their pitiful efforts to censure the ruthless dictator. Lois gagged as she wiped Rough House's blood from her face. Her fingers came away red. A few feet away, Steve Lombard vomited onto the pavement.

He wasn't the only one.

"It's time for heroes who don't just patrol the world," Black Adam declared. "They change it."

He took off into the sky, rapidly disappearing from view. Lois had no idea where he was going next, but she doubted that it boded well for the rest of humanity.

Looks like Black Adam isn't just Kahndaq's problem anymore.

WEEK 4.

GOTHAM CITY.

EVEN when she was on the force, Renee had hated surveillance. It was so boring, it practically redefined the word. "Boring: adjective, tiresome. See also: Surveillance."

She was camped out behind the wheel of her dented red sedan, which was parked across the road from the abandoned building at 520 Kane Street. Cigarettes and coffee rested upon the dashboard, vital necessities for the long hours ahead. The hot and muggy night made her wish she could run the car's air conditioner for a while. Perspiration glued her white T-shirt to her back. Her Smith & Wesson rested securely in her shoulder holster. She rolled down the window to let in a little fresh air.

Stakeouts were hard on the body too. Sitting in the same place, focusing on the same thing for five, six, maybe even *eight* hours at a time definitely gave you a whole new appreciation for over-the-counter painkillers. She rescued a bottle of generic aspirin from the glove compartment and poured a couple tablets into her palm. She washed the pills down with a mouthful of cold coffee.

In theory, surveillance could not be performed alone, at least not well. *Guess that means I've been doing a lousy job of it for the last two weeks,* she mused. Times like this she regretted taking the no-faced guy's money. *That was my first mistake.*

Two weeks so far, and nothing to show for it. She hadn't seen anything that would explain her faceless employer's interest in the old building. Outside, a stray cat crossed the street beneath the flickering light of a malfunctioning streetlamp.

A junked car, parked a little farther down the block, had already been pretty much stripped to its bare chassis. No one stirred upon the trash-covered sidewalks. As far as she could tell, the only person paying any attention to 520 Kane was her.

She lifted a pair of binoculars off the passenger seat beside her. Peering through the telescopic lenses, she took a closer look at the building. Was there anything going on over there?

Nope. Paint was peeling. That was about it.

Sighing wearily, she pulled a notepad off the dashboard and scribbled a terse notation to the effect that there was absolutely nothing to report. She glanced over the previous nights' entries:

Day 9: Nothing.

Day 10: Nothing.

Day 11: Wino urinated on wall. (Wow!)

Day 12: Nothing.

Day 13: Nothing.

Abundant doodles attested to her continuing boredom. She found herself wishing the wino would come back, just to break the monotony. *I'm going stir-crazy in here.* She started to light up a fresh cigarette.

"How many packs a day?" a voice asked her from behind.

"Jeez!" Renee jumped in her seat, smacking her head into the roof of the car. "Ow!" she exclaimed, almost dropping the lit cigarette. Looking back over her shoulder, she saw No-Face sitting in the backseat. "I hate you."

He leaned forward and plucked the notebook from the dashboard. His eyeless face glanced over the notes. "Nice doodles."

"Bite me," Renee replied.

He pointed at his lack of face. "Can't. No mouth."

Ha-ha, she thought sourly. By now, she was almost used to her nameless employer's bizarrely blank countenance, although she still couldn't make up her mind as to whether he was wearing some sort of incredibly sophisticated mask, or if he was just a metahuman freak like Clayface or the Man-Bat. Either way, she had no idea how he could see or breathe.

But apparently that wasn't a problem for him.

"You didn't answer," he reminded her. "How many packs a day?"

She gave him a dirty look. "What're you, my mother?"

"You know, there's cyanide gas in cigarette smoke." His disapproving tone made up for his lack of facial expressions. She took a drag on the cigarette anyway. "That's the same stuff they use in gas chambers."

She blew a puff of smoke in his (non) face.

"Very mature," he commented.

"I thought so," she said, enjoying the moment. Too bad the smoke couldn't make him cough.

He lobbed the notebook back onto the dashboard. She heard the back door open. "Keep up the good work."

"Hey! Wait a minute!" she protested. They hadn't even discussed the pointlessness of her assignment yet. "You saw my notes. There's nothing going on here."

"Not yet. But there will be. I'm sure of it." He got out of the sedan and started to walk away. "We'll talk again later."

"Don't hold your breath!" Renee shouted from the car, not caring if anyone heard her or not. This whole gig was a waste of time anyway. "Four more days, buddy! That's it! Four more days . . ."

He disappeared into one of his damn smoky question marks. She supposed she should be grateful that he didn't set off his portable fog bank inside the car. *And he gives me a hard time about smoking?* She didn't know what kind of chemicals were involved in his vanishing act, but she doubted that they were good for the lungs.

Four more days, she reminded herself.

"Then I'm done."

FOUR nights later, Renee started to drift off into sleep.

It was the rain's fault. A spring shower had started up sometime after midnight, and the persistent beating of the raindrops against the car roof was like a lullaby. Like a gentle, soothing lullaby . . .

Her head drooped back against the driver's seat. Too many late nights and not enough caffeine, along with the muggy atmosphere, made it hard to stay awake. Her eyelids sagged. A black tank top and shorts made up her evening's attire, along with the gun holstered over her shoulder. Dozing behind the wheel, she barely registered the sound of heavy footsteps splashing through the puddles outside.

Footsteps?

She awoke with a start, just in time to see a hulking figure in a heavy overcoat step inside 520 Kane Street. The front door swung shut behind him

"Dammit!" she cursed. She couldn't believe her carelessness and bad timing. Two weeks of waiting for something to happen and she almost slept right through it. *Good job, Renee. Way to earn your money!*

She threw open the car door and dashed toward the building. A raised arm shielded her eyes from the rain. Arriving at the front door, she spotted broken two-by-fours lying upon the sidewalk; the building's mysterious visitor had apparently torn down the boards nailed up over the door. She pressed her back against the front of the building, in order to avoid presenting an easy target, then reached out and gave the door a gentle shove. To her surprise, it swung open easily.

Unlocked, she realized. *So whoever's paying a visit isn't planning on staying long.*

She stepped warily into the darkened interior of the building, which turned out to be an old warehouse after all. Empty crates and wooden pallets cluttered the corners. Broken loading equipment was rusting away. Dust and cobwebs shrouded an abandoned forklift. Rat droppings sprinkled the rough concrete floor. From the looks of things, the deserted warehouse hadn't been a going concern for some time. The glow from the street outside filtered through the filthy windows, giving Renee barely enough light to see by. She kicked herself for not bringing a flashlight.

The one thing she *didn't* see was the big guy in the overcoat. She looked around in confusion. *I couldn't have been more than thirty seconds behind him,* she thought, *so where the hell did he go?* Wiping her wet hair away from her face, she peered into the murky recesses of the warehouse. She listened intently for the man's heavy footsteps. Water dripped onto the floor behind her.

"Don't even think about it," she whispered.

Her faceless employer spoke up softly. "How'd you know it was me?"

"Guy who came in was in front of me," she explained, keeping her voice low. "You're the one who likes to sneak up on people."

"Touché." He came up beside her and extracted a flashlight from his trench coat. A glowing white beam lit up the darkness.

"Question is," she said, "where'd he go?"

"Take a look." He shone the light onto the floor in front of them, revealing wet shoe prints leading toward a brick wall at the rear of the warehouse. The prints were surprisingly large, size triple-E at least. Renee whistled softly. The guy they were looking for was one big customer.

So where was he anyway?

"Curious," her companion observed. The beam from the flashlight fell upon a solid brick wall. A dead end?

"He didn't just vanish," she assumed, thinking out loud. "There's got to be a secret door or something like that."

"A secret door?" He sounded skeptical. "What is this, Dungeons & Dragons?"

"Got a better idea?" She noted a light switch upon the wall. "Let's see if there's still power to these lights." She flipped the switch—and a trapdoor opened up beneath them.

She yelped out loud as gravity seized them. They plunged through the trapdoor into the basement. No-Face hit the floor first, landing flat on his back. He cushioned her fall as she smacked down on top of him. Bright fluorescent lights illuminated the hidden basement. She caught a glimpse of wooden crates piled high against the walls. The flashlight, jolted free from No-Face's grip, rolled across a scuffed steel floor.

He gasped beneath her weight. "Elf needs food badly," he

murmured, sounding dazed by the fall. "Seriously, Renee, you've got to get off of me. . . ."

She wasn't listening. Lifting her head, one hand on the floor, the other splayed across his blank face, she stared in shock at the basement's other inhabitant.

"Oh hell," she muttered.

Green scales glittered beneath the harsh fluorescent lights. For a second, she thought it might be Killer Croc, but even Waylon Jones had never looked so inhuman as the hideous monstrosity standing a few yards away, still cloaked in that same heavy overcoat. Over seven feet tall, and at least four hundred pounds, the creature looked part human, part reptile, and part insect. A chitinous, jade-colored exoskeleton covered its gorilla-sized frame. Bony knobs protruded from its misshapen skull. Multifaceted black eyes were sunken deep into its armored sockets. Segmented claws emerged from the sleeves of its soggy overcoat. Heavy work boots concealed its undoubtedly freakish feet. Saliva dripped from its massive jaws.

"Hnn?" The creature emitted an inarticulate grunt. It looked just as surprised at the humans' abrupt arrival as they were. It turned toward them, clutching a heavy crate in its scaly talons.

Renee rolled off No-Face and jumped to her feet. She drew her Smith & Wesson from its holster. "What the hell is that thing?"

"How should I know?" her employer said. Still stunned from the fall, not to mention providing a cushioned landing pad for Renee, he struggled to get up. A groan escaped his nonexistent mouth.

Roaring like an enraged animal, the monster hurled the crate at Renee. She dived out of the way so that the box smashed into the wall behind her. The crate came apart, spilling out a supply of high-tech guns and rifles that looked like they had been shipped straight from outer space. At least fifty pounds of metal firearms crashed onto the floor, missing her by inches. She fired her gun at the charging monster.

"You wanted me to watch this place!" she reminded No-

Face, shouting over the blare of the gunshots. "I figured you knew what was going on!"

Silly me.

The muzzle of her weapon flared as she gripped the weapon with both hands. Two double-taps, four bullets. All good hits, but they didn't even slow the creature down. Angry growls assailed her eardrums. Moving with unexpected speed, the monster was on top of her in a blur. She didn't even have time to squeeze off another shot. A powerful hand seized her right arm. Sharp claws dug into her skin, drawing blood. She heard bone shatter and knew it was hers from her scream. Excruciating pain raced up her fractured arm. The Smith & Wesson went flying.

A swipe of the monster's arm cracked her ribs and sent her tumbling across the room. The titanic blow knocked the breath from her. She crashed down onto the hard steel floor, landing amidst the jumble of futuristic weapons.

Out of the corner of her eye, she saw No-Face enter the fray. He gave the monster a kung fu kick to the gut, but that only seemed to make the creature more angry. Growling ferociously, the monster grabbed No-Face by the throat and slammed him into the floor. Renee heard his head bang against the steel tiles.

She looked about frantically for her pistol, but all she saw were the weirdo ray guns scattered all around her. They looked like nothing she had ever seen before, outside of movies and television. Were these even for real? For all she knew, the alien ordnance were just props for some new sci-fi blockbuster, but they were the only weapons at hand. She snatched up the nearest firearm and prayed that a trigger was still a trigger. . . .

The monster's claws remained wrapped around No-Face's throat as it yanked the stunned human from the floor. The man's feet dangled in the air, his blank countenance only inches away from the creature's snapping jaws. The monster snarled at the intruder. Drool dripped from its jagged fangs. The inhuman beast was only seconds away from biting the man's head off.

"But how do you really feel?" No-Face quipped.

Skzam! Energy crackled loudly as an incandescent golden beam struck the monster in the back. The shimmering ray instantly vaporized the creature, leaving nothing but a slimy green stain on the floor. No longer held aloft by the monster, No-Face crashed to the ground. He looked up to see Renee standing nearby, the futuristic pistol in her left hand. Her right arm dangled limply against her chest. Glowing white plasma flickered around the ray gun's muzzle. She stared at the weapon, impressed.

"Damn," she murmured.

WEEK 5.

METROPOLIS.

"CURSE you, Booster Gold!"

The armored villain known only as Manthrax shook his fist at the hero before cowardly escaping down a murky subway tunnel. Booster glared at the fleeing terrorist, but stayed behind to finish deactivating Manthrax's insidious bio-bomb. The safety of countless commuters, watching anxiously from a nearby subway platform, obviously took priority.

Or so the televised video footage made it appear.

"We're coming to you live from the Midtown train station," the TV newswoman announced after airing the video clip. Claudia Lanpher stood outside the station speaking into her mike as she faced the camera. "Where Booster Gold just saved thousands of Metropolis citizens from a brand-new masked marauder, as seen in the amateur cam-phone footage you just saw. The exclusive footage vividly captures the villain's attempt to unleash a biological weapon inside the city's busiest subway terminal."

A levitating golden sphere entered the frame. "With us now is Skeets, Booster's robotic sidekick." She turned her mike toward the robot. "Skeets, fill us in. I'm told that Booster abruptly left a crucial endorsement meeting with Promethium Razors when he heard about this crisis. Will that sour your negotiations with Promethium?"

"WE HOPE NOT, MS. LANPHER." Skeets tilted toward the mike. "BUT PRIORITIES ARE PRIORITIES. THE

THINGS BOOSTER DOES ARE NOT ABOUT DOLLAR
FIGURES."

The reporter nodded approvingly. "Skeets, will Manthrax
be brought to justice?"

"YOU BET," the robot replied. "IF THIS ANTISOCIAL
MISCREANT EVER SHOWS HIS MASK IN METROPO-
LIS AGAIN, HE'LL ANSWER TO BOOSTER GOLD!" His
polished exterior reflected the lights of the camera. "YOU
MAY QUOTE ME."

"'CURSE you, Booster Gold'?"

Booster rolled his eyes. Talk about cheesy dialogue!

Manthrax, aka Bob Somebody, shrugged. "I ad-libbed.
That's what actors do." He removed his armored helmet, revealing a face that Booster vaguely recognized from bit parts in
movies and the occasional late-night TV commercial. Booster
also thought he might have seen Bob in a *Law & Order* rerun
once. Just another out-of-work actor, in other words.

The two men stood on the tracks of an abandoned subway
tunnel. Skeets hovered above Booster, projecting enough light
to see by. Security cameras were conspicuously absent. The
nearby platform was deserted. Nervous rats kept their distance.

Booster wrote out a check and handed it over to Bob. Foam
rubber padding bulked up the actor's physique beneath his metallic green and white armor. Flashing lights and circuitry were
just for show.

"I teach a Saturday morning improv class at the Learning
Annex," Bob mentioned as he accepted the check. "You should
stop by."

"This Saturday?" Booster asked. "Love to."

Bob smiled, obviously pleased at the notion of recruiting a
genuine super hero. "Really?"

"Absolutely," Booster said sarcastically. "We can make
brownies after. Maybe braid each other's hair." Bob scowled as
he realized that Booster was making fun of him. "Or, alterna-
tively, Bob—"

"Bill," the disgruntled actor corrected him.

Whatever, Booster thought. "You can go find a horse to choke with the money you just made, then vanish back into the same obscure talent agency where I found you." He reached out for Manthrax's forbidding metal countenance. "I'll take the helmet. Drop the suit off at the same storage locker you picked it up from. Manthrax disappears forever as suddenly as he appeared. We never had this conversation. Everyone wins."

Despite his callous tone, Booster felt a twinge from his conscience. He had never faked a super-heroic stunt before, but what was he supposed to do? He couldn't depend on Skeets' predictions anymore. How else could he nurture his lucrative career unless he manufactured the occasional incident to enhance his reputation? The public had a short memory. He couldn't coast on his past triumphs for long.

Everyone wins, he told himself again. *And nobody gets hurt.*

"*Capisce,*" Bob said, getting the message. A change of clothes waited in the gym bag at his feet. Booster intended to hang on to the "Manthrax" costume just in case he needed to stage an encore someday. Maybe with an actor less fond of ad-libs.

"*Curse you, Booster Gold*"?

Booster decided to cut the guy a break anyway. "Just because I'm a generous soul, let me give you a tip. I'd turn that dough into Promethium Razors stock before the markets close today." Today's heroic headlines were bound to seal the deal with Promethium, and get Booster a much fatter contract than he might have pried out of the stingy company otherwise. And Booster's endorsement was sure to send Promethium's sales through the roof, now that he had famously saved thousand of lives from Manthrax's diabolical plan. *My popularity rating must be in the stratosphere right now.*

He started down the empty tunnel. "Coast clear above, Skeets?"

"AFFIRMATIVE, SIR!" the robot reported. "AND PRO-METHIUM WISHES TO RESCHEDULE. I TOLD THEM TOMORROW."

He gave Skeets a quizzical look. "Why tomorrow?"

"THIS AFTERNOON WE TRAVEL TO ARIZONA. I FI-
NALLY LOCATED, AS YOU REQUESTED, THE LAST
KNOWN ADDRESS FOR DR. RIP HUNTER."

At last! Booster thought. If anybody could get to the bottom
of Skeets' recent spate of inaccurate predictions, it was Rip
Hunter, this era's leading authority on time-travel. For all his
bravado, Booster desperately needed to know whether it was
the robot that was broken—or history itself. *Maybe Hunter can
straighten this out,* he hoped, *so I won't have to fake any more
rescues.* The sooner he got back to genuine super-heroing, the
better he would feel.

"Then we're off!" His feet lifted off from the rusty subway
tracks as he flew down the tunnel. "Don't spend all of that in
one place, Bob!"

The actor's eyes bulged at all the zeroes inscribed on the
check. "I'm not sure I could."

Booster grinned. The future was starting to look bright
again.

Let it never be said I don't pay my villains well!

WEEK 6.

ARIZONA.

NO TRESPASSING, read the sign posted to the sturdy chain-link fence surrounding the remote desert outpost. Razor wire and security cameras topped the fence. Miles of desolate badlands surrounded the compound in every direction. Cacti bloomed amidst the arid landscape. Buzzards circled overhead. Red rock mesas loomed in the background.

"What's he preparing for? World War III?" Booster Gold flew over the fence and touched down in front of a pair of massive steel blast doors. "An underground bunker in the middle of the desert? This is his last known address?"

Despite Skeets' confident assertion back in Metropolis, it had taken them a week to track down this location. The Arizona address the robot had initially discovered had turned out to be merely the first link in a chain of forwarding addresses used to conceal Rip Hunter's true place of residence. Clearly, the celebrated scientist did not wish to be disturbed.

"IN HIS DEFENSE, SIR, DR. HUNTER IS JUST BEING SAFE." Skeets was dwarfed by the size of the looming steel doors. "HE *IS* THE UNQUESTIONED FATHER OF TIME-TRAVEL. OVER SEVENTY-NINE ATTEMPTS HAVE BEEN MADE TO STEAL HIS TRANS-TEMPORAL TECHNOLOGY THIS YEAR ALONE."

I suppose, Booster thought grumpily. The hot sun and blistering temperature did little to improve his mood. He knocked on the steel doors. "Hello? Rip?" He had met the so-called "Time Master" once or twice before. "It's Booster Gold!"

There was no response.

"PERHAPS HE ISN'T HOME?" Skeets speculated. "THAT WOULD EXPLAIN WHY I COULDN'T REACH HIM EARLIER."

"Or maybe he's caught up in one of his projects." Booster examined a futuristic-looking locking mechanism mounted to the door. "Skeets, what kind of a lock is that?"

"AN ATOMIC TIME LOCK, SIR."

Booster fingered the device, looking for some sort of key-pad. "A time lock? When's it set to open?"

"MIDNIGHT, JANUARY FIRST . . . FIFTY-TWO B.C."

Booster groaned. "I hate time-travelers."

Skeets tactfully refrained from pointing out that Booster was no one to talk. "DR. HUNTER SET THE LOCK, BUT ITS COMPUTER CHIPS WERE MANUFACTURED BY KORD OMNIVERSAL. SO, TECHNICALLY SPEAKING, THAT MEANS THE CENTRAL PROCESSOR IS MY GREAT, GREAT, GREAT, GREAT, GREAT GRANDFATHER." A probe extended from the floating robot, plugging into a matching port in the lock. "IT SPEAKS A PRIMITIVE LANGUAGE, BUT I THINK I CAN CONVINCE IT TO OPEN IF I JUST . . ."

Circuits hummed inside the lock. A second later, the blast doors slid open with an audible *whoosh*. A burst of cool air blew against Booster's face. Beyond the doorway, a long metal stair-case led deep beneath the surface of the desert.

All right! he thought. *Now we're getting somewhere.* "You're magic, Skeets."

"THANK YOU, SIR." The robot did not withdraw his probe from the lock. "UNFORTUNATELY, THE LOCK HAS A FAIL-SAFE REQUIRING A CONSTANT HARDWIRE SEQUENCING CODE TO KEEP IT OPEN. I'M AFRAID I MUST REMAIN HERE."

"No problem," Booster said. He started down the stairs on his own. "I'm sure there's nothing to be worried about. . . ."

His words trailed off as he reached the bottom of the steps, where a baffling scene confronted him. Rip Hunter's underground laboratory was in a state of extreme disarray. A transparent Time-Sphere, with seats for four temporal explorers, was cracked like a broken egg. Jagged shards littered the floor around the Sphere, which was obviously not in working order. Layers of dust covered the abandoned workstations and computer consoles. A wardrobe full of period costumes, to be used by Hunter when visiting the past, looked like it had been rifled through. Roman togas, Elizabethan ruffles, chain mail, capes, buckskin, and other antiquated items of clothing lay in a heap upon the floor. Hundreds of clocks, ranging from old-fashioned wooden timepieces to contemporary digital clocks, were scattered around the lab. Every clock was stopped at the same time: 12:52 A.M. The digital displays simply read 00:52. Scribbled notes and newspaper clippings were strewn about like confetti. Booster thought he recognized Hunter's handwriting.

Video screens played key historical events on a continuous loop. Booster recognized the Boston Tea Party, Columbus' ships setting sail, Lincoln delivering the Gettysburg Address, the arrest of Rosa Parks, Elvis Presley's first recording session, the destruction of Pompeii, the assassination of Julius Caesar, the battle of Marathon, the invention of gunpowder, the death of the dinosaurs, and a few scenes he couldn't quite place. History had never been his strong suit. That's what Skeets was for.

A globe of the world, the size of a beach ball, had rolled up against one wall. Large red Xs had been scrawled over the globe, crossing out great chunks of the Middle East, Russia, Korea, India, and China. A chisel had been used to carve a gaping scar where North Africa used to be. Booster gulped as he read the ominous graffiti defacing the globe: WORLD WAR III. WHY HOW?

Even more troubling than the mutilated globe, perhaps, was the classroom-sized blackboard set up in the middle of the laboratory. Nearly every inch of the board's green surface was covered by what looked like the incoherent ravings of a disturbed mind. Chalky white arrows and equations were inter-

spersed with dozens of cryptic remarks and queries. Booster
hastily scanned the board, trying to make sense of some of the
bizarre notations:

Don't ask the Question. It lies.

The scarab is eternal.

Who is Supernova?

When am I?

520 Kane.

Who is Diana Prince?

The four horsemen will end her rain?

I'm supposed to be dead?

Who is Batwoman?

TIME IS BROKEN.

The latter phrase was written in capital letters across the top
of the blackboard, many times larger than the other sentences,
as though it was the fundamental problem from which all the
other puzzles arose.

"Time is broken?" Booster said aloud. He didn't like the
sound of that, not to mention the reference to World War III.
Perhaps Hunter had a good reason for hiding out in the desert
like this? But where—or when—was he? "Rip?"

His call echoed within the subterranean chamber. Water
dripped from a rusted pipe. Booster searched the lab, looking
for some clue to Hunter's whereabouts. Stepping around the
blackboard, he spotted more writing upon the walls in a far
corner of the lab. To his dismay, he saw that a single phrase had
been scrawled onto the walls, over and over again:

It's all his fault.

Huh? Booster thought. "Whose fault? Who . . ."

Taped to one wall was a handful of publicity photos depicting him and Skeets in various heroic poses. The cover of a
recent issue of *NewsTime* depicted Booster triumphantly holding Mammoth over his head. Skeets hovered near the edge of
the photo, shining a spotlight on Booster. The hero's gleaming
smile and wavy blond hair had not required a trace of retouch-
ing. A framed copy of the same cover currently hung on the wall
of Booster's lavish apartment, but this copy had been treated

with considerably less respect. Arrows, drawn with a magic marker, pointed at the photogenic hero and his robotic side-kick. Post-it notes repeated the same damning message.

All his fault.

Booster couldn't believe his eyes. He swallowed hard, un-willing to accept what the crazy scribbling seemed to imply. "Me?"

I broke Time?

WEEK 7.

GOTHAM CITY.

THE Kane family estate was located in one of the ritzier neighborhoods in Gotham Heights. A high wrought iron fence surrounded the grounds of the multimillion-dollar mansion. Imposing stone columns supported the portico in front of the three-story Gothic Revival structure. It was the kind of house that practically screamed, "We Have More Money than You Will Ever Dream of Having, and No, You Can't Come In." Guards were posted at the front gate just in case you didn't get the message.

Tonight the house was host to the annual Kane Family Gala, one of the major social events of the season. Limousines were lined up all along the drive. The elite of Gotham society converged on the estate, eager to see and be seen. The men flaunted tuxedos and expensive haircuts. The women paraded their best furs and jewelry. Hired goons, in fancy suits, kept the local paparazzi at bay.

Just try to keep me out, Renee thought.

She had read about the Gala in the newspaper, while recovering at home from her injuries. Her right arm itched beneath a plaster cast, while another itch nagged at the back of her mind. It had been three weeks since she'd almost died in that waterfront hideout and she still didn't know why. Instead of answers, all she had to show for her investigation were three cracked ribs and a fractured elbow. *That's not good enough,* she thought.

Part of her wasn't sure why she couldn't just let the warehouse mystery go. She was no private eye; she didn't even have a license. Besides, her no-faced employer had only paid for three weeks, and she had already put in more like six now. Plus, No-Face himself seemed to have dropped off the face of the earth. She hadn't laid eyes on him since that fight with the monster. There was absolutely no reason to keep pursuing this matter . . . except that she had maybe one more lead to follow.

Which was why it was time to crash the party.

She felt a flicker of apprehension as she strolled up to the gate, but not because of the beefy security guard posted at the door. *It's been a long time, Kate,* she thought as she peered past the iron bars of the gate at the mansion. *Close to ten years . . .*

"I'm sorry," the guard said brusquely. He sneered disdainfully at her leather jacket, white Oxford shirt, and pressed trousers. This really was her best outfit, but he still seemed to think that she didn't belong here—and was only too happy to point that out. "This is by invitation only."

"Yeah, it always is." She took a moment to light up a cigarette. "Listen, just call up to the house and let Katherine the Younger know that Officer Renee is here."

"That would be you?" he asked dubiously. A few feet away, another guard let a Rolls-Royce through.

Renee wasn't interested in bantering with this clown. "Just give her the message."

It took three minutes to get permission to approach the house and another five to walk up the damn driveway. A metal detector made her glad that she had left her spiffy new ray gun at home. Along the way, she tried to calculate how much money she was passing.

She gave up at fifty million.

The stern-faced butler gave her an even snootier look than the guard at the gate. "This way, please," he instructed, leading her away from the foyer. Polished wood paneling covered the walls. A crystal chandelier sparkled overhead. An antique lever-action rifle was mounted above a doorway in a position of honor. The name was Kane, she recalled, but the money was Hamilton. The Hamilton Rifle Company, to be exact.

Like trying to count the money, you couldn't begin to count the dead.

He escorted her to a cozy den, safely distant from the main festivities. Walnut bookcases, stuffed with expensive-looking first editions, surrounded her on all sides. A large globe rested upon its axis. An antique leather couch and old-fashioned roll-top desk displayed both affluence and good taste. "If you'll wait here, please," the butler said, "Mistress Kane will be with you in a moment." He left, shutting the door behind him.

"Thanks, Jeeves."

Her flippant tone belied the butterflies in her stomach. Now that the meeting was only moments away, she started to have second thoughts. *Ten years is a long time,* she mused, pacing restlessly about the opulent chamber. *Maybe too long.* She had just about convinced herself that sneaking out the servants' entrance was a good idea when she heard the door swing open. A husky voice addressed her from behind.

"If you've come to arrest me, Officer Montoya, I trust you'll be searching me first?"

The photos in the society columns never did her justice. Katherine Kane had the kind of beauty that took your breath away. Lustrous auburn hair cascaded onto her shoulders. A strapless red satin gown clung to her athletic figure. A string of pearls discreetly called attention to her generous cleavage. Perfect makeup subtly highlighted her exquisite features. Piercing brown eyes made Renee's heart skip a beat.

Renee tried to play it cool. "If you insist." Forcing herself to look away, she turned to light a fresh cigarette. "Although that dress isn't likely to conceal anything I haven't seen before."

She didn't see the fist coming until a hard right cross slammed into her jaw. Renee's head snapped to the side. The cigarette and lighter tumbled onto the carpet. A stunned Renee massaged her jaw. Her tongue probed for loosened teeth. She tasted blood in her mouth. Somewhere along the line, someone had taught Kate how to throw a punch.

Good thing I know how to take one, Renee thought.

"You've got a lot of nerve coming here." Kate's vibrant eyes flashed with anger, betraying a temper that Renee remembered well. Her fists were clenched at her sides. "Especially after the last time I saw you."

Renee gave as good as she got. "I assume this means you're still in the closet."

"You self-righteous—!" A furious Kate came at her again, her fingers poised to claw the smirk off the other woman's face, but this time Renee was ready for her. She seized Kate's wrist with her good arm, catching it before Kate's nails could draw blood. They confronted each other face-to-face, their bodies almost touching. Renee could feel Kate's pulse racing beneath her fingertips. Her face was flushed with emotion.

It had been an easy button to push. Renee had always been able to press Kate's buttons, just like she had always been able to press Renee's. That's what had made it so good . . . and why it couldn't last. At least, that's what they'd told each other.

"Not so loud," Renee taunted. "Someone might come in here and get the wrong idea."

She stared into Kate's brown eyes. An endless moment fraught with possibility. The beautiful socialite's gaze seemed to soften. She was breathing hard. A familiar perfume tantalized Renee's senses, throwing her memory back nearly a decade. Old desires surfaced, as strong as ever. Kate's lips parted, and Renee's own heartbeat quickened in anticipation. They leaned toward each other. Renee couldn't believe this was really happening.

It's been so long. . . .

But instead of kissing her, Kate pulled away at the last minute. She wrested her arm from Renee's grip and put some distance between them. "What do you want, Renee?" Her voice was hoarse with emotion. "You're not on the force anymore, so why are you here?"

"Been keeping tabs on me, have you?" Renee asked.

"Don't flatter yourself," she said crisply, regaining her composure. "Father had Commissioner Gordon to dinner last month. It came up in conversation."

Sure it did, Renee thought smugly. Despite everything, it gave her some comfort to know that Kate had not forgotten her completely. *Lord knows I've never forgotten her. . . .*

"I'm asking you again," Kate said impatiently. Her bare arms were crossed protectively across her chest. "Why are you here?"

Renee was both relieved and disappointed to get down to business. "Five-twenty Kane Street. It's in the harbor district."

"Do I look like I spend my time in the harbor district?"

Not exactly, Renee admitted. "You look like you spend your time at Calais on Sixty-third, getting mud baths, massages, and facials. But the building, 520, your family still owns it?"

"I don't know." She shrugged her shapely shoulders. "Possibly. Probably."

"Could you find out?" Renee pressed her.

Kate eyed her suspiciously. "This have anything to do with that cast you're sporting under your jacket?"

Renee was impressed by her observational skills. She'd always thought Kate would make a first-rate detective. "I need to know," she pleaded. "Call it curiosity."

"Why should I help you?"

Her icy tone tore open a scab that Renee had thought long healed. "Because once we thought we were in love with each other." She laid all her cards on the table. "And maybe we even were."

It was the wrong thing to say, something she realized a moment too late.

Kate's face flushed once more. Breaking eye contact, she turned her back on Renee. Perhaps so Renee couldn't see her pained expression? "I think you had better go now."

"Kate . . ." Renee longed to reach out to the other woman, but wisely kept her hands to herself. *I've done enough damage already.*

"Go," the other woman insisted, "before I change my mind and decide not to help you." She looked back over her shoulder, her face a frozen mask that gave nothing away. "You can show yourself out."

Renee got the message. She headed for the door. "You know where to find me."

"Yes . . ." Kate admitted as Renee left the room. She spoke so softly that Renee couldn't be entirely sure that she was hearing her right. "I always have."

METROPOLIS.

A huge crowd had turned out for the opening night of *Aquaman: The Motion Picture*. A line of eager moviegoers stretched around the block, while a handful of protestors demonstrated against the movie's alleged "distortion" of Atlantean culture and history. Police officers stood by to maintain order, even though no one was seriously expecting the demonstration to turn violent. Journalists and photographers were on hand to cover the premiere. The sidewalk outside the theater was overflowing with people—which made this the worst possible moment for a Lex-Corp tanker-trailer to jackknife right in the middle of the street.

Flames erupted from the ruptured tanker, climbing high into the sky. Billowing black smoke blotted out the theater's marquee. Terrified men, women, and children fought to escape from the spreading conflagration, only to find themselves trapped by the crush of the crowd. Overwhelmed cops called for order, but there was little they could do to control the frantic stampede. "Outta my way!" a frightened voice cried out, just one of many in the chaotic din. People were literally climbing over each other in their desperate attempts to escape the blaze. The protestors trampled over their own signs. A hefty movie fan shoved another man aside. "Move, jackass!"

"NO NEED TO PANIC, CITIZENS!" Skeets' amplified voice could be heard above the hubbub. Dozens of faces looked up at the robot with varying degrees of hope and confusion. "READY YOUR CAMERAS . . . FOR ONCE AGAIN, IT'S BOOSTER GOLD TO THE RESCUE!"

Booster came swooping down from the sky. He eyed the burning tanker with genuine concern. This was no hoax; for once, Skeets' prediction had been right on target. Maybe Time wasn't broken after all. . . .

He dived headfirst into the inferno, feeling the heat of the flames licking against his force field and body armor. His fists smashed through the pavement beneath the tanker and kept on going. He disappeared beneath the street, dragging the jagged ends of the broken fuel tank with him, but the smoke and fire continued to climb from the center of the wreck. Helpless bystanders choked on the fumes.

The crowd gasped as the hero vanished into the heart of the blaze. "He didn't stop it!" shrieked a skinny nerd in an Aquaman T-shirt. The lenses of his Coke-bottle glasses reflected the voracious scarlet flames. "We're toast!"

Only Skeets seemed unconcerned. "PLEASE HOLD YOUR APPLAUSE UNTIL THE BIG FINISH," he calmly instructed the people beneath him. "IN TWO, ONE . . ."

Right on cue, Booster rocketed upward from the flames, followed by an enormous plume of water that shot almost two stories into the air. Gallons of water, released from a buried water main, poured down upon the burning truck, extinguishing the blaze. The spray from the geyser rained onto the grateful faces of the nearby civilians, who let out a collective sigh of relief. Jubilant people laughed and high-fived each other. A little girl hugged her teddy bear.

"SUCCESS!" Skeets announced. "AND LET THIS BE A REMINDER, LADIES AND GENTLEMEN. NEVER LEAVE HOME WITHOUT AN OFFICIAL BOOSTER GOLD WIND-PROOF UMBRELLA!"

Thunderous cheers and applause greeted Booster as he descended toward the drenched sidewalk. The artificial rainfall bounced off his force field, keeping him perfectly dry. *Pretty smooth,* he thought, *if I do say so myself.* There were maybe easier ways to put out a burning tanker, but he couldn't think of a more dramatic one. *Superman himself couldn't have handled this crisis any better.*

"**BRAVO, SIR!**" Skeets congratulated him. "**A THRILL-ING SIGHT INDEED!**"

"Booster!" Drawn by the disaster, or perhaps already on hand to cover the movie opening, a throng of reporters swarmed toward Booster. As usual, Lois Lane was ahead of the pack. "Over here!"

"Greetings, Ms. Lane." Booster landed on the sidewalk in front of Lois. Superman had always given Lane the best interviews. Booster figured what was good for Big Blue was good enough for him. "Always a pleasure to chat with the *Daily Planet*'s most prestigious correspondent."

Lois ignored the flattery. "Not a bad rescue. Any comments for our readers?"

"I'm just glad I was able to find a water main in time," Booster said honestly. "Stopping an exploding propane truck is—"

"An amazing stunt," a harsh voice interrupted. Booster turned to see a guy in a trench coat force his way through the crowd. The man looked familiar, but Booster couldn't quite place the face. "But I have a question. How much did it cost you?"

Oh crap! Booster suddenly recognized the man's scowling face. Bob Somebody, or was it Bill? *The actor.* His heart sank. *This could be bad. . . .*

"I have . . . no idea what you're talking about." Stammering, he looked around for a way out. "Interview's over, folks!"

"We'll decide that, thanks," Lois said crisply. Her shrewd blue eyes gleamed at the prospect of a juicy scoop. Turning her back on Booster, she pointed her tape recorder at the newcomer. "Your name, sir?"

"I'm Bill Castell, and I'm an actor." He opened his trench coat to reveal that he was wearing Manthrax's phony armor underneath. "Two weeks ago, Booster Gold hired me to stage a fake—"

"Ms. Lane!" Booster blurted in a panic. He saw his life unraveling right before his eyes. "Don't listen to a word that man says!" He mustered a sternly heroic tone. "He's a proven threat to—"

But Lois had her teeth into the story now and wasn't about to let go. "Go on, Mr. Castell."

"A fake attack on a commuter rail station," the actor continued. "Then his check bounced over the bank building in a single bound!"

What? Booster thought. *How'd that happen?* His finances had taken a bit of a hit when the Akteon-Holt deal fell through, and he was still waiting on the Promethium money, but he hadn't realized that things had gotten so tight. Then again, he admitted to himself, he had been spending lavishly in anticipation of more profits down the road. Apparently, he hadn't been paying close enough attention to the bottom line. And now his sloppy accounting had come back to bite him on the ass.

"I warned him!" Castell declared, taking full advantage of his fifteen minutes of fame. Flashbulbs snapped all around him. Competing cameramen and paparazzi jostled each other for the best angles. He held up a photocopy of the bounced check. "I knew I could go to jail for this, but I'll do it to drag that phony son of a bitch down!"

"Enough, Mr. Castell." Lois turned back toward Booster, her attractive face much more severe than before. She almost seemed to take his ersatz heroics personally. "Booster, is this true? Do you know this man? Was that subway rescue simply a publicity stunt?"

"No!" he lied unconvincingly. "I mean . . . this isn't like it seems. . . ."

Smelling blood in the water, the rest of the reporters charged at Booster.

"Booster! Gary McGraw, WGBS-TV. How much did you pay Castell?"

"Ami Soon, Channel Five! Can you discredit this claim?"

Lois refused to surrender her story to the competition. "Booster! How many of your various death-defying rescues have you staged to improve your marketability?"

Just that one, he thought, but who was going to believe him now? The barrage of questions and accusations left him standing like the proverbial deer in the headlights. Floating overhead, Skeets was unable to come to his defense. The robot drifted away, as though to distance himself from his disgraced master. All on his own, Booster faced the hostile press corps. He didn't know which question to answer, or what on earth he was supposed to say. "I swear, this isn't what it looks like," he mumbled.

Except that it was.

Not getting any good sound bites out of Booster, some of the reporters turned their attention back to the actor in the super-villain costume. "Manthrax" shrugged off his trench coat, the better to show off his incriminating armor.

"Mr. Castell, would you be willing to take a lie detector test?"

"Where did you get that armor?"

"Would you testify in a civil trial against Booster Gold?"

Booster watched the scene unfold like a slow-motion train wreck beyond his power to avert. The falling rain washed his reputation into the gutter. *This isn't fair!* he lamented silently. *I just saved dozens of people—for real! Why doesn't anyone care about that?*

But he knew why, and he knew who was really to blame.

It's all my fault.

WEEK 8.

METROPOLIS.

CHILDREN these days! Mildred Heiney couldn't believe the scene her grandson, Clifford, was making right here on the sidewalk in front of Lacey's department store, all because she wouldn't buy him one of those newfangled computer games. The toddler was lying on the pavement, kicking and screaming and throwing quite a fit, and in broad daylight, no less. His shrill cries could be heard all across Metro Square. She shook her finger at the unruly child. "Listen to me, young man. Your mother may tolerate this sort of behavior, but in my day . . ."

Mildred was vaguely aware of other pedestrians rushing past her with alarmed expressions on their faces. Their reactions struck her as a trifle excessive. Little Clifford wasn't misbehaving *that* much. A large shadow blotted out the sun, and she noticed people staring upward in horror. *What the dickens?*

Before she could look up to see what the matter was, a strong hand fell upon her shoulder. She turned around in surprise to see one of those masked "mystery men" one so often heard tell of nowadays. A blue hood and cape were draped over his head and shoulders, concealing his face, and he wore a skintight white suit that left little to the imagination. Red gloves and boots matched the inner lining of his cape. A bright yellow starburst design was stamped on his chest and forehead. *Who?* Mildred thought. She didn't recognize this new hero at all.

She only got a glimpse of the costumed stranger before he

lit up like the sun. Her eyes snapped shut against the glare, even as she instinctively grabbed onto Clifford's arm. The brilliant radiance faded almost as quickly as it appeared. She opened her eyes cautiously, only to discover that both she and Clifford were somewhere else. Disoriented, and seeing spots before her eyes, it took her a moment to realize that they were now across the street from where they had been only a second before. *I don't understand,* she thought. *How did we get here?*

But that wasn't the only shock in store for her. Looking back toward the department store, she saw that one of the city's many elevated trams had crashed nose-first down onto the sidewalk in front of Lacey's—right where she and Clifford had been arguing. Smoke and flames rose from the mangled remains of the tram, which hung at an angle from the cable overhead. Little Clifford squeezed her hand as he stared wide-eyed at the destruction before them, his computer game completely forgotten. Mildred looked around for the hero who had somehow come to their rescue, but the cloaked man was nowhere to be seen.

"Well, I'll be."

"Who was that, Gramma?" Clifford asked.

"I have no idea, sweetie." She hugged her grandson, grateful to be alive. Tears leaked from her watery eyes. "But whoever he was, he saved our lives."

FIREMAN Fred Farrell thought he was a goner.

He and his crew were trapped inside the burning apartment building. Flaming rubble blocked the way out, while the thick smoke and ash made it almost impossible to see, even with their flashlights. Farrell hacked at the fallen debris with his axe, but his efforts barely made a dent in the deadly barrier. "Watch out!" someone shouted as the ceiling began to collapse above them. The burning beams were going to crash down on them any second. No way was their protective gear going to save them. Timbers cracked as the beams tore loose from the ceiling. Farrell threw up his arms in a hopeless attempt to shield himself.

This is it, he thought.

Suddenly, impossibly, a super hero appeared out of no-where. Through the dense black smoke, Farrell glimpsed a caped figure standing behind them. *Superman?* Farrell thought hopefully, before spying a blue hood over the newcomer's face. The hero's upraised palms projected shimmering rays of golden light that seemed to erase the falling rafters. The fiery timbers vanished as though they had never existed. Farrell's jaw dropped behind his SCBA mask. He lowered his arms, amazed to find himself still breathing.

Maybe we're not goners after all. . . .

Light radiated from the masked figure, cutting through the smoky haze. He waved his arm and a second burst of concen-trated light cleared the rubble blocking the exit. Farrell and his fellow firefighters scurried for safety. "Thank you!" he gasped as he ran past the glowing stranger, who lingered behind, mak-ing sure that all the firefighters got out safely.

Farrell was the last one out onto the sidewalk. He ripped off his breathing apparatus and inhaled deeply of the warm sum-mer air. Flames erupted from the building they had just evacu-ated, but the fireman did not fear for the hero they had left behind. Somehow he sensed that their mysterious rescuer could take care of himself.

"Who the heck was that?" another firefighter asked him. Her sweaty face was streaked with soot.

"Hell if I know," Farrell admitted.

"SUPERNOVA? He calls himself Supernova?" Booster Gold crumpled the newspaper in his fist. Indignation was written all over his face as he railed at the reporter who had come to him for a comment on Metropolis's latest hero. He paced up and down on the pavement outside his apartment building. "I swear, if I have to hear one more word about this guy, I'm going to punch you in the neck."

"SIR, PLEASE!" Skeets said anxiously. "YOUR IMAGE . . ."

"Is in the toilet," Booster groused, "so what damage is left to be done?" His uniform was missing about half of the corporate logos it had boasted before the "Manthrax" scandal last week. "One week, I'm the city's favorite hero. The next, some new Boy Scout has moved in while I'm given the heave-ho!"

Skeets flitted about nervously. **"SIR, THIS MAN'S TAKING NOTES. . . ."**

"'This man' is going to write whatever he feels like as long as it sells papers." Booster unrolled the crumpled newspaper, exposing the front-page headline: "GOLD TARNISHED." An unflattering photo of Booster, taken moments after Manthrax spilled the beans, accompanied the banner headline. Booster glared murderously at the reporter in front of him. "Or have you actually gathered some facts for a change? Huh? What about it?" Passersby gave the disgraced hero dirty looks as he threw the paper in the newsman's face. "Do you know who this 'Supernova' is?"

"No, I do not," Clark Kent responded. "But I guarantee you I'm going to find out."

WEEK 9.

GOTHAM CITY.

"I can't believe we're losing to Star City."

Renee nursed a cold beer as she watched the baseball game on the TV set at Molly's Bar and Girl. Most of the usual crowd was standing outside on the street, watching the Fourth of July fireworks, but Renee preferred air-conditioning to pyrotechnics. She sat at the counter smoking a cigarette. Scrawled question marks covered the cast on her elbow.

"Tell me about it," Jilly the bartender said. She looked up from washing glasses as a newcomer entered the bar. She arched an eyebrow. "Can I help you?"

Someone sat down at the bar beside Renee. She was vaguely surprised to see that it was a young guy wearing jeans, a blue muscle shirt, and a red baseball cap. "A bottle of Lit, please," he asked pleasantly.

"Ooo-kay," Jilly said dubiously, but handed the man a beer.

He glanced up at the TV screen. "What inning?"

"Seventh," Renee volunteered. "Stars five, Knights two." She eyed him curiously, intrigued despite herself. "You do know this is a lesbian bar, right?"

That didn't seem to trouble him. "So no men's room, huh?"

"Smart-ass," Renee said, amused.

"Consistency is everything," he said cryptically. He kept his eyes on the game as he sipped his beer. "By the way, how's your arm?"

Renee recognized the tone, if not the voice. Her eyes narrowed suspiciously. "Who are you?"

"No, I asked you first," he said. "And I'm still waiting for an answer."

That cinched it. Renee's jaw tightened. This was definitely the no-faced asshole.

"You," she accused him.

He turned toward her and touched a finger to the side of his nose. A grin broke out over his face. "Me."

Renee rose from the bar stool, glaring at the nameless stranger. *Now what?* she thought. She honestly didn't know whether she wanted to punch him, walk away, or just sit back down. "I was wondering if I would ever see your face again."

"One of them anyway." He held out his hand. "My name's Vic, but my friends call me Charlie." Renee just glared at his hand, refusing to take it. He shrugged and slipped off his bar stool. "Curious? Full of questions?" Sounding just as infuriatingly calm and smug as ever, he headed for the door. "C'mon. I might have some answers for you."

She flirted with the notion of staying right where she was, but who was she kidding? Answers were even better than A.C.

Scowling, she followed him onto the street. Molly's clientele milled about on the sidewalk, flirting and drinking as they admired the skyrockets going off. A chorus of *ooh*s and *aah*s greeted each spectacular burst of colored flares. Heat and humidity smothered Renee as "Vic" led her down the sidewalk, away from the other women. The scorching weather did little to improve her mood.

"I'm wondering why I shouldn't beat you within an inch of your life, Charlie," she told him. Oddly, though, she felt less angry than she sounded.

He didn't take the threat seriously. "You have impulse control issues, don't you?"

"I thought you were gone for good!"

"Hey, I got hurt in that fight too, you know." He stopped walking and turned to face her. Now that she could see it, there was nothing at all remarkable about his face, which turned out to have blue eyes. Renee pegged his age as being somewhere in the early thirties. "So, you gonna tell me what you learned?"

She couldn't believe the nerve of him. "Your money ran out a month ago, smart guy. What makes you think I'm even still interested in your little mystery?"

"Because you're like me," he said, insufferably sure of himself. "You're curious."

"You almost got me killed!" she protested, giving him an angry shove. "My curiosity doesn't extend that far!"

"Sure it does," he insisted. "Why else are you still looking into it?"

It took a moment for his meaning to sink in. "Wait. You've been spying on me?"

"I wanted to make sure you were all right," he said, actually sounding a bit apologetic. Glancing around, he stepped into a dingy alley off the main street. Renee chased after him, determined to get to the bottom of this. "Who are you?" she demanded. "I mean, just who the hell are you?"

"Like I keep saying . . ." He fished a balled-up wad of pink plastic from his pocket. He tapped his belt buckle, releasing swirling blue fumes. As the smoke enveloped him, he smoothed the plastic over his face, concealing his features. His brightly colored clothing turned an inconspicuous shade of brown. "I asked you first."

By the time the fumes dissipated, No-Face was back.

"Neat trick," she conceded. "How's it work?"

"See? Questions. That's good. That's why I like you." The faceless mask, which blended seamlessly with his skin, distorted his voice. "The clothes and the mask are chemically treated, activated by the binary gas released by the belt buckle."

She took his word for it. Chemistry was never her strong suit.

"Some people call me the Question," he informed her.

The name sounded vaguely familiar. Some sort of vigilante, who used to work out of Hub City? *Hell,* Renee thought, *I can barely keep track of Gotham's freaks.* "Why are you telling me all this?"

"To prove a couple points," he said. "First, that I trust you. Second, that most answers lead to more questions." His blank face confronted her. "How many more do you have now, Renee?"

"Oh, another dozen or so," she admitted. "But mostly I keep coming back to the same ones. What the hell's going on? What was that . . . thing . . . that attacked us? What were those weapons?" She had phoned in an anonymous tip to the G.C.P.D., alerting them to the weapons cache, but that didn't mean that there weren't more of those futuristic firearms out there. "Where'd they come from?"

The Question nodded, like he approved of her queries. "Gotham is being targeted, Renee. What we found was the groundwork for an invasion." His voice took on a more ominous tone. "Gotham City is being targeted by Intergang."

Intent on their discussion, neither Renee nor her companion was aware of a third party eavesdropping on their conversation from five stories up. A cloaked figure crouched on the rooftop overlooking the alley. The scalloped tips of a voluminous black cape fluttered in the breeze, giving the figure the silhouette of an enormous bat. Keen eyes peered down at the alley through white one-way lenses. A determined expression showed beneath a forbidding black mask expressly designed to strike terror into the hearts of criminals. A nocturnal emblem was emblazoned on the figure's chest.

She *wasn't* Batman.

WEEK 10.

SHIRUTA.

"I cannot change the world alone," Black Adam confessed. "Which is why I have summoned Kahndaq's allies here."

He addressed his honored guests in the palace's high-tech reception area. Kahndaqi flags hung upon the walls, while a large holographic representation of the Earth floated in the center of the room. Kahndaq's present allies, indicated on the globe by black with a golden band, included China, Singapore, Iran, Syria, Egypt, North Korea, India, Chile, Zandia, Qurac, and Modora. Conspicuously missing was Bialya, whose corrupt government remained under Intergang's control. *A good beginning,* he thought, *but only the beginning. . . .*

Superpowered champions from throughout the world mingled amongst themselves, accompanied by various aides, advisors, and translators. They sipped on champagne and iced fruit juices as they listened to Black Adam's speech. Among the costumed emissaries, he recognized:

General August-in-Iron from China.

Cascade from Indonesia.

Rocket Red from Russia.

Lady Zand from Zandia.

Ibis the Invincible from Egypt.

Sonar from Modora.

Queen Cobra from India.

Together, they represented a potential alliance with power enough to challenge the Justice League of America and its decadent Western allies. Exactly as he intended.

"Each of you is a representative of your great country," he continued. "And I ask you to deliver a message to your leaders." A short black cape, with golden trim, had been added to his uniform for this formal occasion. "Many have joined our coalition, but many more have been resistant . . . or reluctant to allow others in. As of now, I ask you to forget the political rivalries between one another. Soon we will have the strength to—"

"Stop!" A strident voice, coming from the corridor outside, interrupted his address. Scowling, he turned his head toward the disturbance. *Who dares?*

To his surprise, he saw the nameless young woman he had rescued from Intergang, the one who had so callously been offered to him as a "gift," come charging into the reception hall, pursued by a trio of palace guards. A loose-fitting robe clothed the fleeing maiden. Her dark brown hair flowed behind as she ran from the guards.

"Stop her!" a guard shouted. "Come back here!"

Heading straight toward Black Adam, she jumped through the holographic globe. Laser-generated oceans and continents flickered and fuzzed as her passage disrupted the three-dimensional image. She landed nimbly on the other side of the globe, only a few yards away from Black Adam. Before she could reach him, however, a pair of guards tackled her.

"Let me go!" she exclaimed. The guards struggled to hold on to her. She thrashed furiously in their grip, as when she had tried to escape from her American captors. The girl had spirit, if nothing else.

"A thousand pardons, Mighty Adam," a guard apologized as he and his comrades attempted to drag the squirming woman from the room. He looked profoundly ashamed by the incident. "She threw her dinner in Maqued's face and ran here before we could stop her."

Puzzled by the guard's account, he approached their captive. "What is the girl's problem?"

"My name is Adrianna Tomaz," she blurted defiantly, straining against the beefy guards holding her back. "And you are nothing but a terrorist!"

She spit in his face.

By the gods! he thought. *How dare she mock me before my guests!* His expression darkened as he wiped the spittle from his cheek. Anger flared within his heart. Had he not rescued this maiden from vile captivity? Her lack of gratitude offended him deeply. Were it not for the presence of his distinguished guests, who watched the altercation with varying degrees of embarrassment and amusement, he might have been tempted to strike her down where she stood.

"That was not wise," he informed her ominously.

METROPOLIS.

"SEE for yourself!"

Perry White hurled a newspaper in Clark's face. Smarting from the impact, Clark unwrapped the paper from around his head and took another look at page one. Beneath the masthead of the *Daily Star*, the *Planet*'s chief rival, was a blurry photo of Supernova soaring through the air above the city. "EXCLUSIVE! FIRST LOOK AT NEW HERO!" proclaimed a banner headline.

Clark winced at the sight.

"The *Daily Planet* has nine hundred and twelve employees on its staff," Perry informed him angrily. The apoplectic editor shook his finger at the damning headline. "This is what happens when Clark Kent lets every one of them down!"

"Perry," Clark began, "I tried for an exclusive—"

"Good reporters don't try, Kent! They succeed!" Veins bulged upon Perry's neck. He grabbed the *Star* and waved it in Clark's face. "Superman's been missing for weeks. A new mystery replacement is on the scene. You beg me—beg me!— to give you an exclusive on the investigation. And because you blew it, the *Star* broke the story, not the *Planet*. The *Star*!"

The *Star* was to the *Planet* what Lex Luthor was to Superman. An intractable adversary to be defeated at all costs. Sitting before Perry's desk, like a schoolkid summoned to the principal's office, Clark knew that the other paper's scoop had to be driving Perry nuts. He couldn't blame his boss for being upset. *I really dropped the ball on this one.* Clark awkwardly fingered the Band-Aid on his cheek as Perry continued his tirade.

"Meanwhile, 'reporter' Clark Kent is six steps behind the Pony Express on this." Saliva sprayed from Perry's lips as he glared irritably at the other man. "And what is wrong with your face?!"

"I cut myself shaving," Clark said sheepishly.

"Again?" Perry shook his head in disgust. "If you don't know how to use a keyboard, Kent, tell me you at least know how to use a razor!"

"Kind of," Clark said. These days his face was more delicate than he was accustomed to. He missed using his heat vision to shave. Not that he could explain that to Perry.

"Don't get cute!" Perry scolded him. "This isn't good old Perry, just blowing off steam." His raspy voice took on a more rueful tone. He reluctantly removed an envelope from his desk drawer and handed it to the seated reporter. "Clark . . . I'm . . ." For once, he seemed at a loss for words. "I . . ."

Clark took the envelope. In the past, before the Crisis, he would have peeked at its contents with his X-ray vision. Now he had to open the letter like anybody else. The document inside read Notice of Termination.

Clark couldn't believe his eyes. He looked up at Perry, aghast. "You're firing me?"

"It's not just this, Clark." The editor slumped into his large leather chair, looking miserable but resigned. He massaged his temples with ink-stained fingers. "You've been letting things slide for weeks. Big things."

Clark rose to his feet, determined to plead his case. "Mr. White, I know I've been in a slump. . . ."

"In this business, Kent, two weeks is a slump." His voice held a definite note of regret. "Four weeks is burnout. After seven weeks of watching you walk around like you've forgotten everything you know about reporting, I went against my own better judgment and gave you the Supernova assignment, praying to God above that you could deliver in a timely fashion."

Clark walked over to the picture window overlooking Metropolis. "Mr. White, I can do better."

"No kidding!" Perry's temper flared up again. "That's the point, Kent! I don't know what secret skills and tricks you've been relying on all these years as an investigative reporter. Worse, I don't know where they went."

A flash of light caught Clark's eye. He peered through the window. His eyes narrowed behind his glasses. *Could it be . . . ?*

"You used to be great, Kent," Perry went on, oblivious to the approaching light. Getting out from behind his desk, he paced dolefully across the office. "You used to take risks. You used to put yourself in the thick of news." He sounded like he was trying to convince himself as much as Clark. "Now you play it safe, keep your distance. And that's not the job."

Squinting into the glare, Clark saw a caped figure flying above the city streets. The figure bore a distinct resemblance to the blurry photo on the front page of the *Star*. "So I'm fired." He reached down and unclasped the lock on the window.

"You cost us a lot of credibility," Perry pointed out. His back to Clark, he didn't see the mild-mannered reporter slide the glass pane open. "So far Supernova is still just a headline and a photo. There's still time for the *Planet* to get the first real interview, but it won't be by you. I've reassigned it to Cox. He'll get it somehow."

"You never told me this was my last chance, Mr. White," Clark said as he stepped out of the window onto the ledge. Fear of heights had never been a problem with him.

"I'm sorry, Kent, but—" A gust of wind blew into the room, rustling the newspapers on Perry's desk. Puzzled, he turned around to see Clark standing on the ledge, only inches away from a thirty-story drop. "Great Caesar's Ghost!" he exclaimed. "What are you doing?" Perry rushed toward the window, desperate to keep Clark from committing suicide. "Wait! It's not worth killing yourself, man!" His face went pale as Clark toppled over the edge. Arriving at the window, he watched in dismay as Clark plummeted toward the street. "Kent!"

Clark found falling a peculiar sensation. Gravity, which he had so often disregarded in the past, grabbed onto him in revenge. The wind roared in his ears as the air rushed past him at alarming speed. For a second, he wondered if maybe he had made a fatal mistake. *This always worked for Lois. . . .*

"Easy, mister. I've got you." Supernova swooped out of the sky and caught Clark in his arms. Gravity was cheated once more as the flying hero carried Clark up, up, and away. His all-concealing blue hood muffled Supernova's voice. "Are you okay?"

Thank you, Lois, Clark thought with a grin. This particular stunt came straight from his wife's playbook. "I'm fine." He thrust a miniature tape recorder in the hero's face. "Clark Kent, *Daily Planet*," he identified himself. "Let's talk."

But before he could fire off his first question, Clark heard the sound of heavy artillery blasting somewhere below. *What the devil?* Supernova flew toward the booming noise, which was soon accompanied by frantic shouting and screams of terror. Looking down, Clark saw a formidable-looking armored vehicle rumbling down Memorial Drive. Gun ports and rocket launchers bristled from its dense steel hull. A 120mm cannon protruded from its turret. Panicked pedestrians scattered as the tank opened fire on the buildings facing the streets. Masonry and broken glass exploded outward, adding to the chaos. Police officers fired at the vehicle, but their bullets bounced harmlessly off the ATV's spent-uranium armor. Whoever was manning the tank seemed intent on creating as much devastation as possible.

The Bahdnesian Revolutionary Front? Clark had heard a rumor that the terrorist organization was plotting to hijack the military's new mortar-proof all-terrain vehicle. *Looks like those whispers were right on target.* He frowned at the wanton destruction, wanting to personally take the tank apart. Even though he believed that the loss of his powers was only temporary, he still felt frustrated at moments like this. This was a job for Superman—or at least it used to be.

"Take care, mister," Supernova advised as he swiftly deposited Clark on the sidewalk, safely behind the tank's path. Clark wished the new hero well as, without hesitation, Supernova took off after the tank. A wide-eyed tourist started snapping off photos with his digital camera. Clark hurriedly handed the man a wad of cash in exchange for the camera. He focused the camera on Supernova just in time to catch the flying hero confronting the runaway tank. Dazzling beams emanated from Supernova's eyes, causing a stretch of pavement to *disappear* right in front of the oncoming ATV. Had the asphalt been disintegrated, vaporized, or teleported away? Clark couldn't tell.

In any event, Supernova definitely showed the terrorists that all-terrain was not the same as *no*-terrain. The speeding tank crashed down into the gaping pit and tilted over onto one side. Its armored tread spun uselessly in the air, churning up a cloud of loose dirt and gravel. Glowing like the sun, Supernova landed on the lip of the gap, overlooking the overturned vehicle. His cape flapped behind him as he gazed down confidently upon the immobile tank. Another brilliant eyebeam opened one side of the tank, exposing the trapped terrorists to the broad daylight. They threw down their weapons as a SWAT team closed in to take the felons into custody.

Supernova stepped back to let the police officers take charge of the situation. Clark seized the opportunity to approach the masked hero before he could get away. "Excuse me," he said, taking out the tape recorder once more. "Perhaps we could continue our conservation?"

He already had the first clear shots of Supernova in action. Maybe he could score the first real interview as well? Besides his obligations to the *Planet*, Clark also had a personal interest in finding out more about this new hero. As Superman, he might well have to fight beside Supernova at some point. *Who knows?* he thought. Perhaps Supernova was League material? The world could always use a few more brave men and women to fight the good fight. *Especially after our recent losses.*

"I don't know," Supernova said hesitantly. His blue hood made it impossible to read his expression (at least without X-ray vision), but he seemed wary of the press. He glanced up at the sky, as though wishing he was already aloft. "I should be on patrol. . . ."

"The public has a lot of questions about you," Clark said, appealing to the man's sense of duty. Good public relations was part of the job, no matter what Bruce might think. "It might ease their minds to know more about who you are, what your agenda is."

"I'm just here to help," Supernova said guardedly. Was he simply worried about revealing his secret identity or was there more to his reticence? Still, he wasn't flying away . . . yet. "The public has nothing to fear from me." He seemed to spot something out of the corner of his eye. "That kid . . ." He looked back toward the enormous cavity in the street. Clark saw a curious child approaching the pit. "He's not watching where he's going . . . !"

Supernova vanished in a flash, reappearing a second later in between the little boy and the edge of the gap. "Stay back, pal!" he gently admonished the wandering child. "That's an awfully deep hole in the pavement."

Clark nodded in approval, impressed by the other hero's attitude. Despite being new on the scene, Supernova had an air of experience about him. Would most beginners have thought so quickly to secure the crime scene and look after the by-standers? *I think he's on the level,* Clark thought. He watched as Supernova escorted the boy back to his grateful mother, then took off into the sky. Supernova waved at the cheering crowd below, just like Superman would have done.

A pretty classy exit, Clark conceded. But one question remained. . . .

"WHO's underneath that mask?" Booster Gold vented. He angrily tossed the *Daily Planet* aside, unimpressed by Clark Kent's front-page story and photo. Booster glared at Skeets as, all around them, movers carted the apartment's furnishings away.

Aside from a few nasty smirks, the men ignored the ranting super hero in their midst. None of them asked for his autograph.

"IT'S A MYSTERY TO ME, SIR," the robot replied.

"Yeah?" Booster said sarcastically. "You know what else is a mystery? How I'm going to adjust from living in a penthouse condo to a miserable three-room rental with alley view." He stepped out of the way so a mover could wheel a repossessed jukebox out on a handcart. "Hey, watch where you're going, bub!"

"YOU DO SO SUFFER, SIR."

Booster overlooked Skeets' arch tone. "Largely, if not totally, because this 'Supernova' jerk is stealing my limelight and eroding my endorsement deals." Only a few logos still adorned his uniform, mostly from companies that hadn't gotten around to severing their contracts with him yet. A worker thrust a clipboard at him, and he grumpily signed away his claim on various personal possessions. "This sucks worse than a time warp."

"I UNDERSTAND OUR FINANCES ARE AT A LOW, SIR, BUT PERHAPS IF YOU CHOSE A LESS DANGEROUS LIFESTYLE, A HIGHER CLASS OF REALTOR WOULD BE WILLING TO LEASE TO YOU?"

"Stop confusing me with logic." Booster grabbed onto Skeets and stared into the robot's optical array. "Isn't there anything in those twenty-fifth-century data banks about Supernova's true identity? Zero? Nada?"

"IF ONLY, SIR." Skeets slipped away from Booster's grip. "BUT AS WE'VE SEEN, TWENTY-FIRST-CENTURY HISTORY IS BEGINNING TO DIVERGE MORE AND MORE FROM WHAT'S RECORDED."

Tell me about it, Booster thought.

"PERHAPS INVESTIGATING THAT SHOULD BE OUR FOCUS FOR THE IMMEDIATE FUTURE," Skeets suggested, "SUCH AS IT MAY BE?"

Booster looked around. The movers had departed, taking the last of the furnishings with them. The once-luxurious penthouse had been stripped to the bare walls. He trudged over toward the window and yanked it open. *No point in sticking around,* he thought. He didn't live here anymore.

"Whatever." He launched himself into the sky. Skeets tagged along after him. "As long as I can use whatever we find out to kick Supernova around the block."

"WE'LL TRY OUR BEST, SIR."

SHIRUTA.

ANGRY at being embarrassed in front of Black Adam, the guards roughly returned Adrianna Tomaz to her quarters. An unnecessary shove sent her stumbling into the room, where she fell loudly to the floor. She grunted in pain as her body hit the stone tiles.

"We had better have no more trouble from you," a guard warned her. He sneered at the bedchamber's comfortable furnishings: curtains, cushions, potted plants, and such. "Believe me, there are a lot worse quarters in the palace than this room."

Black Adam viewed the scene with distaste. The bothersome young woman was a victim after all; some allowances needed to be made. Now that his temper had cooled somewhat, he was willing to forgive Adrianna her outburst at the reception. No doubt her emotions had been overwhelmed by all the hardships she had recently endured.

"Enough," he declared. His powerful hands fell upon the shoulders of the guards, who were surprised to find their immortal ruler behind them.

A guard swallowed nervously. "But, Mighty Adam . . . ?"

"Leave us." He dismissed the men, who were only too eager to withdraw from the corridor. Adam paused outside the door, not entirely sure why he was here. By rights, he should be seeing to his guests, yet something about his earlier encounter with Adrianna troubled him. Why should the victimized young woman turn against one who rescued her from shameful bondage? And what could have compelled her to call him a terrorist?

I mean to rid the world of terror, he thought. *Can she not see that?*

Moonlight filtered through lattice windows as he entered the woman's room, which had once belonged to one of his predecessor's many concubines. Elaborate arabesques ornamented the walls. Brightly colored tiles adorned the domed ceiling. He found Adrianna sprawled upon the floor, a few feet short of an antique Persian carpet. She looked up at him with suspicion. Her dark eyes narrowed.

Feeling awkward, he offered her his hand.

She hesitated, then chose to climb back onto her feet by herself. Rather than being annoyed, Adam found himself intrigued by her stubborn independence. Looking at her closely for the first time, he saw that she was indeed as beautiful as the American hoodlums had claimed. Lustrous brown hair framed a lovely face worthy of a bygone queen or goddess. Her bronze skin glowed in the moonlight. Her loose orange robe, tied at the waist by a blue satin sash, failed to disguise her lithesome figure. Large brown eyes reminded him uncomfortably of Shiruta, his long-lost bride. Perhaps that was why her unjust accusation had lingered in his mind.

"Why were you running?" he asked.

She faced him without fear. "I won't be made a prisoner."

"Prisoner? You are not a prisoner." He glanced around at the luxurious bedchamber, which bore little resemblance to the palace's underground dungeons and torture chambers. A canopy-covered divan provided the girl with a soft place to rest her head, should she feel so inclined. The tiled ceiling and ornamented walls were pleasing to the eye. "You are a refugee. After I slew your captors, I asked my aides to take you back home to Cairo. They informed me that your family had been slaughtered when you were taken away, and that your younger brother had been sold into slavery." He sympathized with the girl's loss, remembering the murder of his own family countless generations ago. "You had no one. That is why I offered you refuge in this palace."

She listened to him in silence, a wary expression upon her

face. He tried to fathom what he might have done to make this woman distrust him so. Only one explanation came to mind.

"I apologize," he said sincerely, "for killing your captors and denying you your revenge."

She gazed at him in surprise. "You apologize for *that*?"

Clearly, that was not what had angered her. The Wisdom of Zehuti, the ancient Egyptian god of learning, was among the gifts bestowed upon him by the wizard Shazam. But perhaps not even Zehuti, for all his knowledge, had ever truly understood the mysterious workings of a woman's heart.

He stepped away from the door and gestured toward the open archway. "You are free to leave at any time."

Adrianna marched boldly toward the door, then paused in her tracks. She turned back toward him, as though there was something she had to say before she left. Something that had been preying upon her mind for days.

"You're not going to save the world," she stated.

Once again, her impudence astounded him. What would a mere girl know of such matters? He wondered if he had heard her correctly. "Excuse me?"

"The last few weeks, I've seen and heard about this crusade of yours." She appeared to have given the topic much thought. Her confident voice did not mince words. "It borders on the psychotic."

"Really?" he said archly.

"You're gathering a coalition of other countries that will adopt your Freedom of Power Treaty," she said, accurately enough. Evidently, she was smarter and more observant than he had given her credit for; that much was certain. "Effectively enforcing lethal action against metahuman criminals."

"Some of them have the power to destroy a country," he pointed out firmly. Unaccustomed to being challenged in his own domain, he crossed his arms atop his chest and glared down at her. "If they have the inclination, they must be dismantled."

As I personally dismantled the despicable curs who tried to sell you into slavery.

"But you're targeting America," she protested, unintimidated by his superior strength and stature. "You're trying to build a power base to challenge theirs."

"I'm simply spreading a method of justice that will help protect the people," he insisted, "and ensure that no one will ever lose their family as you have yours." And if America and its overly idealistic heroes got in his way . . . well, so be it. The safety of the world required a force strong enough to do what must be done.

She stepped forward, almost desperate to get through to him. "You're going to plunge the world into war," she warned. Laying an insistent hand upon his arm, she stared urgently into his eyes. "What happened to you? What happened that you have to take it out on the entire world?"

Unhappy with the turn of the discussion, he removed her hand from his person and stepped away from her. *I grow weary of this debate,* he thought irritably. He had not asked for her opinion, nor did he require it. He pointed toward the door.

"You are free to go," he reminded her.

But the infuriating woman seemed in no hurry to depart. "Your problem is that you don't listen to anyone except yourself."

"And your problem is that you are naïve," he shot back.

She refused to give ground, even though he could obliterate her in a heartbeat. "Arrogant," she accused him.

"Disrespectful," he scolded.

"Alone."

Black Adam fell silent, unable to think of an immediate retort. He glumly pondered that final word. That last damning charge, at least, he could not deny.

Allies or no allies, he was indeed alone.

WEEK 11.

GOTHAM CITY.

"YOU really should quit," he began.

Renee rolled her eyes as she reached for the cigarette. *Here it comes,* she thought. *Just like a broken record.* "Let me guess. You used to smoke."

It was a gorgeous Saturday afternoon in Robinson Park. She and Vic sat across from each other at a wooden picnic table, while the rest of Gotham took advantage of the park all around them. Smiling couples strolled hand in hand, or pushed strollers. Teenagers played Frisbee on an open lawn. Lush green foliage and leafy trees provided shade from the sun. Pamela Isley, aka Poison Ivy, was known to frequent this park. Renee had to admit that the crazy plant bitch did good work.

Now if she could just enjoy a smoke without her new friend talking her ear off.

"There's hydrogen cyanide in cigarette smoke, Renee. That's the stuff the Nazis used to murder the Jews in the gas chambers, except they called it Zyklon B." He leaned across the table toward her, intent on making his point. "That's just one of the chemicals. There's benzene. That's a solvent known to cause cancer, leukemia. There's lead, you know, the stuff that'll drive you insane. . . ."

"Charlie . . . " she interrupted him. He could be a real pain in the ass sometimes. Her elbow itched beneath the sports brace that had finally replaced the plaster cast. She lit up the cigarette and blew smoke in his face.

"No," he persisted. "I'm not done yet. I've looked into this, okay? There's cadmium. That's a poisonous metal. It's used to make batteries, which is why they tell you to dispose of them properly. There's formaldehyde, there's acetone, there's . . ."

Tuning him out, she looked past his shoulder. A snazzy silver convertible pulled up to the edge of the park, and she got to her feet, suddenly feeling more nervous than she wanted to admit. She hastily ran her hand through her hair, grooming it, and squashed the cigarette out beneath her heel.

"Here she comes," she informed Vic. "Try not to embarrass me, okay?"

Kate Kane strolled toward them, looking, as usual, like a billion bucks. Sunlight shone through the light red fabric of her designer dress, so that you could almost see right through it. Designer sunglasses perched upon her nose. She carried a stylish clutch that only a clueless plebe would describe as a purse. Golden earrings reflected the radiant sunshine. Renee tried not to stare, or at least not be too obvious about it.

Vic turned around to watch her approach. "Hubba hubba."

"Shut. Up," Renee whispered emphatically.

Kate joined them by the table. She didn't sit down.

"Thanks for coming, Kate."

"Renee," the woman said coldly. The shades concealed her eyes, but she didn't sound terribly happy to be here. She cocked her head toward Vic. "Who's your friend?"

"I'm her partner, Charlie." He leaned toward her, openly admiring her drop-dead gorgeousness. "Pleased to meet you, Ms. Kane."

"Who's yours?" Renee asked. The fact that a sleek young blonde had remained behind in the convertible had not escaped her notice. She told herself it shouldn't bother her.

It did anyway.

"Her name's Mallory. She's a doctor," Kate volunteered. "You don't know her."

Renee let it drop. That wasn't why she was here.

"What do you have for me?"

Kate sat down at the picnic table beside Vic. Reaching into her clutch, she extracted a sheet of paper. "You were correct.

The family does own the property at 520 Kane Street. Like most of our holdings, it's controlled through one of several management companies. We have no direct involvement. . . ."

She started to hand the paper to Renee, only to have Vic pluck it from her fingers. "Thanks."

Kate looked annoyed, but said nothing.

"Is it currently being rented?" Renee asked while Vic examined the paper.

Kate shook her head. "No. At the moment, the property is empty. Up until six weeks ago, though, it was being leased to a company called Ridge-Ferrick Holding here in Gotham."

The name didn't mean anything to Renee, but something else did. "Six weeks," she pointed out to Vic.

"The timing's right," he confirmed. It had been about six weeks since they had nearly gotten their clocks cleaned down at the old warehouse. He got up to go, leaving Kate seated at the table by herself.

Renee turned to leave as well. "Thanks for this, Kate."

"No, wait a minute," she protested. Her tinted shades failed to conceal her confusion. She sprang to her feet. "What's this about? What's going on?"

Renee braced herself. This was going to be the hard part. "I told you, it's something we're looking into."

That wasn't good enough for Kate, who cut in front of Renee, blocking her path. "You're not a PI, Renee. You're not licensed. I checked!" Hands on her hips, she faced Renee defiantly. "And whoever your 'partner' is here, I don't think he's one either."

"Kate—"

"No!" she insisted passionately. "If this is something that concerns my family, I have a right to know! You don't come back into my life after ten years asking for favors without an explanation, Renee!" Her face flushed. Her voice grew more fervent. "You owe me that much!"

Vic studiously looked away, whistling, while the two women confronted each other. Their faces and bodies were only a few inches apart, just like during their encounter at the Kane family mansion a few weeks back. Renee felt her blood heating up once more. Staring at her own reflection in Kate's sunglasses, she steeled herself to do what had to be done . . . for Kate's sake.

"No, I don't," she said brusquely. "I don't owe you anything."

The words hit Kate like a slap across the face. All the fight went out of her as she watched Renee step past her and walk away. "How . . . how can you say that?" She sounded genuinely stunned.

Don't look back, Renee thought as she strode away from the park. She couldn't risk Kate seeing the guilty expression on her face. Better to pretend she didn't care.

"Good-bye, Kate."

"No, that was really smooth," Vic said. "No wonder the women are falling all over themselves for you. We should double-date sometime."

The parking garage was located only a few blocks away from the park. Their footsteps echoed across an upper level of the garage as Renee and Vic headed toward a run-down 1980s VW Vanagon. Sunlight entered through gaps in the concrete pillars. Renee puffed on a cigarette as Vic gave her a hard time about Kate. She was starting to miss his usual antitobacco spiel.

"What was I supposed to do, huh?" she asked him. Frustration tinged her voice. "Bad enough what Intergang will do to us if they find out we're messing with their play. Maybe they'll let us off with being lightly murdered. That's fine. That's my risk. I'm willing to take it, but I sure as hell am not putting Kate in the crosshairs as well."

"Ah, right," Vic said. "I should have seen that. My bad."

Something about his tone bugged her. "What? Should have seen what?"

"That you still have a thing for her."

Arriving at the van, he dug around in his pocket until he located a compact car alarm controller that looked a whole lot newer and in better condition than the Vanagon itself. Rust crept like cancer across the van's dented exterior. Faded bumper stickers helped hold the fenders in place.

"The thing I had for her ended ten years ago," Renee insisted. "And she ended it." She sighed loudly, not wanting to talk about it. "I'm just tired of people I care about dying on me, okay? Better she stays far away from this."

He thumbed the remote and the van chirped in response. He slid open the side door and started to clamber inside. "You're packing a whole lot of guilt for someone so young."

"At least I come by it honestly," she said bitterly.

"Give me a break."

Renee couldn't believe her ears. "What did you say?" Her temper flared as she leaned into the van. Angry eyes looked ready to explode. "What did you just—"

"You heard me." He crouched inside the van, surrounded on all sides by books, magazines, and cardboard boxes stuffed with file folders. Printed labels identified the contents of each box: KENNEDY ASSASSINATION, FLORIDA 2000, LEXCORP, OHIO 2004, HUB CITY, BIG TOBACCO, WAYNE ENTERPRISES, PARADISE ISLAND, ELECTRIC CARS, QUANTUM UNIFICATION THEORY, etc. He leafed through a box labeled INTERGANG #52. "The thing with your partner. You've got to let that go. It'll eat you alive. Trust me, I've seen it before."

Renee clenched her fists. "You don't know anything about—"

"Detective second grade Crispus Allen, murdered three months ago." He reached behind him and snatched a bulging folder from on top of another box. He tossed the file over to Renee. "Corrigan, James, arrested for the killing, but released due to lack of evidence. Case is still open."

Renee caught the folder. A quick glance at the contents confirmed that Vic knew what he was talking about. She snapped it shut before she had to look at the grisly crime scene photos all over again. An overwhelming wave of sorrow and guilt washed away her anger. She bit down on her lower lip.

"James Corrigan killed your partner and then walked." Vic

stopped searching through his files long enough to give her a stern but sympathetic look. "Allen was your friend and your partner and it had to be answered. You owed him that much. So you hunted down Corrigan, intending to kill him. And you couldn't do it."

She slumped against the side of the van, clutching the file to her chest. For once, she didn't worry how Vic knew any of this; all that mattered was that it was true. In her mind's eye, she saw herself back in Corrigan's apartment, pressing the muzzle of her automatic against his skull. Down on his knees, the dirty cop had begged for his life. Corrigan had gunned down Cris in cold blood. He deserved to die. But, at the moment of truth, Renee hadn't been able to pull the trigger. Instead she had just walked away, leaving her partner's murderer to live another day. Twenty-four hours later, she had turned in her badge.

"That's why you hate yourself, Renee Montoya," Vic said. "Because you did the right thing."

Did I? She wasn't so sure.

Lost in thought, she went through one cigarette, then six more, while Vic continued to poke through his overflowing boxes of conspiracy theories. Night had fallen, and the garage's overhead lights come on, by the time she finally heard him crow triumphantly from inside the van.

"Got it!"

He emerged holding aloft a stack of documents and photos. Renee roused herself in order to hear what he had to say. Whatever he had stumbled onto, it had to be better than thinking about Corrigan again.

"Ridge-Ferrick Holding is a subsidiary of HSC International Banking," he explained. "HSC International is Intergang's spearhead, one of the legit fronts they establish to move into new territory. Part R & D, part Human Resources."

Renee arched an eyebrow. "They have R & D?"

"They have 401Ks, Renee." He started laying the documents out on the hood of the van. "This is the *new* Intergang. They're just as happy to kill you in the boardroom as in a back alley. HSC is run by a former agent of the late Rā's al Ghūl."

Renee recognized the name of an infamous terrorist leader once said to command a veritable League of Assassins. "This woman here, name of Whisper A'Daire, and, yes, it's obviously an alias."

He pointed to a color photo of a striking redhead with a cool aristocratic air. She looked slimmer than Kate, but twice as haughty. The photo appeared to have been taken covertly by a long-range surveillance camera. *Pretty glam,* Renee conceded. *But not my type.*

"A'Daire reportedly inherited something from al Ghūl: an alchemical serum capable of turning men into monsters. She also travels with a bodyguard-slash-legman named Abbot. If that's his first or last name I don't know, but the guy's a stone-cold killer."

A second photo showed the scowling face of a dark-haired man who looked to be in his early forties. His cruel eyes, completely devoid of any trace of warmth or compassion, reminded her of any number of hit men and gangbangers she had busted over the years. Heavy black stubble carpeted his cheeks and chin. Bushy eyebrows met above his nose. Renee committed his face to memory.

"If they're here," Vic concluded, "then there's no question that Intergang has Gotham in its sights."

The very idea scared the crap out of her. "So we need to confirm that they're here, and that they're still moving in soldiers and weapons for the takeover."

"Exactly," he agreed.

"And how do you suggest we do that?" she asked.

"Same way I get most of my questions answered." He scooped the papers and photos back together. "Breaking and entering . . ."

"WILL you hurry it up?"

Renee paced across the darkened hallway of the downtown office building. A pair of glass double doors blocked off one end of the hall. A sign above the doors read Ridge-Ferrick Holding, LLC. Through the transparent glass, she could see the empty reception area on the other side. The receptionist's desk was unoccupied, not too surprising considering it was nearly midnight.

"If you can do this faster, please be my guest," Vic replied. Wearing his Question mask, he crouched in front of an electronic card reader mounted next to the door handle. The reader's plastic housing rested upon the floor as he carefully manipulated the exposed wiring.

By Renee's count, they had already committed four misdemeanors and at least one felony getting this far. She figured that should bother her, but somehow it didn't. Maybe "Charlie" was a bad influence on her, but she was curious now and she wanted some answers. Plus, if she was totally honest with herself, she had to admit that part of her was enjoying this. Poking her nose where it clearly didn't belong. Asking the questions that nobody else seemed willing to ask . . .

"Here we go," Vic whispered. Electricity sparked and the double doors swung open. He jumped quietly to his feet. "Camera," he prompted her.

"Got it." She darted forward and blacked out the surveillance camera over the receptionist's desk with a can of spray paint. The hiss of the spray nozzle sounded alarmingly loud in the nocturnal silence.

"Quietly," Vic urged her unnecessarily. They crept furtively down a hallway beyond the reception area. A narrow strip of light shone out from beneath a pair of closed wooden doors at the end of the hall. To her surprise, Renee heard voices coming from behind the doors.

Somebody's working late, she thought.

She and Vic pressed their ears against the doors, the better to listen in. Renee could make out most of what was being said:

". . . for the second stage is scheduled. Arming them won't be a problem, but converting the actual manpower base is going to be more of a challenge."

"We're expecting another shipment from Kahndaq within the month. . . ."

Kahndaq? Renee's eyes widened at the name. If Black Adam was part of this, then things were even worse than she thought. *That guy's in Superman's league.*

And Superman hadn't been seen in months. . . .

A low growl drove every other thought from her mind. She looked away from the door to discover an enormous wolf padding toward them, its eyes glowing red. The shaggy black beast was larger than any wolf Renee had ever seen outside of fairy tales. Its lips were pulled back, exposing ivory fangs. Drool dripped from its slathering jaws.

Oh crap, Renee thought.

The beast lunged at them, hitting her and Vic like a large furry battering ram. The impact knocked the wooden doors off their hinges, sending the two humans tumbling into the conference room. The office's bright lights came as a shock after the shadowy hallway. The wolf's hot breath, stinking of blood and raw meat, blasted Renee's face. Its massive forepaws pinned them both to the floor. She tried not to gag as she struggled for her ray gun.

"That's enough," a female voice declared.

The wolf grunted in disappointment, then began to *change*. Breathless upon the floor, Renee watched in amazement as the beast's sable fur retracted into its skin. Flesh and bone loudly twisted into new configurations. A hairy human chest replaced the beast's lupine torso. Its snout contracted into a stubbly male face Renee had made a point of remembering. The hellish red glow faded from the man's eyes, revealing the same cruel orbs she had noted before. Black trousers emerged from beneath the shaggy pelt. A powerful hand, complete with opposable thumb, closed around her throat. A hairy palm scratched her neck.

A werewolf? The beast's stink lingered in her nostrils. *I'm fighting a freaking werewolf now?*

Abbot effortlessly lifted both her and Vic from the floor. Gasping for breath, she fought to pry the killer's fingers away from her throat even as she instinctively surveyed her new surroundings. A trio of goons in suits sat around a large oak conference table. Charts and reports were spread across the top of the table. A floor-to-ceiling window offered a spectacular view of the Gotham skyline. A string of halogen lamps hung from the ceiling. The goons grinned evilly at the captured investigators. One of them licked his lips.

"Let's have a look at them, shall we?"

The speaker stepped into view. Renee recognized Whisper A'Daire from Vic's surveillance photo. She'd changed her hair slightly, but otherwise the aristocratic beauty hadn't aged a day. A sinuous figure was poured into a slinky black sheath that accentuated its enticing curves. Her low voice had the sound of something ancient sliding across scalding sands.

"Ah, our faceless friend. What a surprise." She smirked at Vic before turning her attention to Renee. Her exotic perfume filled Renee's lungs as Whisper came close enough to touch. She looked the squirming prisoner over like a cobra inspecting a tasty mouse. A cool hand stroked Renee's cheek. "But you, you're new."

The woman's eyes captivated Renee, especially after they underwent a sinister transformation. All at once, they became the eyes of a snake, the pupils slitted and vertical, the irises an iridescent green. A hint of reptilian scales spread across Whisper's neck and shoulders. Renee tried to look away, but the hypnotic eyes held her fast. Her limbs went limp, abandoning their futile struggles. She offered no resistance.

"What's your name, morsel?"

She had no choice but to answer. "Renee Montoya."

Whisper smiled. A forked tongue flicked out and licked Renee's cheek.

Okay, that's gross, Renee thought. The sheer ickiness of it jolted her out of the snake-woman's spell. *Charlie is never going to let me live this down—assuming we live past the next few minutes.*

"Renee Montoya," Whisper repeated. "Nice to have met you, however briefly." She shifted her gaze to her lycanthropic lieutenant. "Mr. Abbot?"

"Whisper?" His hands still clutched the captives' throats.

"They'll have to die, I'm afraid." She stepped over to the conference table and started gathering her notes. The three goons rose from their seats, tonight's business evidently concluded. She stuffed the papers into her briefcase and started toward the door.

"Wait! Wait wait wait," Vic called out hoarsely. "C'mon, don't you even want to know why we're here? What we heard?"

She kept on walking. "That you heard anything is enough to satisfy my curiosity, sir." She glanced back at the three goons, who were closing in on Vic and Renee with bloodthirsty expressions on their faces. "Gentlemen, indulge yourselves."

Her dress rustled as she slithered out the door, leaving the conference room behind her. The sound of her high heels tapping against the hallway floor faded away. Abbot roughly shoved Vic and Renee onto the carpet before following after her. The remaining goons surrounded the prostrate intruders. They growled at the backs of their throats.

Oh Christ, Renee thought. *Now what?*

If she had thought Abbot's metamorphosis was a shock, she hadn't seen anything yet. Bones snapped like broken twigs, and tailored Italian suits came apart at the seams, as each of the three thugs transformed into a different kind of beast. A full-sized gorilla beat its chest. A roaring lion, flaunting a shaggy mane, stood erect on two legs. A spotted leopard-man extended its claws. The tattered remains of their clothing littered the floor as the trio of monsters loomed over the outnumbered humans. A musky odor filled the room. Their feral eyes glowed like hellfire.

"Hey, you know that gun from last time?" Vic said. "Now would probably be a good time to use it."

Not a bad idea, Renee admitted, drawing the weapon. Even still, the odds were against them. Just one of these monsters had nearly killed them both back at the warehouse. Gun or no gun, she figured that this time there was no way they were getting out of this alive. She found herself pining for the good old days when all she had to deal with were mobsters, meth-heads, and the Joker's occasional killing sprees. *When did Gotham become the Island of Doctor Moreau?*

The monsters lunged at them simultaneously. Vic jumped up, meeting one of the attacks with a spin-kick that nailed the gorilla in the jaw. Gun in hand, Renee dived out of the way of the were-lion's slashing claws. She fired the ray gun, but the sizzling beam missed the lion, vaporizing an ugly abstract painting instead. She found herself trapped on the other side of the conference table, far away from the exit. Growling, the lion and the leopard circled her warily. They moved in opposite directions, making it hard to keep an eye on both of them. Her gun swung back and forth as she hesitated, uncertain what to do next. If she targeted one of the cats, the other would be on her in a heartbeat. Heavy paws padded against the carpet. The leopard licked its chops.

Suddenly, without warning, some sort of metal missile came spinning through the air, taking out the hanging lamps one after another. Glass shattered and sparks exploded as the entire room was plunged into darkness. The prowling monsters looked about in confusion.

The missile slammed into the wall only a few inches away from Renee. The scalloped edges of the weapon caught the moonlight coming through the panoramic window. Renee grinned, suddenly feeling a whole lot more hopeful about her chances for survival. She knew a Batarang when she saw one.

I knew it, she thought smugly. *Despite all the talk, the wild rumors. He didn't leave. He's still here. Gotham City will always have—*

A masked figure burst into the room. A lithe body, wrapped in tight black latex, was silhouetted against the crimson lining of a billowing black cape. Flowing red hair spilled out from behind her forbidding mask. A crimson bat-symbol was emblazoned upon her chest, matching her dark red boots, gloves, and utility belt. The scalloped cape spread out like wings behind her.

Batman?

Renee watched in awe as the masked woman threw herself into combat against the startled monsters. A judo flip sent the lion-man flying headfirst into a wall. His head cracked loudly against the thick wood paneling, and he dropped to the floor. She whirled in place, slashing the leopard across the face with the pointed tips of her cape even as she extracted a collapsible staff from her utility belt. Forgetting Vic for the moment, the gorilla pounced at her from behind, but she slammed the length of the pole backward into his throat, then used it to backflip over his head, landing nimbly on the floor behind him. A backhand strike caught the leopard-man in the chin just as he was sneaking up on her. His skull slammed into the wall behind him. Blood sprayed from his mouth.

That's not Batman, Renee realized, her eyes agog. It wasn't even Batgirl. This was an honest-to-god Bat*woman.*

"Hot damn."

So enraptured was she by the breathtaking sight of the woman in action that she almost didn't notice when the gorilla came charging at her instead. Renee drew a bead on the oncoming simian, her finger tensed upon the trigger. She had the shot.

And just like Batman, the masked woman didn't let Renee take it.

"No!" she shouted, jumping between Renee and the beast. She knocked Renee aside with her fist, then nimbly flipped the gorilla through the nearest plate-glass window. The massive ape landed with a thump on a balcony several stories below.

Batwoman's blow knocked Renee to the ground. *Wow,* she thought, impressed. Somewhere along the line, someone had taught this woman how to punch.

How to punch . . .

Renee experienced a sudden moment of déjà vu. She rubbed her jaw, remembering a similar punch only a month ago. She took a closer look at Batwoman, as their rescuer paused to make sure that the two remaining were-beasts were down for the count. A bat-eared mask concealed the upper portion of the woman's face, and opaque white lenses hid her eyes, but there was no mistaking that lustrous auburn hair, nor the athletic body squeezed inside the skintight costume. Renee knew those seductive contours better than she knew her own.

I'll be damned, she thought, lowering her ray gun. *Kate?*

If Batwoman knew her secret identity had been compromised, she didn't acknowledge it. "The police are en route," she said, making an effort to disguise her voice. She unclipped a grapnel gun from her belt and fired it out the broken window. A de-cel jumpline affixed itself to a skyscraper across the street. "I'd appreciate it if you left me out of it."

Renee and Vic watched as Batwoman swung away into the darkness. Bruised monsters moaned behind them. Their unconscious bodies melted back into human form.

"I think she likes you," Vic said.

"Shut. Up."

WEEK 12.

KAHNDAQ.

THE village was dry and dusty. Houses of sunbaked bricks squatted alongside simple structures of mud and straw. An obsolete electric generator wheezed and moaned. A mechanical pump labored to extract whatever traces of water remained beneath the thirsty soil. The omnipresent dust had settled over every surface, rendering the entire community gray and colorless. Hungry livestock, their ribs protruding above their swollen bellies, wandered listlessly, gnawing at the meager desert brush. The hardscrabble setting reminded Adrianna of the small Egyptian village where she had grown up—before Intergang and Black Adam came into her life.

She stood on the outskirts of the town, surrounded by the local villagers. A severe drought had punished this region for years now and taken its toll upon the struggling townspeople, who looked tired, thirsty, and without hope. Reddish dust coated their faces and threadbare garments. Uncertain why they had been gathered here, they milled about listlessly, muttering amongst themselves. Careworn faces testified to years of hardship and deprivation. Scrawny children, their faces frighteningly lean, lacked the energy to play. They clung fearfully to their mothers' skirts, while pleading in vain for something to drink. If they were lucky, their parents rationed out a few precious sips of water.

Life has not been kind to these people, Adrianna thought, deeply moved by the suffering of the hapless villagers. *But perhaps that is soon to change.*

A barren desert, its arid monotony unbroken by even the slightest trace of vegetation, stretched for kilometers before them. A flowing green robe and matching headcloth protected Adrianna from the merciless sun, but offered little relief from the suffocating heat and lack of moisture. Not a single cloud could be seen in the sky. Even though she had been here less than an hour, her mouth already felt dry and parched. She looked expectantly toward the east.

Any moment now . . .

Sure enough, a loud whooshing sound came from the east. A tremendous cloud of dust suddenly appeared on the horizon, rushing across the desert at supersonic speed. Many of the villagers turned to flee, fearing a sudden sandstorm. Their faces filled with terror. Children bawled as their parents prayed for deliverance.

"Wait!" Adrianna cried out to the panicked people. "It's only him. Black Adam!"

Few paid heed to her words, but it didn't matter. There was no time to escape from the approaching storm. A sudden wind whipped up the dust and sand all around them as Black Adam, flying at ground level, zoomed past the gathering, his mighty fists held out before him. So swiftly did he fly that Adrianna barely caught a glimpse of his muscular form before he disappeared from sight. The windblown sand settled in his wake, revealing a deep trench carved into the sunbaked floor of the desert. Wide-eyed villagers gaped in wonder at the freshly excavated furrow. Excitement began to show upon their haggard faces.

The ground rumbled promisingly. Raising a hand to shield her eyes from the sun, she pointed "upstream" back the way Black Adam had come. "Look!" she exhorted the crowd. "Just as I promised!"

Her triumphant words were drowned out by the roar of mighty waters surging down the length of the trench, creating a cascading river right on the edge of town, where none had ever existed before. Adrianna felt the spray of the water against her face, tasted its cool freshness on her lips. The river flowed past her, showing no sign of abating. The roar softened to a soothing murmur.

Cheers and jubilation erupted from the astounded villagers. Men, women, and children raced forward to immerse themselves in the life-giving waters. Little boys and girls splashed each other merrily, getting thoroughly drenched. Laughing men and women enthusiastically filled buckets and bowls from the river. Tears of happiness streamed down the faces of young and old alike, washing away the accumulated dust of too many thirsty years. The flowing river carried their pain away.

Adrianna felt her own eyes moisten in turn. She knelt and helped herself to a sip of water. If it tasted this good to her, she could only imagine what the precious liquid tasted like to the parched townspeople. Their intense emotion tugged on her heartstrings.

"Thank you!" a joyful mother called out to her. She dipped her baby into the cool water, where it giggled happily. "Thank you so much!"

"Thank him," Adrianna replied. She nodded at the sky, where Black Adam could now been seen descending from the heavens. His imposing shadow fell over the spontaneous celebration as he hovered in the air several meters above the newly created shore. He casually wiped the sand from his knuckles. His face maintained a stoic expression as he viewed the scene. Adrianna hoped he understood just how much he had truly done for these people.

"It is he!" a wizened village elder cried out, pointing up at Black Adam. "Our leader . . . our savior!" He dropped to his knees, and the rest of the villagers followed suit. They knelt upon the muddy shore, bowing to the darkly clad figure above them.

Only Adrianna remained standing. "They worship you like a god," she chided him softly. "Is that why you do this?"

Taking her words to heart, he touched down on the ground beside her. He took a kneeling supplicant by the arm and gently brought the man to his feet. "Please," he insisted, "I am not your leader. Not your ruler." He raised his voice to address all assembled. "I only do what I can to help."

Confused but compliant, the other villagers gradually rose from the dirt. Although they continued to cast awestruck gazes in Black Adam's direction, they soon went back to enjoying the miraculous blessing of their new river. He observed the sheer elation with which the grateful citizens greeted the bountiful supply of fresh water. Heedless of their soggy clothes, they danced along the slope of the river. A grinning woman balanced a large, flat-bottomed water jug upon her head.

"I had no idea this village was in such need," Black Adam admitted.

"That's because you've spent all your time and power fighting American heroes and executing American villains." Only days ago, she knew, Black Adam had clashed with Green Lantern when the American hero's pursuit of some foe had carried them over the Sinai Canal, which Adam claimed jurisdiction over. In the end, Green Lantern had departed with his prisoner, but not before exchanging blows with Black Adam over the disposition of the villain. "And gathering allies like chess pieces to consolidate a power base that only serves to escalate global tensions."

He refused to admit the error of his ways. "Do you deny the threats of misplaced power in the hands of those who might do harm to the world?"

"Power doesn't have to corrupt," she insisted. "Look at what you've done these last few days. You changed the course of a mighty river and provided water for hundreds of people. You disarmed fields of mines across Kahndaq's highways. You've made your people's lives better."

He shrugged. "All because you suggested it."

"And that is all I can do," she said humbly. "But someone like you, Adam, you can help in so many ways because of what you can do." She searched his face for some sign that she was getting through to him. He had come so far since they had first met; if only she could convince him to abandon his vengeful crusade. "Why act out of anger when you can act in hope?"

He turned and looked at her, a brooding look upon his face. She sensed the terrible fury lurking within him, never very far from the surface. "For a very good reason."

Sweeping her up into his arms, he launched himself into the sky. She gasped and clung to him as Earth fell away beneath them. Although she was beginning to grow accustomed to this unorthodox mode of travel, she still found it a trifle alarming. Her heart pounded violently within her chest in a not-entirely-unpleasant way. Declining to look down, she concentrated on his chiseled yet saturnine features. *I know there is a good man inside him,* she thought. *He just needs someone to show him the way.*

The speed of Heru carried them swiftly across the country, so that Shiruta—and the great gleaming dome of the royal palace—soon appeared below them. They descended through an open sunroof, landing nimbly upon the floor of Black Adam's office. She breathed a sigh of relief when her sandals touched the floor, yet felt oddly disappointed when he finally let go of her. The entire trip, a distance of several hundred miles, had lasted less than the time it took to brew a pot of tea.

As usual, a horde of advisors and bureaucrats flocked to Adam upon his return. They came bustling up to him, anxiously clutching charts and reports to their chests. The hems of their formal robes brushed against the floor.

"Mighty Adam." A gray-bearded functionary accosted him at once. "The Iranian, Super-Shaykh, has contacted us again. He needs your assistance against the metahuman terrorist group Dark Genesis. They just attempted another strike on Iran's nuclear weapons facility."

"And were they stopped?" Black Adam asked curtly.

"They fled, yes," the aged advisor divulged. "But Super-Shaykh is still in pursuit. He awaits your response."

"Later," Black Adam decreed. Taking Adrianna by the arm, he briskly escorted her toward a nearby exit. The crush of advisors parted reluctantly before their leader's advance, and she caught a few bewildered looks cast in her direction. Puzzled voices whispered and muttered behind her. No doubt the palace's staff were wondering what she was doing to their glorious leader.

Bringing out his better side, I hope.

He led her into a wing of the palace she had never explored before, where an abandoned throne room had been converted into a shrine. Carved into the wall between two imposing stone pillars was an enormous bas-relief depicting a beautiful woman and two young boys. All three figures wore the garb of Adrianna's ancient ancestors and were at least three times the size of her and Black Adam. The woman's slender arms stretched protectively above the boys' heads. Her sculpted eyes were turned upward toward the heavens. A golden scarab was embedded in a pedestal at the woman's feet. Precious jewels adorned the sacred icon.

Adrianna spoke in hushed tones. "What is this place?"

"A few years after the wizard bestowed me with these powers," Black Adam said, "my wife and sons were murdered, killed by an enemy I should have destroyed long before." The bitterness in his voice made it clear that he had neither accepted nor forgiven his family's death. "You must understand. I execute my foes so no one else will feel the emptiness I do. That you surely do as well." His dark eyes searched her face. "Intergang killed your family. They sold your brother into slavery. Where is your anger, Adrianna?"

She averted her eyes from his gaze. "I am not angry."

"You have to feel something," he insisted.

Feeling uncomfortable, she looked into her own soul, but found no answers there. "I'm not sure what I feel," she admitted. A sense of overwhelming loss came over her when she thought of her own family's unhappy fate. "Mostly alone."

Black Adam nodded, as though he understood. Examining her carefully, he seemed to come to a decision. His hand reached out and wrenched the golden scarab from its pedestal, a feat of strength that few could emulate. A heavy rumbling greeted his action as a hidden apparatus awoke from slumber. Stone ground loudly against stone and the entire monument split in two, revealing a long stone staircase that seemed to lead down into the very bowels of the earth. A flickering golden glow could be glimpsed somewhere beyond the bottom of the steps.

"Where does it go?" she asked apprehensively. "A secret tunnel under the palace?"

He shook his head. "It will take us far from the palace," he said cryptically. "And from Kahndaq."

What does he mean by that? Adrianna found herself baffled by this unexpected turn of events. She gulped as she took his arm and let him lead her down the steps toward only the gods knew where. The dusty steps looked as though they were seldom used. She wondered whether anyone besides Black Adam even knew they existed. *Why is he showing me this?*

The shrine was a distant memory by the time they reached the bottom of the steps. They continued down a gloomy tunnel. Torches in sconces cast dancing shadows upon the rough stone walls of the catacomb. Their footsteps echoed within the eerie silence. If she didn't know better, she would have sworn that they were exploring some ancient pharaoh's tomb. No rats or insects seemed to scurry in the shadows.

She held tightly on to Black Adam's arm. "Where are we?"

"This passage leads to the Rock of Eternity," he said, "a fabled place of power outside time and space. Until but recently, it was the home of the wizard who long ago bestowed my powers upon me, but he perished in the recent Crisis. Now another resides here."

Before she could ask who, they came upon a row of grotesque figures lined up along the wall on the left. Leering like malignant djinni, they crouched ominously upon granite pedestals inscribed with their names: Pride, Avarice, Lust, Wrath, Gluttony, Envy, and Sloth. Their petrified expressions seemed to embody all that was evil in the human soul. Bowls of fire burned at their feet. Adrianna shuddered as they walked past the towering idols.

"The Seven Deadly Sins," Adam said. "But you need not fear them. The demons are bound in stone for all eternity."

Was he saying that these weren't just statues, that these were the Sins themselves? She tried to grasp the full implications of this revelation, but before her beleaguered brain could even begin to cope with that concept, he escorted her into a cavernous throne room. Stalactites hung from the ceiling many meters above her. A blazing brazier lit up the chamber, and suffused the air with the scent of some exotic incense. She forgot all about the Sins as her wide-eyed gaze was immediately drawn to the brawny figure seated upon the large marble throne before them. His cape and uniform resembled Black Adam's, save that it was bright red where Adam's garb was dark as night. She immediately recognized one of the world's most famous heroes, second only perhaps to Superman himself.

Captain Marvel.

"Billy," Black Adam addressed the hero. Apparently, they were on a first-name basis.

"Black Adam," Captain Marvel replied. He squinted suspiciously at the newcomer. His tone was far from welcoming. "You should not have come here. Mister Atom. Sabbac. Johnny Sorrow. Every adversary I have has attempted an assault on the Rock of Eternity." He sounded weary but determined. "But the wizard left me in charge, Adam, and the Seven Sins and the power of the Rock are under my watch." He leaned forward upon the throne, his fists clenched in anticipation. "Have you come to steal that power too?"

"Of course not," Adam assured him. He kept his own arms lowered at his sides. "I'm not here to fight. I am not your enemy anymore, Billy."

Adrianna gathered that Black Adam and Captain Marvel had clashed in the past. She hoped Adam's peaceful overture was more evidence of a lasting change in his attitude. Perhaps he might still abandon his misguided campaign to confront the Western powers with his own metahuman alliance?

Captain Marvel settled back onto his throne. "Well, I suppose beating each other up never really solved our problems anyway." No longer on guard against an attack, he seemed to notice her for the first time. "Who's your friend?"

"My name is Adrianna Tomaz," she said, stepping out from behind Adam. She didn't really understand what was happening, but she knew that she had little to fear from Captain Marvel. Word of his heroic deeds and character had reached even her remote village.

"Pleased to meet you." Captain Marvel rose from the throne and came forward to shake her hand. There was something charming about his smile, as though he retained a boyish innocence that Black Adam had lost millennia ago. In a way, he reminded her of her younger brother, Amon. "What brings you two to the Rock of Eternity?"

I wish I knew, she thought.

Adam showed Captain Marvel the golden scarab. "When the wizard believed I had been corrupted by his power, he imprisoned me in this scarab for over three thousand years. But my powers weren't the only ones that dwelt within the scarab." He turned the artifact over, revealing a polished ruby mounted in the underside of the scarab. A golden cartouche housed the smooth red jewel. "This jewel, this amulet, fastened to the back contains the power of another of the wizard's champions from ancient Egypt." He carefully detached the amulet from the back of the scarab. A thin golden chain uncoiled from the top of amulet. "I want to give that power to Adrianna."

"What?" She stepped back from the ruby necklace in alarm. Had she heard him correctly?

Black Adam made his intentions crystal clear. "I want to invite her into the Marvel Family."

The what? She was vaguely aware that, besides Black Adam and Captain Marvel, there was also a Mary Marvel and a Captain Marvel Jr. But what did that have to do with her? "I don't understand," she protested.

"The magicks within this amulet," Black Adam said, "were gathered by Egypt's most powerful goddess, Isis herself. During the Eighteenth Dynasty, the great queen Hatshepsut was gifted with this power. She brought peace throughout her kingdom.

After her death, the powers were returned to the amulet." He held the gleaming ruby out to her. "Where they still are. Waiting for Isis' next champion. You."

She looked to Captain Marvel, hoping he could dissuade Adam from this notion, but instead the World's Mightiest Mortal looked her over thoughtfully. She felt as though her very soul was being weighed in the balance.

"The Sins can find few flaws in her," he informed Black Adam. "And the wisdom of Solomon tells me that she has already had a profound effect on you, one that can only grow with time." He nodded in approval. "She *is* worthy."

"Wait!" she objected. Things were happening far too fast. "I'm not a goddess. I'm just a woman. That's all I want to be."

Black Adam held out the amulet once more. "Think of what you will be able to do," he urged her. "For the people and for yourself. Nothing will ever be able to stop you. You'll never be hurt by anything or anyone again."

When he put it like that, it sounded tempting, and yet . . . she looked back over her shoulder at the Seven Deadly Sins. "But . . . power corrupts."

"It need not. You said so yourself." Gazing into her eyes, he appealed openly to her heart and conscience. There was no mistaking how much he wanted this. "You've only just begun to show me a new way. I need your help. I need someone at my side."

She remembered the river he had brought to the desert less than an hour ago, and the happy faces of the jubilant villagers and their children. There was so much heartache and suffering in the world, and so much that Black Adam could do to make the planet a better place. If he truly needed someone beside him to keep him on the right path, how could she refuse?

"Take the amulet, Adrianna," Captain Marvel said. "Let the words flow into you . . . and through you."

Trembling, she accepted the amulet, holding it in the palm of her hand. The brilliant ruby reflected the shimmering light from the brazier—or was it glowing brightly from within? The amulet felt warm against her skin. A woman's voice, as deep and eternal as the Nile, whispered gently inside her head.

"I hear it," Adrianna admitted. "A simple prayer."

"Say it, Adrianna," Black Adam pleaded. "Say it."

She contemplated the glowing amulet. *Perhaps this was always meant to be,* she thought. *Maybe all my trials and tragedies were intended to lead me to this moment.* She knew in her heart that this was the moment of truth. After this, there could be no turning back. *Very well, then. If this is my destiny, I am ready to accept it.*

She took one last look at Black Adam, then closed her eyes. Her fist wrapped around the sacred amulet. She swallowed hard, then let her lips form the words.

"I am . . . ISIS!"

A mystical lightning bolt struck from out of nowhere. A booming thunderclap rocked the throne room. The force of the lightning drove both Black Adam and Captain Marvel back, but when the blinding glare faded, Adrianna Tomaz was nowhere to be seen.

In her place stood a statuesque goddess taller and more imposing than the woman she had been only a heartbeat before. The ruby amulet had become a jewel-studded tiara crowning her head. Her lustrous brown hair cascaded freely onto her bare shoulders. A brief two-piece outfit, consisting of little more than a few wide strips of white linen, wrapped around her breasts and hips, exposed an Amazonian figure worthy of Wonder Woman. Burnished bronze skin gleamed in the torchlight. Intricate golden jewelry glittered upon her throat, wrists, waist, and sandals. She looked down upon her transformed self in amazement.

"Adrianna?" Black Adam asked, concerned about her reaction.

She smiled at him. "No, Teth-Adam." Even her voice sounded stronger and more confident. "Call me by my new name."

"Welcome to the family, Isis," Captain Marvel said. His boyish smile was almost as bright as her own.

She stretched her limbs, basking in her new abilities. "I can feel Her power inside me, Adam!" Zephyr winds, summoned at will, lifted her off her feet so that she floated several meters above the floor of the cavern. "Nature itself is calling me, asking what it can do to help my crusade."

"I am hoping it will be our crusade," Black Adam said. He rose to join her. Face-to-face above the floor, they clasped their hands together. He looked deep into her eyes. "Help me, Isis. Help me change the world for the better."

"I will, Adam." All her doubts and misgivings were no more. She had found a whole new purpose in life. "I will join you in your mission." Only one thing remained to complete her happiness and put the past behind her. "As soon as we find my brother."

WEEK 13.

FAWCETT CITY.

THE abandoned laboratory looked like a bomb had hit it. Heavy basement doors lay flat upon the floor, as though blown off their hinges by some powerful force. Broken beakers and test tubes crunched beneath Supernova's boots as he explored Dr. Sivana's former hideout, taking care to avoid puddles of foul-smelling chemicals. The infamous scientist was long gone, just as Supernova's sources had reported, but remnants of his twisted genius remained, scattered all over the demolished lab. The masked hero inspected the wrecked devices to see if any of them were salvageable. *Sivana has been missing for weeks,* he recalled. *Who knows what that madman might have left lying around?*

The overhead lights had been shattered, so he provided his own illumination. Supernova's personal radiance lit up the ruins, exposing every murky corner of the lab to view. Unfortunately, the brilliant glare quickly revealed that Sivana's diabolical inventions, from the super-magnet to the minisaucer, were either unfinished or beyond repair. Whatever violence had devastated the laboratory had also reduced the mad doctor's science projects to so much scrap metal and confetti. Supernova lingered over the shredded blueprints of an experimental time machine before tossing the illegible fragments to the floor.

I'm wasting my time here.

He made a mental note to inform the authorities of the hidden lab's location, just so they could properly dispose of

Sivana's potentially dangerous leftovers. Useless or not, he
didn't want them falling into the wrong hands . . . even if he
had more pressing matters to deal with.

A bulletin board caught his attention. News clippings were
pinned to the board, which had been shielded from the blast by
an unfinished robotic torso. Supernova recognized the distinctive typefaces of several major newspapers, including the *Daily
Planet* and the *Gotham Times*. He quickly scanned the headlines of the articles:

"CURSES! FOILED AGAIN!"
FBI raid finds Baron Bug's lab empty

CRIMINAL MASTERMIND SKIPS BAIL, LEAVES LOOT.
Has Ira "I.Q." Quimby outsmarted himself?

"MAD DOCTOR" RIGORO MORTIS VANISHES FROM LAIR.
Neighbors hear "snarling sounds."

"DOCTOR DEATH" FAILS TO TESTIFY.
Mystery of the Disappearing Defendant.

T.O. MORROW GONE FROM LOCKED CELL.
Prison authorities baffled.

DR. CYCLOPS JOINS "EVIL BRAIN DRAIN."
Local super-villain "missing for days," says henchman.

WHERE—OR WHEN—IS DOCTOR TYME?

Looks like someone is rounding up mad scientists, Supernova concluded, *including Sivana himself.* He glanced around
the trashed laboratory. Despite all the damage, there was no
sign of the evil inventor's body—nor any indication that he had

left voluntarily. Supernova guessed that Sivana had joined his missing colleagues. *But where? And what for?*

He took a closer look at the headlines. The one referring to Doctor Tyme intrigued him enough to read further, quickly skimming the article below the headline:

> Doctor Tyme, the crazed scientist behind last year's missing fifty-two seconds, has vanished. Dubbed 'the Tick-Tock Thief of Time,' he disappeared on his way to the high-security metahuman prison on Alcatraz Island after aging three guards to dust in Pelican Bay. When the overturned prison vehicle was found, the driver's watch was off by five minutes. . . .

Supernova shook his head, concerned by the contents of the clipping. *Fifty-two seconds missing,* he thought grimly. According to the rest of the article, that stolen time had never been recovered. *A lot can happen in fifty-two seconds. . . .*

Worried that he was running out of time, he turned to leave the lab and fly back to Metropolis. As he headed to the door, however, his foot accidentally connected with a fallen plastic cylinder and kicked it across the floor. Something rattled inside the tube as it rolled away.

Wait a second. What's that?

Curious, he walked over and picked up the transparent cylinder. Looking inside, he spotted the dried husk of an empty cocoon, only a few inches long. The crumbling specimen glowed faintly, as though radioactive. A peculiar chill ran down Supernova's spine.

Since when did Dr. Sivana, of all people, take up butterfly collecting? He held the mysterious cocoon up before his eyes. Behind his hood, his expression was grave. *And what do you suppose hatched out of there?*

BIALYA.

THE slavery camp was hidden away in the heart of the desert, far from the nearest village or oasis. A chain-link fence topped with razor wire enclosed an ugly concrete building that stood out like a great gray eyesore amidst the endless sand dunes. Hot air rippled above the compound's flat roof. Foul-smelling fumes rose from a belching smokestack, polluting the dry desert air. The morning sun was low in the sky.

The very sight of the camp offended Isis as she swooped out of the sky beside Black Adam. His mighty fists preceded him as he flew toward the camp, while her own arms were stretched out to catch the obedient zephyr whisking her through the air. Her unbound hair streamed behind her as she flew. Despite the gravity of their mission, she found the sensation of flying under her own power exhilarating.

I pray I never become so inured to the experience, she thought, *that I fail to appreciate what a blessing it is.*

Black Adam grabbed onto the edge of the heavy concrete roof and, with the strength of Amon, tore it free of its moorings. Sunlight poured into the factory below, exposing a heartbreaking scene.

Scores of innocent children, some no more than five years old, toiled at long worktables, assembling bits of costume jewelry and cheap plastic decorations. The scrawny, underfed boys and girls wore only filthy rags as they worked in the oppressive heat of the dingy sweatshop; air-conditioning had apparently been judged an unnecessary expense. Scowling adults, armed with truncheons and automatic weapons, sipped on cold sodas and beer as they sullenly supervised the captive children . . . until the ceiling abruptly disappeared overhead. Dust and powdered cement rained down upon their heads. They looked up in alarm.

"Black Adam!" a startled guard shouted. Automatic guns and rifles immediately opened fire on Isis and Adam, but the blistering hail of bullets bounced harmlessly off the heroic duo. Frightened children dived for cover beneath their workstations. Isis caught only a fleeting glimpse of their faces, not enough to tell if her brother was among them. That would have to wait until the slavers themselves were disposed of.

She flew into the building, while Adam hurled the uprooted ceiling away from him. It crashed loudly onto the floor of the desert outside. He followed her into the factory, his eyes ablaze with anger.

"This slavery ring ends now!" he declared fiercely. Isis had no doubt that the pitiful children reminded him of his own murdered sons. He stalked toward the retreating slavers, his fists raised and ready. "As do your wretched lives!"

Isis instantly recalled the brutal way he had disposed of her kidnappers. Noose's blood and brains had literally splattered her robe the day she and Adam first met. "No, Adam," she beseeched him, laying a restraining hand upon his chest. The men's bullets continued to ricochet off her and Adam. "Let them be judged for their crimes in this life. And, when Nature takes its course, the next."

She gazed fearlessly into the blazing muzzles of the guns. "Nothing escapes Nature," she assured Adam. "And as Isis, I *am* Nature." Raising her arm, she gestured at the retreating slavers. "Winds!"

At her command, a furious whirlwind came to life within the factory. The howling tornado snared the slavers, sweeping them off their feet and up into the sky high above the camp. Their panicked shrieks were lost in the roar of the wind, as it stripped them of their weapons and deposited them roughly across the burning sands, where they would have to choose between turning themselves in to the local authorities or dying of thirst and exposure. Alerted by Black Adam's ambassador, a division of United Nations troops was already en route to round the slavers up. Having experienced Nature's wrath, they were unlikely to put up much resistance.

"They deserve more than a few broken bones," Black Adam objected. He began to lift off from the floor, intent on hunting the scattered criminals down personally. His irate tone made it clear that he had several summary executions in mind.

"No, Adam," she entreated him once more. She gently tugged him back down to earth and reminded him of what really mattered. "Not in front of the children."

Now that the angry shouting and gunfire was over, the children gradually crawled out from beneath their hiding places. Timidly at first, then with greater confidence, they flocked to Adam and Isis. Tiny hands reached out to touch their saviors. "Thank you!" said a chorus of childish voices. "Thank you, thank you!"

To her slight amusement, Black Adam looked somewhat at a loss. He was obviously more comfortable wreaking vengeance on his enemies than coping with the heartfelt adoration of dozens of grateful kids. He stood stiffly amidst the children, a stern expression on his face. Isis couldn't help wondering what he had been like with his own offspring, three thousand years ago.

She looked over the children herself, appalled at how dirty and skinny they were. A familiar sadness came over her as she searched their wide-eyed faces. "It's all right," she promised them soothingly. "You're all going home."

"Most of them don't have homes to go to, Adrianna." He walked beside her as they began to lead the children out of the roofless factory. A convoy would soon arrive to ferry them to safety. "Before I retook Kahndaq, the dictator there dragged thousands of children from their homes, forcing them into hard labor and prostitution." He frowned at the memory. "The parents that argued were killed on the spot."

Just like mine were, she realized. "Then . . . then all the orphans of the world will be welcome in Kahndaq. All of them." She stroked the tousled head of a small boy. A powerful gust of wind blew down the wire fence. "All of them we can find . . ."

Black Adam did not miss the melancholy tone that had entered her voice. "Your brother isn't here, is he?"

"No, Amon isn't here," she admitted. Ironically enough, her brother was named after the very god who granted Adam his superhuman strength. "We've spent a week dismantling dozens of slavery camps across Africa, the Middle East, and Asia." And yet her little brother remained missing. "Maybe I need to stop hoping."

"Stop hoping?" He greeted her mournful suggestion with disbelief. He gestured toward the throng of newly liberated boys and girls surrounding them. They gazed up at her with breathless awe and gratitude. "Look at these children, Adrianna. Hope is all they are doing now. You show them hope." He turned toward her, looking deeply into her eyes. "You show *me* hope. And no one has done that in so long, in so many centuries. . . ." His hand gently lifted her chin. "We will find your brother. And we'll free all the children of the world while doing so."

She wanted to believe him, and perhaps she could. It was not so long ago, she recalled, that her own future had seemed absolutely without hope, after Intergang killed her parents and attempted to force her into slavery. Black Adam had changed all that. Single-handedly, he had brought hope back into her life—and given her a glorious new purpose. How could she *not* believe him when he promised that their future was only beginning?

We will find Amon . . . together.

"Isis . . . Adrianna Tomaz. There is something I have for you." To her surprise, Adam dropped to one knee before her. He reached beneath his golden sash and brought forth a sparkling diamond ring. He held the ring out to her, much as he had offered the Amulet of Isis only a week before. "This diamond belonged to Cleopatra, given to her by Caesar on the eve of the Alexandrian War." She gaped at the size of the jewel, which had to be twenty-four carats at least. "I offer it to you, Isis, and I ask you on this morning to be my queen." Following Adam's lead, the children knelt and bowed their heads as well. "To be *our* queen."

Taken aback, Isis was suddenly overcome with emotion. She placed a hand against her heart and felt it beating faster than the wings of a hummingbird. Did he truly mean what she thought he meant?

Lifting his head, he beamed up at her. No trace of his murderous rage could be seen upon his handsome visage, only the hopeful smile of a man in love.

"Will you be my wife?"

Her answer was evident in her smile.

WEEK 14.

SHIRUTA.

IT was a thirty-one-hour flight from Gotham to Kahndaq. You changed planes twice, once in Paris, then again in Algiers. You changed twice because there was no direct service to Kahndaq from the U.S. or Europe.

That's because most people know better than to come here, Renee thought.

Hot, jet-lagged, and craving a cigarette, she peered sourly out of the window of a rickety old bus as it drove them into downtown Shiruta. Vic sat beside her, admiring the scenery. The bumpy ride jolted her already stiff back. Kahndaq seemed to be long on potholes and short on shock absorbers. With every jolt, she had to remind herself why exactly they had come six thousand miles to a foreign country ruled by a superpowered dictator: because Intergang was moving weapons and personnel into Gotham, and Kahndaq was either a source or a link in the chain.

And because, like Charlie, I'm curious.

The bus pulled up to a curb and she realized that they had reached the medina, the walled heart of the city. She let Vic take care of paying the driver with the local currency, while she stepped out of the bus to experience Kahndaq firsthand.

It wasn't what she expected.

Judging from the coverage in the Western press, and Black Adam's sinister history, she had anticipated a Third World hell-hole populated by frightened citizens cowering beneath the oppressive lash of a megalomaniacal super-villain. Instead she suddenly found herself in the middle of a festive street scene. Gleeful men, women, and children crowded downtown Shiruta, practically dancing in the street. Musicians played a cheerful air upon flutes, tambourines, and drums. Fragrant blossoms were strewn upon the streets and sidewalks. The tantalizing aroma of mint tea and spiced lamb wafted from the stands of various open-air food vendors.

She tried to take it all in. The exotic Arabic architecture with its graceful domes and archways. The men in their traditional attire: a fez, a loose tunic, slacks, and sandals. The women in their flowing robes and scarves. Laughing children running and playing amidst the open stalls and donkey carts. Brilliant sunlight cast a golden glow over the merriment, making Renee glad that she had unpacked her sunglasses. Palm trees provided a modicum of shade from the sweltering heat.

Giant banners of Black Adam and Isis hung from every balcony and gateway, smiling down on the celebrants. Renee did a double take.

Black Adam . . . smiling?

Vic joined her on the sidewalk. He dropped their luggage onto the paving stones. "Huh?" he reacted. "Not exactly the Axis of Evil, is it?"

They had only a moment to adjust to their new surroundings before a throng of grinning Kahndaqis rushed toward them. At first Renee thought they were being attacked, then someone draped a flowery garland over her head. *Ohmigod,* she realized, *they're giving us the world's most enthusiastic welcome.* Friendly voices assailed her from all directions. Most of the babble was in Arabic, which left Renee in the dark, but a couple of their new best friends managed to muster some English.

"Welcome!" a teenage boy in a fez greeted them. "Rejoice with us at the start of Kahndaq's new golden age!"

A beautiful young woman bestowed a fresh garland upon Vic, who was thoroughly enjoying their warm reception. "Thank you, thank you very much," he said as the lovely maiden kissed him on the cheek. Renee noted, with just a twinge of jealousy, that the girl had the same haircut as Isis, as did many of the other young women. *Wannabes,* she thought. *Just like all those trendy sorts who copied Black Canary's hairstyle a few years back.*

"Please, share in Kahndaq's blessings!" Kahndaqi men surrounded her, attempting to adorn her hair with lilies and narcissuses. "Come, dance with us!"

"No, really . . . " she demurred, trying to be polite. "You don't have to do this." She was tired and nicotine-deprived and really didn't like being touched, but the men seemed determined to include her in their celebration. She gently attempted to fend them off. "No, thank you . . . No, that's enough. . . ."

Vic smirked at her, amused by her unwanted makeover. "Lovely. Brings out your eyes." He took her by the arm, and she resisted the urge to pound his face into the pavement. "C'mon," he said. "I hired Achmed over there to deliver our bags to the hotel. He has an honest face." Renee wondered if she would ever see her luggage again. "Let's get cracking."

One of Vic's contacts had tracked down the Ridge-Ferrick connection here in Shiruta. A firm called Hni Hnak Shipping, located somewhere in the temple district. According to Vic, Hni Hnak meant "Here to There" in English.

Cute.

Wading through the mob of well-wishers, they began to explore the medina. Vic led the way, consulting a foldout map of Shiruta he had picked up from the Kahndaqi consulate in Gotham. They quickly discovered that the general atmosphere of jubilation was not confined to the courtyard they had just left. Everywhere they went, Renee saw people rejoicing. She hadn't seen a town so giddy since the last time the Joker slipped laughing gas into the water supply.

"What's with all the hoopla?" she asked Vic.

Naturally, he spoke fluent Arabic. "Seems Black Adam has declared a fortnight of feasting in honor of his new fiancée, this woman they're calling Isis."

Renee had read about her in *NewsTime* magazine. Some

sort of Egyptian version of Wonder Woman. As far as Renee was concerned, this new heroine had big sandals to fill if she wanted to replace the missing Amazon princess.

Vic's cell phone rang. The theme from *The X-Files* served as his ringtone. "Hang on," he told her. "I need to take this call."

Renee lit up a cigarette, her first in over twenty-four hours. Cooling her heels, she glanced around the bustling Middle Eastern marketplace. Merchants hawked everything from handwoven carpets to cheap replicas of Isis' jeweled tiara. Donkeys plodded along the cobblestone road. Street urchins chased each other in and out of cramped shops and stalls. Exotic spices scented the air. Excitement over the royal romance could be seen everywhere. A clothing merchant was doing a brisk business selling knockoffs of Isis' costume, even though the skimpy, two-piece outfit wasn't exactly flattering to some of the young wannabes parading through the market. Framed photos of the happy couple were also a hot commodity.

"No, I can barely hear you, Tot," Vic informed his caller. "What's that? The package is on its way? Great." He glanced at Renee. "What, her? Pretty well. There's a lot of untapped potential." He looked away, concentrating on his call. "No, I will. Thanks again, Tot."

He put the cell phone away.

"So who was that?" she asked.

"A friend," he answered. "Name's Aristotle Rodor. Tot, for short. He handles my gear. Calling him a genius is underselling it." The only geniuses Renee knew were criminal masterminds. "He shipped out a Comdex container with some supplies for us. Should arrive sometime next week."

That wasn't what concerned her just now. "You were talking about me."

"I'm not keeping our partnership a secret, Renee." His tone was unapologetic. "He just wanted to know how it was going with you, that's all."

She winced at the word *partner.* Her last partner was currently pushing up daisies back in Gotham. "And how is it going with me?"

"You still have no idea who you are," he said, "but other than that, fine." He paused to haggle with a fruit vendor over a bag of figs. Currency was exchanged. "Fig?"

"You keep saying that," she complained. "I have no idea what it means."

He offered her the bag. "It means, you know, 'fig.' An oblong fruit of the genus ficus . . ."

"That bit about me not knowing who I am, smart-ass." She ignored the figs and took another drag on her cigarette instead.

He took back the bag. "Well, that's the question, isn't it?"

"You're a jerk." Sometimes his cryptic evasions really ticked her off. "You know that, right?"

He shrugged. "It's been noted before."

Finishing off the figs, he consulted his map once more before leading her through the winding streets of the capital. Cobblestone paths passed beneath towering horseshoe gateways. Palm trees sprouted from stone pots placed outside the open doors of the shops. Street signs in Arabic might as well have been written in Kryptonese as far as Renee was concerned. The exotic sights and sounds were like something out of a movie. *Casablanca* maybe, or an Indiana Jones flick. Renee half expected to see a snake charmer at any minute.

"Okay, that was the Old Quarter we just left," Vic murmured to himself. "So the Temple District should be . . . uh . . . that way, I think."

In Gotham, Renee knew the city. She could read the streets and the people. Here in Shiruta, she felt uncomfortably out of her element. Gradually, though, she got the distinct impression that they were heading into a bad neighborhood. Busy boulevards shrank down to a confusing maze of narrow alleys and passageways. Weeds sprouted from the cracked pavement. The joyous crowds and music disappeared, replaced by empty streets populated only by the occasional drunk or beggar. Paint peeled from the porches and doors. Plaster crumbled from the walls, exposing the bare masonry underneath. Abandoned buildings were boarded up. Wilted palms looked on the edge of death. Apparently, not all of Kahndaq was in a rapture over the royal couple's impending nuptials.

Renee felt eyes at the back of her neck. Uncertain of her instincts in this foreign environment, she kept glancing back over her shoulder. Once or twice, she thought she glimpsed a shadowy figure darting out of sight before she could get a good look at him or her. Was she just imagining things, or . . . ?

Vic noted her distracted state. He looked up from his map. "What?"

"Laugh at me and I'll kill you, Charlie, but I think we're being followed."

"Oh, that." He went back to examining the map. "Yeah, he's been on us since we left the airport. C'mon, it's this way." He turned right at a squalid intersection. "At least I think it's this way."

I swear before this is over I'm gonna hold his dead body in my hands. Seething, she clenched her fists. "You didn't think that maybe that info was worth sharing with me?"

"I didn't want you to worry." He glanced up at the sun, barely visible from the cramped alley. "Can you tell which way's east?"

They approached a low one-story building that had definitely seen better days. Empty crates and barrels were stacked haphazardly outside the entrance. Shuttered windows hid whatever might be going on inside. A faded sign, in both English and Arabic, identified the place as Hni Hnak Shipping. Renee thought it looked like the Kahndaqi cousin of that run-down warehouse on Kane Street.

"So who is it?" she asked. "Who's following us?"

Vic responded casually. "Abbot, I think."

"The wolf-man?" She glanced behind her again, but didn't see anyone, human or otherwise. She reached instinctively for her ray gun, then remembered that she had left it behind in Gotham. No way would she have been able to get that gun past airport security. "Just great."

Vic stepped beneath the overhang of the doorway. A plume of smoke enveloped him, and when he turned to address her, his face had completely disappeared. "Shall we?"

"Are you crazy?" His apparent lack of concern over the fact that they were being stalked by a werewolf drove Renee nuts. She pointed to her own skull and twirled her finger. "Is that your problem?"

"There's no such thing as crazy, Renee." He tried the door and found it locked. "Just behavior that society has deemed unacceptable."

Tell that to the Joker, she thought. "Speaking of which, isn't Intergang taking a huge chance setting up in Black Adam's territory? I hear he performs public executions downtown every Wednesday. Draws a huge crowd." She had seen footage of him ripping apart malefactors on the evening news. "Sounds awful risky to me."

The Question kicked in the door. The flimsy doorframe splintered easily. "Unless he's in on it with them."

"There's a lovely thought," she cracked, before following him inside the building.

The smell hit her first, before her eyes could adjust to the murky lighting: the coppery scent of fresh blood, so thick in the air that she could taste it at the back of her throat. An adult male in good health had roughly six quarts of blood in his body. She counted five bodies, which added up to almost eight gallons of blood, most of it splattered over the floors and walls.

"Abbot," Vic whispered. "You son of a bitch."

The shipping office had been thoroughly trashed. Papers were scattered everywhere, spilling out of ransacked cabinets and desks. Overturned furniture and lamps created an obstacle course across the floor. A ceiling fan rotated slowly above the carnage, churning the noxious atmosphere. Crimson droplets spattered against the floor like water from a leaky faucet.

The bodies of the victims weren't in any better shape. They were strewn across the floor and furniture, lying in pools of their own blood. Most of the men had been disemboweled, their guts torn out by the voracious werewolf. The luckier ones had simply had their necks broken. A dead man's face stared up at Renee. His features were frozen in an expression of utter horror.

She removed her sunglasses and took a hard look at the crime scene. It was ugly, but she had seen some pretty brutal stuff in Gotham as well. Killer Croc's last rampage, for example, or the Man-Bat Murders. "What do you think?"

"I think someone didn't want these guys talking to us," Vic said.

"Yeah. Me too." She suspected that the "someone" in question had serpentine eyes and a forked tongue. "If we're going to look around, we'd better do it fast."

The cop inside her screamed at her not to touch anything, but Renee was finding that nagging inner voice easier and easier to ignore. She and Vic picked their way amidst the spreading red puddles. They poked delicately through the scattered papers and other debris. "Any idea what we're looking for?"

He lifted some shipping invoices by their dry edges. "You'll know it when you find it."

"That your way of saying 'I don't know'?" She stepped over a pile of bloody viscera.

"Yeah," he admitted, "but my way is more poetic. . . ."

She noted a pile of cardboard boxes, about the size of cereal boxes, on the floor behind a toppled desk. She crouched to inspect them. The labels were in Arabic, but a visual graphic on the boxes seemed clear enough: a silhouette of a dead rat lying on its back, exed out by a heavy black line. There were at least a dozen boxes of poison, but only three were empty.

"Hmm. Must have had a hell of a rat problem." She stood up and tossed one of the empty boxes aside. "Anything?"

Vic shook his head. "No, nothing." He sounded tired. Renee guessed that the jet lag was finally catching up with him. "Let's get out of here."

"No argument from me," she said. Thanks to Abbot, their one lead had turned into a dead end. She hoped that they hadn't flown six thousand miles for nothing. That would suck, big-time.

They stepped outside into the afternoon glare. She reached for her sunglasses.

"Yaqif!"

A harsh voice shouted at them. Renee turned to see a pair of uniformed police officers rushing toward them from the far end of the street. The cops reached for their sidearms as they yelled forcefully at the two Americans. Renee didn't need her Arabic-to-English pocket dictionary to get the gist of the command.

"Halt! Stop or we'll shoot!"

She realized instantly how bad this looked. Two foreign devils, one of them masked, leaving the site of a gruesome mass murder. No way was this going to end well. Images from *Midnight Express* flashed through her brain.

"Run!" she hollered at Vic, who seemed to have already reached the same conclusion. They sprinted down the street, away from the oncoming gendarmes. Angry shouts pursued. Gunshots rang out. Plaster from a nearby building exploded in their faces.

"Charlie?" she gasped as they fled madly through the maze of alleys.

She could hear him breathing hard behind his mask. "What?"

"Please tell me this isn't Wednesday."

WEEK 15.

METROPOLIS.

THE dingy decor of the East Hope Hotel belied its name. Languishing in the filthy shadows of Suicide Slum, the run-down hotel was a glorified flophouse catering mostly to transients with a few bucks in their pockets. A garish neon sign flickered outside Booster's room, shining through the moth-eaten curtains as he sat on the edge of a lumpy mattress, eating baked beans cold from a can. Unpaid bills littered the top of a bedside table, along with a notice of "Contract Termination" from Ferris Airlines, who had invoked a morals clause in their sponsorship agreement to cut Booster loose. *Like rats deserting a sinking ship,* he thought sourly. *Bunch of fair-weather flyboys.* Gold-tinted spray paint covered the Ferris logo on his uniform.

The latest issue of *NewsTime* rested on the bed next to him. A cover photo of Supernova ("The New Champion of the Metropolis") had been vandalized with a heavy black marker: the hero's hooded face now sported a mustache, buckteeth, and a dagger through the skull. Doodled blood droplets sprayed from the knife.

A laptop computer, primitive by the standards of Booster's native century, balanced upon his knees. On the screen, the *Daily Planet*'s website rubbed his face in his sinking popularity. "SUPERNOVA OUTSHINES FORMER HERO" read the headline above side-by-side head shots of Booster and Supernova. "BOOSTER APPROVAL RATINGS PLUMMET."

On an impulse, he grabbed a bottle of water from the nightstand and poured it over the laptop. Sparks erupted from the keyboard as the computer shorted out. The screen went blank, taking the offending website with it. Skeets, hovering above the bed, let out a startled burst of static. No doubt he found such wanton computer abuse disturbing.

Booster ignored the electronic outburst. "'Former hero . . . '" he muttered beneath his breath. Golden goggles dangled from his neck, revealing pissed-off blue eyes. "I need something big tonight, Skeets. Big and showy to put me back on the map." He looked up at the robot. "What's in the files?"

"I'LL SCAN, SIR. ON THIS DATE IN METROPOLIS HISTORY: A CARJACKING ON THIRTY-THIRD . . ."

"Yeah, that looks like a job for Booster Gold," he said sarcastically. "Please. Next?"

"A POWER BLACKOUT IN THE BAKERLINE AREA . . ."

Booster sighed impatiently. "Skeets, can we get away from the purse-snatchings-and-lost-dog blotter. Give me a comeback mission." He threw up his hands in exasperation. "This is Metropolis! It's a city Brainiac tries to shrink to bottle-sized every second Thursday. Don't tell me nothing is on tonight!"

"AND, FINALLY, A NUCLEAR SUBMARINE CRASH IN MIDTOWN."

"Great . . . if I'm Aquaman!" He rolled his eyes. "A sub accident! Who's gonna notice me at night underwat—" Then it hit him. "Wait. Midtown. How the hell does a submarine end up in midtown Metropolis?"

THE *Curry*-class nuclear submarine was embedded in the slimy flesh of the giant aquatic beast rampaging through the heart of the city. Throbbing blue veins, the size of oil pipelines, bulged beneath the monster's scaly purple skin. A mane of pulsating tendrils, like the fronds of some enormous sea anemone, surrounded a voracious maw large enough to swallow a city bus in a single gulp. Rows of ivory fangs jutted from the creature's jaws. Gigantic tentacles whipped out at the surrounding buildings, knocking loose great chunks of masonry, which plunged down onto the chaotic streets below. Panicked men and women ran away from the beast like extras in a Japanese monster movie. Dense clouds of dust and pulverized cement rose several stories into the air, mixing with the smoke from dozens of uncontrolled fires. An angry tentacle flung a moving van through the ground floor of a ritzy hotel. Terrified screams and moans were drowned out by the horrendous wail of the monster itself, which sounded like the world's loudest foghorn.

"This looks like a job for Supernova," Clark Kent said as he grimly watched the devastation from the top floor of the Daily Planet Building. According to eyewitness reports on the Internet, the sea monster had crawled out of the harbor only minutes ago and was now creating a trail of destruction through Metropolis. The captured submarine was glued to the back of the creature like a prosthetic spine; its breached hull offered little hope that the vessel's crew had survived whatever had befallen them beneath the sea. Clark regretted every life lost, even as he hoped that Metropolis' newest hero would arrive in time to prevent any further fatalities. *I just hope he's up to the task.*

One of the *Planet*'s summer interns sat in front of a computer terminal a few feet away, pulling what info he could off the Web. "The sub's an American SSBN that was attacked in the mid-Atlantic," he reported. "But, Mr. Kent, what is that frigly thing carrying it?"

"I'm counting on you to tell me that, Sanjay!" Clark said urgently. "Try cross-referencing Atlantis and Aquaman." He knew that Aquaman himself was unlikely to make an appearance; from what he'd heard, Arthur had his hands full under the ocean these days.

Sanjay hastily typed the key words into the search engine. "Wow, that was a good guess," he said as a sketch resembling the monster appeared on his monitor. Instead of a submarine, an old-fashioned sailing ship was entangled within the pictured creature. "Here we go! '*Ballostro*: a mythic protocrustacean beast rumored to attach itself to seacraft in search of land prey.'" He looked up from the screen. "I suppose we can wiki out the word 'rumored,' right, Mr. Kent?"

Clark glanced at the screen as he rushed past Sanjay into the corridor outside. The antique illustration certainly seemed to match the behemoth at loose in the streets below. As he hurried to cover the story firsthand, he couldn't help casting a wistful look at the closed door of a little-used storeroom. In days past, he would have used the room to change into his Superman costume. "Ah, storeroom, my old friend. I miss you already."

CLOUDS of dust and smoke obscured the stars, making the fearful night all that much darker. Slithering its way down Fifth Avenue, the sea monster rained destruction down on the city. A gargantuan tentacle grabbed onto a monorail zooming along an elevated track, bringing the streamlined bullet train to a jarring halt. Bodies went flying inside the train, while shrieking citizens stampeded through the streets and sidewalks one story below. Immense muscles flexed beneath the tentacle's leathery hide. Tortured metal screeched loudly as the tentacle tried to wrench the train from the track. Trapped commuters screamed for help.

Looks like I got here none too soon, Booster thought as he swooped down from the sky. He zipped beneath the tentacle and shoved upward, forcibly lifting the pulpy limb off the endangered monorail. He pressed the tentacle above his head like a weight lifter as he hovered in the air high above the street. The smell of raw calamari filled his lungs, nearly making him gag. The monster's reverberating wail pounded against his ear. He strained to keep the tentacle up, up, and away from the stalled train. *I may never eat seafood again,* he mused.

"RELAX, FRIENDS!" Skeets' amplified voice addressed the fleeing crowds. "IT'S BOOSTER GOLD TO THE RESCUE! HERO OF THE PEOPLE. CHAMPION OF METROPOL—"

A second tentacle lashed out, whacking Booster with the

force of a battering ram. He went flying through the air, right into a mammoth bronze statue of Superman, one of many erected throughout Metropolis. Booster smashed through the statue's neck, dislodging its head, before crashing to earth at the base of the decapitated monument. "Look out!" a frantic pedestrian shrieked as chunks of cracked pavement were thrown about from the impact of the hero's hard landing, which left a shallow crater in the middle of a landscaped traffic island. Water spouted from a shattered fire hydrant.

Skeets darted down to assist Booster. "HEAD UP, SIR!"

"'Head*s* up,' you flying anachronism!" Booster corrected him irritably. He sat up at the center of the crater, taking a moment to catch his breath. Despite the protective force field generated by his suit, his head was ringing. "The saying is 'Head*s*—'" A shadow fell over him, blotting out the light from the streetlamps. He looked up quickly, just in time to spot the statue's colossal bronze head falling from the sky. He scooted out of the way only an instant before the larger-than-life bust hit the pavement with a resounding crash. The ground shook beneath his butt. "Oh. I get it. Sorry."

Scrambling to his feet, he ran back toward the rampaging monster. The redwood-sized tentacle had knocked him all the way down to Thirty-Third Street, at least a block away from the oncoming creature. "Any more advice?" he asked Skeets.

The robot kept pace with Booster. "MAINTAIN YOUR FORCE FIELD, SIR."

"Let me rephrase the question," Booster said acidly. "Any more advice *I wouldn't have thought of on my own?*" Looking around for a weapon, he spotted a 1986 Keystone Rambler parked at the curb. An overweight black woman was squeezed behind the wheel of the decrepit car, trying in vain to ignite a faltering engine. The uncooperative car lay directly in the monster's path; no way was she going to get away in time. Fortunately, Booster had another use for the rusty automobile.

"'Scuse me, ma'am." He yanked open the door and physically dragged the heavyset woman out from behind the wheel. "Gonna need this vehicle!"

The squirming woman didn't seem to appreciate the urgency of the situation. She fought him every inch of the way, hanging on to the door of the car as if her life depended on it. "Getcher hands off me, ya perv!" she bellowed at the top of her lungs. "HAAAALP!"

Booster suddenly remembered that carjacking Skeets had predicted earlier. Hadn't that been on Thirty-Third Street? He grinned at the irony. *Sounds like events are right on schedule.* Peeling the woman's fingers away from the open door, he hefted the Rambler with both hands.

"My car—!" the woman cried out.

Booster flung the Rambler at the monster with all his strength. "Here's hoping you filled the gas tank, lady!"

The auto arced through the smoke-filled air before exploding against the monster's side. A bright orange fireball briefly lighted up the night. The smell of burnt fish contaminated the air as the wounded behemoth howled in protest, but the attack only seemed to anger the monster. Its tentacles lashed out at defenseless cars and buildings, smashing them to pieces. Jagged fangs gnashed together within its enormous maw. Smoking metal fragments, which were all that was left of the ancient Rambler, pelted the street and sidewalk. The evicted owner of the car fled in terror, but from Booster, the monster, or both?

Who cares? he thought. *Just so long as she gets out of here, pronto!*

He backed away as the monster charged toward him.

"That didn't make a dent!" Booster observed of his impromptu car bomb. Frustration filled his voice. "Skeets, what are my options?"

"PLEASE MAINTAIN YOUR FORCE FIELD, SIR."

"Yes, Mother!" he snapped impatiently. The monster was getting closer by the second. "Now talk to me about offensive strateg—*Huuh!*"

A monstrous tentacle whipped down, hammering Booster into the pavement. He tasted asphalt and felt every bone and muscle in his body quivering from the blow; it was like getting a full-body massage from Doomsday or Solomon Grundy.

Feeling more than slightly concussed, he crawled out from beneath the tentacle and took to the sky. "Never mind!" he shouted at Skeets. "I have my own plan! What time is the next midtown rail?"

Several of the giant tentacles were still dismantling the elevated tracks. If he was lucky, there was still time to dispose of the beast before the next monorail arrived. The last thing he needed was another trainload of civilians in danger.

"9:19, SIR!"

He dived toward the tracks. "And what time is it now?"

"9:14, SIR!"

"Perfect." Booster grinned past his busted lips. This was just the opportunity he had been waiting for!

ON the street below, closer to the action than was really advisable, Clark watched as Booster touched down upon the tracks. The metallic gold fabric in Booster's uniform made it easy to keep the hero in view, even without telescopic vision. Clark's eyes widened behind his glasses as Booster reached down to grab the electrified rail running the length of the tracks. His heart sank as he guessed what Booster had in mind. "Oh, surely he's not going to . . ." Clark rushed forward, shouting. "Booster, no! A fluctuation like that will blow the . . ."

Clark's warning fell on deaf ears. He could only watch in dismay as Booster wrenched the power conduit free of the tracks. For a moment, there was a blinding flash of electricity as sparks sprayed from one end of the ruptured rail, which Booster clearly intended to use to electrocute the Ballostro. A wary tentacle retreated from the hissing sparks—until the power went out and the entire neighborhood was cast into darkness.

"Midtown power grid," Clark murmured. He sighed and shook his head, disappointed by the other hero's carelessness. *I thought Booster was better than this.*

With no more electrical pyrotechnics to hold it at bay, the swinging tentacle batted Booster off the elevated tracks. He crashed to the street once more, landing in a heap of rubble near a crumpled taxicab. He moaned weakly and clutched his side. Were his ribs cracked or merely broken? Without his X-ray vision, Clark couldn't tell.

Meanwhile, pandemonium was breaking out all around Clark. The sudden blackout had only heightened the terror of the innocent bystanders clogging the streets. Panic-stricken voices cried out in the night:

"What the hell happened to the lights?"

"Ask Booster Gold! Nice goin', hero!"

"I can still hear the monster! I think it's coming!"

"Sydney? Sydney? It's Daddy, honey! Where are you?"

"Can't see a thing!"

Clark stumbled through the chaos. As his eyes gradually adjusted to the darkness, he made out Booster lying on the ground beneath the demolished tracks. Coughing hoarsely, he seemed to be having trouble getting up, let alone helping the hysterical people all around him. Clark clenched his jaw in frustration; at times like this, he hated being nothing more than a mild-mannered reporter. Metropolis needed a hero—and, sad to say, Booster seemed to falling down on the job.

Just when everything looked black, however, a brilliant white light shone down from above. Clark looked up to see Supernova swooping down from the cloudy sky. "Everyone calm down!" The caped hero radiated an incandescent glow that practically turned the night into day. "I'll light the way!"

His timely arrival filled the crowd with hope.

"It's Supernova!"

"Oh, thank God!"

Clark experienced a sense of relief as well. He still had plenty of questions about this new hero, but he was definitely glad to see him. Maybe Supernova would fare better than Booster Gold against the amphibious menace? Clark crossed his fingers.

A beam of light trailing behind him like a comet's tail, Supernova flew over the Ballostro. The multilimbed leviathan vanished in a blinding flash, leaving only the hijacked submarine behind. Enthusiastic cheers greeted the monster's disappearance.

"*Ba-boom*!" A bicycle messenger grinned at Clark. "Supernova, one. Big tentacly thing, zero." He pumped his fist in the air. "That's what I'm talkin' about!"

Clark was equally impressed. *I couldn't have dealt with that creature more effectively myself.* He tracked the flying hero with his eyes, wondering where and how Supernova had acquired his powers and expertise. *Just who are you anyway?*

The emergency over, Supernova descended from the sky. Glowing as brightly as his stellar namesake, he landed on the street in front of Booster, who was still sprawled amidst the debris. Scuff marks dimmed the latter's blue and gold uniform. Torn fabric exposed glimpses of twenty-fifth-century circuitry. His goggles were scratched and cracked across one lens. The last few corporate decals on his costume were concealed by dust and soot. The battered-looking hero was a far cry from the beaming celebrity who had adorned billboards and magazine covers only two months ago. Blood trickled from his swollen lip.

"Hey, Booster!" a bystander called out, adding insult to injury. "You suck!"

Lifting his head, Booster spit a mouthful of blood onto the cracked blacktop. "You're welcome," he croaked hoarsely.

Clark couldn't help feeling sorry for Booster. Even he knew that the public could be surprisingly fickle at times. He shouldered his way through the crowd to get closer to the two heroes.

"It's over, Booster," Supernova said, looking down on the fallen champion. He extended a gloved hand. "Give me your hand!"

"We love you, Supernova!" some exuberant fans hollered in the background. "Supernova rules!"

Booster looked about in confusion. He seemed dazed, and possibly in need of medical attention. Ignoring the hand being offered by Supernova, he climbed unsteadily onto his knees. "Where'd the monster go . . . ?"

"I zapped it away," Supernova informed him. "No need to thank me. The city's safe now, and you are too."

Clark frowned. Was it just his imagination, or was Supernova being deliberately condescending to poor Booster? *That's uncalled for,* he thought. As Superman, he had always striven to treat his fellow heroes courteously, no matter what. Despite his recent missteps, Booster had proven himself in battle before. He remembered Booster coming to his aid in the epic struggle against Doomsday, and fighting against the Secret Society of Super-Villains during the recent Crisis. For all his failings, Booster Gold had earned a little respect.

A nearby teenager obviously disagreed. "Should call him Booster *Fold!*" the boy said loudly. He spat on the sidewalk in disgust.

"Ignore the insults, Booster," Supernova advised. He continued to hold out his hand. "You're not going to pay attention to these people, are you? Of course you're not." There was no longer any mistaking the mocking tone in the glowing hero's voice. "I mean, why start now, right?"

Aside from Clark, the entire crowd snickered and laughed. "Good one!" the bicycle messenger brayed.

That was the last straw, at least as far as Booster was concerned. Launching himself from the ground, he tackled Supernova and knocked the other hero backward onto the street. Gasps erupted from the crowd, some of whom backed away nervously, while others surged forward for a better look. Clark tried to get through the mob, hoping to calm Booster down, but found himself blocked by the press of bodies hemming him in on all sides. The prospect of a fight drew gawkers from all directions.

"SIR, CONTAIN YOURSELF!" Skeets exclaimed.

"Shut up!" Booster snapped at the robot. Kneeling on top of Supernova, his knees digging into the other hero's abdomen, he drew back his fist. "I've had it with this smug bastard! He's pushed me too far!" He pounded Supernova in the face, provoking boos and hisses from the outraged spectators. His own face was flushed with anger. "You can't bully me, you caped creep! You're not the hero in this city! I am! ME!" A force blast fired from his gauntlet. "So you can go to hell!"

Taken by surprise, Supernova failed to defend himself at first, but quickly recovered from Booster's assault. He nimbly sprang out of the way of the force blast, which pulverized the asphalt beneath him instead. "Listen to yourself!" he accused Booster. "You're no hero! You're a billboard!" A scissor-kick connected with Booster's chin, propelling him onto his back. "You turn my stomach! You never had the confidence to earn people's respect, so you tried to buy it! Well, guess what?" He pounced at Booster, his fists clenched. "Metropolis found out the truth about Booster Gold! Staged stunts he can handle, but in a genuine crisis, he—"

"I can do the job!" Booster insisted. A shimmering force-field bubble extended outward from his uniform, slamming into Supernova, who had the breath knocked out of him. He tumbled backward and Booster regained the offensive. "What's your track record, you flash in the pan?" He rocketed at his foe. "Who needs you?"

"ACTUALLY," Skeets observed, "AT THIS MOMENT, HE'S THIS PANICKED CITY'S ONLY SOURCE OF LIGHT!"

But Booster was past caring. Driven by what appeared to be an uncontrollable rage, he delivered an uppercut to Supernova's chin. "You think I'm a joke?" He threw his weight into the blow, staggering his opponent. "How funny am I now? Huh?"

"You're too pathetic to be a joke, Gold!" Supernova taunted him, even as Booster punched him in the face with his left. Supernova's blue hood made it impossible to tell how much damage Booster was inflicting. "You're just a loser!"

This is getting out of hand, Clark thought. He managed to squeeze his way to the front of the crowd, but, without his powers, he knew better than to get between two superpowered combatants. He could only hope that either Booster or Supernova would come to his senses before anyone got seriously hurt.

"BOOSTER!" Skeets paged him urgently. "CONTROL YOURSELF! ACCORDING TO MY SENSORS, WE HAVE AN UNFORESEEN SITUATION. WHEN THE SEA CREA-TURE BREACHED THE SUBMARINE'S HULL, HE MUST HAVE DAMAGED ITS NUCLEAR ENGINES!" Clark tensed, not liking the sound of this. "IT'S LEAKING RADIA-TION INTO THE AREA—AND THE REACTOR CORE IS IN DANGER OF EXPLODING!"

Great Rao! Clark thought in alarm, invoking an ancient Kryptonian deity. He instinctively looked for a place to change, then remembered that he wasn't wearing his Superman uniform under his clothes. He stared helplessly at the lifeless sub, which was perched atop a mountain of rubble where a section of the monorail track had once been. A layer of gray, soundproof rubber insulated its steel-alloy hull. The derelict vessel was over three hundred feet long and probably weighed four thousand tons or so. Curious citizens, who had been poking around the sub, suddenly scurried away in fear.

Clark couldn't blame them.

To his credit, Supernova immediately attempted to take charge of the situation. "Gold, clear the area!" he instructed the other hero, putting their personal differences on hold. He turned toward the radioactive sub. "I'll handle the—"

"NO!" Booster blurted. Rushing past Supernova, he elbowed his rival in the face. "This one's mine!" He soared into the air above the beached submarine. "Skeets, reprogram my suit to process that radiation! If I can route that power directly into my force field and antigrav, we can make ourselves some history and show the new guy who's boss!"

Bright golden tractor beams emanated from his palms, latching onto the massive submarine. A shimmering halo enveloped the vessel from bow to stern. The beached vessel rocked atop the heaped debris.

"Run!" someone shouted. If nothing else, Skeets' an-nouncement of the radiation leak had served to clear out the crowd confining Clark. As his fellow citizens abandoned the site in droves, he hurried forward to join Supernova. The masked hero nodded at Clark, recognizing him from their interview five weeks ago. Together, they watched anxiously as Booster Gold attempted to deal with the crisis at hand.

"Kent, what's he doing?"

"More than . . . my God . . . I ever thought he could," Clark admitted as, before his eyes, Booster landed atop the sub. The glow from his ship-sized force field illuminated the blacked-out city. Clark squinted against the glare.

"Hey, Metropolis!" Booster stood triumphantly astride the sub's conning tower as he addressed the awestruck populace below. "You want a big, shiny star to light your skies. Well, here I am!"

The entire submarine lifted off into the sky, rising rapidly above the imperiled city. Thousands of tons in weight, it looked like the LexCorp blimp, except brighter. Much, much brighter.

"**SIR!**" Skeets shouted desperately. The robot hovered near Clark and Supernova, as if reluctant to get too close to Booster's spectacular display. "**YOUR FORCE FIELD! THE STRAIN ON THE SUIT IS TOO—**"

Booster ignored Skeets' frantic warning. His voice rang out over Metropolis as the glowing sub ascended higher than the skyscrapers overlooking Midtown.

"That's right, every*damn*body! Forget Supernova! The name with the claim to fame is Booster Gold!" Without his telescopic vision, Clark couldn't even see Booster anymore. Even the captured sub was nothing more than a cigar-shaped UFO in the night sky. Clark guessed that Booster was employing some sort of future technology to amplify his voice so that all could hear it. "And I'm back, baby! I'M BACK!"

A moment later, the sub exploded like a supernova above Metropolis. Clark blinked and averted his eyes as, just for an instant, the night was lit up like a summer afternoon. Clark felt the heat of the explosion against his face and guessed that his face was going to be sunburned in the morning, along with those of everyone else out in the open. For a second, he flashed back to that terrible moment, at the end of the Crisis, when he had been forced to fly straight through the heart of Krypton's red sun. The blazing fireball that had consumed the submarine was *almost* that intense.

Booster! he thought, fearful for the hero's safety. *Did his force field protect him or . . . ?*

"THIS WASN'T IN THE RECORDS!" Skeets squawked. **"THIS WASN'T SUPPOSED TO HAPPEN!"** His optical sensors were turned toward the sky. **"SAVE HIM!"**

"We'll catch him, Skeets," Clark tried to reassure the agitated robot, even as Supernova took off into the air. Blue spots danced before Clark's watery eyes, which were still recovering from the blinding glare. He dimly glimpsed a blue and gold figure plummeting from high above the city. "We won't let him fall."

Supernova flew toward the plunging figure. "Oh my God!" he exclaimed through his hood. He reached out to catch the other man. "Hold on, Booster!" He caught the falling hero in his arms. "Hold . . ."

His voice trailed off, and Clark's hopes dimmed. Supernova descended slowly from the sky, his own personal radiance reduced by several degrees. Booster's still form sagged limply in the hero's arms. Clark feared the worst as he ran to meet Supernova upon the ground. Skeets zipped ahead of him. "Is he . . . ?"

Supernova shook his head. "I tried to save him," he said somberly.

"No . . ." Clark whispered. "No . . ."

Although Booster's scorched costume remained intact, all the flesh had been seared from his body. All that was left of Booster Gold was a blackened skeleton inside a loose-fitting costume. Empty eye sockets stared out from behind the cracked golden goggles. The charred skull held little trace of Booster's colorful personality. Born in the twenty-fifth century, he had died only a few years into the twenty-first.

Skeets sidled forward. **"OH, MICHAEL . . ."**

WEEK 16.

SHIRUTA.

A full moon was sinking toward the horizon as Renee skulked through the sleeping wharves. A silent warehouse cast its shadow across a field of stacked cargo containers. She darted from one stack to another, taking care not to be seen. She glanced about warily. After so many years on the force, it felt weird to be the hunted fugitive this time around.

A greasy black rat scurried away at her approach. *The rat's got it right,* she thought. *Stay in the shadows. Only come out at night. Run if you hear anyone coming.*

Survive however you can. . . .

Dirt smudged her face. Her grubby tank top and shorts looked like something one of the local beggars would wear. A scuffed leather satchel was slung over her shoulder. Huge banners, bearing the smiling profiles of Black Adam and Isis, hung from a crane above her head. A series of loud bangs nearly caused her to jump out of her skin. Then she realized that someone was just blowing off firecrackers outside the shipping yard. The citywide jubilation over the impending royal marriage had penetrated even the waterfront district.

This must be what London was like, she mused, *the night before Charles and Di got hitched.*

She crept up to a rectangular cargo container the size of a child's playhouse. A printed label identified the container's point of origin as Gotham City. She rapped softly against one side of the corrugated steel box. "Charlie? It's me."

Nobody answered, and she experienced a sudden moment

of panic. Had something happened to Vic while she was out foraging for food? *No, please, not again,* she thought frantically. Cris Allen's lifeless body flashed across her memory. *Not another partner . . .*

Freaking out, she slid open a metal panel and rushed inside the container. A battery-powered halogen lamp lit up the interior of the box. To her relief, she saw Vic sitting in a lotus position upon the floor of the container. Deep in meditation, he must not have heard her knock before. His unmasked face needed a shave.

Thank God, she thought. "I never thought I'd say this, but I'm glad to see you, Charlie. For a second there, I thought I'd lost you for good."

He emerged from his trance. "I'm with you to the end, Renee," he promised. "We're in this together."

Lucky us.

She glanced around at their home of the last two weeks. The inside of the container had been converted into a make-shift hideaway, complete with a pair of rickety cots. Wooden crates, shipped from Gotham by Vic's buddy, contained spare gear for Vic and even that kick-ass ray gun she had picked up off Intergang back home. Empty food wrappers and plastic bottles littered the floor. Beady red eyes watched her from the box's murkier corners.

"What about you?" he asked. "The kids and I were starting to get worried, Renee."

She eyed the lurking rodents. "The kids give me the creeps, Charlie." Opening the satchel, she took out a bottle of water and a loaf of bread wrapped in paper. She had furtively converted most of her traveler's checks into Kahndaqi currency several days ago; she still had enough cash to pay for food for the time being, but how long would it be before she was reduced to stealing their provisions? They had been in hiding for two weeks now, ever since eluding those policemen outside the trashed shipping office, and she still had no idea how they were ever going to get out of Kahndaq without being arrested. Not for the first time, she wished that there was a local U.S. Embassy she could turn to. Unfortunately, America and its allies had broken off relations with Kahndaq after Black Adam took over the country.

"They still looking for us out there?" Vic asked.

Renee split the loaf of bread with her fellow fugitive. "Everyone's attention's on the king and queen."

"Ah, right," Vic remembered. "Today's the big wedding, right? Black Adam and Isis."

Attracted by the bread, a fat gray rat watched them intently from atop a nearby wooden crate. Vic playfully tossed the hungry rodent a few crumbs. *Don't encourage them,* Renee thought. *Too bad I didn't think to grab one of those big boxes of rat poison from the crime scene.* She remembered the heap of boxes lying on the bloody floor of the office. *God knows they had plenty of the stuff. . . .*

A lightbulb went off above her head, and she instantly lost her appetite. "Get your shoes on," she told Vic urgently, scrambling to her feet. "Hurry!"

He gave her a puzzled look. "What? Why?"

"The wedding." She grabbed the ray gun and thrust it into her satchel. It all made sense now. "Intergang is going to hit the wedding!"

"THIS is crazy, Adrianna!"

Mary Marvel was Captain Marvel's sister, and a super-powered heroine in her own right. She wore a feminine version of her brother's uniform, with a short red skirt instead of trousers. Even though they had only met a few days ago, Isis already thought of the young American woman as the sister she had never had.

"I love him, Mary," she insisted. They conversed in Isis' private quarters in the palace. She stepped behind a translucent screen as she disrobed. A maidservant stood by, holding on to Isis' bridal garments. Isis blushed at the realization that, after today, she would be spending her nights in a different wing of the palace.

Mary sounded unconvinced by the other woman's declaration. "You've known him for . . . ?"

"Thirteen weeks," Isis supplied. "But it feels like a lifetime."

Several lifetimes, in fact. She had lost her family, been shipped to a foreign country, faced a lifetime of bondage, and been transformed into a living goddess . . . all in the space of about three months. Granted, this marriage was a hasty one by conventional standards, but what about her existence was normal these days? What was one more life-changing upheaval, especially when it felt so right? *This was meant to be,* she thought confidently. *I know it.*

"But he's psychotic!" Mary protested.

"He's driven." Isis was not offended by the other woman's blunt appraisal of her intended. She understood where Mary was coming from; Isis recalled, with a twinge of regret, how she herself had once called Adam a terrorist, even spit in his face. But how far they had both come since then!

Mary paced restlessly on the other side of the screen. "He's killed a lot of people."

"But he's saved even more. And he's letting his anger go." She tried to make Mary understand. "Underneath his pain and rage is a man who only wants peace. A man who lost everything he loved and wants no one else to suffer that loss."

Like I did.

"He's the one doing the killing. . . ."

The maidservant helped Isis don her bridal regalia. "But you should see what he's done of late. The lives he's improved. The children that flock to him when he walks the street." Her heart warmed at the thought. "His smile. His smile is always real."

Mary still sounded dubious. "Since when does Black Adam smile?" She peeked over the top of the screen as a new thought occurred to her. "You know, maybe the wisdom of the goddess is messing with your feelings. Perhaps you should change back into your normal self and think about it some more. Just to be sure it's not the magic."

"But that's exactly what this is, Mary. Magic."

She stepped out from behind the screen, now fully clad in her wedding raiment, which resembled a more elaborate version of her usual garb as Isis. Silken white folds draped her statuesque figure. Golden bangles and jewelry glittered upon her arms and ears. A ruby sparkled in her navel. Gilded high heels temporarily replaced her sandals. A long satin train flowed behind her. The maidservant diligently held the tail of the train aloft, to keep it from trailing upon the floor. The bride's dark brown hair was elegantly styled. Black streaks of kohl highlighted her eyes in the manner of her ancient Egyptian ancestors.

"I've already changed back and forth many times," she assured Mary. "And my feelings remain the same." She stood several inches taller than the American teenager; unlike her brother, Mary did not change into an adult when she assumed her powers. "But if you're so intent on questioning them, why did you agree to be my maid of honor?" Her tone was not hostile, merely curious. "Because Captain Marvel asked you to?"

As much as she was grateful to the Marvel Family, Isis couldn't help wishing that her own parents and relatives could have lived to see this day. Alas, she had no family left, except for Amon, who might be dead as well. She deliberately forced such grim musings aside. Today, at least, was meant for happier tidings.

"Well, yeah," Mary admitted, somewhat sheepishly. "He thinks Adam can change. And that you're helping that happen."

"Maybe I am." She laid a reassuring hand upon Mary's shoulder. "But he wants to change. And he *has* changed."

"That's what Billy says too," Mary conceded. "I don't know . . . maybe?"

Just wait and see, Isis thought.

Together, she and Adam would overcome all doubters.

ELSEWHERE in the palace, Black Adam posed in front of a full-length mirror. He scowled at his reflection. "My hair looks terrible."

"Your hair never moves," Captain Marvel teased him. His mischievous tone hinted at a truth that few knew, that the mighty hero was, at heart, just a young American boy named Billy Batson. He regarded his former adversary with amusement.

"It's receding." Black Adam ran a finger along the edge of his dark widow's peak. "Somehow I hadn't noticed."

"I don't think you cared before," Marvel said. The Big Red Cheese, as the Western press had affectionately dubbed him, sat upon an upholstered seat a few feet away. He casually rested his chin upon his palm.

"Can it be fixed?"

"You're over three thousand years old," Marvel pointed out. "Be thankful you still have any hair at all."

Black Adam reluctantly conceded the point. Turning away from the mirror, he lifted his cape off a nearby chair. A tiny brown spot caught his eye. "They couldn't get this bloodstain out," he complained. He vacillated, uncertain whether to wear the cape anyway.

Marvel chuckled. "I can't believe it."

"What?" Adam asked irritably.

"You're nervous. I've never seen you nervous before."

"I am *not* nervous," Adam insisted. He held the cape up before his eyes. "Perhaps no one will notice. . . ."

Captain Marvel's voice took on a more serious tone. "This means you're going to give up that coalition of yours, right? Your crusade to wipe out the world's super-villains with your own private Justice League?"

"It is under consideration," Black Adam admitted. "My time has lately been focused on other matters. Perhaps more fruitful matters." With a sigh, he fastened the blood-specked cape onto his shoulders. *Now is no time,* he decided, *to discuss affairs of state.* "Thank you for coming, Billy. And for agreeing to use your authority as the Keeper of the Rock to wed us."

Captain Marvel rose to his feet. "I was surprised you wanted us here. Not that I couldn't use a break from the Rock of Eternity." He looked distinctly more relaxed than he had been back in Shazam's ancient throne room. "Though I do need to get back before nightfall. You wouldn't believe what the Sins did to the place last time there was a full moon."

Don't be so sure, Black Adam thought. *I know rather more of sin than most.*

He reflected on the irony of the situation. In times past, he and Captain Marvel had been mortal enemies. Yet here was young Billy, his replacement as Shazam's champion, officiating at his wedding. Truly, the Fates moved in mysterious ways. . . .

"My family, all of them, are long gone," he said thoughtfully. He contemplated his boyish American counterpart. "I thought, you have made your Marvel Family. Perhaps it is not too late to make mine."

I'M such an idiot, Renee thought.

She and Vic hurried through the crowded streets toward the palace. Watchful soldiers and security forces patrolled the city, making life more difficult. Spotting an armed police officer up ahead, she grabbed onto Vic's arm and dragged him into the nearest alley. "Don't let them see you!" she whispered urgently.

"They're looking for a man with no face," he reminded her. His mask was tucked into the pocket of his jeans, just in case he needed it later. Thankfully, the police had no idea what his real face looked like. "Besides, if we didn't want to be seen, we should have stayed in hiding."

To her dismay, the alley turned out to be a dead end. A high stone wall blocked the way to the palace. Renee could hear a crowd of excited citizens celebrating on the other side. Middle Eastern music played over loudspeakers.

"Dammit," she cursed. "We're going to have to go over." She started to scale the wall, digging her grimy fingers into cracks in the mortar. She glanced back at Vic, needing a boost. "Help me up."

"What's going on?" he demanded. There had been no time to explain it to him yet.

"The rat poison!" she blurted. "At the shipping place, where we found the bodies?"

He still didn't get it. "You may have noticed that Shiruta has a bit of a rat problem, Renee."

"No, that's not why it was there!" She kicked herself for not figuring it out before. "It's an anticoagulant, Charlie. Suicide bombers use it to coat their shrapnel so that the victims who aren't blown apart will bleed to death!"

She could thank a G.C.P.D. antiterrorism drill for that nasty bit of trivia.

"But Black Adam . . ." Vic began.

She knew where he was going. "Intergang's not after Black Adam himself. He can't be hurt." With Vic's help, she clambered onto the top of the wall, then gave him a hand up. She snatched a shapeless brown robe from a laundry line, the better to blend in with the locals. She hastily pulled the robe over her soiled clothes. "They're going to hit the audience. The bomber's in the crowd . . . !"

ALL of Kahndaq seemed to have poured into the vast courtyard in front of the royal palace. The rejoicing multitude crowded the open patios around the sparkling reflecting pool. Live music played from the domed spires of the palace. The sun god Re had blessed the day with a bright blue sky and golden rays of light.

Quite a turnout, Captain Marvel Jr. thought as he flew above the crowd. His bright blue uniform matched the sapphire sky. A gold-trimmed red cape fluttered in the breeze. The teenage hero found it hard to believe that so many people had shown up to witness the marriage of one of the Marvel Family's oldest enemies. *Heck, I can't believe we actually got an invite.*

Despite his name, Captain Marvel Jr. was no relation to his celebrated namesake. Freddy Freeman was simply a teenage boy whom Captain Marvel had chosen to share his powers with. Billy had done so to save Freddy's life after the innocent teen had been seriously injured by a bad guy named Captain

Nazi. Now Freddy showed his gratitude by using his newfound powers to combat evil alongside Mary and Captain Marvel.

And, apparently, by assisting at a wedding.

He flew ahead of a long procession of children. War orphans, to be exact, rescued by Isis and Black Adam over the last several weeks. At the request of the royal couple, the children were to be given a front-row seat at the proceedings. "Coming through!" Freddy shouted at the milling throng in their path. Most of the men and women below stepped aside to let the orphans through, but a few stragglers weren't getting the message. Too excited to pay attention to the American hero flying overhead, they lingered in front of the procession. Looking around for assistance, Freddy spotted a familiar face waiting in line in front of a street vendor.

"I need you to help me out here, Tawny," he called out to his friend, an eight-foot-tall tiger wearing a neatly pressed white suit. The furry feline stood upright like a man, and seemed distracted by the mouthwatering odors emanating from the steaming lamb kabobs. "I told you to eat something before we left," Freddy scolded the tiger.

"I wanted to save up for the Kahndaqian cuisine," Mister Tawky Tawny explained. The sentient tiger was a longtime friend of the Marvel Family. His whiskers twitched as he licked his chops. "It will only take a minute. . . ."

No dice, Freddy thought. He figured they were already running behind schedule. "I'm in charge of crowd control, man, and you're supposed to be helping."

"But you know how I get when I'm hungry," Tawny protested, reluctant to lose his place in line. "You don't want me to eat a member of the Royal Guard, do you?"

He was bluffing and Freddy knew it. Despite his ferocious appearance, Tawny was a big pussycat at heart. Freddy shook his head. "Just help me clear a path, okay?"

Growling unhappily, Tawny stepped back ahead of the procession. "Let the kids through," he snarled at the slowpokes blocking the way. Not surprisingly, the stragglers were quick to retreat from the grumpy tiger. Together, Captain Marvel Jr. and his feline assistant escorted the homeless children to their place at the front of the crowd, facing the palace. Neither of them paid any attention to one particular orphan, a teenage girl in a green robe. A stuffed backpack clung to her shoulders.

Alone among the elated children, she wasn't smiling.

"LOOK! There they are!"

All heads were turned upward to behold Black Adam and Captain Marvel hovering in the air high above the reflecting pool. Black Adam recalled addressing his people from this very spot a mere four months ago. That speech had been a call to arms, announcing his intention to rid the world of those who would endanger it. At the time, he had never guessed that he would soon be embarking on a far more joyous new endeavor. He searched the sky impatiently for his bride.

It was almost time.

A riotous cheer rose up from the crowd as Isis and Mary Marvel flew into view, joining them above the courtyard. Adam barely noticed Mary's presence, so captivated was he by his bride's radiant appearance. Her womanly grace and loveliness took his breath away. Filmy garments rustled in the breeze, clinging to her supple form. A satin train billowed behind her like the tail of a comet. He chose to take that as a good omen.

"She's beautiful," Captain Marvel whispered to him.

For once, he and Billy were in total agreement.

"Hello, Adam," she greeted him with a smile. They faced each other in the sky, while the Marvel siblings looked on benignly. Her slender fingers reached out and gently stroked his cheek.

"Good morning, Isis." They clasped their hands together. The crowd cheered once more.

RENEE and Vic were the only ones not cheering. *So many people,* she thought anxiously, as they made their way through the packed crowd. Their slow pace frustrated her, adding to the

tension. Her eyes desperately searched the vast assemblage.
How were they ever going to find the would-be terrorist in this
mob scene?

"You said 'bomber,'" Vic whispered. "How do you know
there's only one?"

"The boxes of rat poison," she explained, shoving her way
past a clump of jubilant spectators. Their insistent progress,
and sloppy attire, attracted a few stink-eyes from the people
around them, who were all decked out in their Sunday best.
Many of the celebrants clutched bouquets of flowers, or maybe
just a single red rose. An elderly woman sniffed disdainfully
in their direction. Renee guessed that she and Vic didn't smell
too good. "Only three of them were empty. That's about one
bomb's worth."

No doubt the bombing was in retaliation for that Intergang
mobster Black Adam had ripped apart in Metropolis several
weeks back. The gang's leaders wanted to send the dictator a
message, written in the blood of his subjects.

Gory possibilities flashed through her mind. "Take a look
at this crowd, Charlie. One bomb is all you'd need. A single
blast could kill two hundred people, maybe more."

"Oh, good," Vic said, struggling to keep up with her. "I was
afraid this was going to be easy."

CAPTAIN Marvel glanced down at the exuberant throng. "I
think we have our witnesses," he quipped. "And then some."

And none more important than those children below, Black
Adam thought, *who owe their newfound freedom and happiness to the boundless compassion of the beautiful maiden before me. She is truly a goddess among women.*

Oddly, he felt no guilt at taking a new bride so many years
after the untimely death of his first wife. Or perhaps it was not
so odd; somehow he sensed that Shiruta, wherever her spirit
now resided, would want him to find happiness again after all
these lonely centuries. Kahndaqi tradition allowed a man more
than one wife, after all, provided it brought no disharmony to

his household. He could only hope that someday they would all share eternity together beyond this vale of tears.

He nodded at Billy, signaling him to begin the ceremony.

"Let us repeat the wizard's name in praise," Captain Marvel instructed, "to summon the Virtues."

Ordinarily, the wizard's name would transform them back into their mortal guises, but apparently Captain Marvel's new capacity as the guardian of the Rock of Eternity allowed him to grant them a special dispensation in this instance. Without fear of falling, all four champions loudly called out the name of power.

"SHAZAM!"

Thunder sounded in the clear blue sky and a bolt of en-chanted lightning suddenly appeared before the wedding party. Rather than disappearing in a flash, the coruscating pillar of energy crackled in the air alongside the floating heroes. The pure white light of the stationary thunderbolt was reflected upon the shimmering surface of the reflecting pool forty feet below.

"The Seven Virtues of Man are now with us in spirit," Cap-tain Marvel proclaimed. "Courage, kindness, hope, faith, hu-mility, patience, and love." His booming voice rang out over the courtyard, so that all could hear him. "Do you hear them bless this union?"

Black Adam felt the calming presence of the Virtues. For the moment, they silenced the angry demands for vengeance that never entirely stopped crying out from the darker corners of his soul. He felt happier, and more at peace, than he had in millennia.

"I hear them, Billy," he said sincerely.

"As do I," Isis affirmed. They stared blissfully into each other's eyes, seeing only joy and contentment ahead.

Captain Marvel smiled broadly. "I am delighted that I could be here to see this day. A day when the union between man and woman, god and goddess, looks to spell hope for the future of the world."

* * *

CAPTAIN Marvel Jr. swooped by overhead. Renee waved her arms and tried to get his attention, but all eyes were on the solemn ceremony taking place far above the heads of the spectators. Her frantic cries were lost amidst the hubbub of the crowd. She shared a worried look with Vic. They had been searching for several minutes, but seemed to be no closer to finding the suicide bomber hiding somewhere in the audience. As the wedding neared its climax, she knew they were running out of time.

"Hold on!" she told Vic as a new tactic occurred to her. She climbed up onto his shoulders, causing him to grunt beneath her weight. "Hold still!"

"Hey!" he blurted in protest. "A little warning next time?" He held her ankles in place as she rose to a standing position atop his shoulders, hoping for a better view of the packed courtyard. She tottered awkwardly, trying to maintain her balance.

"Keep me steady!" she pleaded, while she searched the swarm of people ahead of them. A raised hand shielded her eyes from the incandescent white lightning bolt overhead. "C'mon," she muttered fretfully. "Where the hell are you . . . ?"

Her gaze fell upon the rows of orphaned children lined up at the front of the crowd. Her eyes zoomed in on a suspicious backpack strapped to one of the kids' shoulders. Unlike the other children, who were practically dancing with excitement, and laughing merrily amongst themselves, this kid seemed to stand apart from the others. The body language was all different, more subdued, less gleeful. A hooded, olive-colored robe shrouded the figure's slight body.

That's our bomber, Renee realized. Every instinct in her body told her that she had the right person. Then the hooded figure glanced back over her shoulder, revealing a youthful face whose fatalistic expression and somber eyes only confirmed Renee's suspicions. To her shock, Renee spied the winsome features of a girl who looked maybe twelve years old. Thirteen, tops. "Oh my God," Renee whispered. "She's just a kid."

* * *

"I ask all who bear witness to this spiritual matrimony to gaze up at their glory." The words were more formal than was usual for the unassuming Marvel. Adam suspected that Billy was channeling the wisdom of Solomon, or perhaps even the immortal spirit of Shazam himself. "The glory of Kahndaq's champion and his bride-to-be. Look into their light. Behold true love. And pray."

Captain Marvel solemnly addressed the bridegroom.

"Teth-Adam of Kahndaq, do you take Adrianna Tomaz of Egypt, Nature's blessed queen, to be your wife?"

He answered without hesitation. "I do."

RENEE sprang from Vic's shoulders, landing on the floor of the courtyard. Elbowing her way through the crowd, she sprinted toward the hooded girl wearing the backpack. She snatched the ray gun from her satchel as she raced against time. "I see her!" she shouted back at Vic. "It's some kid. They're using some girl!"

Angry protests and curses assailed her as she forced her way forward, roughly shoving uncooperative Kahndaqis to the side. "Out of my way!" she yelled in English, but her foreign tongue fell on uncomprehending ears. She glimpsed the hooded girl up ahead, still several rows away. "She's got a bomb!"

"ADRIANNA Tomaz, also known as Isis, do you take Teth-Adam of Kahndaq, Black Marvel, as your husband?"

Her smile outshone the sun. "I do."

"TAKE the shot!" Vic called out to Renee. She could hear him fighting his way through the crowd behind her. There was no way he could get to the would-be bomber before Renee. It was all up to her. "Dammit, Renee!"

"She's just a kid!" Renee cried out in anguish. Her fingers held on tightly to the grip of her ray gun, which felt impossibly heavy in her hand. She was close enough to the girl that she could hear the teenager praying quietly to herself. Renee couldn't make out the words of the prayer, which sounded like Arabic, but she couldn't help wondering what kind of twisted devotion Intergang had inspired in the girl that would drive her to martyr herself like this. Had she been brainwashed by Whisper A'Daire or something? "I can't shoot a kid!"

Vic refused to let her off the hook. "You're not going to reach her in time!" There were too many oblivious people between Renee and the hooded girl. She pushed helplessly against their unyielding bodies. "You've got to do it, Renee! Take the shot!"

The girl opened the front of her robe, revealing a belt of C-4 plastic explosives strapped around her waist. She removed the firing mechanism from her backpack, touching it to her forehead as she closed her eyes in prayer. Most people were still watching the gravity-defying ceremony above their heads, but a few of the girl's nearest neighbors spotted the explosives and started to back away in fear. The press of the crowd hemmed them in, trapping the terrified orphans well within the bomb's blast radius. The same horde stubbornly blocked Renee's path, unaware that they were only moments away from being blown to shreds. She stared at the suicidal girl through the mass of bodies. Vic kept on yelling at her.

"Take the damn shot!"

CAPTAIN Marvel nodded in approval. "By the gods and goddesses of all universes and all worlds, I now pronounce you man and wife." Caught up by the emotion of the moment, Mary Marvel wiped a tear from her eye. "Now let's have some more lightning."

"GOD forgive me," Renee whispered.

A blast of corrosive energy erupted from the muzzle of the ray gun.

The girl didn't even have time to scream as a searing beam cut through her torso, vaporizing her explosive belt.

Her lifeless body collapsed onto the pavement.

*   *   *

BLACK Adam and Isis embraced passionately. Their lips met and thunder pealed overhead, drowning out every other sound, even the fervent beating of their hearts. Lightning electrified the sky. Lost in the kiss, Adam knew that nothing in heaven and earth could possibly spoil this moment. A glorious new era had begun . . . and perhaps a new dynasty as well.

"MARY, full of grace . . ."

Renee dropped to her knees, emotionally exhausted. Nearby, the bomber's body lay sprawled across the polished stone tiles. Acrid fumes rose from her charred flesh. Blood spread from the gaping hole in her torso. Her lifeless fingers still gripped the firing mechanism. The startled cries of those nearby were lost amidst the deafening thunder and the cheers of the overjoyed populace.

"Just a kid," Renee murmured. Tears streaked her face. She felt sick to her stomach.

A gentle hand fell upon her shoulder. "You didn't have any choice," Vic said softly.

His words did little to comfort her. Disintegrating a scaly man-monster was one thing. Killing a deluded teenage girl was another. She looked at the girl's smoking body.

"Tell her that."

WEEK 17.

CINCINNATI.
OHIO.

CLARK Kent had no memories of his own funeral, of course, but he had viewed TV news footage of the event after he came back to life. Superman's funeral had been a massive affair, attended by pretty much the entire Justice League and every other super hero on the planet. Thousands of ordinary men and women, wearing black armbands that bore his distinctive S-shield insignia, had turned out in Metropolis to bid farewell to the Man of Steel . . . temporarily, as it turned out. Watching the footage much later, Clark had found the proceedings both impressive and deeply moving.

Booster Gold's funeral was something else altogether.

Corporate logos and trademarks were plastered all over the cheap pine casket. "Soder Cola mourns your passing" read one of the stickers pasted to the coffin. Similar sentiments were expressed by labels bearing the logos of Lit Beer, Pep Cereals, and some of Booster's other sponsors. Furthermore, the six pallbearers carrying the coffin out of the chapel were hardly the cream of the super-hero community. Clark recognized:

The Blimp, an overweight member of The Inferior Five, capable of floating slowly through the air. A finned green costume heightened his resemblance to his namesake.

Mind-Grabber Kid, a former teen hero still clinging to what remained of his short-lived celebrity. He mostly signed autographs at nostalgia shows these days.

The Yellow Peri, an amateur sorceress whose spells tended

to go awry more often than not. Clark had first encountered the witchy blonde in Smallville years ago.

Beefeater, a would-be British crime fighter whose elaborate scarlet and gold uniform, resembling that of the Yeoman Warders of the Tower of London, was more impressive than his abilities.

The Odd Man, a clownish-looking individual wearing garish face paint and a motley-colored business suit. He was known (barely) for playing pranks on minor villains.

And Honest Abe, a lanky individual who was a dead ringer for Abraham Lincoln. To be honest, Clark had no idea what his powers were.

The mild-mannered reporter shook his head in dismay. As far as he knew, the obscure heroes meant well, but . . . they weren't exactly League material. A handful of bored bystanders watched the proceedings. They looked disappointed by the costumed turnout. Clark couldn't blame them.

"Classy," he observed. He looked dubiously at Skeets, who was hovering nearby. "Two weeks to arrange this?"

"BELIEVE ME, MR. KENT," the robot insisted, "I'M EQUALLY UNDERWHELMED. BUT THAT'S HOW LONG IT TOOK TO FIND A HOST CITY FREE OF, SHALL WE SAY, ANTI-BOOSTER SENTIMENT."

Clark peered through his glasses at the sorry spectacle. "Skeets, Booster's never even been to Cincinnati."

"EXACTLY," Skeets said. They watched as the coffin was loaded into a waiting hearse. No other reporters were on hand to cover the funeral. "BUT HE HAS NOW, SIR."

Relieved of their burden, the undistinguished pallbearers lingered on the sidewalk. They looked uncertain what to do next. Listening in on their conversation, Clark wondered if any of the costumed mourners had even met Booster before.

"This is chunkage," Mind-Grabber Kid complained. Despite his name, the "Kid" was pushing thirty. A metal helmet and tinted visor concealed his features. "I don't see a single network here." He glanced at the Yellow Peri. "Did your agent promise you media coverage?"

"I don't have an agent," she admitted. A Midwestern accent betrayed her corn-fed roots. Golden bracelets matched her flaxen tresses.

"Really?" Mind-Grabber Kid leaned toward her, eager to make a connection. "If you want to swap numbers, I can hook you up with—"

"No," she said curtly.

A few feet away, the Odd Man chatted with Beefeater. "I didn't know Booster," the clown divulged. "I got this gig off HeroList, which kind of creeps me out." His squeaky voice hinted at years of helium abuse. "Didn't he have any family?"

"Oi," the Brit said with a thick cockney accent. "'E was a time-traveler, remember? 'E won't be born for five 'undred years, guv'nor." A round-brimmed Tudor bonnet capped his head. A white ruff collar circled his neck. His scarlet tunic bore the emblem of the royal crown, above the traditional thistle rose and shamrock. "Oi."

The Blimp offered the two men a ride, and they clambered onto his considerable girth. He wafted into the air, carrying the pair of heroes with him as he slowly drifted after the departing hearse. The Yellow Peri, Honest Abe, and Mind-Grabber Kid had chosen to climb atop the long black limo instead. The blonde waved at the meager crowd as though riding a float in the Macy's Thanksgiving Parade. Abe recited the Gettysburg Address.

"This isn't right," Clark said ruefully. "Booster didn't die in disgrace. He was off his game near the end, but this world is too quick to forget the good some men do." He could only assume that Green Lantern, the Flash, Martian Manhunter, and the rest were too busy saving the world to attend Booster's funeral. He knew that both Bruce and Diana had other matters to deal with at the moment. "I'll write this up for the *Planet* and hope that Perry doesn't bury it under the fold or behind a hyperlink." He glanced at the levitating robot beside him. "Skeets, do you want a ride to the cemetery?"

The robot didn't answer at first, apparently distracted by one of the civilians looking on from the sidelines. Skeets' sensors seemed to be focused on a blond-haired man wearing a loose flannel shirt and jeans. The thirtyish stranger bore a slight resemblance to Booster. Was that what had caught the robot's attention?

"Skeets?"

"I'LL FLY ON MY OWN, MR. KENT," he replied. "I SEE SOMEONE I WISH TO SPEAK WITH."

His journalistic curiosity aroused, Clark watched discreetly as the robot zipped toward the startled bystander. "EXCUSE ME, SIR, BUT YOU SEEM VAGUELY . . . FAMILIAR. MAY I ASK YOUR NAME AND WHAT BRINGS YOU TO THE SERVICE?"

"Who, me?" The man was understandably taken aback by the robot's interest. "I'm Daniel Carter. I'm here 'cause . . . I dunno. Had a lunch hour, felt like I oughta be here for some reason." He took a few steps back from Skeets. "Should I . . . uh . . . know you, or something?"

Good question, Clark thought.

A metal probe extended from Skeets' gleaming carapace. A miniature scanner projected a ruby red beam that swept over Carter's face and physique. "GENEALOGICAL ANALYSIS," Skeets said aloud, his voice briefly taking on a more robotic tone. "SUBJECT: DANIEL JON CARTER. DNA ANALYSIS OF ANCESTRAL LINK TO BOOSTER: 93.2% . . . 95.8% . . . 100%."

Carter scratched his head, thoroughly baffled by the robot's technobabble. His face lit up as an idea occurred to him. "Hey, am I on TV?" He looked around hopefully, as if expecting a camera crew to emerge from hiding at any second. Maybe someone from *American's Funniest Super-Hero Encounters*?

"NOT YET," Skeets informed him. "BUT CONTACT ME SOON AT THE NUMBER I JUST BEAMED TO YOUR CELL PHONE, DANIEL CARTER." The robot flitted away into the sky. "WE NEED TO TALK ABOUT YOUR FUTURE. . . ."

Clark watched the robot head toward the cemetery on its own power. *What was that all about?* he wondered. It sounded like Skeets thought this "Daniel Carter" might be one of Booster's direct ancestors. *Always possible,* Clark supposed. Booster's DNA had to come from somewhere. *Maybe Skeets is just trying to track down Booster's next of kin?*

He made a mental note to find out if Booster had left any sort of will behind. In the meantime, he had to head to the cemetery himself. *Someone* from the Justice League needed to be present when Booster was lowered into the ground, even if Clark could only be there incognito. Whatever his motives, Booster Gold had saved hundreds of lives over the course of his career, both before and after the Crisis. He had lived and died a hero.

He deserved better than this.

WEEK 18.

SHIRUTA.

THE solemn ceremony took place within the royal hall of the palace. Towering marble columns supported the high ceiling. Carved Egyptian hieroglyphs embellished the decorative cornice running along the tops of the walls. Robed courtiers and advisors stood in attendance as Black Adam, with Isis at his side, addressed their honored guests. Or one of them at least.

"On the very day of our wedding," Adam declared, "a vile and sinister attempt to kill hundreds by means of a suicide bomb was averted by your heroic actions in the defense of Kahndaq and her people."

A profound anger simmered within him as he recalled the details of the nefarious plot. Enraptured by the beauty of his bride, and the joyousness of the occasion, he had failed to notice the life-or-death drama that had unfolded outside the palace that day, but his security team had soon made him aware of just how close his people had come to a grisly tragedy. Numerous witnesses, as well as the personal effects of the would-be assassin, had confirmed the foreigners' role in preventing a massacre.

Such valor deserved recognition, which was why he now held a cedar box before him. A pair of gleaming medals rested within the box, atop a black satin cushion. Polished sapphires were lodged in the medals, which were forged of electrum, an ancient alloy of gold and silver prized since the days of the pharaohs. Silk ribbons adorned the medals.

"Thus it is my pleasure to present you and your partner

with the Order of the Scarab, the highest honor Kahndaq can bestow upon those not born of her soil."

Isis took one of the medals from the box and draped it over the head of the man standing before them. "Wear it with pride, Charles Victor Szasz." She smiled warmly at the American as the scarab settled against his chest. "And know that you and Renee Montoya will always be regarded as friends by Kahndaq and its rulers."

"Thank you, your highness." The man wore a neatly pressed suit and tie, courtesy of the palace tailors. His clean-shaven face gazed back at them. He looked relieved not to be a fugitive anymore. "Always nice to have friends."

Black Adam could not fault Szasz' manners. He appeared suitably appreciative of the lofty honor being bestowed upon him.

His associate, on the other hand, was a different story.

"Where is she?" Black Adam demanded crossly. The former policewoman was conspicuously absent, her medal unclaimed. "Or does Ms. Montoya mean to insult myself and my queen with her continued absences?"

Such conduct was inexcusable, even for an American.

"I'm sure no insult was intended to either of you, your highness," Szasz insisted. He awkwardly fingered the medal upon his chest. "Renee . . . is going through a difficult time right now."

"She had no choice," Black Adam said impatiently. For once, a Westerner had shown the courage to do what was necessary; must she now sully that accomplishment by wallowing in useless guilt? Black Adam found her squeamishness just as foolish and infuriating as that of the Justice League. "The girl had a bomb."

Szasz shrugged. "Yeah. Well, let's just say she doesn't see it like that." He shook his head ruefully. "And she's coping in her usual way. . . ."

EMPTY bottles and discarded clothing littered the floor of the hotel room. Heavy curtains kept out the daylight. On the rumpled bed, which hadn't been made in days, Renee lolled atop the satin sheets with a cute Kahndaqi femme named Zalika. Sweat glistened upon the women's bodies. A ceiling fan failed to cool their ardor.

"*Onq ihny,* Renee," Zalika whispered in her ear as she lay atop Renee. Her exotic perfume smelled of sandalwood and jasmine. "*S'alyai mus. . . .*"

"Got no idea what you just said, babe," Renee slurred. So far, the language barrier hadn't posed much of a problem. If anything, it made things simpler. "But I *love* the way you say it."

Drunk on cheap date wine, she sank limply into the sheets, letting Zalika take the lead. The local girl certainly knew what she was doing all right. Renee felt the room shake. Then, beyond the foot of the bed, the wall crumbled. Sunlight poured into room, hurting Renee's eyes. Wincing, she raised a hand to shield herself from the glare. Zalika yelped and rolled off Renee. She covered herself with a pillow.

What the hell?

Black Adam hovered in the air outside the fifth-story hotel room. Powdered stone and plaster caked the knuckles of his clenched right fist. A sparkly medallion dangled from his other hand. He glowered balefully at the two women. "By the gods," he thundered, "what do you think you're doing?"

Zalika hid behind her pillow. Renee didn't bother. "Uhm," she mumbled tipsily. "You don't really want me to answer that, do you?"

"You continue to insult me?" Black Adam's face flushed with anger. He landed indignantly on the Persian carpet. An empty wine bottle crunched beneath his boot. As usual, he seemed annoyingly full of himself. "Do you have any idea who it is you're speaking t—?"

"Oh, shut up!" Renee groused. She felt a hangover coming on, and Black Adam's booming voice wasn't helping any. She sluggishly rolled out of bed and started pulling on her jeans. Squinting into the sunlight, she saw Isis carrying Vic through the sky toward the hotel. A worried expression showed upon the Egyptian woman's face as she and Vic touched down on the floor behind her husband. Vic smirked at the compromising situation Renee had just found herself in. She decided she liked him better when he didn't have a face.

"And you," she accused Vic, shaking a finger at him. "Man, what is it with you, Charlie?" A vivid memory, of a no-faced stranger intruding on her one-night stand back in Gotham, surfaced from her soggy brain. "Every time I'm getting some, you have to crash the party?" She clumsily wiggled into a black tank top, putting an end to the peep show. "You gotta crush on me or what?"

Uninterested in her argument with Vic, Black Adam spun Renee around to face him. "There was a time," he warned her, "when I would have cheerfully killed you for speaking to me as you have."

"Don't let me stop you, big guy." *Once a killer, always a killer,* she figured. The dead girl's face flashed across her memory. She remembered squeezing the trigger of her ray gun. *Just like me.*

Black Adam waved his goddamn medal in her face. "Renee Montoya, you were to receive the Order of the Scarab today. A great honor." He fumed as she rummaged about the room, looking in vain for a bottle that still had a little booze left in it. "But instead of attending the ceremony, I find you here, drunkenly taking pleasure with one of my citizens."

While Black Adam read Renee the riot act, Isis quietly procured a robe from the floor and draped it over Zalika. Keeping a wary eye on her irate husband, she escorted the trembling Kahndaqi babe from the room. Zalika kept her face turned away from Black Adam, no doubt hoping to escape his notice. Renee hoped she hadn't gotten the woman in trouble.

It's not her fault I'm bad news.

"I demand an answer," Black Adam insisted. He looked like he wanted to pop her skull like a balloon. "Do you mean to insult me and my new bride, or is there some other expla—?"

Jesus, Renee thought. *Doesn't this jerk ever shut up?* She angrily swatted the medal away from her. "Get that thing outta my face!"

Black Adam blew his stack. "You push too far, woman!" An iron fist clamped around her throat, cutting off her air. She grabbed onto his wrist with both hands, trying to pry his fingers away from her neck, but it was like trying to bend steel with her bare hands. He lifted her off the floor, giving her the full Darth Vader treatment. Her bare feet dangled in the air. "I am a changed man," he snarled, "but not that changed!"

"Adam!" Isis cried out.

"Renee!" Vic blurted. He started to rush forward, only to be held back by Isis' superior strength. He strained against her slender arm. "Your highness, don't!"

A pitiful gurgle escaped Renee's lips. Her hands fell away, her arms dropping to her sides as she abandoned her efforts to save herself. Starving lungs gasped for air. Darkness swiftly encroached upon her field of vision. Death was only moments away, but instead of her own wasted life passing before her eyes, she saw instead the somber face of the teenage girl in the courtyard, the girl she had burned a hole clean through. The crackle of the heat-ray echoed in her ears as, once again, she watched the deluded teenager drop lifelessly onto the pavement. Fresh blood spilled across Renee's tortured soul.

"That's right, go ahead. . . ." she challenged Black Adam. Tears leaked from her bloodshot eyes. Maybe this was the only way to make the girl's face go away. "Just do it. . . ."

But Isis would not let Black Adam put Renee out of her misery. The Egyptian queen stepped forward and placed her palm against her husband's chest. Kohl-lined eyes entreated him. "This helps nothing," she said softly.

The murderous fury fled his face, at least to a degree. Letting go of Renee's throat, he disdainfully flung her to the floor. Panting for breath, she lay sprawled upon the cluttered carpet. Vic helped her to her feet, and she plopped down onto the edge of the bed. She cradled her aching head in her hands, emotionally and physically exhausted. *Just my luck,* she thought bitterly. *The one time Black Adam shows mercy, it has to be with me.*

Isis came between Renee and Black Adam. She gestured

toward Renee as she spoke to her husband. "Her grief—and your anger—are both misplaced."

"Isis is right," Vic said. He dropped a gentle hand onto Renee's shoulder.

She looked up at him, despair written all over her face. "I killed a kid, Charlie."

"And you're going to be eating your liver—what's left of it—over that for years to come." His face and voice were more serious than usual. "But none of us are talking about *why* that girl was there in the first place." He turned to confront Black Adam and Isis. "And handing out medals, as lovely as they might be, or going on benders with the prettiest lass in Shiruta, doesn't solve the problem. It doesn't even address it." He paused for emphasis. "The problem is Intergang."

Renee lifted her head, taking an interest despite herself. She remembered why she had come to Kahndaq in the first place. And who was ultimately responsible for the would-be bomber's death.

Vic spelled out the mystery for them. "On top of everything else, along with their monster men and high-tech weapons, why are they using kids?"

"A good question, Charles," Isis stated. "It must be stopped."

Black Adam nodded grimly. His simmering rage no longer seemed directed at Renee. His arms were crossed stiffly atop his chest. "Then let us stop it."

Sounds like a plan, Renee thought. A trace of Zalika's perfume still lingered in the room. *Once I sober up, that is.*

WEEK 19.

CINCINNATI.

"IT was, no lie, one of the greatest moments ever in high school football."

Daniel Carter sat in an easy chair in his cruddy apartment as he relived the high point of his life for maybe the one zillionth time. Old football trophies filled the wooden display case to his right. A framed photo of the Manchester High Spartans, circa 1991, was mounted on the wall. A stack of unpaid bills lay unopened atop a cheap particleboard end table.

"A ninety-eight-yard touchdown run put me just over the all-time national rushing record. Half the state came that night to watch me make the history books, and I did." He sipped from a can of Lit Beer before getting to the next part. "And I didn't even get to score with the head cheerleader after." He winced at the memory of a three-hundred-pound linebacker slamming him to the ground. "Broke my leg in four places. Blew my knee *and* my scholarship." Even after fifteen years, the unfairness of it all still stung. "But not all was lost. I grew up to be Evergreen Insurance Company's fifth best term-life salesman." He cracked a bitter smile as he held up five fingers. "Fifth. Out of six."

"IT COULD HAVE BEEN WORSE," Skeets observed. The talking robot floated in front of Daniel. "YOU COULD HAVE ENDED UP A JANITOR AT A SPACE MUSEUM."

What the heck? Daniel thought. "Uh, that's a pretty specific reference."

"IT'S THE PATH YOUR DESCENDANT FOLLOWED.

WILL FOLLOW," Skeets corrected himself. "AFTER A GAMBLING SCANDAL ENDED HIS OWN FOOTBALL CAREER."

"See, I thought just coming home and finding a bippity little robot going through my mail was creepy enough." In fact, Daniel had been out of town on business since dropping in on Booster Gold's funeral two weeks ago, only to find Skeets waiting for him when he got back. *This is why I never called that number he beamed into my cell phone. Everything about this business is too weird.*

He took another swig of beer. "Dude, unless this is the greatest sweepstakes reveal in human history, and you're really a TV camera, I promise I am *not* the droid you're looking for." Part of him kept expecting this whole deal to be some sort of practical joke. "I'm sorry that Booster Gold guy is dead, but he and I were not related. No one in my family was a super hero."

"YET," Skeets pointed out. "BOOSTER—MICHAEL JON CARTER—WAS YOUR DESCENDANT. WE CAME TO YOUR ERA IN PART BECAUSE WE BELIEVED ITS EVENTS TO BE A MATTER OF HISTORICAL RECORD." The shiny golden robot certainly looked like he came from the future. "BUT THAT ISN'T SO. SOMETHING IS AWRY IN THE TIMESTREAM. BEFORE HE DIED, BOOSTER AND I INFILTRATED THE LAB OF A CHRONONAUT NAMED RIP HUNTER TO INVESTIGATE THE CAUSE OF THE ANOMALIES."

Despite himself, Daniel found himself caught up in the bizarre narrative. "What did you find?"

"I'M NOT CERTAIN," Skeets admitted. "MY PRESENCE WAS REQUIRED TO KEEP AN ATOMIC TIME LOCK OPEN WHILE BOOSTER WENT INSIDE. HE CLAIMED NOT TO HAVE SEEN ANYTHING OF SIGNIFICANCE, BUT I'M WONDERING IF HE DIDN'T OVERLOOK SOMETHING." Daniel saw his own face reflected in the robot's metallic sheen. "YOU ARE ONE OF BOOSTER'S ANCESTORS. YOU WILL KNOW."

"This is crazy talk," he protested. "When does Sarah Connor

show up to stop me from inventing Terminators?" He lurched out of his chair and headed for bed. He had wasted too much time on this screwy sci-fi crap already.

"DANIEL!" A note of urgency entered the robot's electronic voice. He followed Daniel across the living room. "IT'S VITALLY IMPORTANT THAT I REGAIN ACCESS TO THAT LAB. ITS BIOMETRIC SECURITY SENSORS 'KNOW' BOOSTER NOW, AND YOU'RE ENOUGH OF A GENETIC MATCH TO FOOL THEM."

He kept on walking away. "Can't help you," he said, wondering if it was possible to get a restraining order against a robot. "I have plans this weekend that don't involve breaking and entering."

"I KNOW," Skeets declared. "A DENTIST APPOINTMENT AND A WEEKLY POKER GAME WITH SOME OF YOUR OLD HIGH SCHOOL BUDDIES. PRETTY EARTH-SHATTERING STUFF. SUPERMAN WOULD BE JEALOUS."

Daniel had never realized that a robot could be so sarcastic. "What, did you read my date book too?" He spun around to glare at the hovering golden orb. "Nice salesmanship, spy guy." He nodded toward the door. "Get lost."

"BUT WHAT IF I COULD PROMISE YOU A MORE THRILLING EXISTENCE, DANIEL?" Skeets caught up with Daniel. "WHAT IF I TOLD YOU I COULD, USING BOOSTER'S DNA, BIOENGINEER A SUPER-HERO IDENTITY FOR YOU?" The robot was only a few inches away from him now, Skeets' glowing sensors practically staring into his eyes. "WHAT IF, IN RETURN FOR YOUR AID, I OFFERED YOU A CHANCE TO RELIVE THAT MOMENT OF FOOTBALL GLORY OVER AND OVER AGAIN FOR ALL TIME?"

Daniel hesitated. He knew he should probably drop-kick Skeets out the nearest window, but what if the robot could actually deliver what he promised? Daniel glanced around his dinky apartment, frowning at the chintzy furniture and high school mementoes. Preserved beneath glass, his old football jersey (#52) hung upon the wall. The jersey, trophies, and other souvenirs seemed to mock his pathetic existence. Thirty-two years old, and what did he have to show for it? Just a dead-end job and a roomful of reminders of what might have been. *Sure, I've fantasized about being a super hero,* he thought. *Who hasn't?* Skeets' offer was tempting. . . . Still, he couldn't help remembering that the robot's last partner had ended up dead. Did he really want to go the way of the late Booster Gold?

"I don't know," he said skeptically. "I'm being asked to entrust my future to a flying toaster. That's a pretty huge gamble."

An electronic chuckle emanated from the robot. "GAMBLING RUNS IN THE CARTER BLOOD."

ARIZONA.

THREE days later, Daniel found himself baking beneath the hot desert sun. Buzzards circled overhead as he faced a pair of ominous steel blast doors. *I can't believe I'm really doing this,* he thought. Sweat trickled down his back, and not just because of the oppressive heat. He was starting to wish that he had never heard of Booster Gold. *I used up all my frequent-flyer miles for this?*

"HOW DOES THE VISOR FEEL?" Skeets asked. The chatty robot had made all the travel arrangements to get them here. A rented jeep was parked outside the chain-link fence behind them. The massive concrete bunker didn't look very welcoming.

Daniel adjusted the gold-tinted goggles. "Featherweight," he admitted. "My contacts are more trouble than this." The goggles and attached blue headpiece only heightened his resemblance to the real Booster Gold. He wore a jacket and jeans over the hero's spare uniform. "You can see through them too. Right?"

"AND HEAR," Skeets confirmed. He inserted a metal probe into the atomic time clock. The dense metal doors slid open, exposing the dimly lit stairway beyond.

Daniel gulped and started down the steps. "What did you call this Rip Hunter guy again?"

"A CHRONONAUT," Skeets said. "A TIME-TRAVELER."

That's what I thought, Daniel thought unhappily. "Just checking." He muttered to himself as he descended the stairs. "What the holy living hell am I getting into . . . ?"

Suddenly, selling life insurance didn't seem all that bad. He wondered if he should have taken out a bigger policy on himself.

The ruined laboratory at the bottom of the stairs did nothing to ease his apprehension. The abandoned bunker looked like a bomb had gone off inside it. A huge crystal bubble had broken into a million pieces. A toppled globe had graffiti all over it. Dozens of dead clocks were stopped at 12:52. A dusty blackboard was filled with loony scribbling. *Time is broken? What the heck does that mean?*

Standing in the center of the trashed lab, he slowly swept his gaze over the wreckage, giving Skeets a good look at the place. He hoped the robot was getting more out of this than he was. "And this would be . . . ?"

"HARDLY ANYTHING BOOSTER DESCRIBED AC-CURATELY." Skeets' voice came to him via a receiver concealed in Booster's headpiece. It sounded like the robot was floating right next to him. "SCAN EVERYTHING. LEAVE NOTHING TO BE PROCESSED BY MY IMAGINATION. BOOSTER TOLD ME *NOTHING* OF THIS, AND IT'S ALL CRUCIAL."

Was it just his imagination, or did Skeets actually sound a little pissed off at his former partner? Daniel started to get a seriously bad feeling about all this. Maybe becoming a super hero was not such a great idea?

"THERE!" Skeets said emphatically. "THE NORTH WALL. MOVE CLOSER."

Daniel saw what Skeets was looking at. The wall in question had been covered with graffiti, apparently by a single individual. Daniel was unpleasantly reminded of Jack Nicholson in *The Shining*, typing the same phrase over and over again, right before he started hacking people up with an axe. A chill ran down Daniel's spine and he looked around nervously, just to be certain that he was all alone in the bunker. Had this Rip Hunter dude gone off the deep end too?

"WHAT DOES THE WRITING SAY?" Skeets asked.

Daniel leaned forward to get a better look. "'It's all his fault,'" he read aloud. "I don't get it." Scratching his chin, he squinted at the repetitive scribbling. "Whose fault?"

A magazine cover was taped to the wall. Hand-drawn arrows pointed at a cover photo of Booster Gold. "It's all his fault," a Post-it note insisted. But was the arrow pointing at Booster, or the robot floating inconspicuously above him? It struck Daniel that his new partner hadn't said anything for a couple of moments now. "Skeets?"

An electronic voice murmured in his ear. **"HE KNOWS."**

Without warning, Daniel heard the blast doors slam shut at the top of the stairs, trapping him inside the bunker. Crimson lights flashed overhead, casting a bloodred radiance over the interior of the chamber. A high-pitched siren went off, echoing loudly within the claustrophobic confines of the underground laboratory. An artificial voice, that sounded not at all like Skeets', stridently sounded an alarm:

"RED ALERT! RED ALERT! LAB ENTRANCE HAS BEEN TAMPERED WITH! RED ALERT!"

"Skeets, what's happening?" Daniel shouted to be heard over the ear-piercing siren. He ran frantically toward the stairs. "Skeets!"

"TRESPASSER DETECTED! TIME-LOOP VORTEX DEFENSE ACTIVATED!"

The air crackled behind him. A whiff of ozone tickled his nose. Peering back over his shoulder, Daniel saw some sort of glowing purple whirlpool forming in the middle of the laboratory. Reality seemed to ripple around the edge of the unnatural phenomenon, as though the very fabric of time and space was being distorted. A powerful suction tugged on Daniel. Loose papers and debris disappeared into the gaping maelstrom.

"Vortex?" He felt the suction growing stronger by the second, pulling him backward toward the time warp. "No!" he gasped as he realized that he had somehow set off the world's scariest burglar alarm. He raced up the steps, fighting the pull of the vortex every step of the way. A rush of wind whipped past his face as he reached the top of the stairs. "Skeets, open the door! Get me out of here!"

He pounded his fist against the sealed doors, which stubbornly refused to open. "Hurry!" he pleaded with the silent robot. "Something's pulling on me! Skeets, please!" The suction began to drag him back down the stairs. He grabbed onto an arm rail, but, unable to withstand the inexorable pull of the vortex, the metal rail came loose from the wall. He tumbled backward toward the lab below. "SKEETS!"

The globe, the blackboard, the shattered crystal sphere, the broken clocks . . . everything in the lab was sucked into the luminous vortex. Clinging to the bottom step by his fingertips, Daniel felt his flesh and bones being stretched like taffy by an irresistible force. His bloody nails scraped against the floor tiles. "You promised me glory!" he reminded Skeets. "You promised me a chance to relive my moment!"

"AND SO YOU SHALL, DANIEL," the robot said at last. **"OVER AND OVER AGAIN, FOR ALL ETERNITY."**

The floor tiles came loose and Daniel was sucked into the heart of the vortex. "Noooooo!" he cried out pitifully as he vanished beyond the event horizon of the time-loop. Upstairs, outside the bunker, Skeets reset the atomic time lock for 1,000,000 A.D.

"I'M SORRY IT HAD TO BE THIS WAY, DANIEL. I TRULY AM." The robot took off across the desert, leaving the bunker behind. **"BUT YOU HAVE SERVED YOUR PURPOSE."**

Skeets had gotten the answer he had come for.

"HE KNOWS."

WEEK 20.

THE Batcave looked like it had been abandoned for months. Tarps covered the equipment and trophies. Dust coated the flat-screen monitor of the primary computer station. Stalactites jabbed from the ceiling. Sleeping bats rustled in their roosts. Water dripped somewhere within the extensive network of caves beneath stately Wayne Manor.

Supernova floated silently down the steps from the empty mansion. His personal radiance lit the way, casting shadows onto the calcite-covered walls of the main grotto. He paused at the bottom of the steps to look around. A quick inspection confirmed what he had already suspected: Batman was not at home, and hadn't been for some time. Nor was there any sign of this mysterious new Batwoman who was rumored to be policing Gotham these days.

Good, the hooded intruder thought. *That makes things simpler.* He glanced at the various tarp-covered trophies scattered around the grotto. *Now then, where could it be?*

Touching down upon the tiled floor, he walked over to the nearest tarp-covered heap. He yanked the dusty sheet off the trophy to reveal a wooden display case containing a number of the Penguin's trick umbrellas. He took a moment to boggle at the very concept of a flame-throwing bumbershoot before moving on to the next exhibit, which occupied a position of honor at the center of the grotto. Clouds of dust were stirred up as he pulled off another tarp, exposing a transparent plastic cylinder holding an empty Robin costume.

Supernova nodded soberly. The brightly colored uniform, he knew, belonged to the second Robin, Jason Todd, murdered by the Joker a few years back. Lately, though, Supernova had heard unsettling rumors that Jason had returned from the dead. *Could be,* he admitted. *Stranger things have happened. He certainly wouldn't be the first of us to survive our own demise. . . .*

Still, the gloomy memorial was not what he was looking for. Turning away from the vacant costume, he tugged a white sheet off another wooden trophy case. Beneath a pane of clear glass, an ominous-looking metal gauntlet rested upon a velvet cushion. Green and purple enamel plating gleamed upon the armored glove. Multicaret chunks of crystal, each a different color, were mounted in the gauntlet's knuckles. Supernova recognized five different varieties of kryptonite: red, green, jewel, blue, and black.

Talk about jewelry to die for, he thought. *Especially if you're Kryptonian.*

The lethal gauntlet had originally belonged to Lex Luthor, Superman's greatest foe, but had come into Batman's possession after the Dark Knight and the Man of Steel joined forces to defeat one of Luthor's nefarious schemes. Supernova had hoped to find the glove in the Batcave—and here it was.

Just what I was looking for.

He reached out and opened the case.

WEEK 21.

BULLETS bounced off the armored carapace of the giant mechanical mantis. Its multifaceted compound eyes glowed like headlights. Spiked forelegs speared hapless security guards as the robot insect rampaged through the hangar-sized secret laboratory. Twin antennae scraped the ceiling.

"No! No! Naughty Mantichine!" its creator cried out frantically. Baron Bug chased after the berserk mechanism. The tail of his white lab coat flapped behind him as he ran. His fingers frantically stabbed at the buttons of a handheld remote control device, which appeared to be doing him no good whatsoever. His face was flushed and perspiring. "Stop, I command you! Stop!"

The rebellious mantis was about to throw a gun-toting guard through a large plate-glass window when a coruscating violet energy beam struck the robot's steel-plated thorax. The amok mechanism was disintegrated on the spot, leaving behind only a charred black stain on the floor tiles. The captured guard fell twenty feet before landing with a thump.

Baron Bug glared angrily at the source of the disintegration beam: a partially assembled robot head mounted on a mechanical lift several yards away. Roughly the size of a freight elevator, the huge metal skull had not yet been concealed beneath a layer of synthetic flesh. High-voltage cables connected the head to the lab's generous power supply. Servomotors and hydraulic conduits dangled from the bottom of the head's titanium neck assembly. A purple glow gradually dimmed within the reflective lenses of the robot's eyes.

"You . . . How dare you!" Baron sputtered indignantly.

"Back to the drawing board, Bugsy!" T.O. Morrow mocked him. The outlaw futurist leaned against the huge robot head. He wore a garish Hawaiian shirt instead of a lab jacket and sipped urbanely on a mai tai. "Didn't I say that your precious Mantichine was no match for my All-Purpose Omnibot?"

A third scientist looked over from his own work space. An acetylene torch flared in his grip as he lifted the face of his welder's mask. "Crow all you want, Morrow. When I complete the Super-Hood Mark II, you'll all be lining up to kiss the butt of Doctor Rigoro Mortis!"

What a stiff, Doctor Sivana thought. He watched the brewing confrontation from a metal catwalk overlooking the ground floor of the lab. Franz Waxman's score for *The Bride of Frankenstein* played over the Muzak system.

Baron Bug was still irate over the loss of his Mantichine. "It's sabotage! One of you has-beens is jealous of my genius." He hurled the useless remote at the floor. "Afraid that Baron Bug will outshine you all."

"Hah!" Morrow laughed. "Your intellect is as weak as your Bug-o-Trons!"

"That's it, Morrow!" Baron Bug stomped across the lab toward the other scientist. Less than five feet tall and balding, the crazed entomologist looked more comical than threatening. "Put up your dukes!"

Sivana decided that this had gone on long enough. "Break it up, boys!" he ordered via a miniature microphone patched into the lab's loudspeaker system. He leaned out over the catwalk's metal rail to address his fellow scientists. "This is no way for the world's greatest minds to behave. We have work to do, or have you forgotten?"

You'd think they'd be more appreciative of the cozy setup we've got here, Sivana thought. Although initially recruited against his will, the fugitive scientist had come to relish the abundant resources that were now at his disposal, thanks to

Intergang's deep pockets and patronage. The elevated walk-way looked out over an enormous industrial facility that made his old lab back in Fawcett City look like a high school shop class by comparison. Robots and death-rays, in various stages of construction, shared space with all manner of revolutionary inventions and experiments, employing the latest state-of-the-art equipment and materials. Right at this very moment, any number of intriguing projects were in progress on the floor below. Doctor Death, late of Arkham Asylum, was brewing up quicker and more undetectable new poisons in an enclosed fume hood. A translucent gas mask partially concealed his ca-daverous features. The lovely Dr. Veronica Cale, a persistent thorn in Wonder Woman's side, occupied the adjacent cubicle, where she was presently splicing genes together in imaginative new combinations. Dr. Cyclops, best known for his notorious "doomsday stare," peered into the Fifth Dimension via a com-plicated array of crystalline lenses. Doctor Tyme, who had a clock face where his eyes, nose, and mouth should have been, wandered all over the floor as he scanned the premises with a portable sensor of his own invention. The minute and hour hands on his face drooped downward to approximate a frown as he shook his head at the readings. Instead of a sensible white lab coat, Tyme wore a ridiculous blue and green super-villain costume, complete with cape. "I seem to have misplaced fifty-two seconds," he called out to his colleagues. "Has anyone seen them?"

The buzz of illicit activity tickled Sivana to no end. *So this is what you get,* he thought, *when the world's maddest scien-tists are given an unlimited budget and encouraged to run wild on the finest mind-expanding narcotics known to man.*

He couldn't complain about the location either. The picture window at the far end of the lab offered a breathtaking view of a pristine tropical beach, complete with swaying palm trees and lavish amounts of sunlight. Ira Quimby, whose celebrated I.Q. had been accelerated by exposure to an irradiated space rock, was lounging on the beach at this very moment, soaking up rays while being attended to by bikini-clad female simula-cra. Ira claimed that the solar energy enhanced his intellect, but Sivana suspected that this was simply an excuse to slack off. *I need to lean on him sometime soon,* he resolved. *Our bene-factors are going to expect a return on their investment.*

Sivana admired the scope of Intergang's ambition—and their wisdom in placing him in charge of the nefarious think tank. Unlike the majority of his colleagues, many of whom were antisocial recluses if the truth be told, Sivana had once been the CEO of his own multimillion-dollar corporation—before Captain Marvel exposed his criminal activities. He was therefore the logical choice to head the operation, at least after Lex Luthor turned down the position.

Luthor was keeping a low profile these days, while rebuild-ing the empire that had been stolen from him during the Crisis. *Probably just as well,* Sivana thought. *I don't need that kind of competition.*

The sound of an approaching helicopter penetrated the walls of the complex. *Right on schedule,* Sivana thought. *We got rid of that malfunctioning Mantichine just in time.* He glanced up at the ceiling as he heard the copter touch down on the heli-pad on the roof. "Look lively, boys and girl," he announced over the mike. "We have company."

And now a word from our sponsors . . .

Heavy footsteps preceded the arrival of Bruno Mannheim, Intergang's undisputed boss. A tailored Italian suit was stretched over his stocky frame. Beefy arms swung at his sides. Pomaded black hair and a pencil mustache did little to civilize his brutish features. Flanked by two sullen bodyguards, he joined Sivana upon the catwalk. His pin-striped suit stood in marked contrast to Sivana's rumpled lab coat.

"Boss Mannheim," the mad doctor greeted him. "How kind of you to visit us."

"This ain't a social call," Mannheim growled. "We're mo-bilizing. And they tell me you have a solution to my problems in Kahndaq."

WEEK 22.

GOTHAM CITY.

"THIS is from three weeks ago, Mr. Mannheim," the pencil-necked flunky explained. "Our spy-eyes over Metropolis spotted Supernova rescuing a small child from a riptide."

A video monitor descended from the ceiling of the conference room. Bruno Mannheim squinted at the footage on the plus-sized screen, which showed the mysterious new hero returning some squalling brat to her mother. The mother, whose bathing suit was clearly modeled on Wonder Woman's skimpy outfit, clutched the soggy child tearfully. Nameless beachgoers applauded in the background as Supernova took to the skies.

"If this footage is three weeks old, Strauss, why am I just seeing it now?" He scowled at the so-called intelligence analyst. Jet lag from Mannheim's return trip to Gotham didn't improve his mood any. "How come I wasn't shown this earlier?"

"It . . . it took us a while to retrieve the recorded data, sir." Strauss swallowed nervously. "We understand that we're under orders to track Supernova whenever he's sighted, but, as you'll see, he did what he always does."

On the screen, the masked hero stared directly into the camera, almost as if he was looking straight at Mannheim himself. A blinding light emanated from Supernova's head and shoulders as the screen whited out before going blank completely.

"He sensed he was under observation somehow," Strauss interpreted the images. "And used his power of disintegration on our cameras." He grimaced at the memory. "It took us three weeks just to reconstruct every pixel and byte that reflected off the satellite before it vanished."

Mannheim considered Strauss' report. "Intergang's billion-dollar comm satellite. Which he saw from hundreds of miles away." He brooded over the facts. "It certainly fits, doesn't it?"

Strauss looked baffled. "Excuse me?"

"Superman, you moron," the ganglord snapped impatiently. "The big blue Boy Scout."

Even though his ambitions were focused on Gotham these days, Mannheim kept a watchful eye over matters back in Metropolis. Having clashed with Superman before, he found it hard to believe that the Man of Steel would really leave his beloved city unguarded for so long, not unless he was dead and buried . . . again. But the Crime Bible had not foretold Superman's demise this year, nor had it predicted that any new hero would rise in Metropolis at this time. The conclusion seemed obvious: Superman was posing as Supernova for some reason of his own.

Who else had the telescopic vision to spot that satellite, Mannheim reasoned, *and the heat vision to destroy it?*

"My orders regarding Supernova stand," he growled at Strauss. "And don't come back until you have some real evidence to show me."

WEEK 23.

BIALYA.

"'For Choice is the domain only of the strong, the way of true freedom. Trapped within thy Law, weak ye are revealed, and thus Choice ain't for ye.' And saying thus, the handcuffs snapped closed, and the beatings did begin. Yea, for forty days and nights did they torture the Detective, until his mind became as broken as his body."

The hooded woman raised her eyes from the leather-bound tome laid open on the pulpit before her. Sputtering torches and candles illuminated a cavernous temple deep beneath the arid desert northeast of the capital. Shadows capered upon forbidding stone walls, into which were carved graphic depictions of murder, torture, slavery, and every other manner of crime and brutality. A black silk ribbon marked her place in the book.

"From the *Epic of Moriarty, Book of Crime*, Chapter Twenty-Seven, Verses Seven through Twelve." She threw back the hood of her ebony cloak, revealing long scarlet hair and slitted yellow eyes. Her slinky black dress, and matching corset, appealed to instincts more sensual than spiritual. A thigh-high slit in her gown offered a provocative glimpse of a lacy black garter belt. "Unto Cain," she preached.

"UNTO CAIN." Her flock, a motley assortment of beast-men and Intergang flunkies, answered her in unison. They bowed their misshapen heads, their assorted fingers, claws, and talons steepled before them in prayer.

No such invocations came from the dozen or so children chained to the stone steps between the priestess and her freakish congregation. Wearing only rags, dirt, and bruises, the miserable kids huddled upon the cold stone floor at the base of the steps. Scrawny limbs and exposed ribs testified to weeks of near starvation. Frightened whimpers escaped their lips as they tried not to look at the throng of chanting monsters only a few yards away from them. Repeated lashings had left welts upon the children's abused bodies.

"Bring forth the boy," the priestess demanded.

How sick is this? Renee Montoya thought as she furtively eyed the unholy ceremony. She and Vic were crouched behind the stone rail of a mezzanine overlooking the ground floor of the temple. Looking away from the enslaved kids, she turned her attention back to the flame-haired femme fatale presiding over the ritual.

"You were right, Charlie," she whispered. "It's her. Whisper A'Daire." Renee's skin crawled at the memory of Whisper's forked tongue licking her cheek. Her hand tightened around the grip of her ray gun. "I should shoot her right now."

"I want a look at the book first," the Question said. His "pseudoderm" mask rendered him faceless once more. Desert gear replaced his usual trench coat. An equipment belt and canteen were buckled around his waist.

"Forget your curiosity," Renee spat. "This is a damn Intergang reeducation camp. The girl I killed came from here, and the naughty nun down there is responsible." *I'll be damned,* she thought, *if I let that scaly bitch brainwash another innocent kid.*

But that seemed to be exactly what Whisper had in mind. Before Renee's appalled gaze, a pair of hulking beast-men dragged a teenage boy out onto the floor of the temple. One of the monsters was a shaggy wolf-man whom Renee recognized as Whisper's lycanthropic henchman, Abbot. His prisoner was a battered Arab youth who looked like he had already endured a couple rounds of beatings. Ugly scars and bruises covered his dusky skin. Disheveled black hair hung before his eyes. His head sagged downward, concealing his face. Trembling legs looked like they could no longer support his own weight.

"Amon Tomaz," Whisper declared solemnly. "For weeks now we have shown you and orphans like you the way of the Red Rage and the Rock. . . ."

Renee started at the name. "Oh my God, it's him. Isis' brother!"

"And while others have taken the Word of Cain to heart, you have not." Whisper closed the book and pulled her hood back over her head. "This is the third time you have tried to run. It will be the last." She nodded at Abbot and the other beast-men. "See to it that his legs never obey him again." She turned away from the pulpit and headed out of the temple. "Start with his ankles."

Growling in anticipation, the huge werewolf grabbed Amon by the throat and lifted him off his feet. Foam dripped from his lupine snout. Before Renee could even think about stopping him, he savagely dashed the teenager onto the hard stone floor. More monsters, sporting various combinations of fur, feathers, and scales, surged forward to join in the carnage. With metal truncheons or their own oversized fists, they pounded the defenseless boy mercilessly. Fresh blood sprayed upon the carved walls of the subterranean temple.

Renee couldn't take it anymore. Even though Whisper was already disappearing down an adjacent catacomb, saving Amon suddenly took priority. She drew her gun and started to climb over the rail. "All right," she told Vic. "On three . . ."

"Stop." To her surprise, he grabbed her from behind, holding her back. A kung fu move trapped her arms behind her.

What the hell? "They're beating him," she protested, trying to break free. "We can't just—"

He clamped his palm over her mouth. "We go down there, we'll die. Simple as that." His voice held none of its usual levity. "It stinks and it's wrong and it hurts like hell, but there's nothing we can do for Amon right now." He held tightly on to Renee as she swore into his glove. "Adam and Isis are on their

way. They can handle this. We can't." She squirmed in his grip
even as she knew, deep in her heart, that he was absolutely
right. "There are some things you just have to accept, Renee."

Like hell, she thought bitterly. Trapped by both Vic's arms
and cruel necessity, she could only watch helplessly as Abbot
and his bestial cohorts beat the living crap out of Amon. The
boy cried out at first, but his feeble protests were quickly replaced by the sounds of cracking bones and the thud of heavy
fists and boots against tender flesh. Renee couldn't even see
Amon beneath the pack of vicious monsters piling onto him.
Biting back sobs and screams, the other children either stared
at the grisly scene with horror, or else buried their heads in
their hands, trying unsuccessfully to hide from the awful sights
and sounds. Would they ever be able to forget this nightmare?
Would they even get the chance?

The beating lasted less than five minutes, but seemed to go
on forever. Just when Renee thought she couldn't possibly
stand another moment, however, the gang of monsters stepped
back from their victim. Amon's pulped body lay facedown
in a puddle of dark, venous blood. His limbs were twisted at
unnatural angles that made Renee's joints hurt just looking
at them. Only the ragged sound of his breathing made it clear
that he was simply unconscious and not dead. Renee guessed
that Whisper intended to keep the crippled boy alive to serve
as a living example of what happened to those who rejected
the cult's teachings. Killing him would've been a mercy by
comparison.

"Here endeth the Lesson," Abbot growled at the other
orphans. The wolf-man took hold of Amon's limp right arm
and dragged the boy down a shadowy stairway. Amon's abused
body left a trail of blood across the dusty stone tiles. Vic waited
until both Abbot and Amon were out of sight before finally
letting go of Renee.

She glared at him. "You really are a bastard."

"Well, I was raised in an orphanage, so you're probably
right." His featureless countenance gave no hint of what he

really felt about what they had just witnessed. He nodded at an adjoining tunnel. "Now let's get mov—"

"CAUGHT YOU!"

Without warning, a huge monster charged at them. Over nine feet tall, with at least four hundred pounds of mutated muscle, the hairless beast-man was as red as a cooked lobster and twice as ugly. Jagged tusks jutted from his lower jaw. Yellow eyes blazed beneath a sloping brow. He had no nose, and only narrow slits where his ears should have been. A tattered loincloth spared Renee a peek at his inhuman private parts. *Thank heaven for small favors,* she thought.

"Oops," Vic blurted, embarrassed at being taken unawares.

Renee took aim at the oncoming ogre. "You were saying something about acceptance?"

"Not quite what I meant," Vic conceded. He leaned backward to give Renee a clear shot at the lobster-man.

"Didn't think so." Squeezing the trigger, she blew a hole right through the middle of the monster's torso. Bulging yellow eyes stared down in confusion at the gaping cavity in his chest.

Would that be enough to stop the beast? Vic didn't wait to find out. Grabbing onto Renee once more, he threw them both over the railing. "Remember to bend your knees!" he suggested as they dropped toward the floor of the temple.

Despite Vic's sage advice, she landed hard on her butt. "Ooof!"

"Cover me!" he shouted, after making a more nimble landing. To her surprise, he sprang for the pulpit behind them. Intergang hoodlums, human and otherwise, drew weapons from beneath their robes and opened fire on the intruders. Bullets chipped away at the elaborately gruesome carvings. Renee ducked behind a bloodstained baptismal font.

"Charlie, what are you doing?" She returned fire with her ray gun. For the moment, the crackling energy blasts seemed to be holding the cultists at bay. Behind her, the shackled children threw themselves onto the floor in order to avoid the gunfire. Renee prayed that none of the orphans would get shot by mistake. She wasn't sure she could live with herself if another child died because of her.

"Going for the book!" Vic explained. He leaped at the pulpit, snatching the heavy tome from its resting place as he hurled past the marble pedestal, then hit the floor in a roll and jumped back up onto his feet. He clutched the book against his chest. "Gotcha!"

Renee questioned his priorities. "I'm not sure now's the time to be boosting your collection!" Bits of stone flew from the font protecting her. The temple echoed with the blare of gunfire. An energy blast disintegrated a gun-toting acolyte, but there were plenty more where he came from. She was seriously outnumbered here, and could definitely use some backup. "Charlie . . ."

"Renee, watch out!" he suddenly hollered from several feet away.

A leopard-man dropped from the mezzanine, landing upon the floor right next to her. Feline claws slashed across her stomach, drawing blood. Gasping in pain, she swung her gun against the monster's skull. The blow stunned the spotted beast-man, but only for a moment. Blood seeped through her fingers as she clutched her belly with her free hand. With a ferocious roar, the leopard-man came at her again. Her gun came up too slowly. . . .

I'm going to die here, she realized.

A thunderous rumble shook the temple. The leopard-man looked up in surprise as a slab-sized chunk of the ceiling crashed down onto his head. Black Adam landed on the slab, flattening the monster. Bullets ricocheted off Adam's back and arms as he shielded Vic and Renee with his own indestructible body. He nodded grimly at the two Americans.

The Kahndaqi cavalry had arrived.

"We came as soon as we could," Isis called out as she swooped down through the hole her husband had opened in the ceiling. At her command, thick roots sprouted from the floor, snaring several of the cultists. Back in Gotham, Renee had seen Poison Ivy pull similar stunts; she couldn't help wondering how Isis would fare against Gotham's most homicidal plant-lover. *My money's on the goddess,* she thought.

The remaining acolytes and beast-men fled the temple. Letting them go, at least for the moment, Isis landed next to Renee. "Are you all right?" Her dark eyes zeroed in on the bloody gash across Renee's stomach. "You're wounded. . . ."

The deep laceration stung like hell, but that wasn't what was important now. "We found your brother, Isis! We found Amon!"

Isis froze as though struck by lightning. "Where?"

"They've taken him below." Renee tried to prepare the other woman for the worst. "Isis . . . he's hurt."

Concern showed on Isis' lovely face, but she did not despair. "I can heal him," she asserted. "Just as I can heal your wound."

She laid her hand gently upon Renee's injured stomach. A purple glow radiated from Isis' slender fingers and the searing pain immediately ceased. *Whoa,* Renee thought. *That feels better already.* The blood stopped flowing as her torn flesh swiftly knitted itself back together. Within seconds, no trace of the cut remained. Only the slash marks in her T-shirt proved that she had ever been attacked in the first place.

How about that? Renee thought. Her smooth skin tingled where Isis had healed her.

Maybe it wasn't too late for Amon after all?

"WE need support now!" a tiger-man growled into a handheld communicator. Three more monsters looked on anxiously. "Black Adam and Isis are here! Repeat, we need—"

Side by side, Isis and Black Adam smashed through a stone wall into a dungeon beneath the temple, where a makeshift medical facility appeared to have been set up. Her heart leaped as she spotted Amon lying atop a crumbling sacrificial altar that now doubled as an operating table. An IV poured cold plasma into his veins. Electronic apparatus monitored his vital signs.

Blessed Goddess, she prayed to her namesake, *grant me the power to save him.*

"Let all of your 'support' come," Black Adam raged. "Let all of Intergang come." A mutated brute with the head of a warthog and the body of a man fired a laser rifle at the avenging champion. A ruby beam bounced harmlessly off Adam's brawny chest, winging an ape-man nearby, before he tore apart the rifle with his bare hands. A titanic blow sent both the warthog and the ape-man flying across the chamber. An instant later, Adam crushed the tiger-man's communicator within his fist, before throwing the feline henchman up against the wall. "I welcome them!"

While her husband dealt with their enemies, Isis rushed to her brother's side. *By the gods!* she thought, shocked by the extent of his injuries. She barely recognized him, so badly had he been beaten. His once-handsome face was now hidden behind fresh cuts and bruises. His eyes were swollen shut, so she could not tell if he was conscious, while the rest of his body also bore the marks of extreme violence and cruelty. In particular, the bones in his ankles and pelvis looked as though they had been reduced to powder. Blood pooled beneath him.

"What did they do to him?" she said, aghast.

Victor Szasz and Renee entered through the breach in the wall. They stepped carefully over the fallen rubble. "Looks like Intergang didn't sell him into slavery like you thought," the Question explained. Isis found his faceless guise disturbing. "They were trying to brainwash him and some other kids into joining their religion of crime."

Isis had never heard of anything more obscene.

"He tried to escape," Renee added.

That sounds like him, Isis thought with a pained smile. Amon had always been a headstrong child, fearless and high-spirited; it was what she had loved most about him. A tear trickled down her face as she gazed down at his vandalized form. Was even the power of Isis enough to repair the damage?

"Adrianna?" To her surprise, his swollen eyelids opened slightly. The whites of his eyes were stained bright red. His lips parted, revealing cracked and missing teeth. His voice was so weak she had to lean forward to hear him. "Adrianna, is that you?"

"Yes, Amon." Her throat tightened as she gently stroked his head.

He struggled to keep his eyes open. A broken nose distorted his voice. "You look . . . so pretty."

Isis fought back a sob. In all the times she had imagined their reunion, she had never foreseen finding him like this. *It's not fair,* she lamented. *If only we could have rescued him earlier . . . !*

"Are these the ones who did this to him, Question?" Black Adam demanded, looking back over his shoulder at the face-less detective. Adam now held both the warthog and the tiger-man up against the wall. His powerful fists gripped their hairy throats.

"Yes," Victor confirmed.

Adam's expression darkened. "Then let *them* feel their bones crushed and shattered. One at a time." His subhuman captives squealed and squawked as he squeezed their necks tightly. The tiger-man's claws slashed uselessly at Adam's mighty arm.

"No, Adam!" Isis summoned a mighty gale, which blew Adam away from the prisoners. Loose dust and debris swirled across the dungeon. "Winds, quell my husband's rage!"

The cyclonic gust slammed the beast-men into the wall, rendering them unconscious. Their grotesque bodies dropped limply onto the floor. Cheated of his vengeance, Adam spun around to confront his wife.

"Look at what these monsters did to your brother, Isis! He is my family now and he is dying!" A murderous wrath contorted his noble features. His fists were clenched so tightly that the blood fled from his knuckles. "They deserve a slow death! Plucked apart like the insects they are!"

"Please," Isis pleaded. Heartsick, she buried her face in her hands. "Too many people here—too many people in the world—are already hurting." Lifting her head, she laid her hands upon her brother's ravaged body. "Amon's wounds . . . the fresh ones cover others from days before. He's been beaten many times before this."

Purple energy coursed over the supine youth, but the eldritch glow swiftly faded away, leaving Amon almost as mutilated as before. Only a few of his more superficial injuries had been healed. "His nerves have been twisted and severed," she sobbed. Kohl streaked her cheeks as she wept openly. "His wounds are too deep even for my powers over Nature."

Raindrops suddenly fell from the roof of the dungeon. Renee looked up in confusion as the unexpected precipitation splattered against her face. "It's raining . . . inside?"

"Isis," the Question said simply. Nature itself was weeping in sympathy with its mistress.

Isis sadly turned away from the bloody altar. Her teary eyes sought out her husband's. "My brother's flesh will heal, Adam, but he'll never walk again."

Her sorrow brought out his gentler side. The anger left his face, replaced by a look of profound sympathy for his wife's anguish. He nodded to himself, as though reaching a decision, and strode past her to approach Amon's bedside. His deep voice addressed the crippled boy.

"Amon, I am Black Adam. Your sister's husband and, by that right, your brother." He placed his palm upon the youth's black-and-blue chest. "We are family."

The Question moved forward to get a better look. "What's he doing to him?"

I don't know, Isis thought. As far as she knew, Adam possessed no healing powers.

"We have a bond now," he declared. Rain spilled down from the ceiling, washing away Amon's blood. "Say my name, brother. Say it."

Through split lips, Amon fought to mouth the words. "Bl-Black . . ."

Sparks flared beneath Adam's fingers. Electricity crackled across Amon's ravaged flesh. His eyes lit up with galvanic fire. Renewed vigor suffused his voice as he shouted:

"BLACK ADAM!"

Thunder rocked the underground chamber as a mystic lightning bolt struck Amon, shattering the altar beneath him. Adam and the others were driven backward by the force of the strike. The blinding flash forced them to blink and look away. Hissing sparks erupted from the life-sign monitors. The IV stand toppled over. Isis would have feared for her brother's life had she not survived a similar thunderbolt in the Rock of Eternity nearly three months ago. Hope surged within her heart. The supernatural rain stopped falling. Could it be . . . ?

Yes! Where once Amon had lain broken and bleeding, her brother now stood tall once more. Not only were all his grievous wounds and injuries healed, but he looked stronger and fitter than ever before. Starvation and torture no longer left their imprint upon him, and his blood-soaked loincloth had been transformed into a sleek black uniform that bore a marked resemblance to Adam's. A golden lightning bolt was emblazoned upon his chest.

Clear brown eyes looked down upon his restored flesh and form. He flexed his arm experimentally, stunned to find it working once more. "I hear voices in my head," he said, visibly baffled by his metamorphosis.

"They are the gods that power me," Black Adam said solemnly. "You now have the strength of your namesake, Amon."

Understanding dawned in the boy's eyes, along with absolute delight. "Yes, and the stamina of Shu! The swiftness of Heru! The power of Aton!" Testing his new abilities, he smashed what remained of the broken altar with a single blow. Solid stone exploded beneath his fist. He sprang into the air, defying gravity. "The wisdom of Zehuti! The courage of Mehen!"

Isis recognized the names of the Egyptian deities who granted Black Adam their divine attributes. She turned to her husband. "How?"

Adam shrugged. "I simply shared a portion of my power with your brother, just as Captain Marvel has done with Freddy Freeman." Isis recalled how Billy Batson had transformed a handicapped American youth into Captain Marvel Jr. "It is something I have always been able to do," Adam explained. "But I never had a family to share my gifts with."

Isis clutched her heart, deeply moved by her husband's strength and generosity. "Amon?" she asked, wondering how he was coping with his transformation. It could be disorienting, she knew.

"I am Osiris," he answered, taking on the name of the ancient Egyptian god of the underworld, who was also the brother of the goddess Isis. His youthful brow wrinkled in confusion as he touched down on the floor before her. "Even though I'm not yet sure what that means."

Black Adam smiled warmly. "It means you are family now, brother."

Fragrant roses sprouted from the walls as Isis joyfully embraced Osiris. "Let these lands bloom with life," she called out. Tears of happiness flowed down her face like the eternal Nile. "For mine has finally returned!"

The reunited siblings hugged each other as Black Adam proudly looked on. All but forgotten in the excitement of the occasion, the Question turned his non-face heavenward.

"Black Adam!" he shouted. "Shazam! Isis!"

Renee scowled at him. She was soaking wet from the rainstorm. "What the hell are you doing?"

"Seeing if it's catching."

WEEK 24.

GOTHAM CITY.

"THOU shalt steal. Thou shalt kill. Thou shalt bear false witness."

Bruno Mannheim stared out through the picture windows of his penthouse headquarters as he contemplated the city he intended to rule with an iron fist. His beefy hands were clasped behind his back. A permanent scowl was etched onto his bellicose features. The mob boss was unafraid to turn his back on an entire roomful of ruthless criminals.

"You think small," he scolded his guests. "For me, Crime is the moral standard, the universal principle, the natural successor to free market consumer capitalism. I'm looking to establish a new world order of Crime, with its own capital city." He gazed approvingly at the diseased urban jungle spread out before him. "Every Caesar needs a Rome. I'm taking Gotham. If you're as smart as you think you are, you'll step out of my way and tell the other local bosses to do the same." His gruff voice brooked no dissent. A crude accent betrayed his roots in the slums of Metropolis. "I'm making this easy. You affiliate with Intergang or you die." He turned and gestured at a massive tome resting closed upon a lectern before him. "You swear upon the Crime Bible or you die."

He waited to see which of his guests would defy him. *There's always a few,* he thought. *The ones whose egos are bigger than their brains.*

"The what?" A masked super-villain, who wore an orange hood over a bright yellow costume, approached the lectern.

Mirage had managed to turn a minor talent at hypnosis into a modest criminal career. "What the hell are you talking about, Mannheim?"

That's Boss *Mannheim to you,* the ganglord thought. He rapped his knuckles against the thick granite binding of the Book. "Cain used that stone to commit the first murder when he battered his brother Abel to death."

"A stone book, very artsy." Mirage failed to appreciate the unholy sanctity of the ancient tome. He peered at the petrified front cover. "Is that blood?"

"Take a closer look," Mannheim urged him. "You'll never see anything like it again."

Mirage bent to inspect the volume . . . and Mannheim slammed the man's hooded face into the unyielding granite. Flesh and bone crunched. Blood and tissue sprayed from the torn cowl.

"Those are your brains trickling onto the carpet, smart guy." Mannheim dug his fingers into Mirage's scalp and yanked his face up from the bloodstained book and pedestal. Then he used both hands to ram the hypnotist's face back down onto the stone volume. Mirage's skull shattered into a bloody pulp. "Guess they weren't worth a crap in the end."

He let go of the gloppy mess and Mirage's lifeless body slid onto the floor. Dietrich Laszlo, Mannheim's personal aide, stepped forward. The thin, officious-looking individual clutched a clipboard against his chest. He beckoned to a waiting janitor, who plugged in a carpet cleaner. "Allow me to take care of that trash for you, boss."

"Bring him down to the kitchens, Laszlo." Mannheim licked his lips. "Building an empire is hungry work."

Startled gasps came from the remainder of his guests. Mannheim smirked as he wiped the blood from his hands with what was left of Mirage's orange hood. It amused him that such hardened felons should be so taken aback by the merest hint of cannibalism. They had much to learn, and he was just the person to show them the light.

He turned to address his guests, who were seated around a

long boardroom table. He knew their nicknames and rap sheets intimately: Magpie, the Ventriloquist, the Squid, John "the Butcher" Morgan, Carl "Junior" Grissom, Ginjer Bread, and other Gotham mobsters. Most of them were still alive, but he had already made an example of some of their more obstreperous colleagues. Wendell Lewis, the so-called Sewer King, was slumped over the table, a letter opener stabbed deep into his back. Kite Man's body had fallen back against his seat, a bright red smear expanding across the front of his ridiculous costume. "Silk" Jefferson's broken neck was twisted at an impossible angle. Magpie, aka Maggie Pye, pushed her chair away from Kite Man's corpse. She lifted her feet to avoid the pool of blood spreading across the floor. Her ashen face suggested that no further demonstrations would be necessary, at least as far as she was concerned. Ditto for the other survivors.

Each of his guests, both alive and dead, had controlled one of Gotham's many warring gangs and syndicates. Conspicuously missing from the summit meeting were the Joker, Two-Face, Scarecrow, the Mad Hatter, and the rest of Arkham Asylum's most famous inmates and escapees. All were too unpredictable to play a part in Mannheim's grand design. He was looking for lieutenants and foot soldiers here. Lunatics need not apply.

"Let me spell it out for you." He took his place at the head of the table. "You Gotham bosses work for me, or we make you extinct. Wipe your names from the annals of crime as though you never existed." He kicked over Jefferson's chair. The pimp's body tumbled onto the carpet. "Dinner will be served shortly."

The smell of spilled blood made his mouth water.

"Enjoy the meat."

WEEK 25.

BOSTON.

It was Halloween, a time for playing at being scared, but tonight the screams were real. Panicked trick-or-treaters and their parents ran shrieking through the tree-lined streets of the city's historic Beacon Hill neighborhood. Pint-sized ghosts, ninjas, princesses, and super heroes fled in terror past rows of elegant Federal-style town houses. Discarded bags of candy spilled onto the brick sidewalks.

A second later, Captain Marvel Jr. crashed into one of those sidewalks, barely missing an eight-year-old boy in a glow-in-the-dark skeleton costume. Shattered bricks exploded into the air, along with a spray of lost Tootsie Rolls and chocolate bars. *Ow,* Freddy Freeman thought. Even with the endurance of Atlas, the crash landing left the young hero momentarily stunned. *That actually hurt.*

"The souls of your innocents will belong to me!" A sixty-foot-tall demon towered over the neighborhood. A taloned hand, that had just batted the World's Mightiest Boy out of the air, reached out for the fleeing children. Curved horns sprouted from the giant demon's brow. His shaggy hide was scarlet. Hellfire burned in his yellow eyes. A bristling blue beard adorned his chin. Cloven hooves pounded the pavement. His sulfurous breath polluted the cold night air. "And thus will begin a century of fire! A hell reborn on Earth, so hot it will melt the flesh off your bones." His booming voice held a thick Russian accent. "So swears Sabbac, King of Devils!"

In fact, Sabbac was a Russian mobster named Ishmael

Gregor who had used black magic to transform himself into Captain Marvel's evil opposite. Just as the magic word "Shazam!" imbued Billy Batson with the powers and attributes of six mythological gods and heroes, the word "Sabbac" granted Gregor the hellish abilities of six arch-demons: Satan, Aym, Belial, Beezlebub, Asmodeus, and Createis. The Marvel Family had squared off against him before. This was hardly the first time Sabbac had gone on a rampage.

Lucky us, Captain Marvel Jr. thought. Wincing from his close encounter with the sidewalk, he sat up slowly and shook the pulverized brick from his tousled black hair. Beacon Hill shuddered beneath the demon's colossal tread. *How many times do we have to beat this guy anyway?*

Mary Marvel touched down on the sidewalk beside him. The night breeze rustled her cape and pristine white skirt. "I told you to wait for me, Junior."

Probably would've been a good idea, he admitted. He looked around for her brother. "Where's Cap—" He caught himself before saying the name that would have transformed him back into a crippled teenager. "Er, Billy? He said he'd be here."

"It's Halloween, Freddy." She helped him to his feet. "Do you know how many extradimensional planes are crossing over into ours tonight?" The question was strictly rhetorical. "Billy's got his hands full dealing with an invasion from the Phantom Zone."

That's a pretty good excuse for not showing up, Freddy conceded. He glanced over at the towering demon and clenched his fists. *Looks like we're on our own.*

To his relief, he saw that Sabbac had not snagged any kids yet. Beacon Hill's narrow streets seemed to be slowing him down somewhat. His sides scraped against the front of the buildings, causing chunks of dislodged masonry to cascade down onto the sidewalks. Trees and gas lamps toppled before him. His hooves left smoking tracks down the middle of Cambridge Street.

Shrill screams alerted Captain Marvel Jr. to the plight of

four small children who appeared to have lost track of their parents in the confusion. Dressed as Captain Marvel, Wonder Woman, the Flash, and Black Lightning, the huddled kids stared upward in fright as a monstrous red hand descended toward them.

"Children, you are mine!" Sabbac roared.

Before either Freddy or Mary could react, a svelte figure clad in fluttering white linen whooshed beneath Sabbac's hairy palm and whisked the kids out of harm's way. The demon's pointed claws closed on empty air. A baffled expression came over his satanic countenance. "What?"

Isis gently deposited the children onto the sidewalk by Mary and Freddy. The wide-eyed kids looked startled, but unharmed. Captain Marvel Jr. blinked in surprise. What was Isis doing in Boston of all places?

And was she alone?

"After all that candy," the Egyptian heroine advised the children, "take care of your teeth and eat some apples." A warm Middle Eastern wind, redolent of exotic spices, lifted her back into the air. "They're Nature's toothbrushes."

Freddy and Mary exchanged puzzled looks. Their gazes followed Isis up into the sky, where two more figures came flying down from the moonlit heavens.

"As they say in America, Sabbac . . ." an exuberant voice called out from above. Freddy watched in amazement as an Arab teenager, wearing a streamlined version of Black Adam's somber uniform, punched the gargantuan demon in the nose. "Trick or treat!"

Who? Freddy wondered.

"A solid hit, Osiris," Black Adam praised the youth. Soaring toward Sabbac like a missile, he rammed both fists into the demon's stomach. Bile spewed from Sabbac's lips. The monster reeled backward.

High above the street, Black Adam, Isis, and Osiris converged upon Sabbac. Even with the infernal might of six arch-fiends at his disposal, the horned devil was clearly on the ropes. He tottered unsteadily upon his hooves. A noxious black ichor dripped from his snout. Osiris' punch had drawn first blood.

"Holy Moley!" Freddy exclaimed.

Mary was just as astonished. "It's a . . . Black Marvel Family!"

Freddy recalled attending the royal wedding in Kahndaq. Could this "Osiris" be Isis' missing brother? *That* must *be Amon.* Freddy didn't need the wisdom of Solomon to figure that out. *Who else could it be?*

"Watch where you send him falling, you two," Isis reminded Black Adam and Osiris. "People live here."

"Not for long, witch!" Sabbac snarled. He charged at the flying trio.

Isis waved an arm and a venerable old chestnut tree defended her. Bare branches awoke from hibernation, grabbing onto the outmatched demon. Gnarled coils snared Sabbac's straining arms and legs. "Nature called to me from thousands of miles away," Isis informed their foe. "You wish to torch its beautiful land." Her lovely face held a look of serene determination. "We will not allow it."

Apparently not, Captain Marvel Jr. thought. He felt funny just standing on the sidewalk, watching the battle from the sidelines. "Should we help them?" he asked Mary.

"I don't think they need it," she replied.

The Black Marvel Family certainly seemed to have the crisis well in hand. The rescued trick-or-treaters crowded past the two original Marvels to watch Isis and family teach Sabbac a well-deserved lesson on the perils of interfering with Halloween. The kids' eyes were as wide as jack-o'-lanterns. Their tiny jaws hung open. "Wow wow wow!" the miniature Flash exclaimed.

Side by side, Black Adam and Osiris zoomed at Sabbac. "Can we do it now? Can we do the Lightning Strike?" the teenager pleaded. "We've been practicing for days!"

Adam smiled indulgently. "Very well."

Wood and bark shredded loudly as Sabbac tore himself free from the branches binding him. He gnashed his jagged fangs. Yellow eyes glowed with malignant fury. He bellowed in rage.

"I will eat your souls!"

"You'll be lucky if you're eating anything after this," Osiris boasted. He slammed his fists into the right side of Sabbac's head at the exact moment that Black Adam barreled into the left. The simultaneous strike ignited a blinding flash of mystic lightning. Thunder rumbled across Boston as the unleashed thunderbolt put Sabbac down for the count. Broken fangs sprayed from the demon's mouth. The fire in his eyes sputtered and went out.

"Careful," Isis said. A powerful gust of wind swept a few stray bystanders out of the way as Sabbac's enormous body toppled down onto Beacon Street. A low moan issued from the demon's lips. Smoke rose from his charred horns.

Cheers and applause arose from the rescued children and their reunited parents. Freddy hesitated for a moment, then he and Mary joined in the clapping. It felt weird to be applauding Black Adam, after all their battles in the past, but there was no denying that Adam and his family had definitely saved the day. Freddy made a mental note to practice that "Lightning Strike" move with Billy and Mary someday. That was a pretty nifty trick!

And the Black Marvel Family weren't done helping out yet. Landing a few yards away, Black Adam and Osiris thoughtfully lifted Sabbac's immense carcass from the pavement and hefted it into the sky. The limp colossus resembled a Thanksgiving Day balloon as it rose above the rooftops. Isis smiled proudly as she wafted ahead of her menfolk. Osiris beamed down at the cheering crowd.

"Happy Halloween, Judeo-Christians!"

The heroes and their captive disappeared into the distance. Freddy wondered if they were planning to transport Sabbac all the way back to Kahndaq or if they were just going to drop him off at the Rock of Eternity for Captain Marvel to deal with. Either way, it looked like Boston was safe for trick-or-treating again—and without him or Mary even lifting a finger.

Wonder if Billy needs any help with that Phantom Zone thing?

On the sidewalk in front of them, the kids Isis had saved started arguing over who got to be their latest heroes.

"I wanna be Black Adam!" the chubby boy in the Captain Marvel costume proclaimed. He pointed proudly at the golden thunderbolt on his chest. A little black dye would easily convert the costume into a Black Adam disguise instead.

"I get to be Isis!" said the little girl dressed as Wonder Woman. Her childish voice mimicked Isis' exotic Egyptian accent.

"No, I do!" another girl insisted, despite the fact that she was wearing Supergirl's bright blue dress and red cape.

The little Flash wannabe stayed out of the fight. Instead he dug through his bag of treats until he found a fresh green granny apple. "Nature's toothbrush!"

None of the children paid any attention to Mary or Captain Marvel Jr. Mary contemplated the starstruck munchkins with a bemused expression on her face. "Is it just me," she asked, "or are you suddenly feeling like yesterday's news?"

Freddy shook his head, not entirely sure what to make of this new Marvel Family, especially now that they had a Black Adam Jr. of their own.

"Nope, it's not just you."

WEEK 26.

THE HIMALAYAS.

WHEN Renee was ten years old, she found a pile of old *Congo Bill World Travel* magazines dumped in the trash behind the tenement where her family lived. Nearly fifty years' worth of them, abandoned like so much garbage. She had carried them up the nine flights of stairs to their apartment. Almost six hundred issues, and she carried them all. Afterward, she couldn't even remember how many trips up and down the stairs it had taken. It was like running a marathon and it had been worth every step.

She had loved those magazines, losing whole days staring at pictures of places she knew she would never go: India, Vlatavia, Egypt, Bhutan. She'd always known she was never going to see the Great Pyramid or the domed kingdom of Atlantis. As of six months ago, the farthest she'd ever been from Gotham was Keystone City, and that was for a prisoner exchange. She'd figured that if she saw the bright lights of Metropolis before she croaked, she could die happy.

All things considered, she thought, *I'm counting myself very lucky right now.*

Cradled in Isis' slender arms, Renee soared toward the snowcapped peaks of the Himalayas. The majestic mountains loomed ahead, while remote plains and valleys stretched out far below her. The icy wind blowing against her face did little to dampen her spirits. A fur-lined parka helped protect her from the cold. A packed duffel bag dangled from her shoulders.

She glanced to the left, where Vic clung to Black Adam's

back, his arms wrapped tightly around the flying immortal's neck. The entire Black Marvel Family was escorting her and Vic on the next leg of their globe-trotting odyssey. Unburdened by a passenger, Osiris flew ahead of both Isis and Black Adam. He did loops in the frigid air, visibly delighting in the sheer joy of flight. At the moment, Renee knew exactly what he was feeling.

Beats flying coach, she thought.

Vic soon indicated that they had flown far enough and the party descended onto the western slope of a towering mountain. Renee's boots sunk into the snow as Isis gently put her down at the base of a steep incline. Nothing but snow and ice surrounded them; Renee guessed that they had to be at least fifteen thousand feet above sea level. The thin air made it hard to take a deep breath, but Renee didn't care. She wouldn't have missed this for all the gay bars in Gotham. She was standing on the roof of the world.

"You're certain this is where you wish us to leave you?" Black Adam sounded less impressed by the awesome scenery. He looked dubiously at the frozen wasteland. "There's nothing for miles. No villages. No settlements."

Vic chuckled to himself. "Yeah, that sounds about right." This whole excursion was his idea, and he was being typically cryptic as to why they were relocating to the Himalayas. Not that Renee was complaining; she was willing to take a breather from tracking Intergang if it meant a side trip to the highest mountains on Earth. *How cool is this?*

"Then we have come to the parting of our ways," Adam said solemnly.

Vic nodded. "Thanks for everything."

"It is we who should thank you, Victor Szasz." Adam shook Vic's hand. "Isis and I owe both you and Renee a great deal. My family counts you as friends."

Osiris expressed his gratitude as well. "A month ago I thought my sister was dead and I would never walk again." His boyish face was filled with happiness. "Now, thanks to you, I have a family—and I can fly!"

Isis kissed Vic on the cheek. She seemed immune to the frigid temperatures, despite her wispy costume. Her slender limbs weren't even showing goose bumps. "May there always be more questions for you to ask, Charlie." She turned and clasped Renee's hand. Her touch was impossibly warm. Flowers blossomed beneath her feet. "And may you find the answers you're so desperately seeking, Renee."

The goddess' compassionate gaze made Renee uncomfortable. She awkwardly let go of Isis' hand. "The only answer I want concerns Intergang and how to stop them from taking over Gotham."

"Then perhaps you are asking the wrong question," Isis replied enigmatically. She cupped her hands before her and a luminous purple glow emanated from her upraised palms. Renee's eyes widened as a bright red rose materialized from the ether. The flower's vibrant color contrasted dramatically with the wintry white landscape around them. Isis handed the miraculous rose to Renee. Her kohl-lined eyes looked deeply into Renee's, as though peering into the hidden recesses of the other woman's soul. "Who are you, Renee Montoya?"

With that, the Black Marvel Family took to the air, leaving Vic and Renee alone on the mountainside. Renee sniffed the fragrant rose. It smelled like springtime. "Hell if I know," she muttered.

Speaking of answers, she decided that it was past time that Vic filled her in on what exactly they were doing here. It was hard to imagine that Intergang had any sort of presence in this glacial wilderness, but maybe Vic was seeing something she wasn't. She opened her mouth to interrogate him. . . .

"Charlie!"

An enthusiastic voice abruptly informed her that they were no longer alone. Looking up from the rose, Renee spotted two men standing on the snowy slope above them. One of them came running toward them, waving his arms to get their attention. An older man wearing a parka, he risked taking a nasty spill as he raced down the slippery incline.

"Tot!" A smile broke out across Vic's face. He waved back at the man. "You made it to the middle of nowhere."

"With the help of several chartered jets and a state-of-the-art GPS system, yes." Breathing hard, the old man came to a halt in front of Vic and Renee, who put his age somewhere in the sixties or seventies. Spectacles and a white goatee gave him the look of an elderly scientist or professor. The flaps of a bushy gray hat covered his ears. "From what we just saw, I think you had the better mode of travel."

"Air Black Marvel," Vic confirmed. "It can't be beat."

Renee glanced curiously at the second man, who seemed to be keeping his distance. Squinting, she made out a bearded, red-haired Caucasian male in surprisingly lightweight clothing. While the rest of them were all bundled up against the cold, the aloof figure wore only a black wool sweater and trousers. He waited silently upon the mountain, his arms crossed atop his chest. He looked younger and more athletic than the panting old man, who was obviously still acclimating to the high altitude. He sniffled as he spoke.

Tot eyed Renee. "Is this your friend?" he asked Vic.

"Absolutely." Vic made the necessary introductions. "Aristotle Rodor, meet Renee Montoya." He gestured at the older man. "Renee, meet Tot."

"Pleasure!" Tot vigorously shook Renee's hand. "I've heard a lot about you."

"Mutual." Even though they had only just met, she got a good vibe from the old man. He struck her as genuinely cheerful and friendly. "I've heard very little about you."

Tot laughed warmly. "That sounds like Charlie." He playfully nudged Vic in the ribs. "You *almost* know what he's thinking at the best of times."

Vic looked up at the standoffish second man. "Richard! You coming down here or not?"

"Going down is easy," he replied. "Right up to when you hit the bottom. Ask any drop of water." He remained in no hurry to join them. "The hard part is climbing up again." He turned his inscrutable brown eyes on Renee. "Isn't that right, Renee?"

She bristled at his attitude. "Charlie, who the hell is this guy?"

"That's Richard Dragon, Renee. He's a teacher, the real deal." Vic started up the hill toward Dragon. "He's the guy who taught me." He looked back over his shoulder at Renee. "And he's just told you that class is now in session."

FAWCETT CITY.

A robot maid, complete with a frilly lace cap, served dessert.

Black Adam and his family sat around a long antique table in the dining room of Dr. Sivana's gloomy mansion outside the city. The remains of a large turkey dinner were spread out atop the white damask tablecloth. A lighted candelabra added to the illumination provided by a hanging crystal chandelier. A roaring blaze crackled in the fireplace. More robots cleared away used plates and cutlery. A mechanical butler sparked and sputtered as though about to short-circuit at any moment. A beautiful blonde woman, in a red satin evening dress, sat across from the Black Marvel Family.

"Thank you so much for coming," Lady Sivana said. "It's been weeks since my husband went missing, and I am so terribly worried about him." Long golden tresses framed her lovely face. "When Superman or Wonder Woman disappears, it's a national tragedy, but when someone like my dear sweet Thaddeus vanishes, everyone says good riddance!"

Black Adam had never understood how Sivana, that hideous gnome of a man, had won the enchanting Venus as his bride, but the ways of the heart could be truly mysterious at times. "I believe I made it clear that your ex-husband was no friend of mine." Although they had both opposed Captain Marvel for years, Adam had always considered the mad scientist an entirely reprehensible specimen of humanity.

"I know, and I don't blame you," Venus said. "Our marriage

ended because of his obsession with Captain Marvel, but despite his madness, my love for him is still there." Moist sapphire eyes entreated them. "Black Adam. Isis. Osiris. I donated twenty million dollars to Kahndaq's Children's Hospital so that you would accept my invitation . . . and consider finding my husband."

Black Adam appreciated the woman's generosity. Her donation would do much to benefit the countless orphans and refugees Isis had taken under her wing. "We will take your request under serious consideration, Lady Sivana."

"Please, call me Venus." She dabbed at her eyes with her napkin. "If you find him . . . if you happen upon him . . . please don't hurt him."

Touched by her obvious grief, he nodded solemnly. "I give you my word."

"This is stupid," Osiris muttered in Arabic. He picked listlessly at his peach cobbler. "What are we doing here anyway?"

Isis patiently addressed her brother. "This is important, Osiris. Our hostess has made a generous gift to our people."

"She only did it so we'd go find that crazy scientist. We should be trying to throw Dr. Sivana in jail, not having dinner with his wife!" He pushed away from the table and jumped impatiently to his feet. "I'm leaving."

"Osiris!" Isis protested, shocked by her sibling's poor manners. "Amon! Stop! Where are you going?"

"Don't you get it?" Osiris stormed toward the exit. "All we ever do is fly around the world, running from one event or adventure after another. I've done everything you've asked of me, Adrianna. Now I need something more."

Isis hurried after him. She laid a gentle hand upon his arm. "You share the powers of Black Adam," she pointed out. "You have a wonderful home. You have a family again." Confusion showed upon her exotic features. "What more do you need?"

Osiris paused and looked back at her. "I need friends."

Caught off guard by this sudden outpouring of emotion, she stood by silently as Osiris fled from their presence. An awkward silence descended over the dining room. Embarrassed by the scene, Black Adam hoped that Venus Sivana did not understand Arabic. He and Isis exchanged a worried look. Neither of them had the remotest idea how to handle this situation.

"Oh, he's just like a little Black Adam Junior!" Venus exclaimed, seeming more amused than offended by the boy's abrupt departure. "Isn't that precious?"

Adam opened his mouth to apologize for Osiris' behavior, but an ominous rumbling noise suddenly intruded upon the meal. Puzzled, Venus peered across the table at her guests. "Is that my stomach growling or yours?"

Before either he or Isis could answer, an enormous crocodile charged into the dining room. Rising onto its hind legs like a man, the huge reptile jumped onto the table, scattering the plates, candles, and silverware. Thick green scales armored the creature's hide. Dorsal fins ran along its back. Snapping jaws revealed rows of pointed teeth. Crimson eyes, with slitted pupils, glared ravenously. A torn shirt and trousers clung to the monster's body. Its swinging tail lashed out, decapitating a robot butler. The automaton's head bounced across the floor, trailing sparks from its shattered neck assembly. Jagged claws tore through the damask tablecloth, scratching the polished wood underneath. The monster grabbed onto the remains of the turkey with both hands and hungrily wolfed it down, bones and all.

"Oh no!" Venus shouted, knocking her chair over as she jumped back from the table. "It's ruining my peach cobbler!"

Black Adam began to suspect that Lady Sivana was just as insane, in her own way, as her megalomaniacal husband. He launched himself into the air. "Isis?" he called out. "What is that creature?"

"I'm not sure." She joined him several feet above the floor. "I cannot make contact with him. Whatever that animal is, it must be a perversion of Nature."

Startled by the flying humans, the crocodile sprang from

the table and crashed through the wall. Running erect on two legs, the monster smashed through one wall after another on its way out of the mansion. By the time Adam and Isis confirmed that Lady Sivana was indeed unharmed, the trail of gaping holes led through adjoining rooms to the shadowy grounds outside. Greasy footprints stained the carpeting and hardwood floors. Adam stared down the length of the escape route the monster had torn through the interior of the mansion. He turned to Isis in puzzlement.

"Where did it go?"

AUTUMN leaves littered the ground of the estate's sprawling gardens, which looked like it hadn't been tended to in years. Weeds clotted the overgrown shrubs and flower beds. Dry brown grass infested the cracks in the cobblestone walkway. Fallen tree branches threatened to trip the unwary stroller. A broken birdbath lay on its side. Dr. Sivana was obviously not much of a gardener.

Probably spent all his time in his lab, Osiris guessed, *building bigger and better super-weapons.* The costumed teenager sat dejectedly on a marble bench beneath a weathered statue of the mad scientist himself. He felt bad for ruining the dinner, no doubt embarrassing his sister and Adam, but why couldn't they understand how lonely he felt sometimes? Isis and Adam had each other, but he was just their tagalong little brother. *I need a life of my own, with friends my own age I can hang out with.*

He was feeling thoroughly sorry for himself, until a snuffling noise, coming from behind a thick bank of hedges, disturbed his moody ruminations. Intrigued, he got up to investigate. He darted around the hedge—where he was surprised to find an unhappy-looking crocodile sitting on a toppled tree trunk. Bizarrely, the croc was wearing clothes and sitting upright like a person. The snuffling sounded suspiciously like sobbing.

"Oh," Osiris blurted. "Hello."

The creature looked up in alarm. He threw his scaly hands up in front of his face. "P-p-please don't hurt me!"

Osiris blinked in surprise. "You can talk?"

"Of course I c-c-can," the beast said fearfully. His gravelly voice fit his bestial appearance.

"But . . . you're a crocodile," Osiris pointed out.

"I was . . . until six months ago, when D-d-doctor Sivana pulled me out of the Nile and brought me here!" Lowering his hands, he pointed at the marble statue of the mad scientist.

Sivana, of course. Osiris had never actually met the infamous doctor, but he had heard all about him from Black Adam. "What did he do to you?"

"I didn't understand what he said back then, but I remember him laughing at me." The crocodile seemed to realize that Osiris meant him no harm. "The next thing I knew I was down in that l-l-lab of his, and he fed me all sorts of things. *Glowing* things. And I grew these." He showed Osiris his hands, complete with opposable thumbs. Then one day he left . . . and he never came back." The croc shuddered at the memory. "I've b-b-been downstairs, trapped in a cage, ever since. I haven't eaten in months." A rumbling came from deep within the animal's belly. "I finally broke out of my cage and I was going to l-l-leave, but the smell . . . Your dinner smelled so good. And I was so awfully hungry." Oily tears leaked from his eyes. "I'm sorry. I didn't mean to scare your family."

The boy's heart went out to the poor creature, an innocent victim of Sivana's crazed experiments. He didn't worry about Black Adam and Isis; they could take care of themselves, and probably Mrs. Sivana too. "Well, they aren't all my family."

"Your friends, then," the crocodile said. He signed plaintively. "I wish I had friends to eat dinner with."

An idea occurred to Osiris as he remembered Mr. Tawky Tawny, the talking tiger who palled around with Captain Marvel Jr. He stroked his chin as he contemplated the homeless reptile before him. "What's your name?"

"I don't have one," the monster admitted.

Osiris grinned. "Do you want one?"

WEEK 27.

IT'S ABOUT TIME, read the sign over the doorway of an unassuming shop facing a quiet side street, just off the main avenue. Inside the darkened interior of the store, dozens of clocks, of every size and generation, confirmed that it was nearly five-thirty in the morning. Grandfather clocks, cuckoo clocks, alarm clocks, pocket watches, hourglasses, and sundials filled the walls and shelves of the quaint little store. Clockwork mechanisms clicked with metronomic precision, counting off the passing minutes and seconds. Digital displays glowed in the shadows.

    5:25:18 A.M.

In the back of the shop, as far as possible from the front door and windows, an unearthly golden glow radiated from behind a counter. The luminous aura emanated from a huddled figure crouched upon the floor like a frightened child. Matthew Ryder's skin and uniform had a bright golden sheen. A nimbus of coruscating quantum energy crowned his head. Gleaming wristbands matched the metallic luster of his flesh. Burnished eyelids were squeezed tightly shut. His arms were wrapped around his knees as he curled himself into a trembling ball of dread and apprehension. The steady ticking of the clocks did little to soothe his frazzled nerves.

    5:25:19 A.M.

Once free to traverse the myriad timelines at will, the being known as Waverider was now afraid to even lift his head to peer beyond the counter. Where his precognitive gifts had previously allowed him to glimpse beyond tomorrow, now the future stalked him like an unseen predator. Along with his colleagues, the Linear Men, Waverider had devoted himself to preserving a single continuous timeline that had suddenly become all too unpredictable—and deadly. Some unknown enemy, beyond his powers to discern, was striking down the guardians of Time, until Waverider feared that he was the only one left. *Who is doing this?* he wondered desperately. *And to what end?*

The ticking clocks held no answers for him. A novelty cat clock, its mechanical whiskers twitching, grinned inanely on the wall above him.

5:25.20 A.M.

A second passed—or did it? Abruptly, the relentless ticking ceased, so that Waverider heard only the rapid beating of his heart. He looked up in alarm at a nearby digital clock.

5:25.20 A.M.

The blinking numerals refused to advance. So did all the other clocks in sight.

"Oh, no," he whispered.

Time had stopped.

Instinctively, he tried to dive back into the timestream, to seek refuge in the future or the past, but his trans-temporal abilities abandoned him. He sprang frantically to his feet, only to find himself anchored to a single moment in time. Dozens of frozen clocks blocked his escape.

He was trapped.

A sonic boom shook the store. A flash of sapphire energy heralded the opening of a space-time rift only a few feet in front of him. Waverider backed away warily. His brain raced through a litany of likely suspects as he tried to anticipate what fearsome entity was about to emerge from the shimmering time warp.

Monarch?

Darkseid?

The Time Trapper?

Parallax?

"Skeets . . . ?"

He blinked in surprise as Booster Gold's robot sidekick materialized before him.

"HERE YOU ARE!" Skeets declared. "WAVERIDER, THE SEER OF HYPERTIME." His electronic voice held a sarcastic tone. "KEEPER OF DIVERGENT TIMELINES."

"By Wells!" Waverider exclaimed, invoking the patron saint of time-travelers. "You're the one Rip Hunter tried to warn us about." He couldn't have been more surprised if Krypto the Super-Dog had suddenly revealed himself as a diabolical mastermind. "The tremors. The paradoxes? *You're* the one splintering the historical mainline!"

"NO," Skeets informed him. "THE CATALYST WAS THE CRISIS, BUT IN ITS WAKE . . . SOMETHING NEW." Bands of quantum energy blasted from the robot, pinning Waverider's wrists to the wall behind him. "I CAN SMELL IT LIKE HONEY. HISTORY'S FERTILE GROUND. THIS YEAR, LIKE WONDERFUL, WET CEMENT. JUST WAITING TO BE MOLDED INTO SHAPE . . ."

Waverider strained against the crackling energy bands. The robot's new armaments had caught him off guard. To his knowledge, Skeets had never possessed such weaponry before.

"WHEN IS RIP HUNTER?" Skeets demanded. "TELL ME NOW OR YOU WILL END UP LIKE THE TIME COMMANDER AND CLOCK QUEEN."

Both chrononauts had recently been erased from history, but Waverider refused to be intimidated. Now that the final confrontation was upon him, he resolved not to cower in fear any longer. "Rip Hunter has survived the onslaughts of Per Degaton and the Lord of Time." He sneered at his cybernetic captor. "A security robot from the future has no chance."

"RIP HUNTER MAY BE THE PIONEER AND INVENTOR OF TIME-TRAVEL," Skeets responded, "BUT HIS PRIMITIVE DEVICES AND WEAPONS ARE STICKS AND STONES COMPARED TO MY TWENTY-FIFTH-CENTURY TECHNOLOGY."

"And yet you still can't find him." Waverider enjoyed a

smile at the robot's expense. "Want to know why?" He glared
defiantly at Skeets. "Rip Hunter spent his entire life preparing
for the kind of adversaries a time-traveler would face. You can
threaten to go back in time and kill him in his crib all you
want . . . but you can't! Rip's true name is a secret. Where and
when he was born and raised is a mystery. And they're secrets
even I don't know."

Skeets zoomed in closer, until he was only inches away
from Waverider's face. Matthew Ryder squirmed against his
bonds in frustration; the robot was close enough to tear apart
if he could just get his hands free! But the energy shackles
refused to release him.

"YOU TALK ABOUT HISTORY. TELL ME, LINEAR
MAN. DO YOU KNOW MINE?" An array of wriggling metal
probes sprouted from hidden orifices in Skeets' gleaming car-
apace. Electrodes and laser scalpels sparked at the ends of the
wiry probes as they extended toward Waverider's captive form.
"DO YOU KNOW WHERE THE GOLDEN METAL THAT
MAKES MY BODY IMPERVIOUS TO THE RAVAGES OF
TIME COMES FROM? DO YOU KNOW FROM WHOSE
CORPSE IT WAS BURNED OFF, AFTER BEING DIS-
COVERED IN A BURIED RUIN FIVE HUNDRED YEARS
FROM NOW?"

Waverider gulped involuntarily. If what the robot was im-
plying was true, then he was about to suffer the fate feared
most by those who traverse the timeways: murder by paradox.

A burst of searing energy tore him apart. Molten gold
splattered across the face of Felix the Cat. Waverider died
screaming.

Time of death: *5:25.20 A.M.*

THE HIMALAYAS.

TIME stood still in Nanda Parbat. The remote mountain village
was cut off from the world of clocks and calendars by sky-high

peaks and vast glacial drifts. A Buddhist temple overlooked a small enclave of thatch-roofed huts known as *ghars*. Wooly yaks were tethered outside the huts. Prayer flags fluttered in the alpine breeze, which carried the chiming of wind bells down from the looming pagoda-style temple. Vic claimed that Nanda Parbat was the real-life inspiration for the fictional Shangri-La. So far, Renee wasn't finding it much of a paradise.

She threw a punch at Richard Dragon, who effortlessly evaded the blow, then flipped her head over heels onto the frosted floor of a spacious ice cavern. The curved walls of the grotto shone like polished glass, so that Renee saw her own reflection every way she looked. Dozens of mirror images, some more distorted than others, captured her embarrassment as she landed hard upon the packed snow and ice. "Oomph!" she grunted, then swore profanely.

Her self-appointed teacher was unfazed by her colorful invective. Richard stood barefoot upon the snow, clad only in a dark T-shirt and a pair of loose karate pants. A brownish red beard obscured his stoic expression. "You must learn to let go," he advised her.

"How the hell do I do that?" She rose painfully to her feet. Despite the winter chill, perspiration soaked through her soiled tank top and sweatpants. Her knuckles were wrapped like a boxer's. Her feet were bare. Breathing hard, she caught another glimpse of her reflection in an angled curtain of ice. No surprise, she looked just as tired and pissed off as she felt. Kahndaq had been a breeze compared to this.

"Acceptance," Richard answered. "Cherish it. The cold, the pain, the frustration, the heartache." His muscular arms were crossed atop his chest. His voice was calm, but stern. "Only when you want it to stay will you learn to release it."

She took out her hostility on the ice sheet, smashing it with her fist. Her reflection shattered into dozens of glittering translucent shards. Blood seeped through the bandages over her knuckles. "If I cherish it, I won't want it to leave."

Flawless logic, she thought, but Richard dismissed it with

a shrug. "Someone else once said the same thing." She assumed he was talking about Vic. "I'll tell you what I told him. Nobody said this is easy."

Tell me about it, she thought. Not for the first time, she wondered what she was doing here, going through all this kung fu crap, while Intergang was up to no good back home. It came as a shock to realize that she hadn't set foot in Gotham for at least three months. *Whose idea was this anyway?* she asked herself. *Oh yeah. Vic's.*

Having evidently decided that he'd humiliated her enough for one afternoon, Richard wrapped up their training session. Renee took a moment to cool down, then put on a turtleneck sweater, her parka, boots, and gloves. She lit a cigarette and took a long drag before exiting the cavern to head back toward the *ghar* she now shared with Vic and the others. A pair of all-seeing eyes was painted on the whitewashed walls of the hut. She scowled at the unblinking eyes.

What are you looking at?

Flickering candles lit the murky interior of the hut. Incense competed with the smoke from her cigarette. The stone floor was sticky from spilled yak butter. As usual, she found Tot hunched over a rickety wooden table, poring over the *Book of Crime.* Reference books were stacked on the floor beside him. His brow furrowed as he scribbled notes onto a thick pad of paper. According to the old professor, the book was a bible of sorts, the foundation of a whole religion based on some twisted theology of crime. The massive tome, which Vic had stolen from that underground temple in Bialya, was apparently filled with prophecies, stories, and fables that preached the virtues of rape, murder, extortion, and blackmail.

Light reading, obviously.

Looking out for Vic, she found him laid out atop a wooden bench, surrounded by scented candles and incense burners. A tray of used acupuncture needles rested at the foot of the bench. He sat up to greet her, only to be stricken by a sudden coughing fit that caused him to double over. Renee flinched at the hacking noises coming from his chest, which sounded like he was coughing his lungs out.

He'd been doing that a lot lately. It had started right after they had gotten here. Vic said that it was the altitude, that he was having trouble acclimating. *Yeah, right,* she thought skeptically. *I'm the pack-a-day smoker, but* he's *having trouble acclimating.*

Over the last week, Richard had made him tea, treating him with acupuncture and pressure points, while Tot had fed him the better part of a pharmacy in pills. Sometimes she caught the men whispering conspiratorially, shutting up whenever she came within earshot. Renee didn't have to be an ex-detective to figure out what was up.

Vic was sick . . . and he wasn't getting any better.

How long has he been fighting this? she wondered. Maybe he had been sick for a while and she had just been too wrapped up in herself to notice. She finished up her cigarette, then ground it beneath her heel. *Sounds like me.*

The coughing fit finally subsided. Looking up from the floor, Vic spotted her worried expression. "Sounds worse than it is," he wheezed.

"I'm wondering how that's possible." Fishing her last pack of cigarettes out of her pocket, she eyed him suspiciously. "When did you quit?"

He cracked a pained smile. "Not soon enough."

An overwhelming wave of grief rushed over her. *Not another partner,* she anguished. *Not again!* The foil pack slipped from her fingers. She felt numb all over.

"How long have you known?" she asked him.

His face was noticeably more gaunt than just a week ago. "About seven months."

Since before the Question first invaded her bedroom, in other words. "How long do you have?"

"Not long." He watched her closely, like she was the one he should be worried about. "Tot says it's metastasized."

"Why me?" Renee buried her face in her hands. Of all

people to waste his last months on Earth on . . . "Eight billion people in the world. Why me?"

He gave her a cryptic smile. "That's the Question, isn't it?"

Perhaps to give Renee a chance to process what he had just told her, Vic got off the bench and walked over to where Tot was working. Isis' magical red rose, still fresh and fragrant even after a week, rested in a vase upon the table. Vic peered over Tot's shoulder at the obscene bible. "How's it going?" he asked.

The old man cleared his throat and read aloud from the open volume. "'The Eighteenth beyond the calling of all saints, sending his Apostle to the land where dwells the lambs of the wise and the foolish . . .'"

"That a literal place?" Vic asked.

Tot nodded. "There was a village in Nottinghamshire, circa 1080 or so, known for its villagers both wise and foolish." His pedantic tone betrayed his academic roots. "The village was called Gatham in Old English. It's where we get the word *Gotham*."

Renee's ear perked up at the mention of her hometown. She wandered over to join the two men. *Is this why Intergang's so interested in Gotham?*

"There's more," Tot said, squinting at the text through his spectacles. "Take a look. 'Absent its Knight-Protector, the Apostle stakes his bloody claim, devouring the heart of the twice-named daughter of Cain.'" Removing his glasses, he chewed thoughtfully upon the earpiece. "Everything points to this being a significant passage. The illustration, the scansion of 'claim' and 'Cain.'"

"As in 'and Abel'?" Vic inquired.

"Indeed," Tot confirmed. "Cain is venerated throughout the text as the bringer of all crime, including the 'most sacred' one, that of murder."

Sick, Renee thought. She leaned forward to get a better look at the pages in question. The bizarre hieroglyphics bore no resemblance to any language she was familiar with, so her eyes gravitated toward the grisly drawing that took up much of

the left page. An intricate woodcut, which resembled something out of Dante's *Inferno*, depicted a large, brutish demon
ripping the heart from the bloody breast of a swooning female
angel.

"Lovely," she muttered.

Something about the illustration, besides the obvious, disturbed her. A chill ran down her spine as she examined the
murdered angel, whose scalloped wings struck her as oddly
batlike. The bloody smear on the angel's chest had a familiar
look to it, like something Renee had seen back in . . .

"Gotham." She stood up straight, her eyes wide with horror.
"Oh no . . . no . . ."

Vic noticed her reaction. "Easy, Renee. What's—?"

"I've got to get a phone," she blurted. "I have to call home!"

Vic shook his head, still not understanding what was at
stake. "There is no phone, Renee. This is Nanda Parbat. Messages come via dreams and telepathy."

Was he joking? Renee didn't have time to find out. "A satellite phone, then. Anything!" Locating her duffel bag, she
started throwing her laundry into it. The Intergang ray gun
weighed down the bottom of the bag. "We have to warn her!"

"Who?" Vic stared at her in utter confusion. Tot looked
equally baffled. "You're not making sense."

"Look at the damn book!" she said impatiently. "Look at the
illustration." The ghastly image, of the leering demon ripping
out the angel's heart, was burned into her brain. "It's not 'Cain,'
Charlie. It's 'Kane,' the daughter of Kane."

Katherine Kane.

Batwoman.

WEEK 28.

GOTHAM CITY.

FOR the first time in months, ever since the police gave up trying to summon the Dark Knight, the Bat-Signal shone in the night sky above the city. The glowing symbol didn't look quite the same as the one Gothamites had once grown accustomed to, though. The spotlight had a slightly more yellowish tint, while the bat-winged silhouette at the center of the luminous orb looked crude around the edges, like an amateur's copy of the original symbol. Renee thought it was obvious that it wasn't the real thing. *Hey, I did my best,* she thought.

"This is not going to work, Charlie." She squatted on top of her partner's beaten-up old Vanagon while pointing their handmade Bat-Signal up at the sky. The makeshift emblem was glued to the lens of a modified halogen flashlight.

"It'll work, Renee." The Question leaned against the side of the van, reading the *Gotham Gazette.* The front-page headline read, "G.C.P.D. UNPREPARED FOR SUDDEN WAVE OF GANG VIOLENCE." His lack of a face did not seem to impede his reading. "That lamp emits over eleven million candela of light." He casually flipped the page. "You're just nervous because you haven't seen her in months."

It was a week before Thanksgiving, and Gotham was much colder than it had been when she and Vic had left the city three and a half months ago. The van was parked on the fringe of Robinson Park, not far from where they had met with Kate way back in July. The park's lush green foliage was all gone now, replaced by skeletal trees whose bare branches extended out over the curb. A winter coat and gloves only partly shielded Renee from the cold November wind. She shivered atop the van, momentarily pining for the dry heat of the Middle East. Her breath misted before her lips.

"I'm nervous because we're throwing a Bat-Signal around in Gotham City." She would have killed for a cigarette, but had gone cold turkey since finding out about Vic. The nicotine craving wasn't helping her mood any. "A guaranteed way to bring half the G.C.P.D. and all the costumed freaks running."

He flipped through his newspaper. "You got another way to reach her?"

A racking cough shook his body. Renee flinched at the ugly sound, which bluntly reminded her that he was dying. The heavy sweater he was wearing under his trench coat helped to disguise how much weight he had lost, but the frequent coughs gave him away. *He shouldn't even be here,* she thought guiltily. *He should be with his friends in Nanda Parbat, not with me, trying to save someone he doesn't know from something we're not sure will happen.*

"None of the other ways worked, and you know it," she muttered under her breath. "Bet the damn butler never even told her I called."

"Moan, moan, moan," Vic mocked her.

Renee scowled at the sky. "Oh, bite me."

"He can't," a husky voice intruded. "He doesn't have a mouth."

Without warning, Batwoman dropped from an overhanging tree branch onto the roof of the van. Startled, Renee almost dropped the flashlight. Batwoman glared angrily at the improvised signal. "Now turn that thing off."

Renee switched off the lamp. "We've been trying to reach you."

"Congratulations," Batwoman said brusquely. Renee recognized the pissed-off tone of Kate's voice as the masked woman jumped down onto the pavement beside the Question. She turned to leave. "Good-bye."

Vic sighed theatrically. "Nobody has any curiosity these

days. You notice that?" He coughed hoarsely into his glove, somewhat spoiling the moment. "She doesn't even want to know why we've gone to this trouble."

"It's too bad, really." Renee nimbly joined him on the ground. "We might have important information. Maybe about Intergang."

"Or how she's prophesied to have her heart ripped out a week from now," Vic added.

That got her attention. Her cape swirled behind her as Batwoman turned around and stalked back to them. "Intergang, I already know about," she said. "Let's hear that second part."

"Picture's worth a thousand words." Vic reached beneath his coat and drew out a Xerox of the gruesome illustration they had discovered in Nanda Parbat. As always, Renee's skin crawled at the sight of the bloodthirsty demon tearing a bat-winged angel's heart from her breast. The more she looked at the grisly woodcut, the more the female victim seemed to resemble Kate in costume. She could practically hear the murdered angel's scream.

"It's taken from something called the *Book of Crime*," she explained as Vic handed the photocopy to Batwoman. "And I'm pretty damn sure that's supposed to be you dying in that picture. . . ."

WEEK 29.

"So much for your prophecy!" Batwoman declared as she rammed her heel down the throat of a frog-faced beast-man. Her gloved hand simultaneously grabbed onto the collar of a fleeing hoodlum. The batrachian mutant choked on her boot, its slimy tail lashing about wildly. The captured hood yelped in alarm.

Looks like I made it to the church on time, Batwoman thought.

The deconsecrated cathedral was tucked away in a squalid slum not far from Crime Alley. Declining attendance, as well as a well-publicized choirboy scandal, had forced its closing several years previously. According to her sources, Intergang's blasphemous Church of Crime had moved in to fill the void left behind by the Gothic cathedral's previous congregation. Stone ribs supported the vaulted ceiling. Moonlight filtered through cracked stained glass windows. A pitcher of fresh blood rested upon the altar.

"Awwk!" the frog-man croaked as Batwoman sprang off him, while simultaneously flipping the human gangster over her shoulder. The thug hit the stone floor with a satisfying *thunk*. Several of his fellow cultists had already felt the female vigilante's fury. Their robed bodies were strewn across the pews and balconies of the desecrated church. Batwoman smiled tightly. Thanks to her, tonight's midnight service was turning into a rout. She was wiping the floor with the various monsters and mobsters. Her flying fists demonstrated exactly what she thought of this so-called religion and its prophecies.

"I've always felt that people should take responsibility for their actions," she lectured her defeated foes. Pausing in the center of the nave, she looked about for a fresh opponent. "Not excuse them by denying that there was any choice in the matter."

"Then you are a fool," a gruff voice said behind her. "Because the Word will not be denied."

She spun around to see Bruno Mannheim emerge from a shadowy nook. He squeezed the trigger of a futuristic handgun and a blast of searing energy dropped her to the floor. Only the triple-weave Kevlar in her uniform saved her from a nasty third-degree burn. Gasping, she sprawled facedown upon the cold stone tiles while Mannheim came up behind her. He savagely yanked on her flowing red hair, lifting her face from the floor. Batwoman grunted in pain.

I just need a minute to recover, she thought. But Mannheim didn't let up.

"Prophecy is upon you," the notorious mob boss preached. He seized her throat with both hands and, with unexpected strength, lifted her off the ground. Her boots dangled in the air as he throttled her. "With your death, Intergang's feast will truly begin." His cruel eyes gleamed with the murderous fanaticism of a true believer. "I shall devour you, just as the Red Rock and the Rage shall devour all of Gotham." His left hand dropped onto her chest, right above her heart. Powerful fingers dug into her costume. "So it has been written, and so it shall come to pass."

"Too bad we're working from a different text," Batwoman whispered hoarsely.

He gave her a puzzled look. "'We'?"

"She means us," Renee said. She and the Question rose up from behind a nearby pew. Renee's own ray gun was aimed right at Mannheim's skull. "Now put the Batwoman down and we won't have to vaporize your ugly ass."

"The Questions?" he murmured in surprise. A look of utter

consternation, and even confusion, came over his brutish face. He stared at Batwoman's backup like he couldn't believe his eyes. "No . . . no, you can't be here, not yet. . . ." He almost sounded as though he was having a crisis of faith. "The Questions have not yet been Answered!"

Questions? Batwoman thought. *As in plural?*

Before she could even begin to figure out what Mannheim was raving about, he suddenly hurled her at the Question and Renee. "Look out!" the faceless detective shouted at his partner. Renee tried to get a clear shot at Mannheim, but was blocked by Batwoman's flying body, which came tumbling through the air toward them. Renee cursed as she ducked out of the way.

Taking control of her fall, Batwoman grabbed onto the back of an empty pew and flipped herself back onto her feet. Now that Mannheim was no longer strangling her, her strength was returning, so she hit the floor running and charged back toward the front of the cathedral. A scorch mark defaced the bat-emblem on her chest.

"Stop him!" Renee hollered at her. Clutching her ray gun, she scrambled back up from the floor. "Don't let him get . . ."

Too late. Batwoman's eyes searched the sanctuary and nave, but Mannheim was nowhere to be seen. He must have vanished down a side corridor while they were all distracted. She glanced around at the criminal casualties littering the church. *At least he left some of his monsters and goons behind.*

"Away. . . ." Renee's voice trailed off. Scowling, she lowered her gun. "I hate it when they do that."

"Tell me about it," Batwoman agreed.

WEEK 30.

KATE'S penthouse apartment occupied the top two floors of a sleek high-rise in one of Gotham's pricier neighborhoods. No doubt it was more private than the Kane family estate, which Renee definitely appreciated. She wasn't sure she could cope with too much company right now, let alone Kate's snooty parents. *That would be a little more than I could handle,* she thought. *Not at a time like this.*

She and Kate watched anxiously from a doorway as Kate's cute young doctor friend practiced her bedside manner on Vic, who was resting uncomfortably in a spare bedroom. An oxygen rig was poised beside the bed, while a nasal cannula helped him breathe. A pitcher of water and a battery of pill bottles rested atop the bed stand. The doctor dutifully checked Vic's pulse. A stethoscope dangled around her neck.

"So, does she make house calls for all her patients," Renee asked archly, "or is this a special arrangement between you and Mallory there?"

Renee hated every minute of this. Hated that the cancer was eating Vic alive. Hated that, even with her best friend dying, she could still be jealous. Hated that all she had left was questions . . . and not one good answer.

"I'm not sleeping with her," Kate said, "if that's what you're asking."

"No?" Turning away from the doorway, Renee wandered across the living room, which was stylishly furnished with black leather furniture, a platinum/silver cocktail table, and mahogany bookshelves. "That wasn't the impression you gave me back in July."

Kate looked annoyed. "I'm not the only one who was looking to score points that day."

True enough, Renee admitted. "Doesn't matter." A framed photo on a mantle showed a shockingly young Kate posing in a West Point cadet's uniform. Renee picked up the photo. "How old are you in this?"

Kate sighed. "I was nineteen." She took the photo from Renee and put it back down on the mantle. Her tone implied that it was ancient history.

Renee wondered if Kate's West Point years had anything to do with her new career as Batwoman. So far Kate had not offered any explanation for why she had adopted the life of a masked vigilante, and Renee had not been pushy enough to pry. She had more important things on her mind these days. *If Kate wants to play dress-up at night and beat up bad guys, that's none of my business.*

Is it?

"Kate?" Mallory joined them in the living room. Her annoyingly attractive face was grim. "I gave him some morphine to help with the pain. You're going to see the onset of delirium soon, with declining moments of lucidity." She placed her stethoscope back into a black leather bag. "You should consider admitting him to a hospital."

"Why?" Renee challenged her. "So he can go and never come out?"

Kate tried to calm her. "Renee . . ."

"He might be more comfortable there, that's all," Mallory explained calmly. No doubt she was accustomed to patients and their loved ones reacting emotionally to terminal diagnoses. Renee remembered dealing with the families of murder victims back when she was still a cop. It was never easy.

This isn't fair, she thought. *We came back to Gotham. We saved Kate's life. But now it's costing Charlie his. . . .*

Kate escorted Mallory to the door. "They're both staying here for now."

"Then I'll see what I can do about setting up hospice care," the doctor volunteered. She gave Kate's hand a comforting squeeze. Renee pretended not to notice.

She listened silently as Kate thanked Mallory and closed the door behind her. Renee stared forlornly out the window at the lights of the city. It was only six o'clock, but the sun was already going down. The smoggy haze of twilight blurred before her eyes as she fought back tears. Kate's graceful footsteps came up behind her.

"I'll take him to the hospital tomorrow," Renee said, feeling crushed and defeated.

"I already told you," Kate insisted. "You and Charlie can stay as long as you like."

Renee turned away from the window. "I'm not going to impose any more than I already have. . . ."

"You were evicted from your apartment," Kate pointed out impatiently. "You hadn't paid your rent in six months." She got right in Renee's face, so that their bodies were only inches apart. Her face flushed. "Where are you two going to go if you leave? You going to live out of Charlie's van?" She threw up her hands in frustration. "Stop being so damn stubborn. Just accept what I'm offering, all right?" She took a deep breath and let her temper cool. Her face and voice softened as her lustrous brown eyes implored the other woman. "Please, Renee."

Renee's throat tightened. How could she turn down a plea like that, especially when it obviously meant so much to Kate? Her ex-lover was standing so close to her now that Renee could inhale her perfume. The intoxicating scent stirred her memory and her senses. Renee felt the blood racing through her veins. *I've missed you so much,* she thought. It was so tempting to reach out for her again, to look for comfort in her strong arms.

"Okay," she whispered.

Kate smiled, visibly pleased that Renee had seen sense. An endless moment hung between them as Renee waited expectantly for . . . what? For a second chance? She gazed longingly into Kate's dark eyes. She held her breath. Her lips parted. . . .

"I have to go out," Kate said abruptly. To Renee's surprise

(and disappointment), the other woman turned away and headed toward her private dressing room. "I won't be back until late."

Oh right, Renee realized. *Time for Batwoman to hit the streets.* She imagined the ominous black cape and cowl descending over Kate's familiar face and figure. Glancing out the window, she half expected to see the Bat-Signal shining in the night sky.

"Don't wait up," Kate advised her.

Renee swallowed hard, trying to conceal her bruised feelings. For a few moments there, she'd really thought something was going to happen between them. *Guess that was just wishful thinking on my part.*

She heard Vic stir in the spare bedroom and went to investigate. He managed to lift his head from the pillow as she entered. He wheezed as he spoke. "She going out to search for Mannheim again?"

"Didn't ask," Renee answered.

"You should always . . . ask the next question," he said haltingly.

"Says the guy who never answers one." She grinned at him. It felt good to banter like this . . . just like before. If it wasn't for his wasted appearance, she could almost pretend he wasn't dying. "You mind if I sit here for a while?"

"I'm afraid I'm not . . . very chatty . . . right now."

"That's all right, Charlie." She assumed a lotus position upon the floor at the foot of the bed. She closed her eyes in meditation. "Neither am I."

Be careful out there, Kate.

WEEK 31.

GOTHAM CITY.

"THIS is me asking you nicely," Batwoman said, smashing the hoodlum's face into the windshield of a parked car. The window cracked loudly, a tracery of thin fractures spreading out from the point of impact like cobwebs. She grabbed onto the gangster's collar and tossed his unconscious body to the pavement. "Should I ask the rest of you *mean*?"

Dirty slush was piled along the sides of the dingy alley. Icicles hung from the eaves of darkened warehouses. An unmarked van was parked in front of an open loading dock; the crooks had been picking up an illegal arms shipment when Batwoman had ambushed them. She had taken out half the gang before the startled thugs even knew was happening. One mob lieutenant was already on the ground, clutching a broken arm. The hoodlum with the smashed face was sprawled in the icy slush. Only two more men remained on their feet.

So far, so good, Batwoman thought. She reminded herself to leave at least one crook conscious enough to answer her questions. *Fun's fun, but I want to get something out of this workout.*

Clothing shredded as the surviving hoodlums began to metamorphose into beast-men. Fur sprouted from their rippling flesh. Bones cracked noisily. Human canines and fingernails elongated into razor-sharp fangs and claws. One of the men took on the aspect of a Siberian tiger; the other assumed the form of a humanoid panther. They hissed and bared their fangs.

Batwoman took the bizarre transformations in stride. By now, she had fought enough of Intergang's mutated monsters to become accustomed to their freakish appearances. According to Renee, some sort of arcane chemical potion was responsible for the gangsters' metamorphic MO. She braced herself for the cat-men's attack while hoping that their devolved vocal cords hadn't completely lost the capacity for speech. She was after bigger prey tonight.

"Where's Mannheim?" she demanded.

To her frustration, the beast-men merely growled in response. Their feline eyes looked past her, alerting her to some lurking danger. *There must be another one behind me!*

She heard the wolf before she saw it. A growl came from the loading dock as, spinning around, she glimpsed a great black wolf lunging at her. Reacting instantly, she rolled across the hood of the car, barely dodging the wolf's attack. Its hot breath steamed in the cold night air. Sharpened claws sliced the fringe of her cape.

Bad dog!

The wolf landed on all fours, then sprang up onto its hind legs. Standing erect, the huge animal morphed into a slightly more humanoid form: half man, half wolf. Batwoman recognized Kyle Abbot from Renee's description. She drew a Batarang from its sheath within one of the scalloped fins of her right glove.

"Mannheim isn't your problem," the wolf-man snarled. "That you continue to live defies the Word of Cain." Flanked by the tiger- and panther-man, he leaped at her, his claws extended before him. "And that cannot be allowed!"

The Batarang flew from her fingers as she dived out of the way. The spinning missile caught the panther across the forehead, slicing open a cut that poured hot blood into his eyes, then ricocheted off the panther's skull to strike the tiger in the throat. The striped beast-man yelped and grabbed clumsily at his neck. The blinded panther flailed about wildly, trying to clear his vision. *So much for those two,* she thought, *at least for the moment.*

Abbot charged past her, and she delivered a vicious kick to his side. He went careening off into the slush, barking like a rabid dog. He angrily wiped the wet snow from his fur as he jumped to his feet. Foam dripped from his curled lips.

"My mistress has sent me to set right what you made wrong."

Batwoman took Abbot's arrival as a sign that she was finally getting somewhere in her campaign against Intergang. She was moving up the syndicate's food chain. "That I'm alive is proof that your insane prophecy was wrong in the first place!"

She figured she could take Abbot, one-on-one. Unfortunately, just at that moment, six more gang members came storming out of the warehouse. Tearing open their clothes, they were already in throes of their own transformations into bears, reptiles, apes, serpents, and God only knew what else. The desolate alleyway echoed with their chirps, growls, and roars. A lupine smile appeared upon Abbot's muzzle.

"Perhaps," he remarked. The army of beast-men swarmed forward. "Take her heart for the Apostle!"

That would be Mannheim, Batwoman guessed, suddenly finding herself severely outnumbered. She planted a heel into the shoulder of a bull-headed minotaur, then vaulted over the heads of the other monsters. Batarangs flew rapid-fire from her fingers. Landing on the ground behind the inhuman mob, she cast an irritated look up at the roof of the warehouse.

"You going to lend a hand here," she called out, "or are you just planning on getting an eyeful?"

So, she knew I was here all along, Nightwing thought. He looked down on the fracas from atop the warehouse. *Impressive.*

Years ago, Dick Grayson had fought beside Batman as Robin, the Boy Wonder. Although he had long ago outgrown the role of a sidekick, he continued to fight crime as the costumed vigilante known as Nightwing. The bat-shaped mask affixed to his face and the somber tones of his dark blue and black uniform paid tribute to his legendary mentor, and he had both loved and lost Barbara Gordon, the original Batgirl. But he had no idea who this new Batwoman was.

Eager to find out, he leaped from the rooftop like the trapeze artist he had once been. A grappling dart, fired by a CO_2-powered launcher in his gauntlet, embedded itself in the wall of a neighboring warehouse. Using the jumpline attached to the dart, he swung down into the fray. His heels crashed into the scaly skull of a human alligator even as Batwoman elbowed a slathering warthog in the throat.

"You have to admit, it's quite an eyeful," he answered her. The downed alligator cushioned his landing as he dropped down onto the pavement. Batwoman cast an annoyed look in his direction, seemingly unamused by his quip. He shrugged apologetically. "What can I say? I've got a thing for redheads."

Barbara had red hair. . . .

"Trust me, I'm not your type," Batwoman informed him. She jumped above a gorilla-man's swinging arm, then snapped the toe of her boot into the ape's protruding jaw. Simian tusks shattered and the gorilla tumbled backward, head over heels.

Hissing, a cobra-man reared up behind Batwoman, poised to strike. Its swollen hood flared dramatically. A forked tongue flicked between its curved fangs. Nightwing's own boot caught the man-snake right in the chin, causing its venomous jaws to snap shut. Back-to-back, the two vigilantes faced off against the shape-shifting hoods. He somehow sensed that he could trust her to watch his back. *She fights like a real pro,* he observed, *like she's been doing this for years.*

His unexpected arrival was more than Intergang's pet monsters seemed inclined to deal with at the moment. Abandoning their stunned and injured comrades, the remaining creatures hastily made for the shadows. Webbed and taloned feet splashed through the slush and icy puddles. Leading the retreat was a large black wolf, which bounded out of the alley on all fours.

"The wolf!" Batwoman shouted. "Don't let him escape!"

Finishing off the punch-drunk gorilla, she started to pursue the werewolf, but the fleeing lycanthrope had already vanished from view. The sound of its racing footsteps were rapidly swallowed up by the noise of the nocturnal city. Batwoman dashed past Nightwing anyway, unwilling to accept that the wolf was probably long gone.

"Whoa there!" Nightwing cautioned. He didn't want haste to make her careless; what if more monsters were lying in wait just outside the alley? He flipped the cobra over his shoulders onto the blacktop, then grabbed Batwoman by the arm. "You'll get another crack at him," he promised her. "Believe me, there's always a Round Two."

They had plenty to deal with right here and now, making sure that the subdued beast-men were down for the count and wrapping them up nice and tight for the G.C.P.D. Besides, if truth be told, he was more interested in getting to know Gotham's latest self-appointed defender than rounding up a few more Intergang tough guys. Batman was still overseas, recovering from the Crisis, but Nightwing knew that Bruce would want a full report on this new Batwoman once he got back to Gotham. This was the Dark Knight's turf after all.

Wonder what her story is, Nightwing thought. Gotham's crime-filled streets seemed to breed masked vigilantes on a regular basis. Besides Batman, there had already been four Robins, two Batgirls, and a Huntress. And who knew what side of the fence Catwoman was working these days. *It's getting so you can't tell the players without a scorecard. . . .*

"Ahem." Batwoman stared pointedly at the hand on her arm.

He smiled and let go. "Nightwing," he introduced himself. New York City was his usual stomping ground these days, but, with Bruce out of town, he had wanted to check on the situation in Gotham himself. "Pleased to meet you."

"Batwoman," she volunteered. Despite being new at this game, she didn't seem at all intimidated by him. Dick admired her confidence.

He looked over her mouthwatering physique, which was

scarcely concealed by her skintight costume. "Yeah," he said in appreciation. "Definitely not a Bat*girl*."

Prone upon the ground, the human cobra tried to slither away. He rustled across a pile of soggy cardboard toward a steaming manhole. Nightwing stepped down on his tail and the serpent hissed angrily. "Guess we should call the cops," he commented to Batwoman. "These freaks are all Intergang, right?"

Since when do mob goons transform into monsters? he mused. That was an ugly new wrinkle where Gotham was concerned. *Clayface and Man-Bat weren't enough for one city?*

"Yes," she confirmed. "They're led by a man named Mannheim." Nightwing nodded, recognizing the name. "I've been trying to find him for the last couple of weeks, but he's gone into hiding." She took out her frustration on the pinned snake-man, kicking the reptile in the head until it stopped wriggling. "I think I scared him."

Nightwing liked her style. "Imagine that."

Mannheim used to run Intergang from Metropolis, he recalled. He wondered what had brought the notorious gangster to Gotham. "If he's the Big Bad, we're going to have to find him." He took it for granted that Batwoman wasn't going to stop hunting Mannheim anytime soon. "I'll start searching in Burnley tomorrow, begin working my way south."

Batman, who tended to be territorial where Gotham was concerned, probably would have told Batwoman to go home and let him handle Intergang, but that wasn't how Dick Grayson worked. His stint in the Teen Titans had taught him the importance of teamwork—and of finding new talent. The way he saw it, the bad guys outnumbered them enough as is. *We can use all the good people we can get.*

Batwoman nodded. "And I'll take Tri-Corner and begin working my way south?"

"Unless you have an objection."

"No." She shook her head and withdrew a grapnel gun from her utility belt. The design was slightly different from the ones used by Batman and his protégés. She fired a grappling hook at an overhanging eave and let a built-in winch carry her up to the rooftops. Nightwing watched her depart, then realized that she had stuck him with cleanup duty. He sighed and extracted a supply of plastic wrist restraints from his gauntlet. He chuckled to himself and set about bagging the mutant menagerie scattered across the icy floor of the alley.

"Nice meeting you too."

WEEK 32.

SAN FRANCISCO.

"ARE we there yet?" the crocodile asked. He covered his eyes with his hands.

"Almost!" Osiris promised as he carried Sobek through the sky. He had named the nervous reptile himself, after the sacred crocodile god of ancient Egypt. Moisture sprayed against their faces as they descended through layers of dense cloud cover before emerging into the sunlight beneath the clinging mist. "Look! There it is!"

Titans Tower rose from an island in the middle of the harbor, within view of the Golden Gate Bridge. Landscaped gardens surrounded the gleaming T-shaped skyscraper, which was home to the world's most famous team of young super heroes: the Teen Titans.

Osiris couldn't wait to meet them.

It was Visitors' Day at the Tower, and throngs of teenagers, tourists, and more than a few adults were lined up to get the heroes' autographs and perhaps have their pictures taken with their favorite Titans. Robin, Beast Boy, Raven, Speedy, Wonder Girl, Cyborg, and Captain Marvel Jr. greeted their fans at the top of a winding stone pathway that led from a ferry dock up to the Tower. A bronze statue of the team's founding members, damaged in the Crisis several months ago, had already been restored. Osiris recognized his fellow heroes from the news. Most of them were teen sidekicks following in the footsteps of their more famous mentors. *Just like me and Black Adam,* he thought. Despite their varied origins, he imagined that he had much in common with the remarkable young people below. *We're sure to be great friends!*

Startled gasps and shouts greeted him as he and Sobek swooped down from the sky. "Hello!" he called out to Beast Boy and the others. "My name is Osiris. I've come to join the Teen Titans."

He deposited Sobek onto the ground in front of the Titans. A plus-sized polyester jogging suit had replaced the tattered rags the crocodile had been wearing when Osiris first found him. He was determined that both he and Sobek would make a good first impression. Nevertheless, frightened tourists and autograph seekers backed away from the large walking crocodile. If not for the reassuring presence of the Teen Titans, he suspected that the petrified mortals would have been fleeing in terror from the menacing reptile in their midst.

"Don't be afraid," he assured the crowd. "This is just Sobek, the talking crocodile." Back in Kahndaq, the palace staff had also been alarmed by Sobek at first. Osiris touched down onto the pathway next to the crocodile. "He's my best friend."

Sobek cowered timidly behind Osiris. "They're still afraid of me."

"They're the Teen Titans," Osiris told the bashful reptile. "They're not scared of anything."

"Yes, they are." Captain Marvel Jr. stepped forward and pointed at Osiris. The golden lightning bolt on his chest matched the one on Osiris' own uniform. "They're scared of you."

"Me?" Osiris said. "That's funny." He was excited to meet his American counterpart again. "My sister speaks highly of you and the rest of the Marvels." He gave little thought to the other youth's accusation. Osiris had seen enough American sitcoms to know that Western teens often teased each other, all in good sport. "I suppose you are joking. . . ."

Captain Marvel Jr. shook his head sadly. "I'm sorry about this, Osiris, but . . ." He looked uncomfortable. "I'm afraid I'm going to have to ask you to leave."

"Leave?" Osiris didn't understand. "But I was hoping I could try out for your team." His eyes searched the faces of the

other Titans, but none of them seemed inclined to challenge
their teammate's decision. "I thought Sobek and I could meet
some more friends. I was hoping you and I . . ." His voice
trailed off as his dreams of friendship seemed to be carried
away by the brisk winter wind.

"I know the changes Black Adam has gone through," Captain Marvel Jr. conceded. "And I know a lot of that has to do
with you and your sister." Osiris heard regret in his voice, but
not uncertainty. His mind was made up. "I was at your sister's
wedding. I saw your family take down Sabbac on Halloween.
But that doesn't change the fact that the head of your family
ripped a man in half on live television in the name of his old-
school brand of justice."

"But I haven't done anything wrong!" Osiris protested. He
couldn't believe how unfair this was. "I've only helped people.
My whole family helps people every day!"

"It's true," Sobek added. "Why, just yesterday Osiris built
a hospital in every village in southern Modora. And he painted
them a lovely shade of green too!"

Osiris appreciated his friend's support. "We're only trying
to make this world a better place."

But as he looked over the faces of the crowd, their suspicious
expressions and fearful postures struck him through the heart
like an enchanted spear. Mothers clung tightly to their children. Scowling visitors clenched their fists, or flinched before
his gaze. Even the other Titans seemed to regard him warily, as
though he might be some sinister super-villain attempting to
infiltrate their ranks. Cyborg's sonic cannon hummed ominously. Speedy, Green Arrow's sidekick, drew an arrow from
her quiver. Wonder Girl unhooked her golden lasso from her
belt. Robin, the Boy Wonder, examined him dubiously. Beast
Boy morphed into a belligerent green gorilla.

Hadn't the Titans been betrayed by a double agent once
before? Osiris vaguely remembered reading about a former
Titan, a girl named Terra, who had turned out to be a wolf in
sheep's clothing. *No wonder they're not willing to trust me!*

At least Captain Marvel Jr. seemed to be taking his pleas

seriously. After mulling it over for a few moments, the American hero extended his hand to Osiris. "Convince the rest of the world of that," he promised, "and I'll help you join the Teen Titans."

Osiris shook the other youth's hand. The deal was less than he had anticipated when he left Kahndaq this morning, but at least it held out some hope for the future. All he needed to do now was find some way to show the world that the Black Marvel Family meant them no harm.

But how on earth was he supposed to do that?

WEEK 33.

GOTHAM CITY.

CHRISTMAS Eve, and the yuletide celebrations were under way in Cathedral Square. A ninety-foot-tall Norway spruce presided over the festivities, its evergreen branches bedecked by over thirty thousand sparkling lights. The magnificent tree was topped by a brand-new Swarovski crystal star, replacing the one Catwoman stole last year. A children's choir, warmly bundled up against the winter chill, serenaded the city with Christmas carols. Their angelic voices rang out across the Square. Last-minute shoppers scurried down the sidewalks, clutching their bags and packages. An avalanche of snowflakes gave all of Gotham a white Christmas.

Batwoman observed the holiday scene from the rooftop of Wayne Tower. Her cape blew in the wind as she took a moment to enjoy the music wafting up from below. *Too bad I can't count on Intergang to take the night off,* she mused. Alas, organized crime was no respecter of holiday traditions—and neither was Bruno Mannheim. *God only knows what kind of perverted holidays are celebrated by the Cult of Crime.*

"Merry Christmas."

The voice startled her, and she spun around to see Nightwing drop lightly onto the snow-covered rooftop. She relaxed and assumed a less aggressive posture, both impressed and dismayed that the masked hero had managed to sneak up on her so easily.

Unlike the Intergang assassin she had dispatched a few minutes ago.

Nightwing glanced down at the unconscious puma-man lying at her feet. The monster's feline muzzle was bloodied. A broken fang rested upon the snow. "Looks like someone is lacking the spirit of the season."

She shrugged. "I think the spirit is upon him now."

Nightwing laughed out loud. "Somehow I doubt that it's visions of sugar plums he's seeing at the moment." He reached behind his back and drew out a small, gift-wrapped package. A bright red bow and ribbon stood out against the metallic green wrapping paper. He held out the present. "For the Bat who has everything."

"Mannheim's address?" she said hopefully.

"Still working on that one," he admitted, handing her the gift. "Go on. Open it."

Batwoman opened the package and peeked inside. A sleek black silhouette rested atop a velvet cushion. "Another Batarang." She lifted the weapon from the box. "How . . . nice."

She hoped she didn't sound too much like a kid who had just gotten socks for Christmas.

"This isn't just another Batarang," he insisted. Her lack of enthusiasm didn't seem to bother him. "This is a *real* Batarang, not one of those homemade models you've been tossing about."

"It's lovely," she dissembled. Embarrassed, she tried to smooth things over. "I don't mean . . ."

He reached out for the Batarang. "Here. Give me." He carefully fingered the weapon, testing its sharpness. "Composite-graphite molded. Unbreakable to ten thousand psi. Laser-honed, never loses its edge." He sounded like a late-night TV huckster extolling the virtues of some new miracle product. "Aerodynamically tested, perfectly balanced, and if you throw it right . . ."

With a flick of his wrist, he sent the Batarang whistling past her head. "Hey!" Batwoman yelped. The spinning missile executed a graceful arc above the Square before swooping back toward Nightwing's waiting fingertips.

"Returning." He plucked the weapon deftly out of the air. "So, no. Not really just another Batarang."

"Wow," Batwoman murmured, genuinely impressed. *Where can I get some more of those things?*

Nightwing handed the Batarang back to her. "Merry Christmas."

She decided not to spoil the moment by explaining that she was Jewish.

THE polished silver menorah gleamed in the window of Kate's apartment as Renee watched the sun come up. Hanukkah had ended the night before. Kate had made a big deal of it, cooking latkes and even laying out jelly doughnuts for dessert. Vic had actually been lucid for most of the meal, even though he hadn't been able to keep any of it down. Kate said she did it because that's how her family celebrated Hanukkah, at least before her dad remarried. That was probably true, but Renee knew that wasn't why she had really done it. Hanukkah was a celebration of a miracle.

And, boy, could we use one of those right now, Renee thought.

"Upon the stair, I met a man who was not there. He was not there again today. I wish to gosh he'd go away."

Vic staggered out of his room, clearly delirious. A fluffy cotton bathrobe failed to conceal just how much he had wasted away over the last few weeks. His gaunt, haggard countenance, with its sunken sockets and cracked lips, was enough to make her miss the blank-faced mask he used to wear. He tottered unsteadily upon his feet. The soles of his slippers shuffled against the carpet.

Lunging forward, he grabbed onto Renee's shoulders. "I've got the answers, Myra!" he said feverishly. His bloodshot eyes stared urgently into hers, but were obviously seeing someone else. "The answer for both of us. It's been so simple, so obvious. Leave Hub City. . . ."

Not for the first time, Renee wondered who this "Myra"

was and what she had once meant to Vic. She was ashamed by how little she knew about the life he'd led before they met. "Charlie . . ." She held on to him gently, afraid that he would fall and hurt himself. His arms felt shockingly light and fragile.

"I know that's what we should do," he insisted. "Mommy told me . . ."

Renee wondered if Vic's mother was even still alive. Hadn't he said something about growing up in an orphanage?

She should have been used to his incoherent rambling by now. He was delirious most of the time these days. It was the only way he could escape the pain. Still, seeing him like this, hearing him converse with phantoms from his past, tore her heart out every time. *It's not fair. He didn't used to be like this.*

"Made out of pseudoderm . . . binder toxic under certain conditions . . . blood poisoning . . ." He ran his bony fingers over his face, as though feeling a mask that wasn't there anymore. "Tot . . . did you know this would happen . . . ?"

"Charlie." She tried to guide him back to his room, but he wasn't hearing her at all. He pulled in the opposite direction. "Let's get you back in bed."

He broke her hold with an elegant jujitsu move. "What's your name? I didn't ever hear your name. . . ."

"It's Renee, Charlie. I'm right here." She wrestled him through the doorway into his room, which was now set up for hospice care. The IV stand and oxygen tanks had been joined by an ample supply of morphine, packaged in disposable syringes. With all the bottled oxygen on hand, she couldn't light up a cigarette even if she still wanted to. A nicotine patch helped keep the craving at bay. "I'm still with you."

Wild eyes locked on hers. For a moment, she thought that maybe he recognized her, but then he shoved her roughly away from him. "I'm sorry. I tried, I really tried. . . . I'm so sorry about Jackie." Weeping, he dropped to his knees at the foot of the bed. Guilt wracked his skeletal features. "I loved her like she was ours, Myra. . . . I loved her like I loved you. . . ."

Renee got down beside him. She wrapped his arm over her shoulders and helped him to his feet, even as he continued to pour out his heart to his long-lost Myra. "I couldn't say it. You could say it, but I never said it. . . ." Tears trickled down his face. "I love you. . . ."

"I love you too," Renee said. She tucked him into bed, making sure the blankets were snug around him. Her weary body dropped into a chair next to the bed. She buried her face in her hands as, exhausted, Vic slowly drifted off to sleep. "Going to play in the snow now. . . ."

Kate appeared in the doorway. She had changed out of her Batwoman gear into a sweater and slacks. Her auburn hair fell past her shoulders. Renee looked up from the chair. *I didn't even hear her come in.*

From the sound of Vic's labored breathing, she guessed that he was down for a while. Moving quietly, so as not to wake him, she joined Kate in the living room. Utterly drained, but too distraught to sleep, she plopped down onto the Italian leather couch in front of the picture window. Kate placed a steaming mug on the platinum/silver coffee table. "Some hot cider might make you feel better," she suggested.

"Only if you added some bourbon to it," Renee said dryly.

Kate shrugged. "I didn't, but I can if you like." She reached for the mug.

"No." Renee pushed her hand away from the cider. Seeking refuge in a bottle wasn't going to do Vic any good; her sojourn in Nanda Parbat had taught her that much. "Seems that all the problems I have when I start drinking are still there when I stop."

Kate sat down beside her, close enough that Renee could lean against her. "You gave him peace. You should be glad for that."

"I am," Renee said. "I just wish I could get a little for myself."

Kate gazed at her, her captivating brown eyes full of sympathy. Reaching out, she gently lifted Renee's chin and bent her head down. Her lips found Renee's, and the two women shared a tender kiss. Over a decade had passed since the last time they'd done this, but, for the moment, Kate's lips were just as warm and welcoming as before. *What does this mean?* Renee wondered briefly, then decided not to worry about it. Right now, it was enough that Kate was here for her. Renee closed her eyes and surrendered to the moment.

"It stopped snowing," Kate said when they finally came apart. Renee rested her head on Kate's shoulder as they cuddled on the couch. The early-morning sunlight glinted off the silver menorah in the window. Candle flames flickered warmly.

"Merry Christmas, Renee."

METROPOLIS.

ICE-skaters looked up in amazement as the Black Marvel Family soared over the Centennial Park skating rink on their way to the Kahndaqi embassy. Christmas decorations adorned the facades of the buildings ahead. Black Adam recalled his last visit to the embassy, when he had executed Rough House before a mob of reporters and demonstrators. Today's excursion had a very different agenda, about which he had serious reservations.

"I remain unconvinced of the wisdom of this move," he said grimly. Leaving the park behind, they flew above snow-covered streets.

"But you've seen the way people look at us outside Kahndaq," Osiris reminded him. Sobek dangled below Osiris as the boy carried the crocodile along with them. Afraid of heights, Sobek covered his eyes with his scaly forefeet. His tail swished nervously. "They're afraid of us! Everywhere we go, the people say terrible things about us. I thought Sobek was going to cry when the Teen Titans wouldn't let us join their team!"

Isis sympathized with her brother and his pet. "A crocodile's tears are nothing to ignore, Adam," she advised her husband.

"Please, Adam," Osiris begged. "Captain Marvel Jr. said I can join the Titans—*if* we can convince the world you've changed."

Black Adam scowled. What did he care of the world's opinion? *I have nothing to apologize for.*

Isis seemed to read his mind. "You tore a man apart on live TV. Rough House was a criminal, but he was still a man. As a result, and because of your efforts to build a power base to oppose the West, you have made many enemies."

"None I cannot defend myself against," he insisted.

"But your enemies have become mine and Osiris'." She glanced over at the innocent youth, who smiled cheerfully at the gaping pedestrians below. A few Americans smiled back, but most shrunk away in fear from the flying boy and the fearsome-looking crocodile. "Do you think he can handle that? And more importantly, should he have to?"

Adam looked at Osiris as well. Perhaps his wife had a point. Was it fair that the carefree youth should be ostracized because of the actions of another? *I have chosen to wage war on evil, regardless of the consequences, but Osiris should be free to forge his own destiny . . . and reputation.*

A large dais had been erected in front of the embassy gates. Kahndaqi flags festooned the stage, while a festive wreath acknowledged that it was Christmas Day in the eyes of the Americans. Despite the holiday, a large crowd had gathered outside the embassy. As during his appearance here last summer, throngs of reporters and protestors were held back by police barricades and security personnel. Unlike before, however, Black Adam saw a few signs in support of his recent activities. WE ♥ ISIS! read one homemade banner. On the other hand, a sign denouncing MAGICAL TERRORISM proved that not everyone had been won over by his family's humanitarian efforts.

He was surprised at the sheer size of the crowd. "Who invited all these people?"

"I did," Isis explained. "The world will see us all as monsters unless we show them otherwise." Her kohl-lined eyes implored him. "For Osiris, Adam."

Reluctantly, he joined his family as they descended toward the stage. Sobek gratefully dropped onto the dais, while the Black Marvel Family hovered in the air a few feet above the platform. Frowning, Adam crossed his arms atop his chest.

"This will cause him great pain," Adam reminded Isis.

"It's okay. I'm ready," Osiris insisted. An aide from the embassy pushed a wheelchair beneath the boy. "I'm ready to show the world!"

"And he does it with a smile," Isis observed proudly. She beamed at Adam. "So can we."

Very well, he resolved. *If this is what my family truly desires, I shall not deny them this chance at happiness.* He owed them that much, for all the joy and satisfaction they had brought into his own life. He raised his voice to address the crowd:

"I have come here today—I have brought my family here today—to show you that underneath the powers of gods long neglected, we are as human as the rest of you." He nodded at Isis and Osiris, who smiled back at him. As one, they recited the magic words that transformed each of them.

"Shazam!"

"Black Adam!"

"Oh Mighty Isis!"

Mystical lightning bolts struck in unison, brighter than any artificial Christmas star. The audience gasped in wonder. Sobek recoiled from a spray of magical sparks. Thunder echoed through the concrete canyons of Metropolis.

When the blinding glare faded, Black Adam and his family no longer levitated above the stage. Instead they stood upon the wooden platform like the mere mortals they had become. Adrianna's gossamer raiment had transformed into a simple cotton dress, while Teth-Adam was clad in the loincloth and striped head cloth of an ancient Egyptian pharaoh. Amon sagged pitifully within the confines of his wheelchair, his mangled limbs no longer capable of supporting his weight. He grimaced in pain, but did not complain. Adam was impressed by the boy's courage.

Their meager garments were ill-suited to the cold of winter. Adam shivered and placed an arm around Isis to warm her. "I realize that it will be very difficult for most of you to look beyond my harsh actions on these grounds many months ago, but let the coming new year mark a new beginning between Kahndaq and the West, one of mutual respect and assistance. My family and I pledge to be worthy of your trust."

A smattering of cheers and applause greeted his declaration. Not everyone in the crowd reacted so positively, but Teth-Adam saw many more friendly faces than he ever would have anticipated. Although he felt uncomfortable being so vulnerable before the world, perhaps this was not such a futile effort after all?

"Thank you," Adrianna whispered as she held him close.

The day was cold, but his heart felt surprisingly warm.

TERREBONNE PARISH. ## LOUISIANA.

BELLE Reve Federal Prison, hidden away in a muggy, alligator-infested bayou, was more than just a maximum-security holding facility for superpowered criminals. It was also the unofficial headquarters of a black-ops government task force code-named "the Suicide Squad."

"Worthy of your trust."

Live coverage of the media event at the Kahndaqi embassy played upon a large flat-screen monitor mounted to the wall of a soundproof chamber deep inside the prison. Black Adam's stirring oration emerged from the speakers. Atom-Smasher recognized Adam's distinctive accent and cadences.

"Listen to him, Waller." Al Rothstein was a former member of the Justice Society of America, now serving time for taking the law into his own hands. A featureless blue hood concealed his face. A stylized atomic diagram was embroidered upon the chest of his dark red tunic. "He's changed."

Amanda Waller snorted in derision. A heavyset black woman in a business suit, she ran the Suicide Squad with an iron grip. "Because he's settling down? Do you really believe a wife, a kid brother, and a talking reptile have turned this magical dictator into a peace-loving preacher?" She shook her head at Atom-Smasher's naïveté. "You were there when he 'liberated' Kahndaq."

Al nodded. In fact, he had fought beside Adam in that struggle, before he'd decided to turn himself in for the crimes he had committed while allied with Adam. "And back then he *never* let anyone see him in his human form."

"So you expect the boys in Washington to breathe a sigh of relief because he's standing onstage in his underwear?" Her mind was clearly made up, and not in Adam's favor. "He's the most powerful international terrorist in the world. He *has* to be brought in."

A third voice entered the discussion, one with a pronounced Eastern European accent. "And now we know he has a weakness. His entire family does."

"Everyone has a weakness," Waller declared. "That's why all of you ended up in Belle Reve."

"But we signed the papers," a fourth voice protested. An Australian accent colored the indignant words. "We join your little team, do this errand, and our life sentences vanish like lightning."

A gleaming metal boomerang whizzed past Waller's head. It ricocheted off the monitor screen before zipping past her again.

Waller didn't even blink. "I heard you were smart," she said scornfully. "I still don't see it."

"You will, gorgeous." The missile returned to its owner's waiting fingers. Captain Boomerang, a cocky red-haired rogue wearing a black leather jacket and his trademark blue scarf, loitered alongside the other inmates Waller had recruited for this mission: Plastique, Count Vertigo, the Persuader, and the Electrocutioner. "As soon as the Suicide Squad wish the Black Marvel Family a happy bloody holiday."

WEEK 34.

NORTHERN CALIFORNIA.

"I see them," Count Vertigo reported. He employed a pair of high-powered binoculars to spy on Black Adam and Isis as they flew over Redwood National Forest. His green velvet cloak swept the mossy floor of the forest. The verdant canopy of the trees concealed him from view. Fog drifted through the lower reaches of the vast redwoods. "Intel was right. They're coming to meet him after his first day at Titans Tower and they're . . ." He hesitated, as though taken aback by what he saw.

"They're what, Vertigo?" Amanda Waller demanded via a comm-link. The mastermind behind the task force was monitoring the operation from her headquarters back at Belle Reve.

"They're holding hands," he divulged. Soaring above the towering sequoias, the romantic couple hardly looked like threats to world peace. Count Werner Vertigo felt a twinge of sympathy for Black Adam; the rightful heir to the throne of his own native Vlatavia, he identified with the forbidding Arab monarch. *But mine is not to reason why,* he thought bitterly. He was only a convict now, not a king. Amanda Waller was calling the shots today.

"Do you have a visual on the boy and his pet yet, Boomerbutt?" she asked another of her operatives.

"Quit calling me that," the young man protested. Over a dozen specialized boomerangs were tucked into the man's belt and jacket pouches. A long blue scarf was draped over his shoulder. He swaggered through the underbrush.

"'Cause 'Captain Boomerang' is so much classier," chortled

a burly figure clad head to toe in futuristic steel armor. His metal gauntlets gripped the haft of a glowing Atomic Axe.

"Shut up, Persuader," Boomerang snapped at his teammate. Extracting a polished silver boomerang from a pouch, he sent it spinning into the trunk of a venerable redwood, where it lodged in the tree's thick bark. Intricate circuitry flashed along the length of the boomerang. "Osiris and Sobek left the Tower five minutes ago," he informed Waller. "They're still in range, but my electromagnetic boomerang will jam their Titans communicators."

"Good," Waller replied. Miniature earpieces conveyed her voice to the entire team. "Then it's up to Plastique and the Electrocutioner to start the fire and give Atom-Smasher his opening."

"We're on it," the Electrocutioner agreed. A black bandanna, with two matching eyeholes, covered the upper half of his face like a mask. His insulated red costume was wired to deliver lethal electrical charges via his metallic copper gloves. "Just remember our deal. We bring in the Black Marvels and our records go clean."

"So what are you waiting for, lover?" Plastique asked. Her hot pink PVC bodysuit gave no hint of the massive explosive energies at her command. Long red hair cascaded over her shoulders. A French Canadian accent testified to her past as a Quebecois terrorist. "I'm the explosive. You're the detonator." She gave him a saucy wink. "Tickle me."

The Electrocutioner grinned back at her. High-voltage sparks crackled around his fingertips. "Yeah, baby!"

He reached out to touch her. . . .

"ADAM! Isis!"

Osiris called out to his family as he saw them flying toward him. His spirits were as high as his altitude, many feet above the treetops. He carried Sobek beneath him, holding on to the crocodile with both hands. The shredded state of Sobek's jogging suit hinted at a furious battle.

"Osiris!" his sister greeted him. "How was your first day?"

"Unbelievable!" he enthused. "Robin gave us a tour. I have my own locker *and* my own Titans communicator!"

Sobek climbed onto his friend's shoulders, having seemingly overcome his fear of heights. "And after we helped Kid Eternity stop the Keeper's plan for controlling the dead, Raven conjured up some wonderful ham and cheese sandwiches for lunch!"

"Sobek ate twelve," Osiris said.

Isis laughed at the crocodile's appetite. "Oh, Sobek."

"Despite our demonstration last week," Black Adam observed cautiously, "many are still condemning my actions in and out of Kahndaq."

It was typical of Black Adam to add a somber note to the conversation, but Osiris chose not to begrudge his brother-in-law his dour attitude. He appreciated everything Adam had already done on his behalf. "Your speech was enough for the Titans to give me a shot." Captain Marvel Jr. had been true to his word, arguing for Osiris' admission to the team. "The world will come around. They'll see all the good we're going to do."

The happy family hovered in midair . . . until a sudden explosion blasted them apart. Stunned by the shock wave, they plummeted toward the forest below. A giant hand snatched Black Adam out of the sky. A gigantic figure expanded in height, until he towered over the mighty redwoods.

"We need to talk, Adam," Atom-Smasher boomed.

"ALBERT?" Black Adam gasped as the colossal fingers closed around him. Dazed by the explosion, he struggled in vain to escape the giant's grip. The Brobdingnagian fist squeezed him like a vise. "What are you doing here?"

"I'm doing what I have to, Adam." His rueful tone made it clear that he took no pleasure in attacking his former comrade. "You can't ignore what you've done in the past. You need to turn yourself in."

He slammed Black Adam down onto the floor of the forest,

over three hundred feet below. The thick mulch covering the ground did little to soften the impact of the blow. Ignited by the explosion, a wildfire spread across the woods, feeding on the dense carpet of mosses and lichens. Frightened birds and animals fled from the flames. Smoke rose from burning shrubs and trees.

Anger flared inside Adam as he rocketed out from beneath Atom-Smasher's hand. A titanic blow sent the oversized hero tumbling backward, toppling a stand of giant sequoias, many of which were almost as old as Black Adam himself. Massive redwoods snapped like twigs. The wanton destruction of the ancient trees only enraged Adam more.

"I will not turn myself in to a hypocritical government to be judged as you have. To rot in a cell while there is still so much work to be done." He had been greatly disappointed in Albert Rothstein when the American had let his squeamish conscience undermine his resolve. Black Adam had no intention of making the same mistake.

"Murder is a sin that can't be washed away," Atom-Smasher insisted. A gargantuan hand reached out for Adam, who dodged the hand with the speed of Heru. He flew out of range of the log-sized fingers.

"I have already asked for forgiveness," Adam said. "In some eyes, that is enough."

Climbing back onto his feet, Atom-Smasher rose to his full height once more. Over sixty stories tall, he loomed like a colossus over the foggy old-growth forest. Fists as large as boulders were raised menacingly. "I don't want to hurt you."

"Albert," Black Adam warned him, "you won't."

He drew back his fist.

OSIRIS landed hard upon the forest floor. The fall alone would have killed any ordinary mortal; only his god-given endurance had ensured his survival. His ears were ringing as he slowly sat up amidst the squashed ferns and fungi. Scorch marks defaced his uniform. Green-tinted sunlight filtered through the dense canopy overhead. Firs and hemlocks were interspersed between the sky-high sequoias. Smoke tickled in his nostrils. He looked about in confusion, unclear what had befallen him. *Are we under attack?*

He spotted Sobek sprawled upon the ground nearby. To his relief, the crocodile appeared to be in one piece as well. Groaning, Sobek massaged his bleeding snout. The explosion had blown away most of his clothing; only a few raggedy scraps clung to his scaly body. His tail twitched spasmodically.

What about Isis and Adam? Osiris fretted. He heard a rustling in the bushes and looked up hopefully, only to see a trio of villains advancing on him instead. He recognized them from the Titans data files Captain Marvel Jr. had e-mailed to him prior to the meeting. The wisdom of Zehuti allowed Osiris to swiftly pluck the renegades' names from his memory.

"There's the kid and his monster," the Electrocutioner snarled at his cohorts. Lightning arced between his outstretched fingertips.

"Suicide Squad's job doesn't include animal control," Plastique objected. Was she the source of the explosion that had knocked them out of the sky? Her file said that she had reformed, but clearly that information was out-of-date.

Captain Boomerang shrugged. "So cook the croc," he said callously.

Plastique aimed one hand at Sobek and beckoned to the Electrocutioner with the other. *No!* Osiris thought, determined to save his friend. He leaped to his feet, but his legs felt like rubber and darkness encroached on his vision. He could barely stand up, let alone come to Sobek's rescue. Plastique was about to kill his best friend and there was nothing he could do!

Before the scarlet-haired terrorist could unleash her destructive blast, however, an immense shadow suddenly fell over the misty grove. Looking up, she yelped in alarm and dived out of the wave just as an enormous body came crashing to the ground. A tremor shook the ground. Fallen logs and leafy redwood sorrels were flattened beneath the fallen Goliath.

Apparently unconscious, Atom-Smasher lay supine across several acres of woodlands. His mammoth chest rose and fell steadily.

"Oh, hell," Plastique swore. Her azure eyes widened as she spotted Captain Boomerang flat on the ground as well. The Australian's right leg was crushed beneath Atom-Smasher's huge skull. An unflung boomerang rested on the mossy sward just beyond his limp fingers. Several more weapons were scattered all around him. He looked dead to the world. "Boomerang?"

The cause of the giant's downfall became clear as Black Adam descended from the sky. His arms crossed atop his chest, he gazed down sternly at the unworthy miscreants who had ambushed his family. His voice was cold and unforgiving. "If you have hurt the boy . . ."

"Adam!" Osiris cried out, fearing that his brother's righteous fury would undo all the work they had done to win the world's trust. "Please don't kill them. . . ."

His desperate plea distracted Black Adam long enough for Plastique and the Electrocutioner to launch another attack. "Tickle, tickle," the male villain said with a smirk. His sparking fingers caressed Plastique's shoulder.

A deafening explosion sent Osiris, Adam, and Sobek flying across the woods.

Not far away, Isis confronted the Persuader. "The trees are crying out," she accused. She could hear Nature itself screaming inside her head. The largest and oldest of the redwoods would likely survive the blaze, thanks to their hard outer bark, but the rest of the forest was being burned alive. A flock of panicked wrens and thrushes flapped wildly through the flaming branches above her. She called on the wind to keep the harsh, black smoke away from her.

"You some kind of Greenpeace fanatic?" the armored villain growled. He swung his Atomic Axe at Isis, scarring the burled trunks of the redwoods as he tried to connect with the Egyptian heroine.

Her superhuman speed and agility kept her one step ahead

of the slashing blade. "That axe is radioactive," she sensed. "It is poisoning the very air around us." Thick roots burst from the ground at her command, snaring the Persuader and the axe. He fought to hold on to his weapon as the gnarled roots sought to wrench it from his grasp. "But the roots of these mighty trees will bury it far beneath the earth where it will do no harm."

But a sudden wave of dizziness overcame her, causing her to drop to her knees. Her command over the roots weakened as she lost all sense of balance. The shrieking forest seemed to spin around her. Nausea gripped her and she clenched her jaws to keep from vomiting. *I don't understand,* she thought. *What's happening to me?*

Count Vertigo came floating down from the sky, looking as though he was walking down an invisible staircase. His voluminous cloak rippled behind him as he descended toward Isis, who realized that the masked villain was somehow inducing her illness. "My dear princess. The surveillance photos don't do you justice." He sounded amused by the sight of her kneeling before him. "You truly are lovely."

"Back off, Count!" the Persuader shouted. He hacked himself free of the tangled roots and charged at Isis. His swinging axe drove Vertigo back. "The tree hugger is mine!"

Osiris lifted his head from the mulch and looked around groggily. The Electrocutioner went flying past him as Black Adam broke up the lethal twosome who had blasted them only moments ago. Plastique directed her remaining energies at Adam, but the explosive bursts only seemed to be slowing him down. *Are we winning,* Osiris tried to figure out, *or are we still outnumbered?* The pervasive smoke and greenery made it hard to tell just how many foes were arrayed against them.

He reached for his Titans communicator to summon reinforcements, only to find a handful of shattered pieces strewn upon the ground around him. "No," he realized. "It's broken. . . ."

An agonized scream came from only a few yards away. "Adrianna!" he cried out, recognizing his sister's voice. Peering through the smoke, he glimpsed Isis scrambling across the ground on all fours, pursued by an armored attacker wielding an enormous glowing axe. She threw up an arm to protect herself and the sharpened edge of the axe sliced through one of her golden bracelets. Her skin sizzled as the irradiated blade cut a deep gash down her arm. A crimson stream gushed from the wound. Pain showed upon her face, which had a sickly greenish tint to it. She looked sick as well as injured.

"They wanted you all alive," the Persuader divulged. He smacked the blunt end of the axe handle into Isis' jaw. Blood sprayed from her lips. He lowered his steel boot onto her back, pressing her face down into the mulch. "But screw that. This is too much fun."

He raised the Atomic Axe high above his head. Osiris realized in horror that the villain was only seconds away from chopping Isis' head off.

"Leave my sister alone!" He launched himself at the Persuader like a missile, his fists out in front of him. Without even thinking about it, he flew straight *through* the armor-clad criminal, tearing the man's body in half. Steel, flesh, and bone came apart noisily. Gory entrails splattered the grove in all directions. The sundered halves of the Persuader's corpse twitched upon the blood-soaked duff before falling still forever.

It took Osiris a moment or two to grasp what he had just done. He slammed to a halt against the trunk of a sturdy sequoia, then turned around to inspect the damage. The first thing he saw was the upper portion of the Persuader's torso, lying lifelessly on the ground. The assassin's hands were still wrapped around the haft of his axe.

By the gods, Osiris thought, aghast at the carnage. *I didn't mean . . . I never meant to . . .* He felt sick to his stomach. He was a killer now . . . just like Black Adam. This was exactly what he had begged Adam *not* to do.

A horrified gasp came from overhead. Osiris looked up to see Count Vertigo floating above the grisly scene. Gore streaked the man's emerald costume. His face was pale behind his mask. Swallowing hard, Vertigo retreated in a hurry, fleeing into the secluded depths of the forest. Osiris let him go. He stared down at his crimson fists, which were slick with the dead man's blood and juices.

Sobek staggered out of the bushes. His vertical pupils widened at the awful sight before him. "Oh dear," the crocodile murmured.

Osiris dropped to his knees beside the Persuader's remains. "You should've . . . you should've left my sister alone!" He buried his face in his hands, his anguished soul crying out in torment. "I wanted to do good. . . ."

Isis laid a gentle hand upon his shoulder. No longer ill, she ignored her own injuries as she sought to comfort her brother. A heavy rain began to fall, as though the heavens themselves were weeping at the tragic chain of events. The downpour swiftly doused the wildfire engulfing the forest.

He looked up at her with tears in his eyes. Isis gazed down at him with compassion, refusing to judge him. But her understanding did little to ease his guilty conscience, even as she knelt to embrace him. He wept against his sister's shoulder, while Sobek looked on helplessly. The crocodile wrung his hands.

Black Adam landed nearby. He flung Plastique's and the Electrocutioner's unconscious bodies onto the ground at his feet. His somber eyes took in the heartbreaking tableau before him.

"Let's go home," he stated simply.

Sobek looked surprised at Adam's muted response, like the crocodile had expected Adam to execute the rest of their attackers on the spot. "But . . ."

"Before anyone else gets hurt," Adam said.

HIDDEN in the underbrush, Count Vertigo breathed a sigh of relief as he watched the Black Marvel Family fly away. The pouring rain mercifully washed the Persuader's blood from his sodden garments.

"They're leaving," he reported.

"That's all right, Vertigo," Amanda Waller replied from

Louisiana. "I never expected the Suicide Squad to actually bring them in. I got what I really needed." Her smug voice held not a trace of remorse for Cole Parker, aka the Persuader. "Video feeds were live and recording."

Vertigo shivered in the rain. He was no saint, but even he was appalled at the woman's cold-bloodedness.

"We pushed the Black Marvels, and they pushed back," Waller said, summing up the mission. "Now we know what they're *really* capable of."

WEEK 35.

METROPOLIS.

CLARK winced as the hypodermic needle pierced his skin. It was an unfamiliar sensation; less than a year ago, the needle would have snapped against his invulnerable flesh. But he still hadn't recovered from the Crisis, which went a long way toward explaining his current predicament.

He sat tied to a chair, his arms cuffed behind his back. He strained futilely against the bonds, which were more than enough to restrain him in his depleted state. His groans echoed off the soundproof walls of a cell in some undisclosed location. A polygraph was attached to his arms and temples. Two burly thugs watched him with sullen expressions, on hand just in case he managed to get loose somehow. They looked unhappy to be spending New Year's Eve this way. Clark wondered if Lois and the others even knew he was missing yet.

"What's that?" he asked as a third man slid the needle out of Clark's arm. "Sodium pentathol?"

His interrogator, a bald-headed Asian man in a business suit, chuckled at the suggestion. "You're mired in the past, Mr. Kent." He placed the syringe down on a metal tray. "That was gaeamytal. It's as close as modern chemistry can come to synthesizing the unique atomic structure of Wonder Woman's lasso." Clark broke out in a sweat. He felt queasy, like there was kryptonite nearby. "Highly experimental as truth serums go; but then, we only have one question for you. One to which you will certainly know the answer, since it concerns the secret identity of your good friend Superman."

Clark's heart sank. Even if his powers were intact, he wasn't sure he could resist any serum that mimicked the magical properties of Diana's golden lasso. He tried to clench his jaws shut, but the drugged muscles refused to respond. His secret was already poised at the tip of his tongue. Was this the day his enemies finally learned that Clark Kent and Superman were one and the same? *I don't know how to stop this!*

To his surprise, the interrogator held up a color photo of Supernova. "Tell me, Mr. Kent. Why is the Man of Steel masquerading as Supernova?"

Relief flooded Clark's system. He laughed out loud.

The Asian man scowled. This was clearly not the reaction he had been hoping for. "We're quite serious, Mr. Kent."

"That's what makes it so funny," Clark explained. "Gentlemen, I have absolutely no idea who's under that mask, but the one thing I do know for certain is this: He is *not* Superman."

And that was nothing but the truth.

"NEUROSENSORS verify that Kent's not lying, Mr. Mannheim."

Bruno watched the interrogation via a closed-circuit camera from his office in Gotham City. Dr. Kim, the Intergang scientist in charge of the operation, reported to Mannheim over the screen. He tugged nervously at his collar.

"The *Daily Planet* has been using Kent to get exclusive coverage of Supernova," Kim insisted. "There's no better source of information."

Mannheim frowned. This entire exercise had been a waste of time and resources. "Drug Kent," he instructed sourly. "Take him back to his home and let him believe he was interrogated by LexCorp." He drummed his beefy fingertips against the top of his desk. "He's of no further use to us."

Kim nodded. "You were so sure. . . ."

Don't remind me, Mannheim thought irritably. He had been all but certain that Supernova was actually Superman in disguise. But apparently that wasn't the case. . . .

"Shut up," he snarled. "And destroy all the evidence."

He cut off the transmission.

WEEK 36.

GOTHAM CITY.

THIS was the death watch now.

They had moved Vic into Saint Luke's Hospital shortly before New Year's, after a nerve-shattering seizure had forced Renee to call the paramedics. Now, thanks to Kate, he was installed in a private room in St. Luke's hospice ward. Renee kept vigil at his bedside, watching him bounce between delirium and agony. Only the morphine kept him from screaming.

"Said take five, Freddie Freeloader, said . . . that's not the cheese, Izzy, that's . . . no, I'm doing . . . all right . . . baby baby baby blues in green . . ."

Renee's eyes teared up. She barely recognized him anymore. A month ago he'd been Vic Sage . . . "Charlie." He'd been funny and smart and a royal pain in the ass. *He was my best friend in the world,* she thought. *Then the cancer got busy.*

"How high is the moon? Huh? Tell me, butterfly. . . ."

She had thought about ending it, about shooting him so full of morphine that he'd just go to sleep and never wake up. But she knew what he'd say if she could ask him if that was what he wanted.

He'd say no.

It's the last big question for him, she realized. *He wouldn't want to miss this. And I'm not going to take it from him.*

Instead she leaned over and brushed the hair away from his eyes. His head lolled forward, his jaw hanging open slackly. Stubble showed beneath the nasal cannula assisting his breathing. Electronic hardware monitored his vital signs. An IV bag

kept him hydrated. A vase of fresh flowers rested on a nightstand, next to a portable CD player. The air smelled of bleach
and antiseptic.

Renee placed his head back against his pillow. An unread
issue of *Congo Bill World Travel* lay open on her lap. The cover
story promised rare photos of Africa's famed Gorilla City, but
Renee couldn't get past the contents page. A cardboard mail-
ing box, liberally covered with stamps and postage marks from
all over the world, sat on the floor by her feet. Similar boxes
were stacked over by the windowsill. An opened envelope
rested atop the latest box. Unable to concentrate on her magazine, she picked up the envelope and skimmed part of the letter
inside:

> though whether this was due to removing them from Nanda
> Parbat or from the depredations of the postal service, I can
> only hope it is the latter. In any event, I have made another
> trip to the sacred gardens of Rama Kushna. As I said in my
> last missive, the flowers enclosed are known to the monks
> for their remarkable curative properties. . . .

Tot's handwriting was as precise and legible as ever. Not
that this was likely to do Vic any good. She picked up the box
and tilted it toward her, so that its desiccated contents poured
into her waiting palm. Instead of magical blooms, crinkly
brown powder spilled through her fingers.

Same old story, she thought bitterly. Tot kept sending the
flowers in vain, hoping they would survive long enough to help
Vic. But they didn't. Outside of Nanda Parbat, their days were
numbered. She glanced at the stack of boxes by the window.
Outside of Nanda Parbat, all of the flowers had crumbled to
dust.

Wait a second. . . .

She stiffened as a flash of inspiration, or maybe madness,
hit her. She clenched her fist so tightly that not a grain of
powder escaped. A look of utter determination came over her

face, transforming her weary features. She nodded to herself as a crazy idea drove all other considerations out of her head.

Outside Nanda Parbat, the flowers were no good.

But inside . . . ?

SHIRUTA.

THE blurry surveillance photo showed Osiris plowing straight through the Persuader in a gory eruption of blood and guts. No one knew who exactly had leaked the photo to the media, but the world's press had given it front-page coverage, including Kahndaq's own Arabic newspapers. Osiris stared bleakly at the damning photo. Even now, two weeks later, part of him still couldn't accept that the killer in the picture was actually him.

But it is me, he acknowledged guiltily. *I really did that. I killed a man. Tore him in half without even thinking about it.*

If only it wasn't so!

He sat alone in his bedroom in the palace. The lights were off, but sunlight filtered through the lattice window from outside. An uneaten meal rested by the door, waiting for the servants to spirit it away. He had barely left his room since returning from America. Captain Marvel Jr. had tried to see him, but Osiris had sent him away. He couldn't face Freddy or any of the other Titans, not after what he'd done. He just wanted to be left alone.

"Osiris?"

Sobek nervously peeked into the room.

"I don't want to talk," Osiris told the lurking crocodile.

Sobek entered anyway, bearing an armload of shiny red apples. "Do you w-want something to eat? I picked these wonderful apples from your sister's garden." One of the fruits tumbled from the pile and bounced across the floor. "They're as sweet as honey!"

Osiris couldn't care less about the apples. He glumly

tossed the newspaper onto his bed. "Adam said it was an ambush, that someone sent those super-villains to try and provoke us." Angry tears spilled from his eyes. "They wanted to show the world that we are nothing more than a family of sadistic murderers!"

"Who would do something so mean?" Sobek asked. His scratched his scaly head. "But you were just trying to save your sister. The world will understand that eventually."

"No, they won't!" Osiris insisted. "They were already afraid of us, even before this happened." The awful truth hit him with the force of a thunderbolt. "They *hate* us, Sobek! And no matter what we ever do, the entire world will always hate us!"

Sobek's head slumped. Unable to refute the anguished teen's argument, he could only hold out a solitary apple. "I don't hate you."

Osiris smiled sadly, grateful for the crocodile's friendship. He took the apple from the reptile's claws. "Thank you, Sobek."

GOTHAM CITY.

"This is a bad idea," Kate said.

A faux shearling jacket shielded her from the wet, heavy snow coming down in buckets onto the small private airfield. A chartered medical transport jet, about the size of a small Learjet, was parked on the icy tarmac, several yards away from the sleek black limo that had conveyed them here, despite the hazardous road conditions. The ambulance from St. Luke's had already departed. Concern showed upon Kate's strikingly beautiful face.

Renee shrugged. She opened a foam-lined metal case and counted the syringes inside one more time. She didn't want to run out of morphine before she and Vic reached their destination. Her own winter gear was considerably less stylish than

Kate's, consisting of nothing more than a rumpled down parka, gloves, and a pair of snow boots.

"Charlie's almost dead as is," she replied. She closed the case and stuffed it back into her duffel bag. "There's not a hell of a lot I can do to make that worse."

"I'm not talking about him." Kate reached out and placed her hand on Renee's arm. "I'm talking about you . . . and I'm thinking this looks an awful lot like denial."

"No," Renee said fiercely, shaking off Kate's grip. "Not denial. *Defiance*." She hoisted the bulging duffel bag onto her shoulder and tried to make the other woman understand. "I've lost too many people, Kate."

That wasn't good enough for Kate. "The jet will only take you so far! There are no flights where you're going! No roads!" She grew visibly frustrated as she tried to talk Renee out of her insane itinerary. "You can't hike a dying man up the Himalayas in the middle of the winter!" She was almost pleading now. "The weather alone could kill you both!"

"I know," Renee admitted. She started to turn away from Kate. Vic had already been loaded onto the jet. The sooner they got going, the better her chances were of getting him back to Nanda Parbat in time.

Kate grabbed onto her arm again, harder this time. "Renee, please! Stay with me, help me fight Mannheim." Melting snowflakes glistened like tears upon her ruddy cheeks. "I just got you back in my life. I don't want you walking out again!"

I don't want to, Renee thought fervently. Reuniting with Kate had been the only bright spot in these last few weeks. Her lips still held the memory of that magical kiss on Christmas morning. *But I don't have any choice.*

"He saved me, Kate. He pulled me out of self-pity and despair. I owe him my life." She gently pried Kate's fingers away from her arm. "If there's even a chance that getting Charlie back to Nanda Parbat will save him, then I'll do it . . . or die trying."

She gazed into Kate's moist brown eyes. This was farewell, maybe forever. She leaned forward and kissed the other woman passionately. Defying the freezing temperature, they hungrily shared each other's warmth. A long moment passed before Renee reluctantly pulled away from her long-lost love. She heard Kate choke back a sob.

"Good-bye," she said and headed for the plane.

WEEK 37.

SOMEWHERE.

"BROKEN is time!"

Rip Hunter threw up his hands in frustration. Glowing white crystals, embedded in the walls and ceiling, illuminated the futuristic laboratory. Bright red sunlight shone through an open window. A flying motorcycle zipped past the window, but Hunter paid it no heed. Instead he paced restlessly across the lab. His bloodshot eyes had a manic gleam. Stubble carpeted his haggard face. His disorderly blond hair looked like it hadn't been combed in weeks, relativistically speaking. His attire reflected a mishmash of diverse eras, so that he wore a vintage World War I bomber jacket over a skintight twenty-third-century space suit. Army boots from Valley Forge stomped across the floor.

"Find can't the right power source for chronosphere the!" Years of time-travel had left him with a kind of temporal Tourette's syndrome. But though the words were scrambled, his impatient tone came through loud and clear. He swept a stack of notes and computer disks off the desk before him, scattering his work onto the floor.

"I've brought everything you asked for," Supernova insisted. He gestured at a nearby workstation, where the fruits of his prospecting were laid out atop a cluttered plasteel counter: Lex Luthor's kryptonite gauntlet, Starman's stellar energy rod, the Shadow Thief's dimensiometer, the radioactive cocoon from Doctor Sivana's abandoned laboratory, an Nth Metal harness, an uncharged power ring, and various other artifacts of

Earth's super-heroic age. He placed an absorbacon headset, salvaged from a crashed Thanagarian warship, onto the counter beside the other relics. "Can't you make something out of them?"

Hunter snatched up the headset and angrily hurled it at the Flash's cosmic treadmill. The alien learning device ricocheted off the treadmill and clanged onto the floor. The treadmill toppled over onto its side. "S'gnhton working!" he shouted. "Nothing!"

"Rip, calm down!" Supernova pleaded. "It's tough enough understanding you when you're linear!"

The distraught scientist struggled to compose himself. "You're thgir." With effort, he spit out the syllables in something resembling chronological order. "I apol-lo-lo-gize. But we. Can't fight. Him yet. What if he sdnifs . . . *finds* . . . us before we're rrrReady?"

"You're Rip Hunter," Supernova assured him. "You're the Time Master." To his relief, the other man no longer sounded like Zatanna on a bender. "I won't worry about deadlines if you can just stay focused."

He wandered over to the window and gazed out over the futuristic cityscape outside. Crystal spires climbed toward the heavens. Alien hieroglyphics adorned holographic signs and billboards. Antigravity cruisers soared beneath a crimson sky. Extraterrestrials of every shape, size, and species crowded the busy streets, which were patrolled by flying centurions. Maglev trains connected soaring temples, palaces, and skyscrapers.

"I realize Skeets has been searching for you," Supernova continued. "He knows you need access to this level of technology, but we're in the last place he'd think to look, if he even knows it exists."

High above them, a transparent dome arched over the gleaming metropolis. The dome looked huge from his perspective; it took effort to recall that the entire city was actually contained in a glass bottle no more than two feet tall. *Welcome to Kandor,* he thought. The Kryptonian city, which had been miniaturized by Braniac generations ago, long before Krypton's destruction, now occupied a place of honor in Superman's Fortress of Solitude.

"For now, we're safe," Supernova insisted.

Belying his words, a sudden tremor shook the city. The collection of high-tech artifacts tumbled off the counter onto the floor. Deep cracks snaked across the vibrating walls. Shards of crystal sprayed like shrapnel. The world seemed to shudder beneath their feet, almost as though the last days of doomed Krypton had finally caught up with Kandor. Loud crashes and screams came from outside. Crowds of alien creatures panicked in the streets below.

"No, oh!" Hunter whispered backward.

"Dammit!" Supernova grabbed onto the window frame to keep from falling. "It's Skeets! It has to be!"

"YOU AND YOUR ERRAND BOY HAVE GOTTEN SLOPPY, RIP HUNTER!"

Impossibly loud, the robot's voice boomed from high above the trembling city. Staring upward, Supernova saw Skeets looming over the bottled city. The floating golden sphere was larger than Kandor itself.

"A TACHYON HERE, A CHRONAL FOOTPRINT THERE. YOU LEFT A TRAIL AND I FOUND YOU!" Skeets bumped against the bottle, tilting it on its side. Supernova nearly tumbled out the window as the floor suddenly sloped beneath him. Tools, relics, and debris slid across the floor into the wall. Rip Hunter gasped out loud as gravity threw him against a counter. A hideous scraping sound reverberated up from Kandor's foundations. Skeets nudged the askew bottle toward the very edge of the pedestal. **"SURRENDER YOURSELF IMMEDIATELY—OR IT'S KRYPTON ALL OVER AGAIN!"**

Hunter shoved himself away from the counter and ran clumsily across the inclined floor. He yanked Supernova's cape from his shoulders. "Hey!" the startled hero protested.

"Prepared we're not a confrontation for!" Grimacing, he wrestled his time-warped syntax into submission. "Size up. And stall him!" He tore open the lining of Supernova's blue cloak and began to pull out heaping handfuls of electronic circuitry. Fiber-optic cables and minute crystal transistors glinted in the faint light. "Leave costume the. So I can reassemble its stiucric . . . *circuits* . . . into something with a little more *oomph*!"

Sounds like a plan, Supernova thought. Not having any better ideas, he began to hastily peel off the costume even as Hunter continued to ransack the cape's lining for spare parts. The all-concealing disguise dropped onto the floor, leaving a dimly lit figure standing by the window. He rescued a pair of goggles from the floor and braced himself for the transition back to his usual dimensions. His fingers were poised above the size controls built into the palms of his gloves.

"Go!" Hunter urged him. "Og!"

The unmasked hero squeezed his fists. The controls clicked and luminous atomic orbitals suddenly swirled around his tensed body, which began to grow larger by the second. Harnessing the incalculable power of a miniature dwarf star fragment, the sophisticated technology, which he and Rip had "borrowed" from Ray Palmer, the brilliant physicist once known as the Atom, instantly increased the hero's height, mass, and density. He flung himself out the window, so as not to explode the lab from within, and zoomed upward toward the sealed neck of the bottle. The solid glass cap seemed to shrink before his eyes.

"FINE," Skeets taunted. "HAVE IT YOUR WAY, HUNTER."

Kandor teetered precariously beneath the hero. Bracing his hands against the bottom of the cap, he pushed it up, up, and away only heartbeats before growing too large for the bottle to contain him. He zoomed out into the glacial vastness of the Fortress of Solitude, while simultaneously regaining his normal size. Polished crystal pillars supported the ceiling of the arctic fortress. The pellucid monoliths angled upward to form what looked like a majestic temple made of solid ice. But the flying hero had little time to admire the Fortress' unearthly architecture as he arced around just in time to catch the bottled city before it plunged off its pedestal. Superman's famed S-shield was carved into the base of the crystal perch.

"Hunter's not your problem, pal," he warned Skeets. "I am." The robot let out a startled burst of static.

"MICHAEL?"

Booster Gold touched down on the translucent floor of the Fortress. His familiar blue and gold uniform was conspicuously devoid of any corporate logos or trademarks. He carefully placed Kandor back onto its pedestal, while glaring fiercely at his former sidekick.

"DNA SCAN: MICHAEL JON CARTER. 100% MATCH." Skeets was taken aback by Booster's apparent resurrection. **"IT—IT IS YOU. BUT HOW?"**

"Tell him everything," Hunter's voice whispered in Booster's ear. He heard fabric tearing in the background of the transmission. Rip sounded like he was ripping the Supernova costume to shreds in his search for crucial components. "It'll buy me some time, and he'll know soon enough anyway."

Booster stepped between Skeets and the fragile bottle city. *Just keep talking,* he told himself. "I've known what's up with you for weeks now, Skeets. When I went into Rip's underground bunker, the clues were everywhere." Like a time machine, his memory carried him back to the chilling discovery he had made beneath the Arizona desert. "I *almost* asked you about it . . . but Rip showed up to stop me."

The elusive Time Master had stepped out of a shimmering temporal rift while Booster had still been reading that damning graffiti on the wall. It was he who had pointed out that the phrase "It's all his fault" referred to Skeets, not Booster. A chronal force field had enveloped both men, shielding them from surveillance.

"I told you Rip wasn't in the lab . . . the first of many, many lies I'd learn to spin. He revealed to me the truth about you . . . and we formed a plan."

Angry at being deceived, Skeets fired a laser blast at Booster, who took evasive action, flying deeper into the silent

Fortress. *That's it,* he thought. *Lure him away from Kandor and all those innocent people.* The laser fire chipped away at the sanctuary's towering crystal pillars. Loose flakes sprayed outward from the once-smooth walls. Booster mentally apologized to Superman for staging a firefight in his home. *I'll have to help him patch the place up—if I come out of this alive!*

"First off, I had to play dumb," he explained, shouting back over his shoulder. "And if you were really yourself, Skeets, you'd be having a field day with that straight line."

His apparently random flight led him right to the Fortress' armory, where Superman had collected weapons from all over the galaxy. Booster plucked a Rannian energy-rifle from its niche on the wall and fired back at Skeets, who zipped out of the way of an azure bolt, so that the blast shattered a crystalline control console instead.

Damn, Booster thought. *I missed.*

"Rip knew that he was destined to face off against you, so he needed the right weapons, but he had to stay hidden until he was prepared to fight. It was my job to gather the necessary materials, and there was no way to do that under your 24/7 observation." He vividly recalled Skeets tagging along with him everywhere he went. "I had to get totally off your radar somehow."

Dodging Skeets' energy bolts, he drop-kicked the levitating robot into a nearby pillar, then ducked behind an alien tank left over from Mongul's attempted invasion of Earth a few years back. The bright red bursts ricocheted off the tank's armor plating. A deflected blast burned a hole straight through a preserved suit of Tamaranean battle armor. Booster shouted over the sizzle of melting metal.

"So we pulled a fast one. Rip explained how I could be in two places at once with the help of time-travel. Then he faked my death, yanking me out of the timestream at the last minute and substituting my own future corpse." Booster remembered feeling the heat of the nuclear explosion, a split second before he slipped sideways through time. Thankfully, he had only caught a glimpse of the charred skeleton Rip had replaced him with. "That's something I'd rather not dwell on, by the way."

He emptied the rifle's cartridge at Skeets, but his blasts bounced harmlessly off the robot's unmarked casing. Out of ammo, he tossed the weapon aside and took refuge behind the turret of the massive tank.

"Suddenly I was twelve weeks back in time, coexisting as both Booster Gold *and* under a new, humbler, more virtuous identity that would, frankly, be the last place anybody would ever look for me." He winced slightly at the assumptions underlying the disguise. *The truth hurts,* he thought, *but what can you do?* "The Booster/Supernova rivalry was designed to throw off any lingering suspicions, and it worked."

He couldn't help wondering what was keeping Rip. He imagined Hunter frantically cobbling a weapon together from the Kryptonian circuitry installed in the Supernova suit. *How long is that going to take?*

"Meanwhile, Rip had me lift the Atom's size-changing belt and gloves from JLA storage, so he could take advantage of the super-science in the bottle city of Kandor. As Supernova, I brought him every super-weapon I could find, from Luthor's kryptonite gauntlet to Hawkgirl's Nth Metal, in hopes of building something that could beat you."

The furious energy bolts stopped whizzing over his head. He guessed that Skeets was holding his fire to hear the rest of Booster's narrative. Curiosity seemed to have momentarily won out over the robot's homicidal agenda. Booster suddenly felt like some sort of sci-fi Scheherazade.

"That's right, buddy," Booster taunted him. "We operated out of this Fortress . . . and don't think we didn't plunder it." He gave the knife another twist. "Where do you think we found the parts and powers for my suit?"

Rip's voice emerged from Booster's earpiece. "Distracted keep him, Booster! I'm my way on!"

About time, Booster thought. *I'm running out of exposition.* Abandoning his position behind the tank, he took off

through the Fortress once more. Over the last few weeks he
had taken the time to memorize the sanctuary's layout, thank
goodness, so he had no trouble circling back toward the trophy
room containing the bottle city. The vengeful robot followed
in hot pursuit.

"Think back, Skeets. Everything Supernova did—*every-thing*—was based on applied teleportation. Every bit of circuitry in that costume was cribbed from . . ."

He flew back into the trophy chamber. Just as he'd hoped,
a full-sized Rip Hunter stood in front of Kandor and its pedestal. A metallic red cube, about the size of a thick paperback
book, rested in the Time Master's grip. A concave metal dish
was mounted to the front of the authentic Kryptonian relic,
which Hunter held before him like an old-fashioned box camera. Booster wondered if Skeets recognized the device.

"Superman's Phantom Zone Projector!"

Rip clicked a switch and a beam of black light targeted
Skeets. The beam produced a photo-negative effect that reversed the colors of the robot's casing and optical sensors. It
also halted his advance, freezing him in place.

"NOOOOO!" Skeets cried out in alarm. Or was it Skeets?
The angry outburst lacked Skeets' usual robotic timbre, causing
Booster to eye the immobilized mechanism suspiciously. Was
there somebody else inside that golden sphere?

The question was possibly academic as Skeets began to fade
from view. The hovering orb started to flatten out into merely
two dimensions. Solid metal became immaterial, so that you
could see through Skeets as though the robot was a ghost . . . or
a phantom.

It's working, Booster thought triumphantly. Back on Krypton, Superman's forebears had banished their worst criminals
to the Phantom Zone, a parallel dimension inhabited only by
bodiless wraiths. With any luck, Skeets would join Krypton's
Most Wanted in endless purgatory, where he would no longer
be able to do any more damage to the timestream.

"That's it!" Booster encouraged Rip. "Crank it up!"

The veteran chrononaut rolled his eyes. "It's a guitar amp

not, Booster." The rush of battle seemed to have stabilized his syntax somewhat. "A prison portal it's a . . . and Skeets is holding on for life dear!"

For a moment or two, Booster thought victory was theirs. But then Skeets began to resolidify. The flattened disk inflated back into a sphere. The photo-negative effect flickered alarmingly. The robot almost seemed to be drinking in the beam from the Projector.

No, Booster thought, horrified. *That's not possible. Is it?*

Hunter poured on the power, pushing the Projector to its limits—and beyond. The device began to shake itself apart, so that Hunter had trouble holding on to it. Smoke seeped from the junctures of the metal cube; Booster smelled the circuitry burning. The black-light beam wavered erratically as Skeets absorbed its power like a black hole.

But more than just raw energy was being consumed. Booster's jaw dropped as he glimpsed a stream of humanoid figures flowing into Skeets. Warped and elongated by a seemingly irresistible pull, the agonized specters wailed silently as, one by one, the condemned denizens of the Phantom Zone exchanged one prison for another. Booster shuddered at the sight. "Rip, what the hell is he doing . . . ?"

"Aaagh!" Hunter yelped as sparks erupted from the Projector, shocking him. He yanked his hands away from the smoking cube, which crashed down onto the floor. It sparked for a few more seconds before shorting out completely. Skeets sucked in the last of the beam before the ebon light flickered out for good. Booster stared mutely at the unstoppable robot, transfixed by the terrifying sight before him:

A trio of Zoners—Kryptonian criminals, presumably—peered out from behind the translucent screen over Skeets' sensor array. Booster made out the contorted features of a pale-faced man with a neatly trimmed mustache and beard. Crowding behind him, their faces equally anguished, were a slinky-looking woman with short black hair and a hulking lummox who reminded Booster of every surly bouncer who had ever kicked him out of a bar. All three prisoners wore matching gray uniforms emblazoned with obscure Kryptonian symbols. Their fists pounded impotently against the inside of the screen, before being drawn deeper into Skeets' voracious core. Booster wondered briefly what the nameless trio had done to be banished to the Phantom Zone in the first place.

Not that it really mattered now.

"Oh my God," Booster whispered. "He's eaten the Phantom Zone."

"I'll go you worse one," Rip said. "A meal not it's for him. Just it's an appetizer!" Producing a handheld console from the pocket of his bomber jacket, he stabbed at the keypad with his fingers. "But a retreat us it bought! You are ready?"

Booster stared at the menacing robot. There was nothing cute or funny about Skeets now. Darksome energy crackled around the robot, whose very presence seemed to distort the fabric of the space-time continuum, causing reality itself to warp and bend all around him. Booster still didn't know what malevolent force had possessed Skeets, but he knew serious trouble when he saw it.

"Yes!" he shouted at Hunter. "Let's get outta here!"

Rip poked a button and a chronal displacement wave swept both him and Booster away, leaving Skeets alone in the vandalized Fortress. The hovering robot consumed the last of the Phantom Zone energy and latched onto the wave before it could fade away entirely.

"OH, NO, NO. YOU DON'T GET AWAY THAT EASILY."

He blinked out of existence.

WEEK 38.

THE bumpy ride jolted her bones, over and over again.

Renee crouched in the back of a grimy army-surplus truck that looked like something out of an old *M*A*S*H* episode. A flapping canvas cover provided only partial protection from the blowing snow and wind outside the truck. An overstuffed ruck-sack sat at her feet. A chilly gust blew a dusting of icy white flakes through a gap in the canvas. She shivered beneath her down jacket and heavy winter clothing.

"AIEEEEE!"

Propped up beside her, Vic screamed in agony. His wasted body had practically disappeared beneath his snow gear. His limbs jerked spasmodically. Gloved hands groped at his head and torso, as though trying to rip out the cancer with his bare hands. Renee held on to him tightly, restraining him.

Time for another shot, she decided. She tugged his jacket down on one side, enough to expose a patch of skin. She kept one arm wrapped around him as she injected another dose of morphine into his veins.

"Aangg ghnn *hurts,*" he mumbled incoherently. "Nhnnn hnnnn."

"I know, Charlie." She withdrew the syringe. "I know it does."

Vic slumped against her as he escaped back into a narcotic haze. She took a quick inventory of the syringes remaining in the scuffed metal case. Frowning, she saw that she was running low on the morphine. Would her meager supply last until they reached their destination? *It has to,* she thought. *For Charlie's sake.*

Worried muttering came from the opposite side of the truck bed, where a trio of local Sherpas eyed her and Vic apprehensively. Renee had no idea what the men were saying, but she couldn't blame them for giving her and Vic funny looks. She imagined that they presented a pretty unnerving spectacle: a screaming foreigner, who looked like he already had one foot in the grave, and a crazed-looking woman with a pack full of drugs. Not exactly the most reassuring of traveling companions.

"Do any of you know the way to Nanda Parbat?" The wary locals gave no sign of comprehending her. "Do any of you speak English?"

She bit down on her lip to keep from crying out in frustration. Vic was dying, dammit, and this was her last chance to save him . . . if she could just get him back to the hidden valley in time.

But that was proving easier said than done.

Retrieving a crumpled map from her pack, she spread it out on the floor of the truck bed. A compass dangled on a cord around her neck and she pulled it out into the open. "Please," she entreated the other passengers. "We're going to Nanda Parbat. It's okay. They know us there." She pointed urgently at the map. "But I don't know exactly what trail to take." She held out the compass. "I could use some help, some directions. . . ."

The men drew back from her, refusing to meet her eyes.

"It's important. I have to get my friend there. To Nanda Parbat."

Only the howling wind responded to her pleas.

I'm on my own, she realized.

The road tilted sharply beneath the truck as it carried her uphill into the Himalayas. Peering out through a gap in the canvas, Renee gulped at the sight of the impossibly high mountains looming ahead of them. Ominous black storm clouds concealed the tops of the peaks from view. For a second, her nerve faltered. Jesus Christ, was she really planning to haul him all the way up there? Maybe Kate had been right. Maybe this was a bad idea.

No, she told herself. *I'm not crazy.* She glanced down at Vic's slumbering form. Even doped up, he grimaced in pain. The bones of his face showed through his skin. He'd lost so much weight he looked like a concentration camp victim. *I can save him. I know I can.*

Even if she had to drag him to the top of the world.

OOLONG ISLAND.

"The Revelation of Apokalips, Book Ten, Chapter Eleven."

Bruno Mannheim held the Crime Bible open before him as he recited from the profane text. The looming exterior of the island's primary manufacturing facility provided a fitting backdrop for his sermon. Blinding flashes of electricity lit up the factory's barred windows. Glowing plasma gushed from towering black smokestacks. Lightning streaked the night sky. Thunder added booming exclamation points to Mannheim's stentorian reading:

"There were Four Ages of Apokalips in Its anguished, bloody morning."

Dr. Sivana and his fellow scientists were gathered on the beach in front of the factory, eagerly awaiting the unveiling of the Four Horsemen. Miscellaneous aides, igors, thugs, and fem-droids filled out the crowd. The threat of an imminent tropical downpour failed to dampen the audience's enthusiasm and impatience. "Thrilling, isn't it?" Sivana commented to T.O. Morrow. He held out a fresh bag of microwave popcorn that he had nuked just for the occasion. "Not that I believe any of this irrationalist nonsense." Apokalips, he knew, was a distant planet ruled by a malevolent alien overlord, but Sivana figured that, from a strictly scientific perspective, extraterrestrial myths were no more reliable than the Earthly variety. He flashed a bucktoothed grin at Morrow. "But Boss Mannheim has such a wonderful reading voice."

"The Age of Hunger," the ganglord proclaimed, "ruled by *Yurrd the Unknown*, in the formless time before time . . ."

The wide front doors of the factory creaked open, spilling an incarnadine glow onto the scene outside. The expectant faces of the congregation were bathed in an unholy crimson radiance. A trio of gargantuan figures emerged from the depths of the factory, stepping out into the night. Hunchbacks in HazMat suits prodded the towering creatures on. The open doors offered a peek at the gruesome scene behind the Horsemen. Mutilated cattle were strewn across the floor of the factory. Bovine blood splattered the walls. A rush of hot air carried the stench of the slaughterhouse. A pallid technician gagged at the odor. *Looks like we missed feeding time,* Sivana thought. He munched happily on his popcorn.

"The Age of War, when *Roggra* sat on a throne of skulls and rivers ran hot and red with blood . . ."

As huge as a tank, the Horseman in question led the pack. He gripped the doorframe as he hauled his mechanized bulk out into the open. Cannons and gun turrets bristled all over his riveted crimson armor. Targeting lasers protruded from metallic hatches on his body. A pair of glowing yellow lenses peered from his burnished red helmet, above his jointed metal jaws. His head was sunk low between his massive shoulders. Gears clanked and servomotors hummed as he scuttled forward, armed and armored to the max. The blazing lenses glared out at the world with unremitting hostility.

"Lord of the Age of Fevers was *Zorrm*. . . ."

Plague tanks bulged upon the creature's back. Winding metal pipes connected the tanks to nozzles in Zorrm's hose-cannons, capable of spraying defoliant, contagion, and corrosion. More humanoid than Roggra, he wore a black leather uniform covered by a network of flexible pipes and valves. A single red eye bulged in the center of his grotesque visage. Throbbing veins pulsated atop a hairless cranium. Breathing tubes were fused directly to his jaws. Toxic waste sloshed loudly with every ponderous step; Sivana thought he recognized elements of Chemo in the monster's design. *That would be Dr. Death's contribution,* he guessed. *Ivan does love his poisons.*

Zorrm's very presence gave Sivana a queasy feeling. He sniffled and wiped his nose on the sleeve of his lab coat. Looking around, he saw that the rest of the audience was looking a bit green around the gills as well. A weakling of a lab assistant vomited onto his shoes. Apparently, the "Lord of Fevers" was already living up to his name. *Atta boy!* Sivana thought proudly. He took his sudden nausea and swollen glands as evidence of a successful experiment. Zorrm was functioning perfectly.

"Then came *Azraeuz,* silent king of the Age of Death, who rode a pale steed across a desert of ash and bone at the black dawn of the Fourth World."

More bestial than humanoid, the final creature carried a gigantic scythe that glowed with lethal energies. The horns and skull of some enormous steer masked his face. Black feathered wings jutted from his shoulder blades. A long, leathery tail dragged behind him. Shaggy legs, complete with cloven hooves, supported the giant monster's weight. A dying rose was engraved upon his bronze breastplate. Sivana wondered if the lovely Veronica Cale was responsible for that embellishment. It had a woman's touch. . . .

Azraeuz limped haltingly, as though suffering from multiple sclerosis. Like his inhuman brothers, he was still adjusting to his newborn existence. He leaned upon the staff of his deadly scythe.

"Before Gods, before the New Gods, the Titans ruled the Void. No flesh can bear their presence, but certain mighty forms are to be constructed through which the Kings may express their shattering cosmic judgment."

The three Horsemen posed behind Mannheim, gazing out at a world that had yet to suffer their prefabricated wrath. Many of the thugs and technicians surrounding Sivana drew back involuntarily. *Pansies,* Sivana thought disdainfully. *This is just what we've been working to accomplish all this time.*

"Only bodies of stone and steel and storm can carry such

Riders and herein is written how such vessels shall be made. . . ."

Sivana admired the scientists' handiwork. It had been an intriguing challenge, using modern technology to bring to life artificial entities that matched the cryptic prophecies of the so-called Crime Bible. The Horsemen were proof positive of what wonders the world's greatest cybernetics experts, terato-biologists, genetic engineers, germ warfare specialists, and plain old mad doctors were capable of, given unlimited re-sources. They were nothing less than the unification of sci-ence and superstition . . . in the form of unstoppable death machines.

Just wait until humanity sees what we've brewed up here! Sivana gloated. *A veritable Monster Society of Evil . . .*

Mannheim also seemed pleased with the results. "Indeed," he declared, clapping the heavy tome shut. "No one in history has ever had the money, the genius, and the ambition to dare what Intergang has done. The Four Horsemen have risen. They have come again!"

"The eyes are based on my death lens designs," Dr. Cyclops boasted to everyone within earshot. He appeared oblivious to the blood trickling from his nose. "That was my idea."

Sivana rolled his eyes. "What do you want, Cyclops? A certificate?"

The Horsemen scanned the crowd with their baleful eyes. They seemed to be looking for someone. Roggra opened his mouth to pronounce a death sentence:

"BLAKK AH-ADUM."

Zorrm nodded in agreement.

"BLACK ADAM MUST DIE."

Sivana cackled fiendishly. *I wouldn't want to be in Black Adam's shiny yellow boots,* he thought, *when the Horsemen make their way to Kahndaq.* He took another bite of popcorn. *Serves Adam right for being such a goody two-shoes lately.*

The crowd applauded with varying degrees of trepidation. People dabbed at bloody noses and ears. Others clutched their stomachs and groaned with nausea. Sneezes and coughs in-

truded on the presentation. Dr. Boris Crabb, a relative newcomer to the island, scratched his head in confusion. Wisps of
gray hair came away from his skull. He counted on his fingers.
"What happened to the Fourth Horseman?"

Veronica Cale brought him up to speed. "Yurrd the Unknown, the hunger-lord, rode out before the others." A silk
handkerchief kept her nosebleed under control as she gazed
uncertainly at the fearsome entities she had helped to create.
Apprehension, and perhaps even a trace of guilt, showed upon
her elegant features. "Oh God, what have we made?"

God had nothing to do with it, Sivana thought. *This is all
our doing.*

The popcorn was delicious.

THE HIMALAYAS.

THE blizzard blew against Renee as she trudged up the icy
slope, toward the heart of the storm. A wool scarf covered her
face. She squinted into the stinging snow and wind. The climb
was murder. Every step was an ordeal. She couldn't even feel
her toes anymore.

I could really use a cigarette right now, she thought. *Good
thing I didn't pack any.*

A pair of wooden poles rested heavily atop her shoulders.
The rucksack was slung across her back. Renee held on tightly
to the poles as she dragged Vic behind her on a makeshift litter.
Strapped down onto the travois, he writhed futilely against his
restraints. "Wh-who-who d-d-do you think you are?" he raged
deliriously. His teeth chattered as he spoke. Racking coughs
punctuated the tirade. "D-don't know anything . . . just . . .
ju-just shoot you in the h-h-head . . ."

Renee heard the pain creeping back into his voice again.
Just keep talking, Charlie, she thought. At least it let her know
he was still alive, if only barely. *Too bad you're not making
any sense.*

"D-d-dump your body . . . butter . . . b-butterflies . . ."

Butterflies? Renee wondered where Vic's fevered memories had taken him. *Somewhere better than here,* she hoped. The glacial wilderness stretched endlessly before her, all the way up into the forbidding black clouds. Second thoughts beset her. Would Vic have been more comfortable back in his cozy hospital room? Was she being selfish subjecting him to this? *Probably,* she admitted. *But I* can't *lose another partner. Another friend.*

Gravity, cold, and exhaustion conspired to slow her down. She paused for a moment just to catch her breath, no easy task at this altitude. She gulped down the thin air, her head throbbing for lack of oxygen. She pulled down her scarf, exposing chapped lips and reddened, windburned features. A metal canteen poured ice water down her throat. She carefully lowered the litter onto the snow and turned around to check on Vic. His withered, pain-wracked face tore at her heart.

"I can't lose you too, Charlie," she whispered hoarsely. "We're in this together, remember? You said we were in this together . . . until the end. . . ."

Renee consulted her compass one more time. She thought she was on the right path, but there was no way to be sure. The blizzard had hidden any tracks or landmarks beneath a featureless white shroud. The cascading snowflakes made it almost impossible to tell where she was going. For all she knew, she was halfway to Tibet by now.

She couldn't help recalling how easily the Black Marvel Family had flown her to Nanda Parbat before. She had flirted with the idea of calling upon Isis and Black Adam for help, but she'd had no idea how to contact them now that relations between Kahndaq and the USA had completely broken down in the wake of that bloodbath in California. Besides, it sounded like Isis and her family had their own problems to deal with these days.

Just as well, Renee thought. *This is my responsibility, not theirs.* She owed Vic that much. *Where would I be now if not for him? Probably drinking and whoring myself into an early grave.* The thought of facing the future without him filled her with dread. *Who will I become if you're not around?*

"We're almost there, Charlie," she said, more out of wishful thinking than anything else. Bending down, she kissed his forehead with her shredded lips. His bloodshot eyes stared past her, tracking the phantoms of his past. Straining lungs whistled damply as he sucked in the frigid air. "You've got to stay with me." She choked back a sob, finding it harder and harder to keep lying to herself about their chances. "It's not far now. Please stay with me."

She lifted the top end of the travois back onto her shoulders and tried to soldier on. Her strength abandoned her, however, and she stumbled forward onto the snow, almost dropping the litter. Landing on her knees, she succumbed to fatigue, just for a second, and closed her eyes, a single moment of weakness that threatened to linger on forever. Hadn't she read somewhere that freezing to death was just like falling asleep? She started to drift off. . . .

No! Her eyes snapped open. *I can't give up. Not now. Not when there's still a chance to save him.*

She looked back at Vic, whose labored breathing seemed to be getting worse by the second. He was gasping for air like a fish out of water. He shivered uncontrollably beneath the heavy blankets Renee had swaddled him in. She hated the awful sounds coming from his chest. His lips were blue.

"I'm sorry, Charlie. So sorry." She crawled over to the litter, until she was kneeling beside his trembling body. The sub-zero temperature seemed to be competing with the cancer to see which could kill him off first. Shrugging off the rucksack, she retrieved the Question's rumpled trench coat from the pack and laid it on top of him like a blanket. An idea occurred to her, and she fished out his old belt buckle. Her thumb found the hidden switch and his rolled-up mask dropped out of the secret compartment into her palm. "Nothing left to keep you warm . . . only this thing."

She gently smoothed the mask over Vic's emaciated

features. His ravaged face vanished beneath the blank pseudo-derm. "Maybe provide some insulation." She fumbled with the buckle, her thick gloves making her clumsy. "Now, how do you . . . ?"

A metallic click rewarded her efforts. A chemical odor accompanied the hiss of Tot's ingenious binary gases as they were released from the buckle. To Renee's dismay, the howling wind carried most of the vapors away, but she blew enough of the fumes onto the mask to glue it to Vic's face. The eerie blank visage stirred painful memories of their earliest encounters. Vic Sage was the Question once more, perhaps for the last time.

"I think maybe I made a mistake, Charlie." Ferocious gusts whipped up the snow around her as she rose unsteadily to her feet and loaded the rucksack back onto her stooped frame. Peering into the storm, it almost seemed as though the swirling white powder was forming icy question marks in the turbulent air. Renee could barely see five feet in front of her. Frostbite nibbled at her extremities. "I think maybe I've gotten us both killed."

Just like Kate warned me, Renee wondered. *Serves me right for not listening to her.* She wondered if she would ever hold Kate again, or if Kate would ever find out what had happened to her. *I never even got a chance to ask her how she became Batwoman.*

She lurched erratically through the snow, dragging the travois and its fragile occupant behind her. Was she even moving in a straight line? Renee had no way of knowing. She tugged out the compass and stared at it in bewilderment.

"Don't know which way to go," she confessed. "I'm lost, Charlie."

In more ways than one.

She slipped on a patch of ice and toppled over onto the snow. *Dammit!* she thought frantically as the upset litter tipped over onto its side. Scrambling back onto her feet, she hurried to make sure Vic was okay. A trail of bright red blood stained the snow behind them. She heard him choking.

"Charlie!"

Righting the litter, she saw that the Question's mask had already begun to peel away from his face. Blood seeped through the false flesh covering his mouth.

Panic overcame her. "Don't leave me," she begged. "Oh God, oh God. Hold on, Charlie." She remembered Detective Crispus Allen's lifeless body lying in a puddle of blood on a moonlit Gotham street, and that time in Kahndaq when she'd thought she had lost Charlie forever. "Hold on, please hold on. I'm here. I've got you. . . ." Her head and shoulders sagged as she bent over him in despair. Bitter tears froze against her cheeks. "I . . . I can't do this again. . . ."

The storm was finally starting to ease up a bit, but it was too little, too late. A sense of utter failure sliced her soul to ribbons, cutting even deeper than the wind.

"You never answered my question," Vic pointed out.

His voice, faint and hoarse as it was, startled her. Her heart missed a beat and she stared at him in amazement. The flapping mask came away from the top half of his face, exposing his sunken eyes and sweaty brow. Alert blue orbs met hers. For the first time in days, he was really seeing her.

He was Vic Sage again, at least for moment.

"Charlie?"

"Get this thing off my face," he wheezed. "Hard enough to breathe as is."

Renee clumsily peeled the rest of the mask away. She let the wind dispose of it; within seconds, the crumpled scrap of pseudo-flesh had disappeared into the snowy wastes. She had no idea what to make of Vic's sudden lucidity. Was this a miracle . . . or a momentary blessing before the end?

Vic grinned up at her. Aside from the blood smeared around his mouth, he almost looked like his old self, at least if you didn't look too hard. "What the hell are you doing, Renee?"

"Trying to get us to Nanda Parbat." She undid the straps binding him to the litter. Tears blurred her vision as she cradled him against her chest. "Trying to *save* you, Charlie."

"But you can't. I told you, some things you just have to accept."

"I can't!" she blurted from her heart. "I need you. I don't know who I am without you!"

Vic's tremulous hand touched her cheek. "It's a trick question, Renee." He coughed up blood. "Not who you are, but who are you going to *become*."

Exhausted by the effort, his arm dropped to his side. He slumped back into her arms. Renee sobbed inconsolably. *Please,* she prayed desperately. *Not now. Not again.*

"Time to change," he murmured with his last breath. "Like a butterfly . . ."

His body shuddered and fell still. His lungs stopped whistling.

Vic Sage had asked his final Question.

The storm died away. The wind stopped blowing. The last of the snowfall settled onto Renee as she sat clutching Vic's limp body. Looking back the way they had come, she saw the trail of blood stretching across the snow behind her—almost in the shape of a question mark. *One last trick, Charlie?* she thought, mourning her friend. It was just like him to leave her with a final puzzle. *How'd you pull that off?*

A bright shaft of sunlight penetrated the overcast sky, lighting up the frozen terrain around her. Turning her gaze away from the bloody question mark, she saw before her a remote mountain valley dominated by an imposing pagoda-style temple. A clutch of familiar huts preceded the temple. The tinkle of wind chimes blew down the valley. Prayer flags waved hello.

"Oh my God," Renee whispered.

The irony was unbearable.

She had reached Nanda Parbat.

WEEK 39.

OOLONG ISLAND.

LIGHTNING flashed outside, causing the lights in the laboratory to flicker. Thunder competed with the Muzak. Driving sheets of rain pelted the plate-glass windows. Turbulent storm clouds concealed the sun and emptied the beaches. Not even Ira Quimby was working on his tan today.

Dr. Sivana looked up from his microscope in irritation. "Haven't those ridiculous Horsemen left already?"

It seemed to Sivana, and he had no doubt that a thorough meteorological analysis would bear him out, that the weather had been the pits ever since the final three Horsemen had come off the assembly line. The Monster Society, as he liked to think of them, had long since lost their novelty value, at least as far as Sivana was concerned. He glared impatiently out the window at the island's pier, where even now Roggra, Zorrm, and Azraeuz were being loaded into an unmarked cargo ship for transport to Intergang's staging area in Bialya. Their deployment boded ill for Black Adam and the rest of Kahndaq, not that Sivana cared. Unlike Adam, he had no sentimental attachment to any Third World pigsty. He was simply anxious to see the Horsemen on their way.

The sooner they're gone, the better.

He cast a baleful look at the overhead lights, as though daring the impudent LED array to brown out again, then turned back to his work. Notes and diagrams, written on everything from graph paper to cocktail napkins, littered the cluttered cubicle. The chemical formula for an unbreakable synthetic cobweb was scrawled on the back of a lunch menu, next to the schematics for an antifrequency "mute ray" capable of deadening all sounds, including, hopefully, the magic word of a certain Big Red Cheese. Hunching over an acid-stained counter, he sorted through the scattered documents, looking for a particular set of notes. Test tubes, beakers, and a half-finished neutron grenade served as paperweights.

"You know what's ridiculous?" An unwanted voice disturbed his concentration. Sivana looked up to see Doctor Tyme standing outside his cubicle. The man's clock-faced countenance looked as absurd as ever, as did his garish cape and costume. "They canceled the *Time Tunnel* revival after only one season." He quivered in outrage. "The CIA knows that's my favorite show!"

Sivana glowered disdainfully at his paranoid colleague. He hoped, for Tyme's sake, that the man had more on his mind than the fate of some inane television program. "Well?" he demanded brusquely.

Bristling at Sivana's tone, Tyme put on a show of pompous indignation. "So, has the 'great' Thaddeus Sivana found any trace of my missing fifty-two seconds?"

That again?

"I wasn't even looking." Sivana nodded at his microscope. "But I did find a world of microscopic naked Amazons who worship *you* as a god."

"What, really?" Tyme elbowed past Sivana in his haste to get to the microscope. "Let me see!" He bent eagerly over the lenses and fumbled with the focus controls. "I *knew* there had to be a world somewhere that values the revolutionary work of Doctor Seymour Tyme. . . ."

His voice trailed off as he quickly realized that there were no nude subatomic sylphs to be seen. Sivana felt embarrassed on behalf of mad scientists everywhere. He shook his head in scornful disbelief. "What are you? An idiot?"

Tyme sheepishly lifted his eyes from the lenses, just as T.O. Morrow wandered into the cubicle to see what all the excitement was about. As usual, the urbane futurist sported a Hawaiian shirt in lieu of a lab coat. His fruity drink had a tiny umbrella in it. "Something interesting?"

Sivana reclaimed his microscope. "I'm looking at Time itself," he explained to Morrow, whom he respected rather more than Tyme. Morrow was a credit to the profession, whose deadly androids had bedeviled even the Justice League on occasion. "Particles of Time. I call it Suspendium." Tyme tried to slink away unnoticed, but Sivana wasn't about to let him off so easily. "Maybe you'll think twice about interrupting me again," he called after the humiliated scientist. "You pathetic worm!"

"That reminds me, Thaddeus," Morrow commented. He leaned against the wall of the cubicle, stirring his drink. "You never did tell us what happened to Mister Mind. Shouldn't he be here with us?"

Dubbed "the world's wickedest worm" by the tabloid press, Mister Mind was actually the larval form of an ancient Venusian life-form. The alien caterpillar was an inveterate foe of Captain Marvel—and a former ally of Sivana's.

"I'd forgotten all about him," he admitted. In fact, Sivana had been experimenting on the tiny extraterrestrial when Intergang's subhuman henchmen had forcibly recruited his services. The details of that rather intriguing project came back to him swiftly. "Mind was trapped in larval form, denied his full potential. I wanted to see what would happen if I irradiated the slimy little creep with Suspendium rays to accelerate his natural processes. . . ."

"And?" Morrow prompted.

Sivana shrugged. "Then a couple of monsters turned up to drag me here." The last time he'd laid eyes on the small green caterpillar, Mind had been sealed inside a transparent containment cylinder back in Sivana's old laboratory. "I have no idea what became of Mind, but the Suspendium's been acting tricky for months now. . . ."

He reclaimed his microscope, just as an unexpected ray of sunlight brightened up his work space. Looking up, he saw the sun shining outside for the first time in a week. He also noted that no surprise, the nameless cargo ship had left the pier, taking the three Horsemen with them. Stormy black clouds followed the ship out to sea.

"Finally," Sivana muttered.

Maybe now he could get some serious work done.

WEEK 40.

SHIRUTA.

SUNLIGHT shone down on the palace gardens. Fragrant lilies and narcissuses bloomed amidst the verdant shrubs and arbors. Refugee children, rescued from captivity, joyfully chased each other down the winding paths. The orphans' laughter elicited a faint smile from Isis as she strolled through the garden with Black Adam and Sobek, but only briefly. Despite the idyllic setting, her heart was heavy.

"Osiris has still not left his room," she lamented to Sobek. "He will not speak to Black Adam or myself about what happened in America." She shuddered at the memory of the Persuader's gruesome death—and of Osiris' horrified reaction afterward. Nearly six weeks had passed, yet the consequences of that terrible day still haunted them all.

Sobek sighed heavily as he trudged down the path. His reptilian appearance no longer frightened the children, who had grown accustomed to the talking crocodile's presence. A fresh jogging suit clothed his body. "Osiris talks to me about it, Lady Isis. He's my f-friend."

"And what does Osiris say?" Black Adam inquired. Isis knew he shared her concern for her brother. "Perhaps if I should attempt to speak with him again . . . ?"

Sobek shook his saurian skull. "I think a visit from you would only h-hurt right now. He believes—" He snapped his jaws shut in midsentence, as though he had already said too much.

"What?" Adam demanded. "What does he believe?"

The crocodile stared glumly at his bare feet. His slitted pupils refused to meet Adam's gaze. "He believes the power inside him m-made him kill. That he's *c-cursed*. That all of us are cursed."

Isis gasped and lifted her hand to her mouth. *The power inside him,* she thought. *Black Adam's power.* For a fleeting instant, she briefly considered the possibility that Amon might have inherited Adam's murderous wrath as well as his godlike attributes, but she hastily rejected the idea. *It can't be true. Osiris was born of Adam's compassion, not his anger. . . .*

"That's absurd," Adam said, scowling.

"He is a boy," she reminded him hastily, lest he take offense at the notion. "He is trying to rationalize something he did. Something he feels incredibly guilty for."

The image of her brother, liberally splattered with the Persuader's blood, rose unbidden from her memory. She had no doubt that the villain's sundered remains were seldom far from Osiris' thoughts as well.

Adam nodded. "I understand that, Isis, but my powers did not make him kill." He looked down at his own hands, perhaps remembering the first time he killed a man, millennia ago. "He has the wisdom of Zehuti to tell him that. How can he believe such nonsense?"

Sometimes even the greatest wisdom is not enough to ease a guilty conscience, she thought. But before she could open her mouth to say as much, a thunderous boom shook the heavens. Dark storm clouds came rushing up from the south, blotting out the sun. Lightning cracked open the sky. Rain poured down upon the gardens. Drenched children ran for cover.

"By the goddess!" Isis looked up in alarm. Goose bumps broke out across her skin. She sensed at once that this was no natural storm. Within seconds, she was soaked to the skin.

"Rain?" Black Adam sounded confused. "There were no clouds in the sky a moment ago." He held up his cape to shield Isis from the storm. His dark eyes questioned her. "Did you—?"

"No," she assured him. Whatever this unnatural tempest was, it was not her doing. Some other power was at work here.

She called upon the power of Isis to calm the air above them, but the turbulent weather resisted her efforts. The wind and rain defied Nature itself.

"The gardens!" Sobek cried out. "What's happening to our beautiful gardens?"

Peering out from beneath her husband's cape, Isis stared in horror at the formerly lush flowers and shrubs. The unexpected downpour should have been a blessing to the plants, but the driving rain had exactly the opposite effect. Before her eyes, the fresh blossoms withered and turned brown. Rotting petals fell to earth, to be washed away by the torrential rain. They disappeared down polished stone gutters.

She reached out to lay her healing touch upon a wilting narcissus. But though she felt the goddess' power flowing through her, as strong as ever, it had no effect upon the fragile flower, which continued to suffer from some terrible unnamed malady. The freakish rain seemed to be poisoning the garden, beyond her power to save. She tried healing a second blossom, only to meet with an equal lack of success. Isis had not felt so helpless in months. She spoke in a hushed tone.

"They're dying."

DAYS later, Osiris soared through the storm, seeking proof of what he already feared. Everywhere he looked was more evidence that all of Kahndaq was cursed.

His sister knelt in the muddy ruins of what had once been her gardens. Heavy raindrops streamed down her face like tears as she struggled to grow a single flower from the blighted soil. A purple glow shimmered around her extended fingertips, yet not a single green sprout answered her call. Her shoulders sagged in exhaustion. Her elegant face was haggard and drawn. The deadly rain had not stopped for nearly a week and showed no sign of ceasing anytime soon.

Forgive me, sister, Osiris begged silently. Although her sorry state tore at his heart, he could not bring himself to face her. *I never meant to bring this evil upon us.*

Leaving the palace behind, he flew over the city. He saw

quickly that the curse was not confined to his family alone. Food was already running short, as both crops and livestock wasted away almost overnight. Only a meager supply of rotting fruits and vegetables were available in Shiruta's many markets and outdoor bazaars. Even these pitiful foodstuffs drew large, unruly crowds, which threatened to erupt into violence at the slightest provocation.

"My child is dying! She needs food!" A crazed man, his own face gaunt with hunger, forced his way through a mob of angry citizens to snatch an overripe melon from a fruit stand. Before he could escape with his prize, however, the street vendor drew a knife and stabbed the desperate father in the chest. A woman screamed as the bleeding man tumbled against her. Another customer grabbed onto the melon and tucked it beneath his robe. Greedy hands tried to pry the precious fruit from him. The vendor cursed and slashed at the crowd with his knife, defending the rest of his produce. Blood spilled onto the cobblestone streets. Deep puddles turned red.

For a moment or two, Osiris considered intervening. Then, to his relief, a regiment of Kahndaqi police rushed onto the scene. Shouting commands, and cracking skulls, the officers broke up the riot . . . at least for the moment. Osiris guessed that similar scenes were taking place all over Shiruta. The starving city was like a powder keg, primed to explode.

He flew on, grateful to have been spared from having to deal with the violence himself. He didn't trust himself to use his powers anymore, not after what he had done to the Persuader. *I don't want any more blood on my hands,* he thought. *I can't risk killing someone else!*

Alas, famine was not the only predator stalking Kahndaq. Not far from the maddened bazaar, he beheld a nightmarish scene outside the city's largest hospital. Sick and dying patients were lined up for blocks outside the overcrowded facility. Frantic doctors and nurses performed triage on the ever-growing throng of patients, who appeared to suffer from all manner of noxious diseases, including cancer, leprosy, bubonic plague, smallpox, polio, and many other contagions that had not afflicted these lands for generations. Open sores and pus-filled boils scarred suffering flesh. Tumors disfigured faces and bodies. Clotted lungs wheezed for breath. Osiris saw a moaning woman, pronounced beyond hope by an exhausted physician, left to die alone on a sidewalk in front of the hospital. Many more victims looked to share her fate.

The gods themselves have forsaken us, Osiris thought despairingly. He looked away in agony, knowing there was nothing he could do to save the plague-ridden multitude. *There are so many . . . !*

But the hospitals weren't the only places overflowing in Kahndaq.

So were the cemeteries.

On the outskirts of the city, he came upon an even more dismal sight. Black Adam, his dark hair soaked by the endless rain, plowed through the earth with his bare fists, digging a mass grave large enough to accommodate a veritable army of the newly dead. Hearses and ambulances carted corpses by the truckload to the desolate setting. Priests and mullahs presided over countless funerals. Grieving friends and relatives wailed for their dead. Lost in sorrow, none of the mourners noticed Osiris hovering above the graveyard, hidden amidst the churning clouds and rain. Black Adam was too intent on his Herculean labors to even glance at the sky.

I've seen enough, Osiris decided. Tears leaked from his eyes as he squeezed them shut, unable to take any more. With the speed of Heru, he zoomed back toward the palace, but he could not outrace the dreadful truth he had just witnessed. Famine, pestilence, violence, and death were abroad in Kahndaq and he alone was responsible. *I brought these plagues upon us with my own bloodstained hands.*

Sobek was waiting for him upon the roof of the palace when he finally reached home. The cold rain sluiced down the crocodile's scaly hide. His blue polyester Windbreaker was zipped up tightly against the downpour. He wrung his clawed hands anxiously as he watched Osiris descend from the stormy sky.

"This is all my fault," the teen said. He stood upon the

edge of the rooftop, as though tempted to hurl himself over the brink. Screams, shouts, sirens, and the blare of gunfire rose from the city beyond the palace walls. "If I had not murdered that man, I would have been able to keep these corrupted powers under control."

Sobek looked puzzled. "Do you really th-think your magic powers did this, Osiris?" The concept seemed too difficult for his simple mind to grasp. "You k-k-killed but one."

"And those around me will forever suffer because of it." Osiris envied his friend's childlike naïveté. He wished that he too could be unburdened by the awful truth. "I am *cursed*. Kahndaq is cursed." He cast a mournful look at the unsuspecting crocodile. "You may be as well, my friend."

Fear showed in the reptile's eyes. "That would be terrible!"

WEEK 41.

"PONDERING the insoluble?"

Tot entered the hut to find Renee contemplating the rose Isis had given her nearly four months ago. Even after all this time, the bright red blossom remained as fresh and vibrant as ever. She lifted it from its vase upon Tot's desk. The Crime Bible, and the professor's copious notes on the text, shared the desktop with the vase. Sunlight penetrated the window curtains. Incense flavored the air.

"How your flower can continue to live without food, water, or soil?" He unzipped his heavy parka and tossed his floppy hat onto a bronze idol of Ganesh. Bitterness tinged his voice. A scowl deepened the creases in the old man's face. "Wondering what keeps it going, maybe? Or just asking why it, like you, is still alive . . . and Charlie isn't?"

Renee gently returned the rose to its vase. "I remember when Isis gave it to me." The former Gothamite looked as though she had gone native, trading her old winter gear in for a heavy cotton *gi*. Her long hair hung loose over her shoulders. A turquoise pendant dangled from her neck. A bracelet of bodhi beads was wrapped around her left wrist. "I think she knew Charlie was sick. I think she knew there was nothing she could do for him."

"I can't speak to that," the scientist said gruffly. "Where have you been?"

She shrugged. "I was on the mountain. With the monks." Her voice was uncharacteristically calm. A serene expression suggested that she had finally come to terms with Vic's death. Her stay in Nanda Parbat seemed to have taught her acceptance.

But, as Vic had taught her, appearances could be deceptive.

"You just walked off," Tot accused her. "We cremated Charlie's body, and you left without a word." Renee realized belatedly that Vic's mentor was feeling abandoned. "Not to me. Not to Richard."

Despite her placid demeanor, she flinched slightly at her teacher's name. "Where *is* Richard?"

"At that ice cave of his," Tot muttered. "He wants you to meet him there." The professor sat down at his desk and reached for the Crime Bible. Apparently, he was done scolding her for the time being. "Now, if you'll excuse me, the rest of these *Cantos of Crippen* won't translate themselves. . . ."

She left the old man to his work.

"RICHARD?"

Spring had finally come to the Himalayas, so that a flood of golden sunlight followed Renee into the cavern. Glancing around, she spotted her own face reflected in the polished planes of the cave walls, but saw no sign of the enigmatic Richard Dragon. "Professor Rodor said you were expecting me?"

"Two weeks eating rice with the monks of Rama Kushna, a change of clothes, and you think that does it?" His voice echoed off the cavern walls, mocking her. "Or is this just a case of fake it 'til you make it?"

One minute, she couldn't see him at all. The next, he seemed to be all around her, his bearded face scrutinizing her from dozens of icy reflections. It took Renee a moment to locate the real Richard amidst the countless mirror images. Without warning, he threw a *wu shu*–style punch at her head, which she barely managed to block in time.

Whoa! she thought. *What's with the sneak attack—and the sarcasm?*

Instinctively, she directed a counterpunch at his gut. "Charlie wanted me to carry on for him." Richard easily deflected the blow, even as she tried to justify her time at the temple. She snapped a side-kick at him. "That's what I'm trying to do."

"No," Richard said, seeing straight through her bullshit. "You're doing what you always do when faced with loss and guilt." His voice was as calm as Renee wished she could be. "You've just changed the props you use." He caught her kick, trapping her right leg. "A *gi* instead of a bottle. A kick instead of a kiss."

Renee bounced awkwardly upon one leg. "I'm *not* denying my grief," she said, more defensively than she had intended. Raw emotion shredded her voice as her Zen facade began to crack. Her flushed face scrunched up.

"Just because you're feeling it doesn't mean you've *accepted* it." He executed a smooth takedown, sweeping her left leg out from beneath her. Her butt slammed against the ice-cold floor. "You want to honor Sage? Then stop running from yourself."

Before she could stop him, he took her head in both hands and forced her to turn her gaze on her own myriad reflections. Instead of acceptance, the distorted faces in the ice displayed a dozen different blends of confusion, anger, hurt, and humiliation.

Renee hated the sight of them.

"Deal with who you *are*," he challenged her. "So you can see who you can *be*."

But all Renee saw was a miserable, unhappy woman who had let herself down, along with everyone she had ever cared about. Vic, Cris, Daria, Kate. She had failed them all when it mattered, as a partner, a friend, or a lover. Vic had spent his last precious months on earth trying to save her from herself, and in the end she hadn't even been able to pay him back. She had let him die right on the doorstep of what might have been his deliverance. Why had he picked her anyway? What a waste . . .

Staring bleakly at the reflections, she tried to look herself in the eye. But the prospect of seeing her own guilt and worthlessness gazing back at her was more than she could bear.

"I can't!"

She twisted her head free of Richard's grasp, and violently jerked her gaze away from the damning self-portraits. Reeling, she clambered to her feet and staggered out of the cavern, leaving Richard and his reflections behind her. The looming peaks of the Himalayas dwarfed her own petty problems, but not enough to ease her anguish. No longer hidden beneath a pose of philosophical detachment, her naked pain lay exposed beneath the vast blue sky.

"Deal with who you are," Richard had said.

Please, no, she thought plaintively. *Anything but that!*

THE monks at the temple said that Rama Kushna was the living voice of all that is and was not, the perfect countenance smiling upon us all forever. Renee wasn't sure exactly what that meant, but she kind of liked the idea of God being a woman. Certainly, the temple's gardens were like a little slice of heaven. Tucked in amidst the glacial plains and snowcapped peaks just beyond Nanda Parbat, the open sanctuary overflowed with lush fruit-bearing trees, fragrant orchids, and birdsong. Monks in saffron robes tended to the gardens, treading along stone pathways worn smooth by the passage of countless pilgrims. Prayer wheels, mounted on wooden spindles along the paths, were spun by the monks as they went about their duties. With every rotation, the rolled-up sutras inside the embossed bronze cylinders were symbolically recited. Libations of yak butter or oil were offered at various small shrines throughout the gardens. Renee gave one of the wheels a spin as she entered the garden.

Why the hell not? she thought. *When in Rome . . .*

She had come to the temple to be alone with her thoughts, but found another woman sitting on a stone bench beneath a flowering bamboo tree. Blue jeans and a flannel shirt identified her as another Westerner, perhaps a mountain hiker between youth hostels. Lustrous black hair cascaded down the slender back of the woman, who seemed to have a knack for attracting the local wildlife. An orange-bellied squirrel nestled upon her lap, while a bevy of native birds serenaded her. An iridescent pheasant perched on her shoulder, while plump white snow-cocks clustered on the bench beside her, or milled about at her feet. It was like a scene out of a Disney movie.

Who's this? Renee thought, intrigued. *Snow White?*

The birds and squirrels fled at her approach, showing them-selves to be excellent judges of character as far as Renee was concerned. She sat down at the opposite end of the bench and shrugged off her down jacket. Having abandoned her whole Zenner-than-thou act, she had traded in the *gi* and Tibetan jew-elry for her usual winter attire. She reached automatically for her cigarettes, then remembered that she didn't smoke any-more. *Bummer.*

Lost in thought, the other woman did not immediately acknowledge Renee's arrival. They sat in silence for several moments before Renee finally tried to get a conversation going. "So," she asked lightly, "what's a nice girl like you doing in a spiritual retreat like this?"

The stranger turned toward Renee, who was caught off guard by the woman's breathtaking beauty. Sapphire eyes shined from a face that put the Venus de Milo to shame. A smile lifted the corners of her luscious lips, which didn't look the slightest bit chapped despite the arduous trek she must have taken to get here. Her porcelain skin was smooth and unblemished. *Goddamn,* Renee thought, trying not to stare. Her heart belonged to Kate these days, but you'd have to be dead not to notice the stranger's striking good looks. The ex-quisite face also looked somewhat familiar. *Maybe some sort of international supermodel?*

"I'm waiting for a friend," the woman volunteered, speaking English with just a trace of a Greek accent. "We're supposed to be meeting here, but I'm afraid I'm early." Her melodious voice was captivating. "Bruce's going to help me . . . start a new life, I suppose you might say."

Renee caught a note of regret in the woman's tone. "The old one not working out?"

"Not exactly as I hoped, no." She sighed ruefully. Sorrow filled her eyes as she gazed out into the distance, as if looking back the way she had come. "I killed a man."

The shocking admission caught Renee by surprise. *Maybe not a model, then.* "You have a choice?"

"I tell myself I didn't."

I know how that goes, Renee thought. She remembered the would-be suicide bomber in Kahndaq, the brainwashed girl whose life she had been forced to end. There were still times when she felt certain that there had to have been another way to stop the girl, if she had just been faster, or smarter, or less of a failure. But what that way was she had no idea.

"And yourself?" the woman asked her. "Why are you here?"

"I was . . ." Her throat tightened. "I was trying to save my friend's life." She dropped her head into her hands. "He had cancer."

The woman nodded solemnly. "You have my sympathies," she said with what sounded like genuine compassion.

"Yeah," Renee muttered. A few months ago, she realized, she probably would have hit on this gorgeous stranger, hoping to drown her sorrows in some tawdry fling or one-night stand. But not anymore. Vic would have wanted her to work through her grief, not numb herself with meaningless sex and booze. And she owed him too much to cheapen his sacrifice like that, even if that left her torn apart by emotions she didn't know what to do with.

She jumped to her feet, unable to sit still any longer. "I get so angry," she confessed. "I just want to scream, you know? I'm here in Nanda Parbat for heaven's sake, and still Charlie dies of cancer." She threw up her hands in frustration. "All these miracles in our world, all the monsters and magic, and he dies of cancer anyway." She looked to the other woman for answers. "I mean, can you explain that to me? Does that make any kind of sense to you?"

"No," the stranger replied. She rose to her feet to join Renee upon the pathway. "But it was not my experience, so I cannot interpret it for you."

Renee clenched her fists, wanting to hit something. "There's nothing to interpret," she said bitterly. *There's no point to any of this.*

"Certainly there is," the woman contradicted her. Several inches taller than Renee, with an athletic figure of Amazonian proportions, she gazed down at Renee with such profound wisdom and mercy that Renee was instantly reminded of Isis at her most goddesslike. "You are looking for reason, and you are looking for it without. But the only reason you will find will be the reason *you* bring to the experience . . . and that can only come from looking within."

Renee swallowed hard. The depth of the other woman's gaze was almost more than she could take; it was as though Rama Kushna herself was staring into her soul. "It's not that I don't want to look," she insisted. "I'm *dying* to look. But I'm afraid of what I'll see there."

"Then that is all the more reason to do it." The woman gently laid her hands upon Renee's shoulders. The sleeves of her flannel shirt rode up, revealing a pair of bulletproof silver bracelets upon the stranger's wrists. Renee gasped in, well, wonder as she suddenly realized who the other woman was, and where she knew her face from. "It's a simple question," Diana said. "Which will have the greater rule over you, your fear . . . or your curiosity?"

WEEK 42.

NANDA PARBAT.

RENEE sat in the lotus position upon the floor of the ice cave. She had the frozen grotto to herself, just as she had for at least a week now. Far from the entrance, deep within the stygian darkness in the lower depths of the cavern, it was easy to lose track of the passage of time. Hunger gnawed at her; she hadn't eaten or slept since entering the cavern days ago. Her muscles were stiff from holding the same position for so long. Her uncombed hair felt matted and greasy. The unwashed *gi* made her skin itch. She felt woozy, light-headed.

And yet she kept on sitting.

An unlit candle rested on the floor in front of her, next to a pack of wooden matches. She reached for the matches, then hesitated. *Am I ready for this?*

Even after a week of fasting and meditating, she still hadn't worked up the nerve to face her reflections once more. Sitting alone in total darkness, slowly wasting away, seemed preferable to looking deeply into her own eyes in search of . . . what? Proof that she really was the weak, worthless human being she had always suspected she was?

"Which will have the greater rule over you?" Wonder Woman had asked. *"Your fear . . . or your curiosity?"*

Renee knew which one Vic would choose.

Taking a deep breath, she struck a match against the side of the box. The sudden flare of ignition sounded like a rocket going off in the subterranean hush. Renee leaned forward to light the candle, then hastily closed her eyes as the glow of the candle lit up the grotto. The smell of burning yak oil filled her nostrils.

She kept her eyes squeezed tightly shut. Her heart was pounding wildly. *No more stalling,* she scolded herself. *Here goes nothing.* She took a moment to steady her heart and breathing. *This is for you, Charlie.*

Her eyes opened.

As before, it was like being in the middle of a fun-house hall of mirrors. The flickering light of the candle cast dozens of reflections onto the polished walls of ice. Multiple facets captured her from every conceivable angle. Swallowing hard, Renee stared at the reflections, expecting to see her own anxious face looking back at her.

But there were no faces to be seen. The myriad reflections showed her oily black hair and soiled garments, but where her eyes, nose, and mouth should have been, there was only a blank expanse of flesh, just like the mask Vic used to wear.

What the hell? Renee thought. Her eyes bugged out. Her jaw dropped. *Am I hallucinating? What's this supposed to mean?*

She had come looking for herself, but had found only . . . the Question.

WEEK 43.

SHIRUTA.

BLACK Adam's long-dead family was carved in stone upon the wall of the imposing shrine. Few visited this lonely wing of the royal palace. No courtiers or servants observed Osiris and Sobek as they approached the large sculpted figures. Towering stone pillars flanked the intricate bas-relief. Subdued lighting revealed a deep crack running down the middle of the monument.

"How long do you think this journey is going to be?" Sobek asked. A half-eaten loaf of bread and a dusty jar of olives were cradled in the crocodile's arms. "I don't th-think I brought enough snacks."

"You and your bottomless stomach!" Osiris snapped. "Stop thinking about food all the time." Didn't Sobek understand how serious this was? "All of the meat in Kahndaq has spoiled. The water has made the people sick. Our land is dying, and you're worrying about snacks!"

Sobek flinched at his friend's harsh words. He looked guiltily at the food in his arms. "I'm s-sorry," he stammered.

Osiris instantly regretted lashing out at the poor reptile. "I'm sorry too. I didn't mean to yell at you, Sobek." He stared glumly at his own hands, which still felt like they were coated in the Persuader's blood. "This is all my fault. I've cursed Kahndaq because of what I've done."

He had spent weeks trying to figure out a way to make things right again. Now his guilt had brought him to the shrine before him. *I need to purify myself on a pilgrimage.* He ran his finger along the crack splitting the monument in two. "My sister said Adam opened a doorway to the Rock of Eternity through these statues. Look, you can see the crack."

But how was he to open it now?

"Maybe you just need to say the magic w-word?" Sobek suggested.

Osiris considered the notion. "Like what?"

"Sh-sh—" The crocodile seemed hesitant to say the word aloud, but Osiris guessed what he meant.

"Shazam?"

No lightning flashed, but a sudden rumbling greeted the name of the ancient wizard, who had first bestowed Black Adam's powers upon him. Just as Osiris had hoped, the looming statues split down the middle, revealing the hidden stairway beyond. Worn stone steps seemed to lead down into the very bowels of the earth.

"Great thinking, Sobek!" Osiris praised his friend. "The powers Adam gave me must allow us access."

The crocodile eyed the murky staircase with obvious trepidation. "It's dark down there."

"I can see torches on the wall ahead," Osiris said. "Come on!"

Overcoming his fear, Sobek followed Osiris down the long staircase until they reached the bottom of the steps. Blazing torches, mounted in sconces along the tunnel ahead, lighted the way before them. Shadows danced upon the rough-hewn stone walls. Their footsteps echoed loudly as they neared the end of the tunnel. Hideous stone demons squatted along the wall to their left, their leering faces illuminated by the braziers burning at their feet. Osiris recognized the Seven Deadly Sins from his sister's description.

"Hello?" he called out. "Captain Marvel?"

He entered a vast cavernous chamber, where he found Earth's Mightiest Mortal seated upon a bulky granite throne. To his surprise, and discomfort, Mary Marvel and Captain Marvel Jr. stood alongside the throne. He hadn't expected to find them here too.

"The wisdom of Solomon told me that you would seek me out eventually," Captain Marvel said solemnly. "We've been waiting for you."

Captain Marvel Jr. stared at him anxiously. "Where have you been, Osiris? The TV news shows . . . they show you flying right *through* a super-villain." He shook his head in disbelief. "I told the Titans it was staged. That it couldn't have been you."

Osiris stepped forward, prepared to take the heat like a man. "It was me, Freddy," he confessed. It broke his heart to disappoint Captain Marvel Jr. like this, especially after his former teammate had vouched for him to the Titans. "I did not mean to hurt anyone like that, but . . . they were about to kill Isis."

That didn't seem to matter to Captain Marvel Jr. "The Department of Meta-Human Affairs is investigating the Teen Titans for ties to *terrorism* because of you," he said angrily. Osiris wondered if Freddy blamed himself for trusting Osiris too quickly.

"The Suicide Squad provoked the Black Marvels to sway public opinion, and you know it," Mary Marvel pointed out, coming to the newcomer's defense. "Osiris isn't to blame for all of this, Freddy."

"No one forced him to *kill* anyone," Captain Marvel Jr. insisted.

Sobek tugged on Osiris' shoulder, obviously anxious to leave. He looked nervously at the petrified Sins. "I don't like it h-here."

"This is my only hope," Osiris reminded the timid crocodile. The Marvel Family, he recalled, were empowered by a different pantheon of gods than those who had imbued Black Adam with their divine attributes. Maybe Solomon, Hercules, Atlas, Zeus, and the others could lift the curse that had infected all of Kahndaq?

Captain Marvel rose from the throne. "I allowed you entry into the Rock because the Sins didn't want me to," he explained. "They know you have a good soul, despite what you've done."

"It's his powers," Osiris tried to make them understand. "It is Black Adam's powers that are doing this to me and Kahndaq." He lowered his head in shame. "Ever since I . . . murdered that man, our entire nation has suffered. The grave-yards are overflowing."

Captain Marvel contemplated the heartsick youth. He appeared uncertain what Osiris wanted from him. "What can I do?"

"The powers you share have made you a family. Mine has only poisoned ours." Osiris held out his hands in supplication. "I beg you to rid me of this curse. Take away my powers."

"Your powers were a *gift*," a deep voice rebuked him from behind. Osiris spun around to see Black Adam and Isis come striding into the throne room. Adam's face and voice were stern. "They were not a curse!"

"Black Adam!" Sobek exclaimed. "Isis!"

Osiris felt caught in the act. "How did you know—?"

"You left the cavern open behind you," Isis explained. She looked more worried than angry to find him here. She gave the Marvel Family an apologetic look, as though embarrassed at barging in like this.

Black Adam laid a heavy hand upon Osiris' shoulder. "Come back to the palace," he said firmly. "This is a matter for our fam-ily, not theirs." His tone was severe. "Why would you come here when our country is in desperate need of your strength?"

"Kahndaq is suffering because of *you*!" Osiris blurted, pull-ing away from Adam's grasp. "I am suffering because of you!"

Without thinking, he slammed his fist into Black Adam's chin. Sparks flew as the blow sent Adam flying into the stone wall above the Seven Sins. Shattered chunks of rock and cal-cite rained down on the demons' heads. Wrath smiled broadly.

"Osiris!" Isis was shocked by her brother's behavior. "Stop this!"

"Can't you see it, sister?" he pleaded. "His dark powers

may have made me walk again, but at the price of my very soul." Isis was clearly blinded by her love for her husband. "They have corrupted me and all of Kahndaq. In time, they may even corrupt you!"

Black Adam rose up from where he had fallen, behind the row of granite Sins. His dark eyes smoldering with anger, he started to shove Pride and Wrath out of his way. "Move aside, Sins." Centuries-old stone ground ominously.

"Keep your temper in check, Adam," Captain Marvel admonished him. He and Mary Marvel flew over the Sins and grabbed onto Black Adam from behind. "The Rock of Eternity is *my* home now, and I'm not going to let you crack it apart. Or carelessly free the Seven Deadly Sins of Man." They struggled to restrain Adam. "You fight us and I'll banish you to the Rock of Finality."

Mary Marvel raised an eyebrow. "The Rock of Finality? What's that, Billy?"

Osiris had never heard the term before either.

"I'll show you when you're older," Captain Marvel promised. Now was apparently not the time to explore the subject further.

While his family wrestled with Black Adam, Captain Marvel Jr. took it upon himself to restrain Osiris as well. He twisted the other teen's arms behind his back, but that did little to quell the anguish surging inside Osiris. "You did this to me, Adam!" he accused his infamous brother-in-law. "You infected me with your power and anger!"

"Calm down, Osiris," Captain Marvel Jr. ordered. It was hard to believe that they had fought together as allies only two months ago. Everything had gone wrong since then!

"You don't understand," Osiris sobbed. "I am *cursed.*" He fought to break free from Freddy's hold. "Let me go." His expression darkened in frustration, so that he looked more like Black Adam than ever. Isis came running up behind him. "Let. Me. Go!"

He savagely threw his elbow back, hoping to connect with Captain Marvel, but the blow collided with his sister's face instead. She was hurled backward, almost striking Sobek as well. The sound of her hitting the hard stone floor echoed across the throne room.

A hush fell over the torch-lit chamber. Concerned for his wife, Black Adam stopped grappling with Captain Marvel and Mary. "Isis!"

Osiris froze, struck with horror at what he had just done. *Again!* he realized. Despair washed over him. *I lost control again!*

"Adrianna?"

To his relief, Isis got up off the floor. But his heart sank at the sight of the blood streaming from her torn lip. *How hard did I hit her?*

"You're . . . bleeding," he moaned. "I made you bleed." Sensing that the violence was over for the time being, Captain Marvel Jr. cautiously let go of Osiris, who barely noticed. His sister was all that concerned him now. "Are you all right?"

Isis wiped the blood from her chin. "No," she said sadly. Her gaze took in the whole sorry scene. "Thousands are dying by starvation and disease within Kahndaq. Every time I try and grow crops within our borders, they dry up and die." She shook her head in dismay. "When our people need us most, we're fighting."

She walked over to her brother. "These powers, Osiris, have enabled us to do things that have made so many others safe and happy. They are not a curse. Something that brings my brother back to me when I believed he was lost forever could *never* be a curse." She looked deeply into his eyes, without any trace of anger. "Something has invaded Kahndaq. Something unseen and evil. Help Black Adam and me find it. Help us stop it." Her brown eyes brimmed with tears. "Don't turn your back on your family."

Osiris did not know how to respond. His throat tightened, but the words would not come. *I never meant to make you cry,* he thought as he accepted his sister's loving embrace. *I don't want to disappoint you now.*

Leaving the Sins and the Marvels behind, Black Adam flew

over the heads of the statues to join Isis and Osiris in the center of the throne room. Sobek looked on anxiously, wringing his scaly hands.

"I know it is hard to accept what happened," Adam said gently. His voice softened as he tried to get through to Osiris. "It is hard to live with what you have done. But you have more than taken responsibility for it." He spoke as one who knew much of life . . . and death. "And it was you and your sister who showed *me* how to do that. You urged me to reveal my humanity to the world . . . and make myself a better man. Now we are asking you to do the same, my brother."

Osiris could tell that Adam's words were sincere. No matter what tainted power might flow through his veins, the older man truly regarded him as a brother.

If only that was enough . . . !

"I'll try," he said.

Isis smiled and wiped away her tears. Encouraged by her response, Sobek crept forward to reunite with his adopted family. "I could really go for some hummus and lamb right now."

"Oh, Sobek!" Isis laughed out loud.

Black Adam nodded approvingly. "Let us return to our home." He turned to leave the cavern.

"Wait," Captain Marvel said. "The situation in Kahndaq sounds pretty serious. Perhaps my family and I can help?"

Black Adam shook his head. "Thank you, Billy, but no." Pride loomed behind him. "Kahndaq is our responsibility. We can tend to our homeland on our own . . . now that we are a family once more."

They departed the Rock of Eternity.

THE next day, Sobek found Osiris standing forlornly atop the palace. The toxic rain had stopped falling, only to be supplanted by a blistering drought and heat wave. The sun blazed fiercely in the sky above Osiris. The air rippled above the streets and rooftops of the suffering city. Tormented by guilt, the youth stood on the brink of a high terrace, as though on the verge of throwing himself over the edge. *Not that such a leap could truly hurt me,* he thought bitterly. *With my powers, I can only hurt others.*

"What are you doing up here?" the crocodile asked. "I th-thought you were meeting Black Adam and Isis." He observed Osiris uneasily. "Your sister was going to try to dispel the heat again. . . ."

Osiris looked out over the horizon. "I'm not going. I'm leaving Kahndaq."

"W-w-what?" Sobek scratched his head in confusion. "But what about what you said? At the Rock of Eternity?"

"I said what they wanted to hear," Osiris admitted. "That's all. Adam may be able to live with what he did, but I can't." The awful sound of his elbow slamming into his sister's face played over and over in his memory. He saw again the blood dripping from her injured lip. "As long as I have these cursed powers, I need to be far away from anyone else."

"B-but that's it, Osiris!" He sounded desperate to change his friend's mind, to keep Osiris from leaving. "You *can* rid yourself of your powers. Just speak Black Adam's name and free yourself of the curse."

Osiris hesitated. Could it truly be as simple as that? *Once I change back, I could vow never to say the magic words again. I could stay Amon forever.*

"But then . . ." Sobek winced at the full implications of what he had just suggested. He placed his claw over his snout, perhaps wishing he had kept his jaws shut. "Oh, Osiris, you will not be able to walk. . . ."

Osiris glanced down at his legs. Although they were strong and sturdy now, he still remembered the pain he had felt when Intergang's beast-men had crushed his bones to powder in that hellish temple beneath Bialya. He recalled how weak and crippled he had felt, only ten weeks ago, when he had briefly shed his powers before a gaping crowd in Metropolis. Did he really want to stay that way for the rest of his life?

"Of course, Sobek! That must be my penance." It all made

sense now. This was the only way to make things right again. "Maybe then Kahndaq will be free from death and disease and hunger!"

The loyal crocodile did not try to dissuade him, now that his mind was made up. "S-say it, my friend."

"Step back," Osiris warned. Moving away from the ledge, he strode to the center of the terrace and looked up at the sky. He took a deep breath and braced himself for what was to come. Despite his newfound conviction that this was his only hope, he trembled at the enormity of the sacrifice he was about to make. But there was no turning back, not if he truly wanted to atone for his crimes.

"Black Adam!"

A mystic thunderbolt struck the youth, momentarily hiding him within its blinding glare. But then the brightness faded, and Amon Tomaz collapsed onto the rooftop. A simple cotton robe had replaced Osiris' heroic uniform. Twisted limbs sprawled limply across the ceramic shingles. Amon felt a dull ache coming from his mangled legs, but he didn't care. He smiled through the pain, free at last of the unnatural abilities that had made his life a misery.

"The gods," he murmured. "Adam's vengeful gods . . . they're gone. I don't hear their voices anymore." For the first time in months, he felt like himself again. He gazed up at the nearby crocodile. "You were right, Sobek! Perhaps my life will return to normal now. Maybe I will be happy again, and all of Kahndaq will be as well."

He reached out to his friend, figuring that Sobek would lift him up from the soggy rooftop and help him inside, but instead the crocodile just stared at him with a strangely inscrutable expression. For the first time, he felt uncomfortable in the creature's presence. "Sobek?"

Without warning, the reptile lunged forward and sank his teeth into Amon's throat. Blood sprayed across Sobek's snout as his jaws clamped down on the crippled boy's neck. No longer invulnerable, Amon's flesh was torn apart easily by the crocodile's jagged teeth.

He's killing me! Osiris realized in shock. He didn't understand, but he knew that his only hope was to regain his powers right away. "Bla-Black . . ."

Sobek didn't give Amon a chance to complete the invocation. His powerful jaws bit down hard, crushing his victim's larynx. Yellow eyes glinted with cold reptilian glee as he released his grip on Amon's throat. Licking his chops, he gazed down at the helpless boy. Amon gasped for breath. Blood gushed from his wounded throat.

"I'm not so hungry anymore," the crocodile said.

WEEK 44.

SHIRUTA.

THE heat wave continued, despite Isis' strenuous efforts to cool the land. She and Black Adam hovered in the air high above their palace. He clenched his fists in frustration; his strength was useless against the torrid temperature.

"I keep trying to summon rain," she lamented, "but the clouds dissipate almost as soon as they form." A drawn face testified to her fatigue. Perspiration glistened upon her bare arms and legs. "Something has been affecting my powers for weeks now."

Adam nodded grimly. "Something has been affecting all of Kahndaq."

"Thousands are dying of thirst, hunger, and disease. Violent riots erupt in the streets." Her weary eyes beseeched him. "You have refused to ask the outside world for help, but we have no choice. We must do something."

He was forced to agree. Although it galled his soul that he could not protect Kahndaq on his own, he could no longer deny that their own powers were insufficient. "Let us return to the Rock of Eternity," he declared. Perhaps Captain Marvel and his family could succeed where he had failed. *For the sake of my people, I will even appeal to the Justice League if I must.*

He wondered crossly what had become of Osiris. He had expected the boy to join them, but apparently Osiris was still brooding over his imagined "curse." Adam thought it unwise to let the boy wallow in his guilt this way, but Isis had urged him to be patient with her brother, and he had deferred

to her judgment in this matter. Besides, it was doubtful that
Osiris' presence would have made any difference today. The
malign forces besieging Kahndaq were greater than any single youth could overcome.

But from whence did this evil truly spring?

Abruptly, a mystical thunderbolt exploded up from the
rooftop of the palace, jolting Black Adam to his marrow. He
froze in midair, transfixed by the surging electricity.

"Adam!"

Isis swooped to his side, but he was not in need of rescue.
Instead he felt a rush of power course through his veins and
sinews. Magical energy crackled around his levitating form.
Lightning arced between his gleaming metal wristbands.
Sparks flashed along the thunderbolt emblem on his chest. His
eyes burned with eldritch fire.

"Adam?" Isis eyed him with concern. "Are you—?"

"I feel . . . stronger," he informed her. He flexed his muscles
experimentally. At first, the sudden influx of power puzzled
him. Then the truth hit home like a second bolt from the blue.
Apprehension showed upon his brooding features. "They have
returned to me."

Isis had not yet made the connection. "What have?"

"The powers of Osiris," he said somberly. The golden glow
faded from his eyes as he grasped the full implications of what
had just transpired. The wisdom of Zehuti warned him to take
care. He cast a worried gaze at his wife. "Something is wrong."

Isis gasped out loud. From the sudden look of fear upon her
face, he realized that she too understood that this ominous
event boded ill for her brother. "Amon!"

The thunderbolt had come from the roof of the palace
below them. He and Isis dived from the cloudless sky down to
the source of the magical blast: a level terrace surrounded by
four domed towers. A quick glance confirmed their worst
fears. A sob tore itself from Isis' throat as they spied the mutilated body of Amon Tomaz lying upon the bloody shingles.
The corpse's shattered limbs, and shredded garments, made it
clear that Amon had been in mortal form when he died. Bite

marks suggested that some carnivorous beast had been feeding on the youth for hours before he finally expired. His mouth was frozen in a silent scream. Adam saw to his disgust that the boy's tongue was missing. There was no way he could have summoned his powers to save himself. *By the gods,* Black Adam vowed, *someone will pay for this atrocity.*

Isis dropped to her knees beside her brother's body. "No!" Tear-filled eyes looked up at Adam. "Please, do something!"

His heart ached for her loss, remembering the deaths of his sons millennia ago. He yanked his cape from his shoulders and laid it over Amon's ravaged corpse like a shroud. There was little he could do to ease his beloved's pain, but at least he could spare her the sight of her brother's grisly remains.

Helping her to her feet, he took Isis in his arms. She sobbed against his shoulder. "Why did he change?" she asked despairingly. Amon had been all but indestructible when in the guise of Osiris. "Why did he change back?"

A gravelly voice answered her. "Osiris believed his powers were the cause of Kahndaq's misery." Sobek came crawling across the rooftops on all fours. Fresh blood was smeared across his saurian jaws and teeth. His tail swished across the polished ceramic shingles behind him. "What a fool."

"Sobek!" Isis cried out, surprised by the crocodile's presence. Adam realized that Sobek must have been hiding behind one of the nearby turrets.

The crocodile licked her brother's blood from his chops. "For all he tried to do to sweeten his soul, his flesh tasted like rotting chicken." His callous tone mocked her grief. "He was too stringy." A reptilian tongue flicked over his incisors. "He's still stuck between my teeth."

"It was you?" she asked, aghast at the monster's treachery. "How could you?"

Rising to his feet, Sobek warily circled Black Adam and Isis. An elaborate suit of armor clothed his scaly body, replacing the polyester jogging suits he had always worn before. He greedily eyed the body beneath the cape. "I was hungry," he explained. "I'm *always* so awfully hungry, and only the flesh of a Marvel can satisfy me." He shrugged his shoulders. "That's the way they made me."

They? Black Adam realized that some unknown enemy had planted the perfidious reptile among them. Although eager to avenge Amon's death, he held back in hopes of learning more from the loquacious lizard. *Who are "they"?*

"I told Osiris that I had no name," Sobek declared, "but I lied. I am Yurrd the Unknown. I am *Famine.*"

Yurrd? The name meant nothing to Adam. But, like all of Kahndaq, he had grown far too familiar with famine over the last few weeks. Could this demon truly be responsible for the empty stomachs of his countrymen? *All the more reason, then, that this accursed creature not live another day!*

"Osiris was your friend!" Isis accused the reptile. At her command, rustling vines snaked up the sides of the palace. A blast of angry wind nearly knocked Sobek off his feet. "He saved you from Dr. Sivana's lab!"

The crocodile laughed harshly. "I *said* I'd been left there after Sivana disappeared, but that was another lie." A wicked grin stretched beneath his snout. "I was delivered to Sivana's mansion only hours before you arrived."

Black Adam recalled Sobek's unexpected appearance during their dinner with Lady Sivana. He wondered whether the mad scientist's wife had been in on the deception. Perhaps her plea for their assistance in locating Sivana had only been a ruse?

"You were all so desperate to help the poor and unfortunate," Sobek jeered, "so a plan was hatched to infiltrate your inner circle by posing as a confused and frightened animal. We knew that your Black Marvel Family wouldn't be able to resist having their own version of that insipid talking tiger."

Nature's fury flashed in Isis' dark eyes as her sorrow gave way to rage. Bristling with jagged thorns, the animated vines rose above the edge of the rooftop. "We treated you like family!" she thundered at Sobek. "We *loved* you!"

"Love?" The crocodile spat out the word. "What does a reptile care of love? My blood is cold!" He glared malignantly at Black Adam. "Intergang offered you riches for safe passage through Kahndaq. They urged you to ally yourself with our puppet government in Bialya. But you refused, and now you and your family are a threat to Intergang's ever-growing religion of crime!" He stalked toward them, his clawed hands raised before him. "That's why we were brought here."

"We?" Black Adam raised his own fists in anticipation. *I should have known that Intergang was behind this,* he thought fiercely. *They will pay dearly for the heartache they have caused, beginning with this loathsome creature.*

But Sobek was no longer alone. A sonic boom heralded the opening of a sudden rift in time and space. A trio of monstrous giants emerged from the rift, which instantly closed behind them. Over twenty feet tall, they dwarfed both the humans and the crocodile. Black Adam quickly took stock of these new adversaries.

One was a mechanized monstrosity, boasting an impressive array of high-tech weaponry. Cannons served as the creature's arms. Crimson armor covered every inch of his body. The roof trembled beneath its elephantine tread.

The second was a hideous cyclops, with but a single bloodred eye gazing out from its scarred visage. Instead of cannons, metallic valves and hoses were mounted to the monster's arms. Pipes connected the hoses to enormous steel tanks affixed to the giant's back.

The third was like a demon out of ancient myth, with the wings of an enormous hawk, the legs of a goat, the arms and torso of a man, the tail of a jackal, and the yellowed skull and horns of a dead steer clamped over his face. He clutched an imposing steel scythe, like the Grim Reaper of Western folklore.

"Behold my siblings," Sobek boasted. "Roggra, Zorrm, and Azraeuz. Some call us 'The Monster Society,' but we truly embody the Four Horsemen of dread Apokalips. Our influence is the true source of Kahndaq's misery over the last month." His burnished armor proclaimed his warlike intentions. "But we are through hiding!"

Together, the fiendish quartet pounced on Black Adam and Isis. The impact drove the couple and their attackers through the roof of the palace into the royal bedchamber below. They crashed down onto their own marital bed, smashing it completely. Broken pieces of stone and plaster fell from the jagged gap in the ceiling. Feathers and wooden splinters went flying.

Sobek sprang at Black Adam, his jaws snapping at Adam's throat. "Let me tell you how I ate Amon!" the crocodile taunted. "How his organs popped in my mouth like fresh grapes!"

The monster's cruel words only fueled Adam's wrath. With superhuman swiftness, he grabbed hold of Sobek's jaws with his bare hands. Powerful muscles strained as he began to pull the jaws apart.

"You are done talking, lizard."

Sobek croaked in pain. His front claws pawed frantically at Adam's chest, but failed to penetrate the champion's impervious chest. The crocodile was not attacking a helpless cripple now, nor would he ever be eating anything again. Greasy tears leaked from his eyes.

"Adam?" Isis said uncertainly. She seemed conflicted between her divine mercy and a very human desire for revenge.

"These are not men," Adam stated bluntly. Unlike his wife, he had no doubts about what was to be done. "Sobek said it himself. They are monsters . . . and they will be treated as such."

Calling upon the strength he had reclaimed from Osiris, Black Adam tore Sobek's jaws apart. Cold reptilian blood sprayed against Adam as the deceitful crocodile spasmed through his death throes. Adam hurled the scaly carcass away from him in disgust.

Yurrd the Unknown was no more.

His fellow Horsemen howled in protest. Rising from the wreckage of the bed, their inhuman craniums scraped against the vaulted ceiling of the violated bedchamber. The armored giant, who looked more machine than flesh and blood, charged Adam.

"I am Roggra!" he declared. "I am War!"

Tackling Adam, his merest touch ignited an explosion that brought down the wall behind Adam. They tumbled through the breached wall into another chamber of the palace. A cloud of dust and smoke momentarily blinded Adam. He broke free from Roggra's mechanized grasp and staggered backward away from his foe. Shattered masonry crunched beneath his boots. He wiped the dust from his eyes.

A massive cannon slammed into his face. "I have the power of all the world's soldiers and bombs," Roggra proclaimed. The muzzle of the cannon flared and a tremendous blast propelled Adam through a solid marble column into the wall beyond. "Those are *my* gods, and they are infinitely more deadly than the senile deities who empower you!"

Dazed, Adam shook his head to clear his thoughts. His hand went to his aching brow and came away stained with red. He tasted salt upon his tongue.

War had drawn first blood.

Isis and the remaining Horsemen faced each other within the ruined bedchamber. The one-eyed giant stomped toward her, while his skull-faced companion looked on in silence. Toxic chemicals sloshed inside the tanks and hoses that were arrayed upon Zorrm's immense frame. He smelled of rot and gangrene. Isis sensed the Horseman's unclean nature at once.

"Your body is made of nothing but viruses and bacteria. You are Pestilence itself." Ropy vines descended through the hole in the ceiling. More tendrils entered through the windows to defend her. "All these diseases, all these plagues afflicting Kahndaq, stem from you!"

The fetid cyclops opened its jaws, as though to answer her charges. Isis braced herself for Zorrm's heartless retort. Her loyal vines reared up around the advancing Horseman, like serpents preparing to strike. They whipped the dusty air.

But no words escaped the monster's lips. Instead he vomited a stream of viscous green slime onto Isis, dousing her with his foul effluvia. Isis recoiled in horror, her gorge rising at the sour-smelling mucus clinging to her face and limbs. Gagging, she frantically wiped it away from her eyes and mouth, but feared that she had already been contaminated by the infectious spew, which was literally swimming with every germ known to man. *Goddess preserve me,* she prayed fervently. *The plague is upon me!*

In retaliation, the vines lashed out at Zorrm. Thick green tendrils coiled around his limbs and torso, squeezing as tightly as a boa constrictor. Thorns jabbed at his livid face and flesh. The aggressive vines distracted the Horseman from his attack on Isis, forcing him to defend himself against the topiary assault. He spewed more vomit at the vines scratching his face, which were eaten away as though by acid. Dying branches hissed and sizzled as they dissolved against his leather armor.

Isis felt the plants' pain, even as a thousand diseases invaded her own immortal form. Nausea, even worse than that which had been inflicted upon her by Count Vertigo, gripped her stomach. A sudden fever left her shaking and sweating. Painful cramps racked her entrails. Her throbbing head felt as though it was being stabbed repeatedly by a red-hot poker. Breathing became difficult as her lungs filled with fluid. Every muscle ached. Her throat was sore. She sneezed and coughed violently.

Save me from this Pestilence, she begged the powers of Nature. *Don't let him near me again!*

The surviving vines grabbed onto Zorrm and threw him far away.

ROGGRA'S cannon boomed again.

The blast hurled Black Adam out of the palace into an enclosed courtyard outside. Decorative fountains and pools had dried out beneath the oppressive sun. Somehow managing to stay on his feet, he staggered unsteadily across debris-strewn tiles. Blood dripped from numerous small cuts and scrapes. His black hair was disheveled and powdered with dust. His distinctive garb was torn and scorched. His bare knuckles were raw and red.

Whirring and clanking, War pursued Adam into the court-

yard. His cannon automatically reloaded, and Black Adam
threw up his arms to protect himself. A bomb-burst exploded
against his upraised wristbands. The golden metal shattered
into a million pieces. The earthshaking impact jarred Adam to
his bones. He teetered upon his heels, on the verge of losing
his balance. He lacked even the strength to flee.

Roggra prepared to fire again. . . .

Salvation arrived in the unlikely form of Zorrm, who came
flying between them as though flung by a catapult. A titanic
blast, meant for Black Adam, struck Pestilence instead. Dying
vines were blown away from the monster's smoking frame.

Isis? Adam guessed, grateful for the respite.

His wife appeared upon the ruined terrace. To his dismay,
he saw that her graceful form was liberally coated with some
vile green ichor. She threw out her arms to command the
elements.

"Winds!"

A mighty zephyr plucked the fallen debris from the ground
and threw it at War and Pestilence with tremendous force.
They went tumbling across the spacious courtyard.

She stumbled over to Adam's side. He couldn't help notic-
ing how ill she looked. Her face was ashen. Burst blood vessels reddened her eyes. "Adam," she said hoarsely. Her quaking
body clung weakly to his. Her flesh was hot to the touch. "My
blood runs cold. Can you feel it?" She looked back over her
shoulder. "Death is here."

He followed her gaze to where the fourth Horseman—
Azraeuz—stood watching them from the ragged gap in the
wall. A bovine death's-head masked his features. His ebony
wings were folded against his back as he held his gleaming
scythe aloft. His eerie stillness was more unnerving than his
brothers' vicious attacks.

Black Adam found it hard to gaze at Azraeuz for long. His
eyes watered and stung, blurring his vision, until he was forced
to look away. Isis also averted her eyes. She rubbed at them
with her fists, trying to clear her sight.

"You have been marked by the stare of Azraeuz, the Silent

King," Roggra stated as the malevolent war-machine righted himself and came clanking toward Adam. Paving stones cracked and splintered beneath his ponderous tread. Mechanical arms extended from open compartments in his armor. "He has chosen you for Death and you will suffer through it."

Steel pincers yanked Black Adam away from Isis and launched him back toward the palace. Smashing headfirst through the wall, Adam skidded across the floor of a vast, sepulchral chamber. Stunned, it took him a moment to realize that he was now within the shrine he had erected to his long-lost wife and sons. He lay sprawled at the feet of a marble replica of Shiruta and their two boys. His battered face flushed with anger. *How dare Sobek's evil brethren profane this sacred place!*

Roggra stomped into the shrine. The metal pincers seized hold of Adam again and lifted him from the floor. The Horseman held Adam's face up to the sculpted images of his dead family.

"War has always been your undoing," Roggra gloated. "Your wife and children died in a battle you were not here to fight." That much was true; Mighty Adam had been fighting evil in Egypt, on behalf of the wizard Shazam, when his homeland had been overrun by a merciless invader. "Your oldest son begged for his life. He was a coward."

Lies! Adam thought vehemently. This unholy being was obviously a creation of modern science, not ancient sorcery. Roggra had no knowledge of what had truly occurred in that bygone era. He knew only the historical tidbits his creators had fed into his artificial brain. *My son was no coward!*

In the vandalized courtyard, Isis rubbed at her eyes, which still smarted from looking at the Angel of Death. Half-blinded by her own tears, she heard ponderous steps behind her, along with the sloshing of toxic fluids. *Pestilence!* she realized, spinning around a moment too late. Poison gas sprayed from Zorrm's inexhaustible supply of biohazardous waste.

Already feeling weak and feverish, she choked on the

fumes. She fell to the ground, clutching her throat. Her wheez-
ing lungs sucked at the air. She retched onto the cold stone
tiles. Hungry insects burrowed up from the arid soil. Cock-
roaches and beetles scuttled over her supine body, eager to
begin consuming her flesh even before she died. A swarm of
buzzing flies nipped painfully at her skin.

Azraeuz approached at a measured pace. The shaft of his
scythe tapped against the broken tiles. Zorrm backed away,
bowing his head to his more funereal brother. "I have spread
my diseases across her and inside her," he told Death. "She is
ready for you."

THE Horseman smashed Adam into the statues, shattering them.
Adam grabbed onto the carved faces of his sons before they
could crash to the floor with the rest of the fragments. Still holding on to Adam with his pincers, Roggra aimed all his guns and
cannons at the back of his captive's skull.

"Will you beg for your life as well?"

Never! Adam vowed. Wrenching his body around, he
plunged both his fists into the Horseman's armored chest. Torn
metal shrieked, and sparks flared, as, still gripping the marble
shards, his hands sank wrist-deep into the monster's torso. He
found something warm and fleshy deep inside Roggra's mechanized chassis. He pushed harder, forcing his fists through the
pulpy mass. Roggra squealed in pain.

"Will you?" Adam challenged him.

An oily yellow fluid leaked from the corners of Roggra's
hinged jaw. "S-stop. . . ."

"War is nothing new to me." Black Adam sneered at his foe.
"A being who embodies it does not impress me."

Clenching his jaws, he swung his arms open, ripping
Roggra right down the middle.

AZRAEUZ loomed over Isis' fallen form. His cloven hooves
scraped against the ground. His huge black wings spread out
behind him. No mercy showed in the cavernous depths of his
empty eye sockets. He reeked of death and decay. His seg-

mented tail swished across the pavement. Supporting himself upon his scythe, he bent low and reached out for Isis. She felt the icy touch of his fingers against her face.

Throbbing black veins spread across her flesh, emanating outward from where he touched her. Agony pulsed through her body with every beat of her heart. Bleeding sores tore open her once-smooth skin. Insects infested the wounds, feeding on the exposed tissue. Flies laid their eggs in the open sores. She groaned pitifully.

Pestilence crept closer, the better to savor her demise. Isis heard a gun being cocked nearby. Part of her prayed that Roggra's powerful firearms would swiftly put her out of her misery. *Forgive me, Adam, for leaving you alone as you were before.* She turned her head to look into the face of her executioner.

But instead of War, she saw Black Adam standing boldly behind Zorrm. He aimed one of Roggra's severed arms at Pestilence like the cannon it was. The muzzle flared and the gun went off with a deafening boom. Zorrm's head exploded from his shoulders. His headless body toppled onto the ground.

Bless you, my husband, Isis thought gratefully. For once, she did not question the severity of Adam's actions. *The Earth is well rid of such an abomination.*

Azraeuz' wings flapped loudly as he instantly flew to avenge his brothers. The sharpened tip of his scythe sunk into Black Adam's side. Adam grimaced in pain, gritting his teeth to keep from crying out. His bloody fist slammed into the Horseman's face, cracking the skeletal visage.

Take care, beloved, Isis thought, fearing for her husband's life. *Beware his fatal touch.*

Death's fingertips grazed Black Adam's cheek. Almost instantly, the telltale black veins began to spread across his face. . . .

No! Isis thought. *Not Adam too!*

With one last burst of divine power, she reached down to the very core of the world and summoned fiery vengeance from underground. "Earth, remove him. . . ."

A geyser of red-hot lava erupted directly beneath Azraeuz. The volcanic explosion hurled him high into the air, away from Black Adam. Above them, the burning Horseman arced across the sky like a blazing comet. Scarlet flames rushed over his great black wings. Isis prayed that the purifying fire would consume the lethal entity until no trace of it remained. There had been too much Death already . . . or perhaps there had not been enough.

Exhausted, she collapsed against the ground.

"Isis!"

Adam rushed to her side. He furiously swept the voracious insects away from her body. Sores and swellings disfigured her unforgettable face and form, but beneath the diseases ravaging her body he could still see the woman he loved . . . the woman who had brought him peace and happiness for the first time in countless centuries. *This cannot be!* he thought in anguish. *The gods could never be so cruel!*

Despair tormented her. "All we tried to accomplish . . . all my brother tried. . . ."

"I will take you to the Rock of Eternity," he promised, clutching her hand tightly. Her feverish skin was hot and dry. Her pulse throbbed feebly beneath his fingers. "Perhaps Billy will be able to . . ."

She shook her head. "I see it now. Why your way . . . kept Kahndaq and its people safe."

"Do not give up hope," he commanded her. "You taught me never to abandon hope."

Hot tears streaked her face. A bitterness entered her voice that he had never heard before. "I was wrong."

Adam didn't want to hear it. "I believe in you."

"I was wrong, Adam," she insisted. "It was never you that needed redemption. It was the rest of the world." A palsied hand reached up to stroke his face. "You tried so hard . . . for a world that did not deserve our mercy . . . that put our family through so much pain. . . ." Her expression hardened. A light went out of her eyes. When she spoke again, her voice was cold and unforgiving:

"*Avenge us.*"

Her heart stopped. Her trembling body went limp. A bolt of golden lightning shot from her eyes. The power of Isis fled her dying body, returning to the heavens . . . perhaps for all time. All that was left behind was the lifeless body of a woman named Adrianna Tomaz.

Her final words echoed in Black Adam's brain.

He clenched his fists.

NANDA PARBAT.

ONE minute, the rose was as bright and fresh as ever. The next, it died right before Renee's eyes.

Seated at Tot's desk, she looked up from the Crime Bible in surprise. The diabolical tome lay open before her, revealing a grisly woodcut image of screaming victims throwing themselves into a fiery pit in the middle of a distorted cityscape. Renee had been poring over the illustration, searching for any possible Gotham landmarks, when a falling brown petal caught her attention.

What the hell?

More petals, all crinkly brown, rained down onto the open pages. She reached out for what was left of the rose, but it crumbled to dust in her hand, disintegrating like Dracula in the sunlight. The fallen petals also blackened and fell apart, faster than any natural process of decay could account for.

A shiver ran down Renee's spine. *I don't understand,* she thought. Isis' magic had sustained the rose for over four months now. How could that magic fail now, unless . . .

"She's dead," Renee realized. "Isis is dead."

Tot and Richard looked up from their seats by the hearth. They watched somberly as she let the powdery remains of the rose trickle through her fingers. Neither of them offered any other possible explanation for the flower's freakish demise. Richard's eyes narrowed as he observed Renee's reaction to the news. He nudged Tot, who got up and left the room.

"Whatever happened," she guessed, "it can't be good." She gazed thoughtfully out the window, a worried expression upon her face. "Adam and Osiris . . . what will they do now? How will they cope?"

"Find out," Richard said.

"Huh?" She turned toward her teacher. What was he suggesting?

"Go and find out," he said simply.

Tot reentered the room, bearing a bundle of clothing. Renee recognized some of her own laundry, as well as Vic's old fedora and trench coat.

"There are lots of answers to be found in Nanda Parbat, no question about it." He rose from his seat. "But none of them are going to satisfy you. Not one of them is the one you're looking for."

Tot set the bundle down on the desk. "I took the liberty of treating your normal clothes with the same reactive compound used in the coat and hat. You'll also find in your belongings a bottle of specially formulated shampoo that will likewise react to the binary gas, altering its color. The actual adhesive for the mask is now part of the . . ."

"No," Renee said firmly, crossing her arms across her chest. She saw where Tot and Richard were going with this. "I'm *not* him. I'm not going to *be* him."

The old professor was visibly annoyed by her reaction. "Believe me, Ms. Montoya, I'm painfully aware of that fact."

Richard stepped between them, playing peacemaker. "Of course not. You're going to be yourself," he told Renee. He lifted Vic's hat from the desk. "That's the way it should be. That's what Sage wanted."

He faced her across the desk, his voice as calm and confident as usual. Renee eyed him skeptically, but was willing to listen to what he had to say. *Go ahead,* she thought dubiously. *Make your case.*

"You saw your reflection in the cave, Renee. You saw yourself without ego, without distortion, selfless and ideal."

Without a face, you mean. "I don't know *what* I saw, Richard."

"Sure you do," he said with a sly grin. "It just makes you uncomfortable. It scares you." That didn't seem to bother him. "It should."

"How reassuring," she replied sarcastically, while Tot watched the discussion intently. "Is this another lesson about letting go? Cease being myself to *become* myself?"

"Lovely paradox," he commented. "A lot like life."

Big deal, she thought, still resisting the idea. "Well, I don't need a mask for that."

Richard contemplated the fedora in his hands. "You're going to find, like Sage did, that some questions can only be answered by wearing a mask." He leaned forward and lightly placed the hat on her head. "Just as there are some that can only be asked when you remove one."

The brim of the hat cast a shadow over her face, hiding her features. Renee tried to imagine herself wearing the Question's trademark trench coat and mask. *That's not me,* she thought. As a Gotham City cop, she had worked with plenty of masked vigilantes: Batman, Robin, Catwoman, the Huntress. But she had never wanted to be one. *That's Kate's scene, not mine.*

She reached up to remove the hat, then hesitated. What would Vic want her to do? Why else had he spent so much time preparing her?

"Start in Kahndaq," Richard suggested. "See where that leads you."

WEEK 45.

SHIRUTA.

BLACK Adam stood before the open balcony, looking out over the city below. His hands were clasped behind his back. Night had fallen outside. The darkened sky seemed to match his mood.

"It started raining the day she died," he said grimly, "and it has not stopped since. The people say these are her tears. They say Isis weeps not for herself nor for her brother nor even for me, but rather for all of Kahndaq and her people."

He turned to face Renee, who had just been escorted into the throne room. Water dripped from her trench coat as she removed her hat. A black armband, purchased from a street vendor, let her share in the city's mourning. *I still can't believe Isis is really dead,* she thought.

"She weeps," Adam continued, "because she can no longer walk among them." He inspected his visitor. "Sage is not with you."

Renee held on to Vic's hat. "He died."

Adam nodded, unsurprised by the news. "She said he would."

Turning away from Renee, he gazed out at the city once more. She joined him at the rear of the balcony. Neither of them looked at each other.

"Why are you here, Renee Montoya?"

She knew better than to place a comforting hand upon his arm. "I wanted to see if there was anything I could do."

"You?" His voice took on a bitter edge. His expression darkened.

Renee understood that she was taking a serious risk here. An angry Black Adam was a dangerous Black Adam, and he had never exactly been the president of her fan club. But somebody had to talk to him, before he took his pain and fury out on the rest of the world. "I know what it's like to lose the people you love." She looked him squarely in the eye. "To have the world turn on you for no reason."

"You know *nothing*," he spat.

"Almost nothing, sure," she conceded. "But I know about this. I know about the guilt and self-loathing at being the one who survived. I know the rage at not having been able to prevent what happened."

He snarled in warning. His fists clenched at his sides, and Renee remembered the last time she had faced a pissed-off Black Adam, when he'd caught her lolling in bed with that local girl. At the time, she had goaded him recklessly, not caring what happened to her, but this was different. She didn't want to provoke Adam. She wanted to help him. *Whether he wants me to or not.*

"And I know the shame that comes from believing you've failed those most important to you. . . ."

Black Adam grabbed onto her by her face. His fingers, which were capable of ripping her head from her shoulders, dug into her cheeks. "You have *always* presumed too much," he growled. "Now you presume a friendship that does not exist."

"*Isis* was my friend," she insisted, only too aware that she could be moments away from death herself. When Black Adam lost his temper, people tended to get dismembered.

But he merely tossed her aside. Skidding across the floor on her butt, Renee realized that she had gotten off easy. Adam was seriously restraining himself.

"And it is in her memory that I will allow you to leave here alive," he said. "I do not require your help, and I do not want your pity." His feet lifted off from the floor, so that he hovered in the air above Renee. It was only a matter of inches, but that short space seemed to define an unbridgeable gulf between them. "Look to your own affairs, and leave me to attend to

mine." He peered down at the mortal woman as she got up off
the floor. An icy cold rage seemed to emanate from him, chilling Renee to the bone. "The last of the Four Horsemen who
murdered my wife and brother has fled to Bialya, where he has
been given aid and comfort by the government. A government
bought by Intergang, much as they tried to buy their way into
Kahndaq."

He floated out over the balcony. "But Intergang has *other*
targets, do they not?" He glanced back over his shoulder at
his unwanted guest. "Isn't it time you went home, Renee
Montoya?"

With that, he launched himself into sky.

Renee was suddenly very glad that she wasn't in Bialya.

BIALYA.

"THIS is a betrayal, Mister Mannheim!"

Colonel Sumaan Harjvati, President-for-Life of the glorious
nation of Bialya, railed at the enormous flat-screen monitor
taking up one entire wall of the presidential war room. Epaulets
and medals adorned Harjvati's khaki military uniform. A thick
black beard sprouted from his florid features. An automatic
pistol was holstered to his hip. Aides, advisors, and generals
clustered around the spacious chamber, whispering nervously
amongst themselves. Harjvati shook his fist at the screen.

"I'd choose your words carefully, Mr. President." Bruno
Mannheim, live from Gotham City, glowered from the jumbo-
sized screen. Smaller monitors, situated around the room, ran
TV coverage of the funeral services in Kahndaq. Captain Marvel and the rest of the Marvel Family could be seen serving as
pallbearers for Isis and Osiris.

Harjvati ignored the ganglord's warning. "Our whole nation embraced your religion of crime, your new world order!
You said it was prophecy, and that Bialya's role in deploying
your Four Horsemen would remain secret!"

He pointed an irate finger at the looming figure of Azraeuz, who was lurking at the rear of the room, glaring ominously at all assembled. The last of the Horsemen still bore the scars of his battle with Black Adam. Scorch marks defaced his armor. The tips of his wings were singed. Armed soldiers, members of Bialya's elite Sovereign Guard, kept their weapons trained on the unearthly apparition, while trying hard not to look Azraeuz in the eyes.

"Why has Death arrived at our doorstep, Mister Mannheim? Why does he hover over us in silence?" Perspiration beaded upon his balding dome. "Is this part of your prophecy too?"

On the screen, Mannheim looked distinctly unsympathetic to Harjvati's plight. A massive map of Gotham City occupied the wall behind him. A circle had been drawn in the center of the map, over the very heart of the city. Harjvati didn't even want to know what that signified. *Gotham is Mannheim's territory,* he thought. *All I care about is my own country!*

"Prophecy's a funny thing, Mister President," Mannheim said with a smirk. "You tried contacting Dr. Sivana?"

Of course I did! Harjvati thought. "The Oolong Complex is refusing all incoming communications. They appear to be in lockdown!"

"Then it looks like you've got a problem." Mannheim glanced at his watch. "Especially since the funeral services in Kahndaq just ended."

Harjvati knew what that meant. "Black Adam will be on his way here." More sweat streamed from his pores. He dabbed frantically at the perspiration with a monogrammed silk handkerchief. "You must help us! My army won't be enough!"

"That's what I'm trying to say," Mannheim said. He casually lit a cigar and blew smoke at the screen. "Nice knowin' ya."

The screen went blank as Mannheim abruptly cut off the transmission. *Traitor!* Harjvati thought. *Turncoat!* He opened his mouth to demand that contact with Gotham be restored. "Get me—"

Black Adam flew through the screen, exploding out of the

heavily fortified walls of the war room. A high-pitched shriek escaped Harjvati's lungs as he ducked beneath the flying debris. Generals, soldiers, and terrified cabinet members dived for cover. Azraeuz screeched like a wild animal as he retreated via the rear exit. The Horseman's fearsome scythe cut a bloody path through any soldiers unlucky enough to get in his way. Gunfire ricocheted harmlessly off Death's scorched armor.

No! Harjvati thought. *This isn't fair!* He wished that he had never heard of Intergang, let alone accepted their bribes and support. What was the good of being President-for-Life when that life could be cut short in an instant? *I have to get out of here!*

A powerful hand grabbed onto the dictator's neck, lifting him from the floor. His feet dangled in the air as he found himself face-to-face with Black Adam. The other man's saturnine features were as hard and unyielding as the pyramids. Iron fingers tightened around Harjvati's throat.

"The Four Horsemen did not come from Bialya!" Harjvati lied desperately. He tried to pry himself free from Black Adam's grip, but not even a crowbar would have sufficed. "I beg of you! Mercy!"

Black Adam's implacable black eyes were those of an executioner. "This is mercy," he declared. "It will be quick."

He hurled Harjvati up at the ceiling, where the dictator's head splattered like a soft piece of fruit.

FRAGMENTS of skull and brain clung to the ceiling even after Sumaan Harjvati's lifeless body hit the floor. But pulping the buffoonish president provided Black Adam with little satisfaction. Harjvati had been nothing but a pawn in Intergang's ruthless play for world domination. Isis' true killers lay elsewhere.

No matter, Adam thought. *They shall not escape my justice.* Bullets bounced off his face and chest as Bialya's Sovereign Guard sought to avenge their leader. A grenade exploded uselessly at his feet. His fists clenched, he flew straight into the midst of the soldiers. *And all who oppose me will suffer the same fate. . . .*

Moments later, he burst through the walls of the presidential fortress out into the open square beyond. Fresh blood soaked Black Adam's sacred garb, which remained unmarred by the feeble efforts of Harjvati's defenders. To the military forces stationed outside the palace he looked like some bloodthirsty *afreet* out of their childhood nightmares.

An entire battalion of tanks and missile launchers awaited Black Adam, nor were these decrepit Cold War relics; Intergang's generous support had allowed Bialya to upgrade its armed forces significantly. Over a dozen state-of-the-art Luthor-Corp battle cruisers, complete with spent-uranium armor, were pitted against a single unarmed man. Laser targeting beams swept over his body.

Black Adam sneered in contempt.

Without pausing for an instant, he plowed right through the row of tanks. One after another, the armored vehicles exploded from within. Tank guns and mounted artillery tried to retard his progress, but the high-explosive rounds detonated harmlessly against him. Black Adam ripped one tank in half, causing it to blow up, before flying onto the next. Choking black smoke soon filled the square. A panicked general urged his troops onward. The braver of his soldiers fired wildly at Black Adam; many others fled in terror from their immortal foe. Flying shrapnel posed a threat to everyone except Adam.

"Where is the Horseman?" the general cried out in frustration. Mere mortals were obviously no match for Black Adam; only Intergang's inhuman creation stood a chance of stopping him. "Where is Death?"

A burning chunk of metal slammed into his body, answering his question . . . at least in the abstract. The flying tank chassis killed half a dozen of his lieutenants as well. A mangled heap of steel served as their headstones.

Yes, Black Adam thought, his eyes on the lookout for Isis' murderer. *Where is Death?*

BELLE REVE.
LOUISIANA.

FRANTIC aides briefed Amanda Waller on the crisis.

"Echelon has picked up fresh transmissions out of southern Bialya, all within the last twenty minutes." Count Vertigo was visibly shaken by what he'd heard. His own country had been destroyed by the Spectre years ago. "It's . . . it's a slaughter. . . ."

Another voice piped up. "Checkmate and NSA satellites positively confirm Black Adam's presence in country, but whether he's responsible . . ."

"The State Department has shut down our embassy in Bialya," a third voice reported. "All American personnel are to be evacuated immediately."

Too little, too late, Waller thought grimly. *We should have forced a regime change there months ago. And in Kahndaq too.* She sorted through the mug shots on her desk, picking out a new Suicide Squad. So far, she hadn't found anyone in custody strong enough to bring the rampaging superhuman down. *I knew Black Adam was a loose cannon, and now he's gone off . . . just like I predicted.*

The prison's official warden came running into her office. "I have the White House on line one," he announced shrilly. "The Pentagon is on line two."

"Hold my calls," Waller barked. "And get me the Justice Society!"

BIALYA.

THE fighter jet crashed into the center of a crowded bazaar.

Flames erupted within the market, consuming shops, merchants, and customers alike. The few survivors choked on the smoke as they pulled themselves across the shattered pavement. Shocked men and women called out for their loved ones. Confused children cried for their parents. The moans and screams of the dying and the injured filled the air. Blood poured across the cobblestones. Billowing black fumes hid the moon and stars.

Black Adam strode out of the heart of the blaze. A torn jet wing crunched beneath his boots. Bloody tracks charted his progress across the wreckage. His dark eyes scanned the horizon. In the distance, more jets were impaled atop the spires of wrecked skyscrapers and mosques. Fireballs spewed into the sky.

Adam didn't even know what this city's name had been. He had left the ruins of the capital far behind him and was now making his way across the entire country. The wisdom of the gods might have informed him of his precise location, but Adam didn't care enough to listen. All of Bialya would pay for sheltering the Horsemen. Let others make a list of the dead.

I have had my share of burials, he thought. *And more.*

He paused for a moment, his unquenchable rage ebbing slightly. An overturned flower cart, now being devoured by blossoms of bright orange flame, lay directly in his path. A single yellow rose floated in a crimson puddle, its delicate petals soaking up the blood. The fragile flower reminded him of all he had lost.

Isis . . .

He knelt down beside the puddle and plucked the rose from the blood. For a second, sorrow unmanned him and a solitary tear leaked from his cheek. There had been a time, not so long ago, when he had finally found true happiness.

A bottle smashed against the back of his head, disturbing his grief. "Murderer!" an hysterical voice cried out. "Demon!"

Black Adam rose to find a mob of vengeful Bialyans advancing on him. The crazed civilians were obviously possessed of more fury than sense. They brandished knives, clubs, handguns, and rifles as they sought to stamp out the menace in their midst. Shots rang out. Lead bullets flattened themselves against his impervious flesh. Their lust for revenge reminded Adam of his own.

"Avenge us. . . ."

So Isis had beseeched him as she had lain dying in his arms. He would not deny his wife her last request. No power on Earth could stop him, let alone this pathetic mob.

"You!" he accused the ungrateful rabble. Isis had devoted her life to saving the world's people, and look how they had repaid her. The spirits of Osiris, Shiruta, Gon, and Hurut joined Isis inside his skull, crying out for justice. "You took them away again. You took them all away!"

He crushed the bloody flower in his hand.

"Where is the Horseman?" He flung himself into the crowd, determined to wrest the truth from them even if he had to take every man and woman apart one by one. "Where is Death?"

A bloody crimson haze descended over his vision.

All he saw was red.

MANHATTAN.

"CONTAINMENT?" Power Girl exclaimed. "Are they out of their minds?"

Before the Justice League, there was the Justice Society of America, Earth's original super-hero team. Now composed of gray-haired veterans and their younger protégés, the JSA was ready to take on any threat to world peace, especially when the League was not available.

Like now, for instance. The so-called Infinite Crisis had left the League in disarray. Superman, Batman, and Wonder Woman were all MIA, while their various teammates were either missing as well, or coping with the fallout from the Crisis. Hal Jordan, John Stewart, and Earth's other Green Lanterns were all off in space, on peacekeeping missions throughout the galaxy. Hawkman and Supergirl had been lost in space during the Rann–Thanagar War. Aquaman was busy rebuilding Atlantis. Bart Allen, the youngest surviving Flash, was still recovering from his battle with that evil Superboy from another dimension. Martian Manhunter was reputed to be on a top secret undercover mission. . . .

So it's up to us, Alan Scott thought. Earth's first Green Lantern, he presided over the tense meeting taking place in the JSA's Manhattan headquarters. His teammates—Flash, Wildcat, Hourman, Stargirl, Mister Terrific, Doctor Mid-Nite, and Power Girl—were gathered around the marble round table in their conference room. They looked worried, but ready to go. *As soon as the UN gives us the go-ahead.*

"We're told that the Security Council will have a further decision within the hour," he informed the team. Black Adam's status as a foreign leader, not to mention his Freedom-of-Power treaties with various hostile nations, made this whole situation politically dicey. No one wanted to start World War III. . . .

But Adam might not give us a choice.

That wasn't good enough for Power Girl. She paced restlessly on the other side of the table, too worked up to sit still. The buxom blonde heroine's fiery temper matched her heat vision. Her eyes flared as brightly as the red sun of her native Krypton. "There won't *be* a Bialya in an hour!"

"Believe me, Karen," Green Lantern said. "We know that better than anyone."

Emerald flames flashed within his power ring.

BIALYA.

AN airport smoldered in the distance. Toppled skyscrapers jutted at odd angles, like gigantic works of modern art. A crashed 747 had been ripped asunder, spilling its human cargo out onto the rubble. Still bodies littered the streets. Broken glass glinted amidst the shattered steel and concrete. Garbage rotted along with the corpses. Countless fires ate away at the foundations of the ruined buildings. The crash of falling timbers and beams occasionally disturbed the sepulchral silence of the murdered country. Screams and gunfire no longer echoed in the night. There was only the crackle of the flames, and the keening of the wind as it passed through the broken buildings. Bialya had become a ghost town, inhabited by only a single restless spirit.

Black Adam wandered through the wasteland, dazed and muttering to himself. The bodies of his victims were strewn in every direction. Scarlet rivers flowed into the sewers beneath whatever city this was. His knuckles were caked with blood.

"Where . . . are . . . you?" His eyes searched fruitlessly for his prey. He had been fighting and killing for what felt like an eternity now, and yet the last of the Horsemen continued to elude him. Frustration overcame him and he rocketed through an empty high-rise with such force that the entire building flew apart. "WHERE ARE YOU?"

The remains of the skyscraper crashed to earth, raising a huge cloud of pulverized concrete. Black Adam hovered hundreds of feet above the wreckage. His shoulders sagged and he cradled his face in his bloody hands. He could not rest until he had slain his wife's killer, but how much longer must he search? He should have never let Azraeuz escape Kahndaq in the first place. *I should have made certain he was dead before.*

The cawing of birds came from somewhere overhead. Surprised by the sound, he lifted his gaze and beheld scores of vultures and crows circling in the air above him. As he watched in morbid fascination, they descended and began feeding on the corpses populating the streets below. He rose higher and saw that yet more scavengers were coming to join in the feast. Indeed, it seemed as though the eaters of carrion were circling above the entire nation. All of Bialya had become a meal for them.

And flapping amongst the vultures, his great black wings spread out behind him, Azraeuz presided over the banquet. His lethal scythe sliced through the smoke rising up from the ruins as the fourth and final Horseman spoke at last.

"With every murder . . . with the death of every man, woman, and child . . . I have grown stronger."

He swooped down out of the sky, tackling Adam in midair, and sending them both crashing toward the earth. The force of their landing dug a deep trench across what, ironically enough, appeared to be an abandoned cemetery. They slammed into a string of granite headstones, smashing the weathered markers into dust. Rotting coffins and skeletons were uprooted and tossed about. The pungent reek of Death filled Black Adam's nostrils. Squawking vultures scattered in alarm.

"All thanks to you," Azraeuz gloated. His voice was like the rattle of dry bones as he rose from the freshly furrowed trench and swung his scythe at Black Adam. The edge of the blade slashed across Adam's chest, drawing blood. "I knew you would bring your unreasoning rage here. You were certain to give in to it without that female meat at your side, whispering her sentimental platitudes into your ear." The scythe whistled through the dusty air. "I knew you would feed me with spilled blood and stopped hearts." He raised the scythe high, preparing to separate Adam's head from his shoulders. "Now I hunger for *your* death, mortal!"

Black Adam caught the blade with his bare hands. The razor-sharp edge sliced through his skin, making his hands slick with blood, but he did not let go. "You make false claims," Adam hissed through gritted teeth. "You are not Death." He swung the blade down and around so that it jabbed straight into Azraeuz' gut—and out through his back. "I am."

Letting go of the blade, Adam grabbed onto the Horseman and pulled him close.

"Shazam!"

A lightning bolt zapped down from the sky, striking both him and Azraeuz. The lightning transformed Black Adam back into his mortal guise, while electrocuting the Horseman at the same time. His body jerking spasmodically, Azraeuz let out a howl of agony as his flesh fried upon his bones. Smoke rose from his feathered wings. The smell of burning meat supplanted the putrescent odor he usually exuded. Charred black skin flaked off his body.

Teth-Adam, clad in an ancient Egyptian loincloth and headdress, savored his enemy's torment. But he was not through with the Horseman yet.

"Shazam!"

A second thunderbolt hit the pair. Azraeuz' bronze armor melted, fusing to his carbonized flesh. Still impaled upon his own scythe, which had acted as a lightning rod, attracting the mystical energy, he crashed to the ground. Viscous green tears leaked from the sockets of his skull as he whimpered in pain. Teth-Adam became Black Adam once more.

His superhuman strength restored, Adam wrested a jagged tombstone from the ground. "Now, monster, you are going to answer every question I ask."

Azraeuz attempted to crawl away, dragging himself through the damp graveyard dirt. The feathers had been burned away from his wings, leaving only the bare pinions behind. The blade of the scythe jutted up through his shoulder blades. His cloven hooves scraped against the ground.

"You are going to tell me where I can find your masters."

Black Adam drove the pointed tip of the headstone into the Horseman's back, breaking his spine. Azraeuz' charred tail twitched once, then fell limp. He reached backward, groping for the headstone, but merely sliced his fingers upon his own scythe. The scorched pinions spasmed violently.

"And then, almighty 'Death' . . ." Black Adam placed his hand against the back of the Horseman's head and drove his bony face into the mud. His fingers poked through the monster's skull. Embalming fluid flowed from the wounds. "I am going to spend the rest of the night slowly ending your life."

Destroying the last Horseman would not completely avenge Isis' murder. The creature's masters still had to answer for their crimes.

But it was a good start.

WEEK 46.

OOLONG ISLAND.

"RED Alert!"

Crimson lights flashed and warning klaxons sounded inside the main laboratory. Panicked scientists dashed to their battle stations as the island's sensors picked up a humanoid figure zooming toward the tropical atoll at close to the speed of sound. A holographic wall monitor identified the figure as Black Adam, who had clearly discovered the origin of the Four Horsemen—and was hell-bent on revenge.

"He sterilized Bialya," Rigoro Mortis whispered, aghast. The puny scientist seemed to shrink a few inches more. "One million men, women, and children in less than twenty-four hours . . ."

"Just think what he'll do to us!" Veronica Cale added. All the color drained from her exquisite features.

Only Dr. Sivana appeared untroubled by Black Adam's approach. He rubbed his hands together in fiendish anticipation. "Oh, I've been waiting for this for a long, long time. The Black Marvel himself at my mercy!" He cackled eagerly. "Bring it on!"

The other scientists gazed nervously at the oversized monitor. On the screen, Black Adam flew straight into a deluge of scalding chemicals. His silk uniform bubbled and sizzled, but he kept on flying, leaving a trail of steam behind him. His clenched fists tore through the corrosive clouds.

"He survived my acid rainstorm!" Doctor Death gasped. He lowered his gas mask, revealing pointed ears, bushy eyebrows, and a satanic goatee. He grabbed onto a fuming vial of poison like a child clutching his security blanket.

"But the Perimeter Force Shield is designed to withstand a direct asteroid strike," Baron Bug desperately reminded his colleagues, "of the sort which brought about the extinction of the dinosaurs!"

His words did little to reassure Doctor Tyme, who paced back and forth across the laboratory. The hands of his clock face spun hysterically. "How can you be so calm, Sivana?" he accused their leader. "The most dangerous living being on the planet is mere miles away from our soft, vulnerable guts." His blue cape flapped pathetically behind him. "And I still haven't found my lost fifty-two seconds!"

Talk about a cuckoo clock, Sivana thought. He counted down to Black Adam's arrival. "Five hundred miles away. Three hundred. One hundred . . ."

"We're all going to die," Cale moaned. A most unflattering display of guilt compromised her beauty; rumor had it that she'd been having nightmares ever since the unveiling of the Four Horsemen. "We *deserve* to die."

A tremendous sonic boom shook the lab. "The Perimeter Force Shield has shattered!" Baron Bug announced. "Black Adam is here!"

"Just give me a moment," Rigoro Mortis pleaded. His hairless dome was slick with perspiration. His hands trembled as he clumsily attempted to screw together a handheld control console that looked like a cross between a PlayStation joystick and an old-fashioned TV antenna. Loose screws slipped between his fingers. He swore in Latin as they bounced across the floor.

Sivana savored the other scientist's anxiety. "Sweating, Mortis? Now you know what it's like having the Marvels on your heels." None of these lesser lights appreciated what he had been up against all these years. "He has the power of *six* gods. Think about that!"

"Oh yeah!" Mortis snapped back. "Well, I'm an atheist and I have the powers of ultra-science at my disposal, in the form of the Super-Hood Mark II! The greatest killer android the world has ever seen." He finally succeeded in fitting the control device together. "He'll save us!"

He stared up at the screen, where Black Adam could be seen closing in on the island. Before Adam reached the coral ridge surrounding the atoll, however, a monstrous figure rose up from the sea below. Over fifty feet tall, the Super-Hood Mark II was a hulking artificial humanoid who bore a distinct resemblance to Boris Karloff in *Frankenstein*. Pasty white pseudoflesh covered its hairless cranium. A sneer occupied its brutish countenance. High-tech cannons rotated upon its arms. Swollen plastic tanks, filled with a transparent gel, bubbled upon its back. Crude stitches held its scalp together.

Doesn't look all that different from the Mark I, Sivana thought dubiously. *Mortis is a real one-trick pony.*

A mammoth arm aimed at Black Adam. The attached cannon sprayed the sticky gel at its target, coating Black Adam with the goo. The giant's other hand grabbed onto the immobilized immortal. Heat-rays shot from the Super-Hood's sunken eyes, setting the gel ablaze. Black Adam went up in flames.

"See!" Mortis crowed, dancing excitedly. "Super-flammable liquid plastic plus thermo-vision!"

Unimpressed, Sivana leaned back against his chair and sneered. "All you're doing is making him mad." His hands were clasped behind his head. "And when he gets mad, he makes you dead."

Sure enough, Black Adam was making short work of the Super-Hood Mark II. Heedless of the red-hot flames enveloping his body, he twisted free of the android's grip, tearing off Super-Hood's right arm in the process. The dismembered giant sheared away from Black Adam as explosions erupted from his shoulder. Mortis' grotesque creation tumbled backward into the sea, disappearing beneath the waves. The android's synthetic green blood formed an oil slick atop the water.

So much for that ill-conceived monstrosity, Sivana thought smugly, even as another of the mad scientists stepped up to bat.

"Time for Baron Bug to save us all!" The crazed cyber-entomologist tapped frantically at the keypad of his remote control device. "Oh God, oh God," he muttered under his breath. "Where are my Insectrons?"

He let out a sigh of relief as a swarm of mechanical insects appeared on the screen. Buzzing furiously, the robotic bees, hornets, and wasps rushed toward Black Adam, who hurled Super-Hood's severed arm at the first wave of Insectrons. The limb exploded against the bugs, wiping out several at once. Mangled steel wings and feelers splashed down into the sea.

But Baron Bug had been very industrious during his stay at Oolong Island. Yet more Insectrons assailed Black Adam, biting and stinging every inch of his body. He slapped and swatted at them with his mighty hands, crushing them by the handful, but they threw themselves against him with suicidal determination. The largest of the Insectrons, a hawk-sized Robo-Wasp, clung to his back. A foot-long radioactive stinger stabbed repeatedly into his back.

Howling in pain, Black Adam dived toward the ocean and plunged beneath the waves. Underwater spy cameras caught him as he struggled to pull the Robo-Wasp away from his back. Intent on ridding himself of the vicious Insectron, he did not appear to see a gigantic steel Mega-Scorpion, roughly the size of a nuclear submarine, scuttling across the ocean floor toward him. Searchlights beamed from the Scorpion's glittering crystal eyes. The pilots of the manned robot could be glimpsed on the other side of the eyes.

"Attention, Mega-Scorpion crew!" Bug shouted into a microphone. "Attack at will!"

Reaching back behind him, Black Adam ripped the Robo-Wasp in half and angrily hurled away the pieces. Blood from his wounds turned the seawater red around him, but the Scorpion's high-intensity spotlights cut through the scarlet haze. Black Adam faced the oncoming creature defiantly, like some mythical Titan pitted against a primeval beast. The Scorpion's pincers snapped at him.

"Do you really think that toy of yours will stop him?" Cale

mocked the Mega-Scorpion. She sounded resigned to her fate. "Black Adam killed *Death*, the Pale Horseman. What does that make him?"

The bone-crushing pressure of the deep did not slow Black Adam down. He caught hold of one of the enormous pincers with both hands and began to wrench it apart, just like he had Sobek's jaws so many days ago. The Scorpion's stinger jabbed at him, but he deflected the blows with the robot's own front claw. The pincers snapped to pieces. Sparks flashed underwater as the entire limb short-circuited. The pilots inside the cockpit drew back in terror as Black Adam launched himself straight for the vessel's glowing eyes. A cruel smile played upon his face as he drew back his fist. . . .

"Mayday! Mayday!" the pilots screamed over the laboratory's PA system. "He sees us! He sees—" A deafening crash cut off the men's shrieks. Static, then silence, came over the loudspeakers. A hush fell over the laboratory.

"My Mega-Scorpion . . ." Baron Bug whimpered. His stooped shoulders slumped in defeat.

All right, Sivana thought. *Who wants to take a crack at him next?*

Dr. Cyclops rose to the challenge. "Don't worry," the one-eyed scientist insisted. "He can't find the island if he can't see it." He hunched over the keyboard of his desk computer. "My unparalleled lens technology bends light all around us."

Ira Quimby strolled into the lab, looking remarkably relaxed and well tanned. A Hawaiian shirt, Bermuda shorts, and sandals made him look more like a beachcomber than an evil scientist. "He can still *smell* it, and *hear* it, my dear doctor." He peered over Cyclops' shoulder as he contemplated the computer's display screen. "If I may contribute a suggestion, perhaps you might consider turning your null-light lenses *away* from the island and *toward* our adversary's eyes?"

"Smart thinking, Quimby," Sivana admitted. Perhaps all that sunbathing really had boosted Ira's intellect.

Quimby grinned. "Well, they don't call me 'I.Q.' for nothing." He removed his mirrored sunglasses. "Granted, we should be safe as long as the blast doors hold, but it always pays to anticipate every outcome."

"Amen," T.O. Morrow agreed.

On the screen, Black Adam burst from the lagoon surrounding the island. The last of the burning gel had been washed away from him, but his costume was still torn and charred. He clutched a twitching steel stinger in one fist and a blackened human skull in the other. He tossed them aside with equal disdain.

With godlike swiftness, he zipped out of the range of the cameras. A second later, heavy blows pounded against the solid-steel blast doors protecting the main lab complex. Nervous scientists jumped at the ringing blows. The dense promethium alloy began to warp inward. The impressions of powerful knuckles bulged through the metal.

"That won't stop him," Cale predicted. "Nothing can."

White-faced scientists began to scurry toward the emergency exits. Sivana opened his mouth to call them back, but Ira Quimby beat him to the punch. The mutated super-genius jumped up onto the head of an unfinished robot and attempted to rally his frightened colleagues.

"Come on, now," he exhorted the various mad doctors. "Don't be scared, fellas! We've all been here before." His savvy gaze swept over the fleeing scientists, who halted their disorderly retreat long enough to hear what he had to say. "Let's face it, some of you boys look like you've been bullied all your lives."

Doctor Death nodded reluctantly, and was soon joined by most of the other mad doctors. Their expressions darkened as they recalled countless petty humiliations inflicted on them by their intellectual inferiors. Bitter resentment, never very far from the surface, began to overcome their panic at Black Adam's progress so far. Only Veronica Cale looked unconvinced by Quimby's stirring oration.

He goaded them further.

"Now the ultimate big, bad bully's right outside, knocking

on the door. Do we run? Do we hide? Or do we get even?" He pumped his fist in the air. "This time, we have the weapons. We have the gang!" He shook his fist at the bulging door, even as Black Adam's titanic blows continued to reverberate throughout the lab. "This time it's our turn to kick some ass!"

Cheers and applause greeted Quimby's speech. Sivana decided that the criminal mastermind had missed his calling.

He should have gone into politics, Sivana thought.

BLACK Adam slammed his fists into the massive steel door before him. His knuckles bled, matching the countless burns and lacerations scarring his flesh, but the pain only stoked the murderous wrath blazing within his chest. It had taken hours to coax the secret of the Horsemen's origins from the dying Azraeuz, but the effort had been well worth it. Isis' true murderers—the architects of Kahndaq's misery—lay behind this final obstacle . . . and no mere wall of steel would spare them from his justice.

Throw whatever technological trickery you have at me, he challenged his unseen foes. *Your feeble science is no match for my righteous fury.*

He threw all his might into one more blow, and the "impenetrable" blast doors finally surrendered before the strength of Amon. Torn from their hinges, the doors crashed down onto the floor beyond. A harsh metallic clang echoed loudly.

Black Adam strode across the threshold into what appeared to be an enormous laboratory. Workstations divided the ground floor, while elevated metal catwalks ran along the upper walls of the facility. Armed guards and beast-men patrolled the walkways, but Adam barely gave them a glance. He was after Sivana and his diabolical cronies today, not mere foot soldiers.

I never trusted that myopic madman, Adam thought of Sivana. *I should have rid the world of him years ago.*

To his slight surprise, the mad scientists stood their ground, as though daring him to venture farther into their domain. He sneered at their balding craniums and stunted physiques. The information he had extracted from the Fourth Horseman,

coupled with the wisdom of Zehuti, allowed him to identify
them all by name. He was unimpressed by their fearsome rep-
utations; despite their vast intellects, they were all merely mortal in the end. And he was so much more.

A few of the scientists shrank away from him, looking
ready to flee at a moment's notice. But a smirking American in
beach attire, whom Adam deduced to be the notorious Ira
Quimby, attempted to bolster his comrades' courage.

"Don't worry," he said confidently. "I've been thinking
about this and here's how it'll go." He glanced at the scientist
to his right, a freakish-looking individual with but a single eye
above his nose. "Paging Dr. Cyclops."

The one-eyed scientist raised an elaborate ray gun that
projected a beam of blinding black light at Adam's eyes. The
world turned dark as the infernal ray stole his sight from him.
Black Adam staggered forward, groping blindly with his
hands. The footsteps of the scientists scattered in all directions.
He snarled in frustration.

"Someone get him while he's blind!" Cyclops hollered
shrilly. "Get him!"

More footsteps circled him warily. Black Adam caught
a whiff of acidic fumes coming toward him. He heard liquid
sloshing in a beaker. Another set of footsteps seemed to stag-
ger beneath the weight of some heavy device. He heard the
hum of motorized components powering up. He smelled ozone
in the air.

"Where is he?" Doctor Tyme shouted frantically. The gears
of a clock ticked where Adam estimated his face to be. "I can't
see a thing out of this freaking mask!"

"Aim your Suspension Ray to the left, Doctor," Quimby
advised him. "That's it."

A sensation like static electricity rushed over Black Adam's
body, making every hair stand up. He tried to lunge at the ticking Tyme, but his muscles refused to move. *What devilry is
this?* he thought angrily. He could still feel his limbs—he
wasn't paralyzed—and yet he could not budge an inch, almost
as though he was trapped in a single instant of time. *Let me*

loose! he raged silently, but the words caught in his throat. *By the gods, when I get free, you will pay for this indignity!*

If he got free . . .

FROZEN in time, and blinded to boot, Black Adam was right where they wanted him. Ira Quimby nodded in approval. "Now then, we have among our number some distinguished old pros. Evil geniuses who have faced the entire Justice League single-handed." He turned toward yet another member of the Oolong Island brain trust and smiled knowingly. "Tom? Time for you to grandstand, I presume?"

T.O. Morrow rose from his seat. He put down his daiquiri and fished a slender silicon wand from his back pocket. "Ahem," he began. "Somewhere around the fifty-second century, people will learn how to unfold the hidden dimensions of space." He aimed the wand at Black Adam and flicked a switch. All the lights in the laboratory flickered and went out. Only the sunlight from outside illuminated the sprawling complex. "I invented tesseract technology when I was fifteen, gentlemen. Using this device I can open an area the size of a football field inside that invulnerable brain of his."

Tyme's Suspension Ray shorted out, but it was no longer needed. Black Adam screamed and clutched his skull. His bloodshot eyes bulged from their sockets. Agonized cries went unheard by the gods.

"It takes a lot of power for a split second," Morrow expounded, "but it's all we need." Black Adam collapsed onto the floor. Painful spasms racked his body. Morrow clicked off his wand and the lights came back on. "Now then, gentlemen, indulge yourselves."

The other scientists ran toward the prone figure, eager to get their licks in. They gleefully kicked Adam in the face and ribs, revenging themselves on all their past persecutors, super-human and otherwise. Doctor Death poured a beaker of acid over Adam's head. Baron Bug shoved a mechanical tarantula down his throat. Dr. Cyclops punched him in the eye.

Ira Quimby watched the beating from his perch atop the

robot skull. He beckoned to the guards, who hustled down from the catwalks to take Black Adam into custody. They grabbed Adam under his shoulders and lifted his face from the floor. Quimby nodded at Veronica Cale, who came forward bearing a glittering crown of electronic circuitry. Unlike her nerdier colleagues, the glamorous female scientist had little interest in abusing their captive. She just looked relieved to be alive.

Quimby continued to provide the expert commentary.

"And now the lovely Dr. Cale will apply the Neural Crown, which will reroute all the electrical impulses his battered brain sends to his body."

He smirked as she pressed the crown down onto Black Adam's skull and activated the electrodes. Bright blue sparks arced between the silvery spikes of the crown. Black Adam stiffened in shock, then started twitching uncontrollably. His bloody eyes rolled wildly.

"It's done," she said bleakly.

Exhausted by their efforts, the frenzied scientists backed away from their vanquished enemy. They looked at each other in amazement, as if they still couldn't believe that they had actually come out on top. Ira Quimby basked in his triumph.

"Let's all feel a real sense of accomplishment," he urged them. "We've conquered our fears in a very real way." He stepped down from his perch and slapped a grinning Doctor Death on the back. He peered through the assembled scientists at Dr. Sivana, who came forward at last. "And dear old Thaddeus will take over from here." Quimby shrugged. "That's how I saw it working out anyway."

Sivana clapped quietly. The other scientists parted to let him through. The wizened old doctor looked around at his victorious colleagues. An insidious smile lifted his lips.

"I hate you all," Sivana said. "I want you to know that. But together we've done something I could have never achieved on my own."

He crouched over to look Black Adam in the face. A trickle of bloody drool dripped from the defeated champion's lips.

"Oh, foolish Black Adam," Sivana cackled. "You shouldn't have come here, should you? Not after all we've put you through." He gestured to the guards. "Bring him to my private laboratory," he instructed the beast-men. "And heat up my acid baths."

He rubbed his hands together.

"I've been planning for this moment for a very long time. . . ."

WEEK 47.

GOTHAM CITY.

"FOR I have given unto thee all the tools to bring about my desires, the same gifts used by Kürten, Crippen, and Gacy. . . ."

The Cathedral of Hate, located deep beneath the city, was far grander than that underground temple in Bialya. Torchlight illuminated the wide central nave leading to the gilded sanctuary at the west end of the profane church. Carved serpents wound around the marble columns supporting the vaulted ceiling. Luridly colored frescos depicted the greatest crimes in history, from the murder of Abel to the destruction of Coast City. Life-sized statues of legendary saints and apostles, such as Rasputin and Vandal Savage, occupied recessed niches along the walls. Individual shrines paid homage to each of the Seven Deadly Sins. A choir composed of involuntary castrati sang glorious hymns to evil.

"That which is used to flense, grind, pierce, and burn . . ."

Whisper A'Daire read from the Crime Bible, which was laid open on the marble pulpit before her. The illustration accompanying the text depicted an enormous fire pit opening up in the heart of a ravaged city. Doomed souls plunged into the pit, condemned to eternal torment. The grisly woodcut promised great things ahead.

"Ahhh!" An anguished cry interrupted her sermon. "Hurts . . . it hurts—*nhn*—I don't know anything—*nhngg*—I've never even seen her. . . ."

The pain-wracked moans came from the hapless Gotham

police officer strapped to the altar a few feet away. The rookie's blue uniform had been reduced to shreds by the ministrations of Whisper's subhuman servitors. His abused flesh bore evidence of the torturer's craft. Beast-men capered around the bloody altar. Pincers, branding irons, flails, and other sacred implements were grasped in their claws, paws, and talons. A scorpion-man preferred to use his own stinger.

To each his own, Whisper thought.

Equally brutish congregants, representing every genus of the animal kingdom, knelt before the dais. Their feral eyes gleamed with predatory glee. The werewolf, Abbot, crouched among the first row of the worshipers.

"So that ye might learn the truths which are hidden, that ye might pull secrets from the very hearts that hide them . . ."

Reciting the verses from memory, Whisper crossed the dais to the altar. She drew an ornate dagger from a sheath between her breasts. A scarlet cloak and corset flattered her figure. Forged on unholy Apokalips itself, the blade was used only on the most sacred of occasions. She raised it high above her head, its jagged point aimed at the lacerated chest of the unwilling sacrifice.

"Please, I'm begging you. . . ." The rookie stared in horror at the dagger poised above him. Whisper wondered if his insignificant life was already passing before his eyes. "I don't know where she is. . . ."

Her slitted pupils dilated. A forked tongue flicked between her lips. No matter how many times she performed this rite, it never ceased to fill her heart with unholy fervor. "And so see my Kingdom rise anew upon the Earth. In Cain's name."

"I don't know Batwoman . . . !"

She plunged the dagger into the policeman's heart. The congregation growled in unison.

"IN CAIN'S NAME!"

BRUNO Mannheim did not turn around as Whisper and Abbot entered his office. He stared bleakly out the picture window

overlooking Gotham, his Neanderthal forehead resting against
the cold plate glass. "It didn't work, did it?"

Whisper used a towel to wipe the rookie's blood from her
hands. She had come straight from the cathedral, not even taking the time to change out of her gore-splattered raiment. Abbot,
now in human form, followed behind her, carrying the *Book of
Crime.* She regretted being the bearer of bad news.

"We'll make a new offering tomorrow," she promised. The
policeman's entrails had yielded no new omens. "Divination is
uncertain, you know this—"

He cut her off abruptly. "And it will fail tomorrow. The
same way it's failed every night since she escaped me!" Turning away from the window, he grabbed her roughly by the
shoulders, just the way she liked it. Whisper knew she should
fear Mannheim's wrath, but that only made the moment more
thrilling. "Everything is prepared but this last piece of the
prophecy! Gotham stands ready to burn to ashes, but I *must*
have the Twice-Named Daughter's heart to kindle the holy
flames!"

"And you shall, Brother Bruno." She stroked his face to
mollify him. The caresses seemed to please him, although his
scowl persisted. "We know the Book cannot be wrong, for the
Word is perfect in its cruelty. The error must come in our in-
terpretation of the prophecy, not in the prophecy itself."

"Or in a lack of faith," he agreed sullenly. They were both
true believers.

Behind them, Abbot placed the Crime Bible down on
Mannheim's own marble lectern. The act attracted the ganglord's attention, and he broke away from Whisper to snarl at
her henchman. "Again and again you fail to find her, Brother
Abbot. Ever since that one night when you fled from her in
terror."

"Nightwing came to her assistance," Abbot reminded him
impatiently. He was clearly tired of having to keep explaining
this. "I was outnumbered and outfought."

"You should have trusted the Word to be your strength,"
Mannheim accused him.

Abbot stood his ground. "This would be the same 'Word' that prophesied you killing her five months ago?" He sneered at Mannheim. "We all know how that worked out for you, Bruno."

"Blasphemer!" Flushed with rage, Mannheim charged at Abbot. The two men slammed into the long boardroom table, shattering it. Lupine fangs sprouted from Abbot's gums as he started to change into a wolf-man again. He growled furiously at Mannheim, fighting back. "I'll take *your* heart!" Mannheim threatened as they grappled savagely. The tussle carried them across the office. They crashed against the lectern, knocking the Crime Bible from its stand. It fell toward the floor.

"Stop it, both of you!" Whisper shouted. She dived for the falling book, but got there too late. The Book landed with a thump upon the carpet. "In Cain's name—"

Her eyes widened as she gazed at the Crime Bible, which had fallen open to that symbolic representation of Mannheim ripping Batwoman's heart from her chest. Could there be any clearer omen than that? She gasped out loud as inspiration struck her like a blast of hellfire rising up from the abyss.

"Cain," she whispered. "It's her name."

Snatching up the Book from the floor, she rushed between Mannheim and Abbot. By now, Abbot had completed his lycanthropic transformation. Mannheim's tailored suit had been rent by the wolf-man's claws. Heedless of the danger in getting between the murderous combatants, she thrust out her arm to separate them.

"Don't you see?" she exclaimed. "It's her name! Cain! We focused on the illustration and saw only the Batwoman! But the true meaning is in the words. 'The Twice-Named Daughter of Cain!' One name is Batwoman, the other is Cain."

Mannheim instantly grasped what she was saying. His beef with Abbot forgotten, he shoved himself away from the growling werewolf. Excitement deepened his voice. "We find the woman with the name of Cain. . . ."

"Exactly." Whisper nodded eagerly. "There can't be many women in Gotham with the name, the resources, and the training to become Batwoman. And once we know who she really is, it will be a simple matter to place her heart in your hands!"

BIALYA.

THE entire country was a graveyard. The capital lay in ruins. Emergency relief units from around the world swarmed over the corpse-strewn rubble, assisted by the Justice Society of America. Jay Garrick, the original Flash, searched the devastated landscape at super-speed, resembling a blurry red streak until he finally skidded to a stop in front of Green Lantern. His winged silver helmet made him look like a middle-aged Mercury, straight out of classical mythology. His weathered face held a grim expression. He shook his head soberly.

"I haven't found a single survivor," he reported.

"Neither has my ring," Green Lantern said. Emerald flames emanated from his power ring, forming an enormous green fist that lifted a collapsed building from the surrounding debris. To his dismay, he found only corpses beneath the toppled highrise. The dead bodies were everywhere, lying atop the rubble or buried beneath pulverized steel and timber. Equally horrific vistas, he knew, could be found all across the murdered nation. "Over two million dead."

Shaken by the carnage, he let the flaming hand evaporate. The fractured skyscraper crashed to earth, raising a cloud of dust. Not far away, Mister Terrific, Power Girl, and the rest of the team did what they could to uncover more bodies. Doctor Mid-Nite, the Society's resident physician, treated overstressed aid workers for exhaustion and dehydration.

Wildcat tossed a mangled metal street sign aside. The grizzled former heavyweight boxing champion wore a furry black cat costume, complete with whiskers, that would have looked ridiculous on anyone else. "Ya really think Black Adam did this on his own?" he asked gruffly.

"I've never seen him unleash anything like this," Green Lantern said, "but the satellite images Amanda Waller gathered . . ."

Wildcat snorted in derision. "You're not seriously listenin' to Waller, are ya?"

"I may not always agree with her methods," Green Lantern said, "but her footage matches what info we've received from other sources." The veteran hero had deep connections to the American intelligence community. "If Black Adam has truly gone berserk, we're going to need all the allies we can get."

"I'm glad you feel that way, Alan," a new voice said. An anonymous figure on the horizon suddenly increased in size and height, until he towered over the other heroes and relief workers. A dark blue cowl concealed the giant's face, but Green Lantern recognized him instantly.

"Atom-Smasher?"

"I want back on the JSA," Al Rothstein declared. He had once been a member in good standing of the Justice Society, before he helped Black Adam liberate Kahndaq from its former dictator. Now the young hero had blood on his hands. "Waller issued me a pardon." His determined voice boomed over the ruins. "I want to help you find Black Adam."

GOTHAM CITY.

WHEN Renee had last left Gotham, nearly three months ago, the city had been blanketed in snow. Now March was exiting like the proverbial lamb, bringing a hint of spring to the air. Vic's trench coat hung open as she took the elevator up to Kate's penthouse apartment. Her duffel bag was slung over her shoulder. She counted the floors impatiently, looking forward to a warmer reception here than the one she had recently received in Kahndaq.

I'm lucky I got out of there alive, she realized. *Especially after what Black Adam did next.*

The old Renee would have blamed herself for the slaughter in Bialya, but her current self refused to wallow in guilt over her failure to console Black Adam. The vengeful superman had been a stone-cold killer for over three thousand years; it was doubtful that anyone could have gotten through to him after Isis was killed. *At least I tried,* Renee thought. *I can live with that.*

The elevator door slid open and she hurried out into the hallway. She couldn't wait to see Kate again. Her steps quickened as she approached the door to the penthouse. It was dark out, but maybe Batwoman was not on the prowl yet. She reached the door, then froze when she realized it was already ajar.

"Kate?" she called out apprehensively. A cop's instincts put her on alert. Pushing open the door with her foot, she cautiously entered the apartment. Her ray gun was tucked away in her duffel, but Renee didn't have the patience to dig it out right now. Her right hand found the light switch, but the overhead lights failed to come on. Another bad sign.

As her eyes adjusted to the gloom, streetlights from outside exposed a ghastly scene. The penthouse had been totaled. Broken glass and timbers were strewn about the living room. Expensive furniture had been overturned. Leather upholstery was slashed and torn. A stiff breeze rustled the curtains over the shattered windows. Tufts of fur and feathers blew about the suite. A broken tusk was embedded in a fallen bookshelf, not far from a piece of severed tentacle. Blood splattered the walls and ceiling, and pooled upon the carpet. The gory stains still looked wet.

Renee gasped out loud. Her duffel bag dropped onto the floor.

This was more than mere evidence of a struggle. From the look of things, Kate had fought hard against a small army of beast-men before they had finally beaten her into submission. "Kate," Renee whispered hollowly. The fact that no body was visible provided meager comfort. She knelt beside the nearest puddle of blood. There seemed to be an awful lot of it. . . .

"They took her," a male voice confirmed. Renee looked up to see Nightwing standing on the sill of the broken picture window. The curtains flapped around Batman's protégé, whom Renee had met on occasion back during her days on the force. "We're going to get her back."

If she's still alive, Renee thought. *And Mannheim hasn't yanked her heart out yet.*

WEEK 48.

GOTHAM CITY.

GOTHAM had way too many warehouses, at least as far as
Renee was concerned. Heavy crates were piled high on wooden
pallets as she and Nightwing invaded yet another murky storage
facility in search of a lead on Kate's current whereabouts. The
masked vigilante machined across the floor like an acrobat, letting his lightning-fast hands and feet put the fear of the Bat into
a gang of motley beast-men. Renee was right behind him,
watching his back.

"Where is Mannheim?" she demanded. "Where?"

A warning shot from Renee's ray gun drove back a snarling pack of were-creatures. The futuristic firearm matched the
black-market ordnance being unloaded by the shape-shifting
Intergang thugs. Renee couldn't help remembering her first
battle with the beast-men, in a shadowy warehouse much like
this one. Then she had fought beside the Question instead of
Nightwing, but that wasn't all that had changed over the last
ten months or so. Now Vic was dead, and Kate might be too.
Renee wore Vic's hat and trench coat in memory of her friend,
but her face was still her own. She wasn't ready to put on the
Question's mask just yet.

Maybe she never would be.

This is taking too long, she thought impatiently. She and
Nightwing had spent the last several days combing the city for
Kate, hitting everything from swanky mob-controlled night-
clubs to skeezy strip joints in the worst parts of town. This dock-

side warehouse was only the latest stop on their whirlwind tour of Intergang hangouts, but Renee prayed that it wouldn't turn out to be another dead end. For all they knew, Mannheim was going to sacrifice Kate any night now, if he hadn't already. . . .

All because of that damn prophecy, she thought. Renee still wasn't sure she actually believed in any of that Crime Bible mumbo jumbo, but that didn't matter. *What counts is that Mannheim and his creepy cult believe it.*

A few feet ahead of Renee, Nightwing slammed a puma-man's whiskered snout into the lid of a large wooden crate, which splintered loudly. Renee spotted a minotaur trying to pry open another crate to get at the weapons inside, so she squeezed off another blast from her ray gun, disintegrating both the crate and its lethal contents. Another burst sent the bull-headed monster and his cronies scrambling for the exits.

Not so fast, Renee thought. *Not until one of you tells me where Kate is.*

KATHERINE Kane was not looking her best.

After nearly a week in captivity, her Batwoman costume was torn and filthy. Heavy iron shackles weighed down her chafed wrists and ankles. Her utility belt had been stripped from her. A split lip testified to her rough treatment at the hands of her captors. Scabs and bruises, many of them left over from her losing battle at the penthouse, formed a black-and-blue mosaic over her battered flesh. Her long red hair was matted and badly in need of a shampoo. The rough stone floor of her cell was cold and unyielding. Her stomach growled pite-ously; she had been served nothing but water and gruel for days now. Still, she would have gladly traded a three-course meal for one good Batarang.

How long have I been here anyway? she wondered. Locked away from the sun, starved and beaten, it was hard to keep track of the time. *Has it been five days already? Six?*

Whisper A'Daire leered at her with the sort of salacious delight usually reserved for female wardens in women-in-prison movies. Her feral associate, Abbot, looked on with a scowl on his face as Whisper delicately fingered the red inner lining of Kate's soiled cape.

"No, this just won't do, not for such a special occasion. The garb is fine, but the *condition* . . ." Her nose wrinkled in distaste. She peeled away Batwoman's mask, exposing Kate's face. Two swollen black eyes offered further evidence of abuse. Whisper ran her gaze over the other woman's tight black costume. "Of course, white is traditional for virgin sacrifices, but that hardly matters in your case."

Bitch! Kate lunged at the other woman, determined to wipe the smirk off her face. But her reflexes were slowed by too little food and too much brutality. Whisper deftly stepped out of the prisoner's reach, while Abbot bludgeoned Kate from behind. She collapsed onto the floor. She swore out loud, infuriated by her own weakness. Abbot dug his heel into her back to keep her from getting back up again.

"No more of that," Whisper declared. She knelt down beside Kate, who caught a glimpse of a hypodermic needle in Whisper's hands. *No!* Kate thought. *Get that away from me!* She tried to wriggle out from beneath Abbot's foot, but Whisper surged forward with the speed of a striking rattlesnake. The hypo jabbed into Kate's neck.

A narcotic numbness spread quickly through her veins. Kate struggled to resist the drug's effect, but within seconds she was too groggy to even remember why she was fighting back. Her bones seemed to dissolve as she melted limply against the floor. Her eyes rolled back until only the whites were visible. The last thing she was aware of, before succumbing completely, were Whisper's cool fingers stroking her cheek.

"That's more like it," she said. "Let's clean her up."

THE slimy tentacles of an enraged human octopus reached out for Nightwing's head. Suckers the size of silver dollars glistened upon the underside of the tentacles, while the creature's chitinous beak clacked angrily. Gripping a hard plastic escrima stick in each hand, Nightwing batted the aggressive tentacles away, but the crazed cephalopod had eight limbs to the hero's two, putting Nightwing at a severe disadvantage. A pair of tentacles caught hold of Nightwing's right arm and flung him into the side of a large steel cargo container. Dozens of surplus pallets were stacked precariously on top of the container. Renee winced in sympathy as Nightwing hit the container hard enough to leave a dent. The upper tentacles grabbed onto his face and pulled at his skin. He let out a pained grunt.

"Hey, Squid-Face!" Renee called out. "Heads up!"

A golden beam shot from her stolen ray gun. The bottommost pallet atop the damaged container vanished in a burst of light. An avalanche of wooden planks cascaded down onto the octo-man. A loud *squish* turned Renee's stomach as the creature's trunk and tentacles were trapped beneath a heap of heavy timbers. Hot plasma rose like smoke from the muzzle of her high-tech pistol.

I never did like calamari, she thought. Nightwing yanked a limp tentacle away from his face. The suckers left angry red rings on the skin around his bat-shaped mask. He gazed down at the defeated octopus-man, who whimpered beneath the fallen pallets. "Thanks for the save," he said to Renee.

She glanced around the warehouse. The fight appeared to be over. The few beast-men who were still conscious had evidently chosen to make tracks rather than risk ending up like the squashed were-octopus. She hoped the trapped monster wasn't injured too badly to answer any questions. *What was the point of trashing this place if it doesn't get us any closer to Kate?*

Blinking lights caught her attention, and she looked up at the dented shipping container, whose door was now ajar. Inside the container was some sort of high-tech device that looked like a cross between a neutron bomb and a large industrial drill, big enough to drill straight through to China. Lighted panels and gauges flickered over the surface of the device. It hummed softly.

Uh-oh, she thought. *I don't like the looks of this.*

* * *

BLOOD and brains dripped from Bruno Mannheim's hands.
He wiped them off with a towel, then angrily hurled the towel
onto the carpet. A framed blowup of the Fire Pit drawing from
the Crime Bible now adorned the wall of his office. His eyes
held a manic gleam as he stared at the sacred illustration. He
ground his teeth in agitation. An angry vein pulsed against his
temple.

"Every single word as the Book commands us, Whisper! All
for tonight, to spill the holy blood tonight!" Instead of his usual
tailored suits, a scarlet robe, with golden trim, clothed his stocky
frame. The vivid hue of the ceremonial garment hid the spattered bloodstains. The sacred dagger was tucked into the sash
around his waist. "This wasn't supposed to happen."

The body of a dead frog-man lay at Mannheim's feet. His
skull had been pulped beyond recognition by the mob boss'
bare hands, just because the unfortunate amphibian had been
the bearer of bad news. *Typical,* Abbot thought. He regarded
the volatile ganglord with barely concealed contempt. *I've had
about enough of this lunatic's tantrums.*

Abbot waited by the office door, which was guarded by a
pair of smelly ape-men. He kept his distance from Mannheim,
but Whisper hurried forward to mollify their leader. A flash of
jealousy added to Abbot's sour mood. He was starting to wish
that he and Whisper had never gotten involved with this insane
cult. Bruno Mannheim was no Rā's al Ghūl, that was for sure.

Why couldn't Whisper see that?

"Calmly, Brother Bruno," she purred into Mannheim's ear.
Like him, she had already donned her priestly regalia. Her
slinky black gown rustled as she moved, like a serpent in the
grass. She gracefully stepped over the mess on the carpet. "The
sacrifice awaits you even now."

"What does that matter now?" Mannheim ranted. According to the frog-man, a key element in their grand design may
have already fallen into the hands of their enemies. "I should've
carved the Twice-Named's heart from her breast the moment
she was in our power!"

"And defied the Word by doing so," Whisper reminded him. In theory, the sacrifice could only be performed under the right conditions and circumstances. They had already missed one such opportunity months ago, when Batwoman escaped them.

At least that's what we thought, Abbot thought bitterly. His doubts had started then, the first time the Book's so-called prophecies had turned out to be about as reliable as a cheap fortune cookie. Now, of course, Whisper claimed that they had simply misinterpreted the prophecy. Abbot's lip curled into a sneer. *Yeah, right.*

"We were not ready to unleash the Fires, Brother." She rested her chin on Mannheim's shoulder as she pressed her sinuous body against his back. Her arm draped itself around his bull-like neck. "It is tonight that you are destined to welcome the rule of Rage with the Twice-Named's heart in your hand. Her death will mark the dawn of Intergang's dominion over the world. A world devoid of virtue, devoted to the worst of humanity. A world much like Gotham City itself, before the coming of the Bat."

Her seductive blandishments failed to appease him. "How am I gonna do that when one of the Keys is lost?"

"Brother Abbot will recover the Key," she promised him, "and all shall come to pass as written."

Speak for yourself, Abbot thought. He was tired of keeping his mouth shut. "And if it doesn't? If, once again, the Book is wrong? What then?"

"Blasphemy!" Mannheim raved, his face turning purple. Whisper tried to restrain him, but he tore himself away from her arms and lunged at Abbot. He backhanded the other man across the face. "The Book is not wrong! The Book is *never* wrong!"

"Bruno," Whisper pleaded.

"No! Send others to recover the Key." He nodded at the ape-men, who took hold of Abbot from both sides. Alarmed, Abbot struggled to break free from the simians' powerful grip. "Your dog's time is done here." Mannheim rammed his fist into Abbot's gut. "I'll see him carved apart for his heresies!"

* * *

NIGHTWING seemed to share Renee's concern about the mysterious device they had just found inside the shipping container. Opaque white lenses concealed his eyes, but there was no mistaking the worried cast of his mouth and jaw. He squatted down on his haunches to examine the machine while Renee looked on. She fidgeted restlessly.

"So how did you find out about Kate anyway?" she asked him. Given that they had met in Kate's vandalized apartment, there was obviously no point in trying to conceal Batwoman's secret identity.

"She didn't *tell* me who she really was, if that's what you're asking," he commented. "She just made it easy for me to figure it out." He glanced up at Renee. "Her way of saying she trusted me, I think."

Renee nodded. "That sounds like her." She wondered how much Nightwing knew about their stormy history. Not that it really mattered. She gestured at the ominous-looking device. "So what do you think?"

Nightwing stood up. "I think it's a bomb of some sort, and I should probably stop messing with it." He cautiously stepped away from the device. "Stuff like this is better left to experts. We ought to call in the G.C.P.D. to handle this."

"I'd rather not be here for that," Renee told him, "if you don't mind."

He looked her over. "That's right. You used to be a detective, didn't you?"

"I'm *still* a detective," she said forcefully.

Is that why you chose me, Charlie? That need to ask the question? The need for answers? Or was it something else? A way to fight your own demons?

Turning away from the blinking device, she squatted down in front of the pinned octo-man. The tips of the monster's upper tentacles twitched feebly against the floor. He smelled like sushi gone bad. She gagged at the stench even as she gave him her most intimidating interrogation stare. More than willing to play the bad cop, she grabbed onto his beak and forcibly lifted his head from the floor. She looked ready to rip his tentacles off one by one to get what she wanted. It wasn't an act.

"Where's Mannheim? Where's the woman he kidnapped?"

"It's too *shhllpp* late!" the octo-man slurped. "You will *blplll* burn, all of Gotham will burn!"

A shadow fell over Renee. "He's right," another voice rumbled behind her. "And it will begin with you!"

Diving instinctively to one side, she drew her gun. A burst of red-hot flames struck the floor right where she had been kneeling only a second before. A quick scan revealed four new beastmen on the attack, led by an honest-to-goodness dragon-man, complete with glittering bronze scales, the head of a prehistoric lizard, dorsal fins, and a flailing tail. Dragonhead perched atop a nearby stack of crates, glaring down at Renee and her prisoner. A cone of fire erupted from the creature's jaws. The blast barely missed Renee, incinerating the octo-man instead. The burning were-creature shrieked in torment as the heap of wooden pallets turned into a funeral pyre. "GNNHHAAAAAAAAAAAAA!!!!"

"Montoya!" Nightwing shouted as he leaped up and kicked Dragonhead across the jaw. "The device! Don't let them activate the device!"

A human-vulture hybrid, with a wattled throat, a hooked beak, and dark black wings, was already flapping toward the mystery device. A shaggy sasquatch and a snake-tressed gorgon followed close behind their avian accomplice, charging at Renee. She smacked her gun across the face of the gorgon, then sprinted after the vulture-man. Her soles pounded against the concrete as she raced past the smoldering remains of the octo-man. The nauseating smell reminded her of that time the Firebug torched the Gotham Fish Market. . . .

Recovering from Nightwing's kick, Dragonhead belched flames at the hero, who seemed to catch a piece of the blast before he sprang out of the way. Renee hoped that Nightwing's snazzy costume was seriously fire-resistant. "Ahhh!" he yelped as he landed clumsily at the fire-breathing reptile's feet.

"Light the Inferno, brothers!" the dragon roared. "The time is now!"

Renee was gaining on the buzzard, until the sasquatch tackled her from behind. He hit her like a giant hairy linebacker, knocking her off her feet. Crashing toward the floor, she saw the vulture-man swoop down into the open cargo container. Three-toed feet touched down right in front of the humming machine. Renee threw her arms out in front of her; instead of trying to break her fall, she fired off another burst from her ray gun. The incandescent golden beam burned a hole straight through the buzzard's right pinion. He screeched in pain.

Winged him! she thought as she hit the ground. The impact knocked the breath out of her and jolted the ray gun from her grasp. The sasquatch's bulk pinned her to the floor, while the gorgon chased after the fallen weapon. The writhing snakes atop the beast-woman's head hissed like burning fuses.

Sorry to let you down again, Charlie, she thought, frustrated by her failure. *You tried your best, in what little time you had left. Maybe you should have chosen another student. One less selfish and self-absorbed . . .*

She was still dazed when the sasquatch stood up and yanked her to her feet. Grinning wickedly, the gorgon waved Renee's own gun in her face. A forked tongue reminded Renee of Whisper A'Daire. She was getting pretty damn sick of this never-ending freak show.

The bigfoot's rancid breath blew against the back of Renee's neck. Drool dripped from his prognathous jaw. A sloping brow made him look like the Missing Link. "Shoot her," he growled at the gorgon.

A few yards away, Dragonhead had his scaly tail wrapped around Nightwing's throat. Grimacing, Nightwing tried to pull the constricting coils away from his neck, but wasn't having much luck. The left corner of his uniform was badly scorched. Sucker-marks still blemished his face. His feet dangled in the air as the dragon's tail lifted him off the floor.

"Don't you get it, meat?" Dragonhead jeered. Nightwing swung an escrima stick at the monster's slitted eye, but Dragonhead easily blocked the blow with his right paw. Tiny red flames started to curl around the corners of the reptile's mouth as he got ready to roast Nightwing for good. "The outcome was already decided. This was all written long ago."

A guttural new voice intruded on the scene. "Then you probably should have seen this coming, hadn't you?"

Without warning, a furry black wolf-man pounced onto Dragonhead's back. Lupine fangs sank into the reptile's scaly neck. Dragonhead reared backward in surprise. His flaming breath shot uselessly at the ceiling, sparing Nightwing.

What the hell? Renee thought. She instantly recognized Abbot, Whisper's lycanthropic henchman, but what was he doing on their side all of a sudden? Her subhuman captors appeared equally stunned by the werewolf's unexpected arrival. The gorgon looked confused, uncertain what to do next. *Just so long as she doesn't pull the trigger . . .*

Caught off guard by Abbot, Dragonhead must have loosened his grip on Nightwing, who took advantage of the respite to kick himself free of the monster's tail. Cold blood sprayed across the warehouse as the wolf-man tore out a chunk of Dragonhead's shoulder with his teeth. Nightwing followed up with a flying kick across the reptile's face. Jagged incisors cracked to pieces, but the enraged dragon seemed angrier at the werewolf on his back. "Heretic! Infidel! Betrayer!" Dragonhead spit out chunks of broken enamel. Spraying saliva smelled like kerosene. "You shall—!"

Furious blows from Nightwing's plastic batons cut off the threat in midsentence. Abbot slashed his claws across the dragon's neck. A bloodthirsty howl issued from his throat.

There's something you don't see every day, Renee thought. *A werewolf fighting a dragon fighting a super hero . . .*

The two monsters threatening Renee didn't know what to make of this shocking turn of events. The gun-toting gorgon looked away from Renee to check out the bizarre clash going on only a few paces away. The sasquatch's sunken eyes were also glued to the fight. Even the snakes on the gorgon's head were distracted.

Renee saw her opportunity and took it. She savagely kicked the gorgon in the crotch, then snatched the ray gun back from the snake-woman's grip. Before the sasquatch even knew what was happening, she shot him in the bigfoot. He let go of her abruptly and stumbled backward, clutching his perforated foot, while the gorgon groaned weakly, doubled over in pain.

Wishing she was pistol-whipping Whisper A'Daire instead, Renee whacked the gorgon in the side of the head, putting her and her serpentine hairdo down for the count. She turned to deal with the sasquatch, but Nightwing beat her to the punch. An escrima stick ricocheted off the floor to hit the crippled beast-man right below the chin. The sasquatch dropped like a shag carpet onto the floor. *How about that?* Renee thought. *Who knew Bigfoot had a glass chin?*

She looked over at her allies and saw that Dragonhead had also been taken care of. The fire-breathing monstrosity lay in a pool of his own blood, his flames thoroughly extinguished. Was he still breathing? Renee was in no hurry to check. She had more pressing matters to worry about right now.

Like Abbot, for one.

The wolf-man stood over the prone body of his victim. Nightwing watched him warily, poised to defend himself at the first sign of an attack. Renee kept her gun raised. She hadn't forgotten that shipping office in Shiruta, where Abbot had massacred all those people. She trusted the lycanthropic hit man about as much as she trusted the Joker.

"The save buys you an explanation," Nightwing told him, "but not a lot more."

"You want a bloody explanation?" Abbot snarled. Fur and fangs melted away as he morphed back into his human guise. Now that her life was no longer in immediate jeopardy, Renee noticed that Abbot looked like he'd been through a hell of a fight. His right eye was missing, and one ear was partly torn away. Cuts and scrapes and bruises covered his naked body, more than his brief tussle with Dragonhead could account for. Someone had worked him over pretty badly. "I'm sick of prophecies, that's my . . ." His remaining eye lit up as a sudden thought struck him. "Wait a sec. . . . Where'd that buzzard get to?"

Crap! Renee thought. She had forgotten about the vulture-man too. Spinning around, she spotted the wounded beast-man dragging himself up against the scary mechanism. There was a smoking hole in his wingspan, but that didn't stop him from wrapping his talons around a stainless steel lever. His hoarse voice held a fanatic's fervor.

"To the shiv, the gat, and the Red Rock, in thy unholy name . . ."

Dragonhead's alarming instructions flashed through Renee's brain.

"Light the Inferno."

"No!" Nightwing exclaimed. He and Renee dashed forward to stop him, but Abbot grabbed onto both of them and dragged them backward, away from whatever doomsday weapon the mutated cultist was trying to activate. Even in human form, Abbot was unnaturally strong. *Dammit,* she thought. *I knew we couldn't trust him!*

"Let go!" Nightwing protested. "We've got to stop him!"

"Too late!" Abbot barked. "Get down!"

They hit the floor only a second before the suicidal buzzard pulled down the lever. A sudden burst of heat flared against Renee's face as the device ignited, instantly consuming both the vulture-man and the cargo container. A pillar of liquid flame shot through the roof of the warehouse and up into the night sky.

Way, way up.

Flat on the floor beside Nightwing and Abbot, Renee couldn't look away from the blazing column, which cast a red-hot glow over the interior of the warehouse. She shuddered as she recalled that *other* etching in the *Book of Crime*: the flaming pit at the center of a damned city. Was this what Intergang had been planning for Gotham all this time?

And what did this mean for Kate?

"It's growing," Nightwing realized as they backed away from the flames and got to their feet. "It looks like it's spreading."

"It is," Abbot confirmed. He looked sickened by the sight. "Just not the way you imagine it. It's not going out." He pointed at the base of the pillar, which was busily burning its way through the concrete floor of the building. "It's digging down."

FLEEING the unbearable heat inside the warehouse, the unlikely trio relocated to the rooftop of an adjacent building. From that vantage point, Renee was able to see that the towering pillar of fire was just one of six skyscraper-sized torches lighting up the night. The burning columns were arrayed throughout the city, from the Upper East Side to Chinatown. Fire engines rushed from one blaze to another. Screams and sirens wailed over the crackling of the flames.

"Gotham burns tonight," Abbot stated. "Each device tears into the foundations of the city, igniting everything it touches. By dawn, a pit of fire will roar at your city's heart."

Renee recalled the apocalyptic illustration once more. "It doesn't make sense," she objected. "If Intergang wants Gotham, why turn it into a fire pit?"

"Because Mannheim believes everything in the Crime Bible is true and *must* come to pass." The disgust in the werewolf's voice made it clear that he was no longer a believer.

"What about Kate?" Renee asked. "The Twice-Named Daughter of Cain? Is she still alive?"

Abbot nodded. "Her heart is supposed to unite the flames and open the pit. Mannheim intends to sacrifice her at dawn."

"Over my dead body," Renee said fiercely.

Abbot was unimpressed by her bravado. "Easy enough for him to do, girl. Bloody hell, even if you can save her, it won't be enough."

"Then stop wasting time," Nightwing demanded. "And tell us what will be."

Renee stepped away, putting some distance between herself and the men. She felt destiny, and Vic's enigmatic agenda, closing in on her—or maybe it was just her future taking shape. *Who am I, Charlie? Who am I going to be?* Richard Dragon's words of wisdom echoed in her brain. *"Some questions can only be answered by wearing a mask."*

"Each device has to be shut down," Abbot explained to

Nightwing. "Otherwise they'll simply burn where they stand until nothing is left."

Nightwing took Abbot at his word. "We'll split up," he declared, taking charge. The sucker-marks on his face had finally faded away. "You and Montoya go after the devices. I'll—"

"No," she said firmly. Her gloved fingers found the hidden switch on her belt buckle. A balled-up wad of pseudoderm dropped into her hand. Tot's patented binary gases billowed out from the buckle. The swirling fumes smelled like baby powder and cardamom. She unfolded the mask and began to smooth it over her face. "It's got to be you two who go after the devices."

The pseudoderm bonded to her face as though it belonged there. Renee experienced a flash of claustrophobia as the artificial flesh covered her mouth, nose, and eyes, but the anxiety swiftly passed. She was surprised at how good it felt to be so empty and so free.

Who am I? Who am I going to be?

The two men stared at her in surprise as the last of the fumes wafted past them. The gas reacted with the chemicals in her hair and clothes, changing their color. Her dark brown hair turned pitch-black. The trench coat went from tan to slate gray. Renee Montoya's distinctive features had disappeared beneath a smooth expanse of skin.

Good question.

"I'll take care of Mannheim," the Question said.

Nightwing took her transformation in stride. She guessed that he was used to all manner of masked heroes and villains. "You'll be going to rescue Kate alone," he pointed out. "Would you really die for this?"

Her blank face looked back at him.

"Wouldn't you?"

FOR the first time in years, she was going back to church.

Gotham Cathedral had been closed ever since the Crisis, when a freak meteor storm had trashed Cathedral Square and the surrounding neighborhoods. Scaffolding and opaque canvas tarps now covered the exterior of the looming Gothic edifice. A metal sign hung upon the chain-link fence surrounding the construction site:

CATHEDRAL SQUARE RESTORATION PROJECT
"Rebuilding the spiritual heart of Gotham."
REOPENING SUMMER NEXT YEAR
Brought to you by your friends at
Ridge-Ferrick Construction

Towers of flame, burning in the distance, cast an incarnadine glow over the Square. The crimson radiance made it seem like the sun was already rising, but the Question figured it was still at least thirty minutes until dawn. She hoped that would be enough.

For Kate *and* the city.

Taking one last look at the sky-high torches, she silently wished Nightwing luck and crept toward the cathedral. The padlock securing the wire gate proved easy enough to pick, while Richard's training gave her the finesse to slip past the scaffolding and tarps undetected. Peering through her eyeless mask, she spotted a jackal-headed beast-man standing guard just inside the cathedral. The canine sentry sniffed the air suspiciously.

Looks like I'm on the right track, she decided. *Guess Abbot was on the level.*

She picked up a nearby piece of rebar. Being careful to stay downwind of the jackal-man, she came up behind him and cracked the rebar against his skull. He dropped onto the worn marble floor of the vestibule. His tongue lolled from his muzzle. His tail twitched against the flagstones.

Time to let sleeping dogs lie, the Question thought. *Hope PETA doesn't find out about this.*

She cautiously entered the heart of the cathedral, and frowned behind her mask. The vaulted chamber, once a lovely monument to Gothic architecture, had been thoroughly gutted and vandalized. Obscene graffiti was scrawled upon the walls, along with blasphemous murals depicting high points in the unholy history of Crime: Cain slaying Abel, Judas betraying Christ, Sweeney Todd applying his bloody razor to the throat of an unsuspecting customer, Holmes and Moriarty grappling at the brink of the Reichenbach Falls, Blackbeard laying siege to Charleston, Booth assassinating Lincoln, Bonnie and Clyde on a killing spree, the Joker beating Robin to death, Lex Luthor discovering kryptonite, an evil Superboy on a rampage, Jack the Ripper, Leopold and Loeb, Cheshire, Scarface, Lizzie Borden, Rā's al Ghūl. . . . Everywhere she looked was more evidence of Mannheim's twisted religion, glorifying mass murder, torture, and every other heinous crime. *I'll be damned,* she vowed, *if Kate's murder joins this sickening hit parade.*

A large hole had been carved into the floor of the sanctuary, where the dais and altar used to be. Firelight emanated from deep within the hole. Smoke rose through a ragged gap in the vaulted ceiling.

The Question proceeded down the nave to the edge of the cavity. Snatches of a profane invocation emerged from the hole. She recognized the sly, sibilant voice even before she got close enough to peer down into the depths below.

"Bound and gagged, hostage and victim, prisoner and slave," Whisper A'Daire chanted, "thus do we offer the fool's flesh, that of your wayward daughter, your lost wolf. . . ."

The overly familiar cadences made the Question's skin crawl, but not as much as what she saw as she furtively peeked over the edge.

The Cult of Crime had transformed one of the cathedral's underground crypts into an unholy temple that reminded Renee of the one she and Vic had infiltrated in Bialya, back when there still was a Bialya. The rotting bones of past sacrificial victims occupied niches carved into the walls of the desecrated catacomb, but she barely registered their presence. Instead her attention was seized by the terrifying sight of Kate lying, chained and gagged, atop a large stone sarcophagus that now served as an altar. She was dressed as Batwoman, but her mask and utility belt were missing. Her luxuriant red hair was elegantly coiffed. Beauty makeup failed to entirely conceal her swollen eyes and busted lip. Rusty chains bound her to the lid of the coffin. Wide-awake, she squirmed and tugged at her bonds, but to no avail. A black silk gag kept her from shouting at her captors.

Bruno Mannheim, his brutish anatomy incongruously garbed in a flowing crimson robe, stood over Kate's supine form. He held aloft a fancy-looking golden dagger. Whisper A'Daire, wearing the same "naughty nun" outfit she had sported in Bialya, was positioned behind a nearby lectern, where she read aloud from the *Book of Crime*. A circle of low flames surrounded the ceremony. No other congregants appeared to be present.

"And saying such, the Killer drew his shiv 'cross the Whetstone of Brutus once, twice, thrice, and using its edge did test it on hisself. . . ."

In accordance with the lurid text, Mannheim sliced his own thumb with the gleaming blade. Kate glared at him with both fear and fury as he rubbed the thumb beneath her eyes, smearing his blood across her face. The silk gag muffled her protests. The Question shuddered at the degrading scene; if not for her mask, she would have looked just as pissed off as Batwoman.

"Splitting the skin of his thumb, and anointing the frail with his claret . . ."

The Question had heard—and seen—enough. She drew the ray gun from beneath her coat.

Remember Shiruta, Charlie? The girl I killed, the Intergang suicide bomber?

"And seeing the razor cut quick and right, he readied hisself to the wet work before him. . . ."

Mannheim raised the knife with both hands. He stood poised to bury the point of the blade in Kate's chest.

"In Cain's name, we commend this offering, the heart of the Twice-Named Daughter. . . ."

The Question calmly aimed the gun at Mannheim.

What goes around, comes around.

"That the fires of your hate and pain may blaze on Earth . . ."

Her finger tightened on the trigger—just as a pair of beast-men tackled her from behind. She fired off a shot, but the blast went wild, disintegrating one of the slumbering skeletons instead of Mannheim. Savage growls filled her ears as she tumbled forward over the edge.

Damn! She landed roughly on the dusty stone floor of the crypt, just outside the flaming circle. The two monsters—a horned satyr and a were-grizzly—pounced down after her. Startled, Mannheim stepped back from altar, lowering the dagger. Whisper darted out from behind the lectern. Her slitted eyes widened at the sight of the faceless intruder. *Oh well,* Renee thought. *At least I kept hold of my gun this time.*

"I told you!" Mannheim shouted. The Question's abrupt appearance obviously upset him. "I told you, Whisper!"

The outraged priestess didn't argue the point. "Kill her!" she commanded the beast-men. "Kill her!"

The bear-man and the satyr charged at the Question, who dropped them with one shot each, while Whisper came at her from the side. Iridescent scales spread across Whisper's exposed skin as she took on a more serpentine form. Folds upon her throat inflated into a cobra's hood. Fangs extended from her gums. Venom sprayed from her lips.

The caustic saliva burned right through the Question's glove, stinging her skin. She yelped in pain as her gun slipped from her fingers. Whisper sprang at the Question, her jaws open impossibly wide. "Foolissssh girl!"

She charged into the Question, shoving her up against the wall. Renee threw her forearm up beneath Whisper's chin in order to keep the snake-woman's fangs from her throat. Bones rattled in the limestone niche behind her. The circle of flames danced between them and the altar. The Question glimpsed Kate struggling atop the ponderous stone coffin.

"Her blood will ssspill here," Whisper hissed. A forked tongue flicked between her lips. Her slender legs melted together, forming the tail of an enormous serpent. Half woman, half cobra, Whisper now resembled a lamia out of classical mythology. The Question fought to keep the monster's venomous fangs at bay. "It isss written in the Vile Book!"

"I'm doing a rewrite," the Question said. Adapting a martial arts move she had learned in Nanda Parbat, she flipped Whisper into the ring of fire. The lamia shrieked in agony as the flames raced over her inhuman body. The scaly tail thrashed frenziedly as Whisper threw herself away from the fiery circle. Hissing furiously, she slithered away into the catacombs.

That's one less snake to worry about, the Question thought. She hastily scooped up her gun from the floor. To her alarm, she realized that she had lost track of Mannheim in the confusion. *Where is he?* she thought frantically. Gun in hand, she whirled around toward the altar. *What about Kate?*

"The Word is perfect," a gruff voice intoned. "My faith without question."

The Question saw Mannheim plunge the dagger into Kate's chest. Her mouth was still gagged, but her body arched in agony. Mannheim's eyes blazed in exultation.

"NO!" Renee screamed. She fired the pistol and a brilliant yellow blast grazed Mannheim's thick skull. He toppled backward, away from the altar, leaving the golden blade embedded in Kate's chest. "No no no!"

Racing death, the Question rushed to the altar. Four short bursts from the ray gun disintegrated Kate's chains, freeing her, but the horrified detective feared that she was already too late. "Please, Kate, hold on. . . ."

Not again. Not this time.

She glanced quickly at Mannheim. The mob boss appeared to be down for the count, sprawled upon the floor at the very edge of the flaming circle. A tendril of white smoke rose from a nasty-looking burn on his temple. His pomaded black hair was singed above one ear. His once-crazed eyes were now closed at last. Part of Renee wanted to kick his ugly face in, but it was Kate who needed her full attention now.

"You're not doing this," she insisted, carefully tugging the gag away from Kate's mouth. "You're not dying. . . ."

But the grisly sight before her seemed to mock her pleas. The dagger was buried deeply in Kate's chest, precisely in the center of the bat-symbol on her costume. There wasn't a whole lot of blood visible yet, but the Question knew a mortal injury when she saw one. Her memory flashed back to Crispus Allen lying dead on a street not terribly far from here, and of Vic Sage expiring in her arms amidst a plain of bloodstained snow.

No. This time is different. It has to be!

"Gotta get the knife out," she murmured. Her fist closed around the hilt of the dagger.

"No . . ." Kate weakly lifted a hand to stop her. "That'll make it worse. . . ." She looked up at the Question. Somehow she seemed to recognize Renee despite the disguise. Her fingers lightly grazed the pseudoderm. "Where'd your face go . . . ?"

"You're looking at it," the Question said, choking back a sob.

"Not for long," Mannheim growled. Blood leaked from his wounded skull as he grabbed onto the Question's throat and yanked her away from Kate. She croaked loudly as Mannheim's powerful hand squeezed her larynx. "I'm going to rip it clean off your head!"

"Renee!" Kate gasped, too weak to intervene.

Mannheim pivoted, catapulting the Question into a wall. Dusty skeletons shattered on impact, rattling down onto the floor. Still maintaining a tight grip on her gun, the Question twisted her body in time to keep from breaking any of her own bones. But that didn't keep her head from spinning. She staggered groggily across the floor of the crypt. Chances were, she was already suffering from a concussion.

Oh, this is bad in so many ways.

Mannheim strode through the fire toward her. His crimson robe appeared irritatingly flame-resistant. "By the way, I'll take my gun back now." He grabbed onto her gun arm and twisted it painfully, until she was forced to release the weapon. "If you don't mind."

"Hey," the Question said shakily, "all you had to do was ask."

Unamused by her flippant response, he pitched her headfirst into the side of the altar. She slumped down onto the floor. Kate tried to reach for her, but the movement obviously caused her excruciating pain. A sharp intake of breath hinted at her anguish.

"Funny," Mannheim snarled. He marched toward the Question, coming between her and the altar. His massive frame blocked her view of Kate. "Let's see if you make a funny pile of dust."

The Question tilted her heard to peer past the looming gangster. "I wouldn't do that," she whispered hoarsely.

"You wouldn't?" Mannheim sneered down at the faceless woman. He raised club-sized fists. "And why not?"

He stiffened abruptly. His troglodyte features contorted as the point of his sacred blade suddenly protruded from the center of his chest. Dark arterial blood streamed down his robe.

"She wasn't talking to you, Bruno," Kate explained, kneeling atop the altar. Her hands let go of the dagger's hilt. Her chestnut eyes flashed vindictively. "She was talking to *me*."

Mannheim toppled forward, landing facedown upon the floor. The hilt of the dagger jutted from his back. Kate, the last of her strength evaporating, started to tumble off the altar, but the Question jumped up to catch her before she hit the ground. She collapsed into Renee's arms.

This time it's different. . . .

Kate glanced down at her chest, where her bat-insignia rapidly disappeared beneath a spreading crimson oval. Blood trickled from the corner of her mouth. "Think maybe . . . I shouldn't have done that. . . ."

With the blade no longer sealing the wound, Kate's lifeblood began to gush from her heart. "Stay with me," the Question urged as she gently laid Kate back down atop the altar. Her gloved hand pressed down on Batwoman's chest, applying pressure to the wound. "Stay with me."

Dawn's light began to creep into the crypt from the stained glass windows and shattered ceiling above them. Since they were not being engulfed by a bottomless pit of flame, the

Question assumed that Nightwing and Abbot had managed to locate and disarm all six of Intergang's infernal devices. The sirens of the fire engines slowly died away outside.

Her hands stayed atop Kate's bleeding chest, while she silently recited the same mantra over and over again.

This time it's different. . . .

WEEK 49.

OOLONG ISLAND.

"My name is Doctor Thaddeus Sivana," the mad doctor said. Spotlights shone down on his hairless cranium as he addressed the television camera. A uniquely modified microphone transmitted his voice to every TV set, radio, computer, and iPod on the planet. "And I represent a coalition of the greatest scientific minds of the twenty-first century."

It had been over a week since they had been able to raise their sponsors in Gotham. The scuttlebutt was that Boss Mannheim was dead and Intergang in complete disarray. *Guess that makes us free agents,* Sivana thought, *which means that we need an alternative source of funding.* Hence today's force-fed infomercial.

"We have in our possession the world's most dangerous living weapon. He killed over two million men, women, and children in a single night. Then he vanished."

The robotically controlled TV camera panned over to capture an eye-catching shot of Black Adam being held captive in Sivana's personal laboratory/torture chamber. Black Adam was shackled to an upright operating table. The Neural Crown upon his brow sent epileptic tremors through his convulsing body. His face was contorted in agony. A string of drool hung from his quivering bottom lip.

"We have Black Adam."

A red light blinked atop the camera as it swiveled back toward Sivana. A sinister grin stretched across his gargoyle-like visage as he addressed his worldwide audience.

"Now, how much am I bid?"

"HE's not merchandise," Green Lantern declared hours later. The Justice Society stood atop a glider composed of cool emerald flames. The glider hovered in the air outside the force-field dome defending Oolong Island. His power ring tapped into the island's broadcasts, projecting a miniature image of Sivana's leering face. "We're here to take Black Adam into custody, by force if necessary."

Mister Terrific stood beside Green Lantern on the platform. Despite Sivana's devious efforts to route his original trans-mission through a bewildering maze of satellites, servers, and global communications networks, it had taken Michael Holt only a few hours to trace the signal back to its source. His patented T-Spheres orbited his head; the baseball-sized com-puters used holographic displays to provide Mister Terrific with a constant flow of fresh information. Not for nothing was the brilliant African-American inventor and athlete known as the third smartest man on Earth.

"You found me more quickly than I expected," Sivana con-ceded. "I'll give you that. But you'll also find that this island's defenses are state-of-the-art and then some. No one is taking Black Adam from us without coughing up a king's ransom!"

"We'll see about that," Green Lantern said. He directed a beam of emerald energy at the force shield. Radiant green flames raced across the surface of the invisible dome, defining its borders. He nodded at his teammates. "Go to it."

The Justice Society went on the offensive, combining their powers in a determined effort to break through the force shield. Hourman popped a Miraclo pill, giving him superhuman strength for exactly sixty minutes. His energized fists pounded against the field. Stargirl used her Cosmic Rod to blast the dome with concentrated stellar energy. Power Girl focused her heat vision on the same portion of the dome. The Flash punched the wall a thousand times a second. Doctor Mid-Nite stood ready to provide medical assistance if necessary. Mister Terrific's T-Spheres scanned the field with their sensors.

"We're making progress," he reported. The motto "Fair Play" was emblazoned on the sleeves of his Kevlar jacket. A T-shaped black mask adhered to his face. "Stargirl, increase the amplitude of your stellar blasts. That should increase the disruption to the energy lattice."

"You got it, Michael!" Courtney Whitmore called back. The perky blonde teenager adjusted the settings on her Cosmic Rod, a glowing metal staff that harnessed the energy of the stars themselves. "Whatever it takes!"

Wildcat paced atop the emerald glider. He slammed his fist into his palm. This sort of super-science was not his forte; he couldn't wait to get down to some old-fashioned fisticuffs. "Hurry up, guys and gals," he muttered in a thick Brooklyn accent. "I've got skulls to crack."

You and me both, Green Lantern thought.

"MAINTAIN the shields!" Sivana ordered the other mad doctors. He stood upon the catwalk overlooking the main floor of the central laboratory. A large picture window offered him a panoramic view of the battle being waged just beyond the shore. His fellow scientists stared intently at their monitors, or else looked to him for instructions. Fear showed upon their ashen faces. Every one of them had been on the receiving end of a super-hero beat down more than once and was in no hurry to experience the same again. Security guards and lab assistants scurried about, frantically shoring up the island's defenses, many of which had already been damaged by Black Adam's attack three weeks ago. "Don't let those muscle-bound oafs intimidate you," Sivana exhorted his colleagues. "Hold your posts!"

Despite his pep talk, Sivana was less than sanguine about their prospects. If Black Adam alone could smash through the force field, he had to assume that the combined resources of the Justice Society would also break down the barrier eventually. *The hell with it,* he thought. *I'm not hanging around for this.*

"Where's that teleport control?" He fished the remote control device from the pocket of his rumpled lab coat. The hand-held remote was programmed to activate a teleport link to the all-purpose Omnibot, currently in geosynchronous orbit over their heads. He visualized the giant robot cruising serenely above the blue white curve of Earth, far above the tempest descending upon Oolong Island. The cockpit installed in the robot's transparent brainpan seated two, which was one more seat than Sivana wanted or needed. A co-pilot would only slow his escape.

There was just one catch: To use the teleporter, he would have to lower the force field over the island, which would leave his fellow scientists and the rest of the base's personnel completely vulnerable to the JSA's assault.

Tough, Sivana thought. He took a final look at the immense, high-tech facility and let out a heavy sigh; it had been a cushy gig while it lasted. He shut down the force field and tapped the emergency escape code into the remote. *Sayonara, boys!*

A shimmering dematerialization beam whisked him away.

"THE shield's down!"

Doctor Death's panicked cry was quickly echoed by the shouts and curses of the remaining scientists. Anxious eyes looked to the catwalk, only to discover that Doctor Sivana was no longer overseeing their defenses. Dr. Cyclops' single eye bulged from its socket. Baron Bug whimpered and crawled under his lab counter. Doctor Tyme's minute hand spun hysterically upon his clock face. Ira Quimby raced upstairs to look for Sivana. Frozen with fear, Rigoro Mortis was as stiff as a board. Veronica Cale looked almost relieved.

Time to go, T.O. Morrow decided. *This place is going to be crawling with angry super heroes any minute now.* He gulped down the last of his peach daiquiri and put the glass aside. *Good thing my Omnibot is powered up and ready to go.* He pulled open the top drawer of his filing cabinet and reached for the Omnibot's remote control device, but his fingers found only air. The drawer was empty. Someone had taken the remote.

"Sivana," he realized instantly. The crafty old coot had betrayed them all.

He kicked himself for not thinking of it first.

WITHIN seconds, the Justice Society poured into the complex. Fierce fighting broke out as the Intergang guards fired at the invading heroes with a mixture of handguns, Uzis, and laser rifles. "Stand your ground!" Ira Quimby shouted from the catwalk, having literally taken Sivana's place. "We beat Black Adam! We can beat these insufferable do-gooders!"

Don't bet on it, Green Lantern thought, leading the charge into the lab. Hot lead and energy blasts ricocheted off a wall of emerald flames that bulldozed through the hail of gunfire like a battering ram. Scanning the scene for the most dangerous threats, he spotted T.O. Morrow whipping a blinking metal wand out of his back pocket. Green Lantern reacted with the speed of thought, binding Morrow's arms to his sides with luminous green chains. *I don't know what that gadget does,* Alan Scott thought, *but I'm not giving Morrow a chance to use it against us.*

He concentrated his willpower and the chains tightened around the fugitive futurist. "Drop the wand," Green Lantern ordered his prisoner. Meanwhile, out of the corner of his eye, he caught glimpses of the heated battle raging around him.

In a blur of super-speed, the Flash single-handedly disarmed the guards in a matter of moments. Their weapons ripped from their hands by an irresistible force, the demoralized mercenaries, many of whom hadn't been paid in weeks, quickly surrendered.

A one-eyed scientist, whom Alan identified as Dr. Cyclops, aimed some sort of black-light ray at Doctor Mid-Nite. "In the land of the blind," Cyclops ranted, "the one-eyed man is king!" Clearly he was unaware that Dr. Pieter Cross could *only* see in pitch blackness. Doctor Mid-Nite hurled a Blackout Bomb at Cyclops. Inky black smoke blinded the scientist, but not the crime-fighting physician, who delivered a karate chop to the mad doctor's neck with surgical precision. Cyclops' single eye rolled up until only the white could be seen.

Doctor Death hurled a fuming beaker of acid at Power Girl's face. "Please!" she jeered as the acid and broken glass splashed harmlessly against her invulnerable skin. "Like that's supposed to bother me?" A gust of super-breath blew the goateed scientist into the wall behind him. A shelf's worth of glass retorts and graduated cylinders crashed down onto him. "I've had bikini waxes that stung more."

"Your time is up, Hourman!" a clock-faced crook taunted Rick Tyler as the hooded hero ran toward him. An hourglass full of Miraclo tablets dangled on a chain around Hourman's neck. A beam from Doctor Tyme's ray gun washed over Hourman, who suddenly seemed to jump forward sixty seconds in time. "You're powerless now!"

That didn't seem to worry Hourman, who slammed his fist into Tyme's goofy countenance anyway. The face of the timepiece cracked down the middle. The minute and hour hands went flying off in separate directions. An alarm bell chimed as Hourman literally cleaned Tyme's clock. He wrested the gun from the villain's grip. "I don't need super-strength to take out a creep like you."

Tyme moaned upon the floor. "If only I had those fifty-two seconds . . . !"

Huh? Green Lantern thought. *What on earth is he babbling about?*

"Defend me, my Insectrons!" Baron Bug commanded from beneath a counter. A swarm of mechanical bees and wasps rose from a worktable and toward Mister Terrific, who just happened to be invisible to all electronic cameras and sensors. The Insectrons buzzed right past him, leaving him alone as he grabbed onto Baron Bug's collar and dragged him out into the open. Capturing the scientist's remote, Michael Holt quickly deduced its function. A press of a button caused the robotic swarm to drop lifelessly onto the floor, where they were crushed beneath the feet of fleeing sentries and lab assistants. Their metallic exoskeletons crunched loudly.

"Chicken much?" Stargirl swept the floor with a low-level blast from her Cosmic Rod, stunning over a dozen retreating accomplices with one smooth move. Using the staff in a gymnastic fashion, she nimbly pole-vaulted over a heap of unconscious bodies after Veronica Cale. "What a bunch of losers!"

"I surrender!" Cale cried out, raising her manicured hands above her head. Guilty tears streaked her mascara. "After what we created, we deserve everything we get."

"Me too," Rigoro Mortis added, sounding more intimidated than contrite. With the Super-Hood, Mark III, only a pile of notes and blueprints, the balding scientist had nothing more up his sleeves. His voice quavered. "I give up too!"

That left Ira Quimby up on the catwalk. Wildcat swung up onto the walkway with feline agility. A meaty fist grabbed onto the collar of Quimby's sweaty Hawaiian shirt. "Forget it, chum," Wildcat growled, spinning the scrawny super-genius around. "You're not going nowhere." The costumed prize fighter scowled beneath his whiskers. He looked disappointed that he hadn't had a chance to punch someone yet. "Where's Black Adam?"

While Wildcat gave I.Q. the third degree, Green Lantern finished up with T.O. Morrow. The constricting green chains finally forced Morrow to drop his wand, which Green Lantern incinerated with a burst of emerald fire. *So much for that,* he thought, then rendered Morrow unconscious with a mild jolt of energy. Dissolving the chains, Green Lantern took a moment to survey the battlefield. From the looks of things, his teammates had won an easy victory. The sprawling lab complex looked like a cyclone had hit it, but the fighting appeared to be over. Proud of his comrades' skill and courage, it took Green Lantern a moment to notice that someone was missing.

"Wait a minute," he called out to the others. "Has anyone seen Atom-Smasher?"

LET *the others mop up the floor with those nutty professors,* Atom-Smasher thought as he sprinted through the building, leaving the battle behind. He had no doubt that the JSA would be able to handle Doctor Sivana's diabolical think tank without his assistance. *I need to find Black Adam.*

Despite their differences, he and Adam went way back. They had liberated Kahndaq together, fighting side by side. Adam was like a brother to him. A stern and unforgiving brother, perhaps, but a kindred spirit nonetheless. They had both known tragedy in their lives, and sought solace in vengeance. The other difference between them was that Al Rothstein now regretted his bloody past. He figured Adam deserved the same shot at redemption.

"Adam?" he called out loudly. He had shrunk down to normal human proportions, the better to search the sprawling lab complex. He ran through sterile white corridors, searching for his friend. Open doorways offered glimpses of bizarre weapons and inventions under construction, including a kryptonite guillotine, a fifth-dimensional torpedo, a portable black hole projector, and a subterranean locomotive for boring to the center of the Earth. Sealed airlocks were marked with cautionary labels warning of radioactive and/or biohazardous materials. A refrigerated storeroom held a sickening collection of eyeballs, hearts, and other human organs, preserved in formaldehyde. The specs for a life-sized plutonium android were scrawled on a blackboard, next to the ingredients for the ultimate nerve gas. None of which was what Atom-Smasher was looking for. "Adam, can you hear me?"

"Albert . . . ?"

A pain-wracked voice came from the other side of a locked steel door. KEEP OUT! ordered a handwritten sign taped to the door. TRESPASSERS MAY BE DISSECTED.

That sounds like Sivana, Atom-Smasher thought. *Increas-*

ing his mass by 10 percent, he slammed his shoulder into the door, knocking it off its hinges. He charged into the chamber beyond, then froze in his tracks, taken aback by the ghastly scene before him.

Black Adam was still trapped upon the mad doctor's operating table; his convulsing limbs clamped down by thick promethium bands. A blinking crown of circuitry, which Mister Terrific had theorized was some sort of neurological disruptor, continued to induce epileptic seizures in the captured superman. Steel cables and pulleys suspended the operating table above a frothing vat of noxious chemicals. A profusion of probes and electrodes monitored his vital signs, while robotic arms employed diamond-tipped drills, flamethrowers, buzz saws, cattle prods, and laser scalpels to test the limits of Adam's invulnerability. His black tunic and trousers had been sliced to ribbons. Ugly purple welts and bruises showed through the torn fabric. Exposed flesh was scalded and burned. A tray of bloody surgical instruments sat atop a nearby counter. High-voltage defibrillator paddles were cradled upon a crash cart, the better to keep Sivana's unwilling guinea pig alive. Anesthetics were conspicuously absent.

"Oh my Lord," Atom-Smasher whispered. The caustic fumes from the vat stung his throat and nostrils. He shuddered to think how long Adam must have been inhaling the corrosive vapors. "What has that bastard been doing to you?"

And for weeks, no less.

Atom-Smasher didn't care what Black Adam may or may not have done. Nobody deserved this kind of torture. Not even the world's most dangerous mortal.

"Help. . . ." Adam pleaded, through cracked and bleeding lips. His hoarse voice held only a whisper of its usual deep timbre. His bruised face furrowed in concentration, as though it was taking all his strength and willpower just to stay focused on the other man. Bloodshot eyes entreated Atom-Smasher. "Release me. . . ."

"Hang on," the giant hero said. He tripled in height and

weight, so that he could reach over the acid vat to grab onto the hanging operating table. He scanned Adam's restraints, wondering where to begin. Maybe the steel shackles?

"The crown . . ." Adam's eyes turned toward the intricate device girding his skull. "Neural crown . . ."

Atom-Smasher nodded. "Got it." He reached to remove the crown, then hesitated. Unbidden, images of the devastation in Bialya flashed through his brain. He recalled the stink of millions of rotting corpses. He couldn't believe that Adam had really been responsible for that atrocity. The man he knew would never have committed such a crime.

And yet . . .

"Adam, about Bialya." His eyes searched the other man's face. "Tell me you didn't do what they say you did. Waller doctored that satellite footage, didn't she? The same way she edited that footage of Osiris killing the Persuader." To Atom-Smasher's disgust, Amanda Waller had spliced in reaction shots from Osiris' brief, happy stint with the Teen Titans to make it look like the youthful hero had enjoyed dismembering the axe-wielding super-criminal. He figured she had pulled a similar trick with the footage from Bialya. "It was the Fourth Horseman who killed all those people, right? You chased him to Bialya, but he murdered everyone before you could stop him."

It was the only explanation that made any sense. Adam wouldn't commit genocide, not even after his wife was killed. From what Atom-Smasher knew of Isis, that's the very last thing she would have wanted Adam to do in her name. Adam had to know that.

Didn't he?

"Yes," Adam confirmed. "It was . . . the Horseman."

I knew it! Atom-Smasher thought. The world had always misjudged Black Adam. *I'm the only one left who understands what kind of person he really is. He's not a monster, just a man who's known too much tragedy in his life. Like me.*

"And if I free you now, you're not going to do anything crazy?"

Adam shook his head, the simple motion obviously requiring a Herculean effort. "Just want to . . . go back home," he assured Atom-Smasher. "Grieve . . . for my family . . ."

"Of course." Atom-Smasher sympathized with Adam's loss; he had lost his own mother to the heartless machinations of a fiendish super-villain. In addition, he couldn't help feeling responsible, at least in part, for all the sorrow Adam had recently endured. Everything had started to go wrong for Adam and his family after that bloodbath in the redwoods. *This is partly my fault,* Al Rothstein thought. *I should've never joined the Suicide Squad on that damn assignment.*

His mind made up, he plucked the Neural Crown from Adam's brow and tossed the sadistic gadget into the acid bath below. *Good riddance,* he thought. Adam's muscles immediately stopped spasming. In control of his own body once more, he strained against the steel bands pinning him to the table. Atom-Smasher tugged on the restraints as well, adding his own strength to Adam's, and the promethium bonds shattered. He lifted Adam from the table and gently placed him down on the floor, several feet away from the edge of the acid bath. "Are you all right?" he asked his friend.

"I am better." Black Adam teetered unsteadily at first, weakened by nearly a month of debilitating abuse, but quickly began to regain his strength. "Thank you, my friend." He flexed his biceps experimentally, making a fist. "Your actions . . . shall not be forgotten."

Something in his tone set Atom-Smasher on edge. He started to say something, but was interrupted by a clamor from outside. The unmistakable sounds of combat penetrated Sivana's private chamber of horrors. Atom-Smasher recognized the distinctive zap of Stargirl's Cosmic Rod, and the crackle of Green Lantern's emerald flames. The noise was getting louder by the moment. He realized that there was no time to lose.

"The Justice Society is here," he warned Adam urgently. "You've got to get away." There would be time enough to clear Adam's name later, before a violent confrontation could get out of control. "You need to leave here before someone gets hurt."

Adam laughed bitterly. "I cannot possibly be hurt any more than I have already been, thanks to Intergang and Sivana." Scowling, he looked to the west. "Gotham City, I have learned, is Intergang's new capital."

Gotham? Atom-Smasher didn't like the sound of this. "You said you were just going to go home to Kahndaq," he reminded Adam. "To mourn Isis and Osiris."

"Did I?" Adam's expression darkened ominously. "Perhaps you only heard what you wanted to hear." He gave Atom-Smasher a warning look. "I go to fulfill my wife's dying request. Do not try to stop me."

Before Al could ask what he meant, Black Adam rocketed into the air like a missile, smashing through the ceiling. Pieces of shattered steel and concrete splashed down into the acid bath, dissolving instantly. The spray from the vat splattered against Atom-Smasher's legs, stinging his skin. Smoke rose from his scorched trousers.

Attracted by the commotion, the Flash zipped into the chamber. He stared up at the gaping hole in the ceiling. Even though Jay Garrick was the only member of the JSA capable of matching Adam's speed, he was unable to fly. Bound to the ground, he could only squint upward at the sky. "Was that . . . ?"

"Black Adam," Atom-Smasher divulged. He shrank down to normal size. "He got away from me."

"Hell," the Flash swore, taking him at his word. The two men waited silently for their teammates to catch up with them. Atom-Smasher wished that he could confide in the older man, but he kept mouth shut instead. He doubted the Flash would understand.

Please tell me, he prayed, *that I didn't just make the biggest mistake of my life.*

WEEK 50.

AROUND THE WORLD.

BLACK Adam had just crossed the International Date Line, en route to North America, when a sudden blow sent him tumbling backward into the Southern Hemisphere. He fell from the heavens like a fallen angel, coming to rest in a vacant lot outside Sydney, Australia. The earthshaking impact of his landing was picked up by seismometers all across the continent.

What? He rose angrily from a deep crater. *Who dares?*

"That's far enough, Adam," Captain Marvel declared. Accompanied by both Mary Marvel and Captain Marvel Jr., he descended from the sky until he hovered only a few yards above Adam's head. His broad face looked graver than Adam ever recalled seeing it before. "You need to answer for what you did to Bialya. This ends today."

The sight of the Marvel Family, still intact while his own family had been ruthlessly slaughtered, enraged Black Adam. He launched himself into their midst, lashing out furiously with his fists. The violent struggle carried them across the city, blasting through the defenseless streets and buildings. Flames and explosions erupted in their wake. "Do not presume to dictate to me, Billy!" Mary and Freddy grabbed onto Adam, hoping to restrain him long enough for Captain Marvel to knock him out, but Adam tossed them aside. "Look to your own family's safety!"

A volcanic punch sent Captain Marvel Jr. flying away from Sydney and across the Indian Ocean. Knocked senseless by the stupendous force of the blow, he crashed into the base of a monumental pyramid outside Cairo, Egypt. He collapsed onto the desert sands, nearly nine thousand miles from where Black Adam had hit him.

Seconds later, Mary Marvel splashed down into the reflecting pool outside India's famed Taj Mahal. Startled tour guides pulled the unconscious American heroine from the water. Baffled onlookers stared up at the heavens. More timid souls fled the scene, half expecting more bodies to come hurling down from the sky. Suddenly, it was raining super heroes. . . .

That's two down, Black Adam thought.

BACK in Sydney, Captain Marvel suddenly found himself facing Black Adam on his own. Smoke rose from the collateral damage of their titanic clash. The city's world-famous Opera House was in ruins, its overlapping concrete shells flattened to the ground. A few miles away, the Harbour Bridge, colloquially known to the locals as "The Coat Hanger" due to its distinctive arched design, no longer connected the central business district and the North Shore. Its wide lanes had been sliced across the middle. The huge steel arch was a tangle of twisted metal beams and girders. Fire trucks, ambulances, and other emergency vehicles raced through the demolished streets. The Tasmanian Devil, Down Under's most famous super hero, was out cold atop a decapitated high-rise. Tanks and missile launchers, dispatched by the Australian military to defend the capital, had been reduced to so much scrap metal. Overturned vehicles cluttered the streets. Mangled cannons and gun turrets bore the imprint of Black Adam's bare hands.

Lightning flashed as the World's Mightiest Mortals traded blows atop the remains of the Opera House. "Stop this!" Captain Marvel shouted. He wobbled unsteadily upon his feet. Blood dripped from his split lip. His knuckles ached from slamming repeatedly against Black Adam's invulnerable face and chin. Marvel had fought Black Adam before, but he had never seen his ancient Egyptian counterpart this berserk.

Adam's murderous rage only seemed to increase his already formidable strength, which he no longer had to share with Osiris. Looking into Adam's hate-crazed eyes, Captain Marvel found it hard to believe that he had actually presided over Adam's wedding only eight months ago. "Let me help you! Tell me what you want!"

"To avenge my family!" Black Adam snarled in response. "Starting with Gotham City!"

He hurled himself into the air, intent on wreaking more havoc elsewhere. Moving with the speed of Mercury, Captain Marvel intercepted him high above the city. The two men crashed together like opposing missiles. They grappled furiously in midair as their superhuman speed and momentum carried them far away from Sydney and the entire continent of Australia. They rocketed across the Pacific toward Asia.

America was less than an hour away.

NOT even the Flash could keep up with the conflicting news reports coming in from all around the globe. Egypt. India. Australia. Black Adam's genocidal rampage appeared to be spawning turmoil and damage everywhere at once. The press was already calling it "World War III."

The Justice Society arrived in Sydney only to find that they were too late once more. "Damn," Green Lantern muttered under his breath. Ever since Adam had somehow eluded them at Oolong Island, he had managed to keep one step ahead of them. A platform of glowing green flames supported his teammates as they gazed down at the devastation below. "My God. It's like the city has been through Armageddon."

"It's not the only one," Wildcat pointed out. "Wars are breakin' out between Black Adam's allies and enemies. Gonna be more fightin' soon over what's left of Bialya and Kahndaq."

Mister Terrific monitored the news reports coming in from his orbiting T-Spheres. The computerized orbs projected text and images before his eyes. "Why else do you think they're enforcing a global curfew until Black Adam is apprehended?"

"*If* he's caught," Power Girl said impatiently. She flew alongside the emerald platform, her scarlet cape flapping in the breeze. "So far he's been kicking the butts of everyone that's been able to catch up with him. The Global Guardians, the Doom Patrol, the Marvel Family . . ."

Wildcat raised his dukes. "Just give the JSA one round with that nutcase and that'll be a whole different story."

Let's hope so, Green Lantern thought. As much as he admired his friend's feisty attitude, he knew that they had one hell of a challenge before them—and that the outcome was by no means certain. *Of all times for Superman, Batman, and Wonder Woman to be AWOL . . . !* Still, the Justice Society had been defending the world long before the Big Three came along. *If we have to, we can do it again.*

"You may get your wish, Wildcat," Mister Terrific said. He scanned the holographic display floating in front of him. "Black Adam's just been spotted over Hong Kong."

Green Lantern nodded at the information. Concentrating his willpower, he sent the emerald platform soaring north at supersonic speed. A translucent green bubble protected his passengers from the physical stresses of the flight. "Contact the Chinese government, Michael," he instructed Mister Terrific. "Request permission to cross their borders in pursuit of Black Adam." With the world situation already deteriorating, he didn't want to provoke Beijing any more than they had to. "And notify our allies of Adam's current whereabouts. Tell them to meet us there!"

It was time to stop Black Adam, before he could do any more damage.

CHINA.

OVER four thousand miles long, the Great Wall of China stretched across the hilly landscape of northern China, winding its way atop lush green mountain ridges. The huge stone ramparts had been constructed to defend the Middle Kingdom from foreign invaders, but its ancient builders had never anticipated a menace like Black Adam.

This isn't working, Captain Marvel realized. Undulating hills and valleys rushed by beneath them as he and Black Adam hurled through the sky, locked in combat. The wisdom of Solomon informed him that continuing their duel could only result in yet more random destruction to any city or country that got in their way. *We're too evenly matched. I need to find another way to defeat him.*

A squadron of Chinese J-10 fighter planes joined the battle. Air-to-air missiles exploded against the two men, blasting them away from each other. Black Adam angrily grabbed onto the wing of one of the fighters and sent it spinning out of control into the other planes. Pilots frantically ejected from their aircraft, but a few were not able to escape in time. An enormous fireball consumed them before Captain Marvel even had a chance to go to their rescue. Smoking metal fragments spiraled toward crash landings ten thousand feet below. The Chinese casualties served as more proof that Black Adam's quest for vengeance was turning the entire world into a disaster area. Captain Marvel could only imagine the carnage in store.

Unless I stop him once and for all.

An idea occurred to him, but unfortunately it meant having to abandon the fight. *How can I do that?* he wondered anxiously. Black Adam started to fly away, only to find Captain Marvel blocking his path once more. A roundhouse punch, fueled by the strength of Hercules, sent Black Adam tumbling back the way they had come. *The minute I leave Adam to his own devices, he'll zoom straight to America. Gotham City will be doomed. . . .*

Then a bolt of emerald fire blasted up from below, striking Black Adam in the back. He howled loudly, more in anger than in pain, and glared down at the source of the flames. "Who dares?"

Hope flared in Captain Marvel's heart as his own eyes widened at the sight below.

Led by Green Lantern and the rest of Justice Society, a small army of costumed super heroes had gathered on top of and above the Great Wall. Besides the JSA, Marvel spotted Green Arrow, Black Canary, the Teen Titans, Plastic Man, Metamorpho, Black Lightning, Steel, Vixen, and at least a dozen other heroes forming a defensive line along the length of the Wall. Their determined faces made it clear that every one of them intended to stop Black Adam or die trying.

"It's over, Adam," Green Lantern said. A fiery green megaphone amplified his voice. "This is as far as you go."

But could the assembled champions actually succeed in halting Black Adam's bloody crusade? Captain Marvel wished them luck, but feared that even the JSA and their allies would not be enough. Still, these reinforcements might slow Adam down long enough for Marvel to put his newly formed plan into effect. *This is my chance,* he realized. *I have to take it.*

He threw a feint at Black Adam, deliberately giving his adversary an opening. Adam took the bait and delivered a brutal undercut that sent Captain Marvel rocketing up toward the heavens—just where he wanted to go. Once he was safely out of sight, he accelerated under his own power and sped beyond the bounds of mortal reality straight toward the realm of the gods.

If he was lucky, maybe he could cut off Black Adam's powers at the source.

ADAM sneered at the force assembled against him. *Let them come,* he thought defiantly. *My wrath cannot be denied. Gotham City will be nothing more than a smoking crater when I am done with it, as will any other city, hamlet, or nation that dares to harbor Intergang and its minions. Sivana too will pay, even if I have tear apart the entire world to find him.*

The flying heroes came at him first. Green Lantern led the charge, followed by Power Girl, Firestorm, Bulleteer, Stargirl, Beast Boy, and others. A giant emerald fist grabbed onto Adam, holding him in place while the other heroes assailed him. Bulleteer, her sturdy body encased in living metal, ricocheted off his skull. Firestorm seared him with atomic fire. Stargirl, riding her Cosmic Rod like a teenage witch upon a broom, jolted him with a blast of stellar energy. Power Girl slammed into him with all her Kryptonian strength. Beast Boy attacked him in the form of a large chartreuse pterodactyl. Hawkgirl swung her mace against his nose.

"Get him on the ground!" Green Lantern shouted. "Then the others can pitch in."

"Yeah, let's bury his ass!" Firestorm chimed in enthusiastically. A halo of nuclear flames crackled atop his scalp. His voice betrayed him as naught but a callow youth.

Against his will, the airborne heroes succeeded in driving Black Adam into the fortified earthworks at the base of the Wall. Bricks and mortar erupted upon impact. He fought to break free of the emerald fist, but the glowing fingers squeezed him more tightly than a mummy's wrappings. Hourman, Liberty Belle, the Flash, Black Lightning, Obsidian, Vixen, and others piled onto him. Fists, electricity, claws, and living shadows besieged him. An explosive arrow detonated against his brow. Black Canary's sonic cry battered his eardrums.

Another gigantic fist, this one composed of flesh and blood, hammered him into a paved parking lot at the base of the wall. A twenty-foot-tall giant, his face hidden behind a blue hood, towered among his other attackers.

"Is this your new 'Suicide Squad,' Albert?" Adam spat defiantly.

"That was a mistake," Atom-Smasher admitted. His booming voice could be heard even over the tumult of battle. "Just like the mistake you're making now. Why are you doing this? You told me you just wanted to go home!"

Black Adam didn't care what Atom-Smasher, or any other so-called hero, had to say. His vengeance was all that mattered. Exerting his strength to the utmost, he broke free from Green Lantern's flaming fist and flew straight at Atom-Smasher. His outstretched fists collided with the giant's chest, knocking him off his feet. The falling colossus crashed into an oncoming wave of heroes, including Aquagirl, Doctor Mid-Nite, Plastic Man, and others. Black Canary, Wildcat, and Green Arrow dived out of the way. Metamorpho transmuted into vapor an instant before being crushed. Raven vanished in a puff of black smoke.

"I do what I need to do," Adam said.

THE ROCK OF ETERNITY.

THE Phantom Stranger, Madame Xanadu, and Zatanna were three of the most powerful mystics on Earth. Now they convened within the cavernous throne room of their deceased colleague, the wizard Shazam, as they waited upon the will of the gods.

They did not have to wait long.

The Rock of Eternity shuddered as Captain Marvel came smashing through the ceiling into the throne room. A burning brazier toppled over, spilling glowing coals across the rough stone floor. A stalactite fell from the ceiling, threatening to impale Madame Xanadu, but the dark-haired fortune teller deftly stepped aside so that the rocky spike missed her by inches. The Seven Deadly Sins of Man trembled inside their petrified shells.

Captain Marvel slammed into the floor, cracking the foundations of the hidden chamber. Steam rose from his head and shoulders. The Phantom Stranger and Zatanna stepped forward to help the hero to his feet. The force of his landing left a deep impression in the floor. Madame Xanadu, her blind eyes covered by a silk bandanna, stood to one side. A green satin dress, slit high on one side, sheathed her slender figure. She restlessly shuffled a deck of Tarot cards.

"I take it they said 'no,' " she surmised.

"Emphatically," Captain Marvel confirmed. He took a moment to catch his breath. "I petitioned the gods of ancient Egypt to sever their ties to Black Adam before it was too late . . . and they just laughed at me." The faces of the arrogant deities, some of whom sported the heads of beasts, were seared into his memory. Horus had been particularly obnoxious. "Apparently, he still has their blessing. They refused to make Adam mortal again. They won't send the lightning."

"Well, that sucks," Zatanna said. A reserve member of the Justice League, the celebrated show-biz magician wore a costume better suited to a Vegas stage show than the Rock of Eternity. Her trademark top hat, tuxedo top, and fishnet tights were a big hit with her fans, few of whom realized that her sorcerous powers were for real. "I never did like that pantheon."

The Phantom Stranger nodded grimly. The brim of his black fedora shrouded his inscrutable face in shadows. He wore an indigo cloak over a conservative black suit and white turtleneck. A golden pendant, engraved with arcane cabalistic symbols, rested upon his chest. Not even the wisdom of Solomon held the secret of the Stranger's true nature and origins. "Is there no way to force the transformation?" he asked.

The three mystics looked expectantly at Captain Marvel. With Shazam dead, he was now the inheritor of the wizard's legacy—which, for better or for worse, included Black Adam. The renegade immortal was his responsibility.

"Let me think," Captain Marvel said.

CHINA.

JOHN Henry Irons, better known as Steel, crouched upon the rooftop of a Ming Dynasty watchtower as he made a few last-minute adjustments to a large homemade missile. His niece, Natasha, tapped upon the keyboard of a nearby laptop. Matching sets of burnished steel armor granted the two inventors extraordinary strength and protection. An atomic-powered sledgehammer rested at John Henry's feet. A second hammer belonged to Natasha. Bright red indicator lights flashed upon the surface of the gold-plated missile.

"C.O.M.P.U.T.O. is online, Uncle John," Natasha reported.

She tapped a final command into the missile via a wireless connection. The teenage prodigy took after her brilliant uncle.

"Thanks," Steel said. An S-emblem was riveted to his breastplate. A red cape paid tribute to his inspiration: Superman. "Without your help, it would've taken me months to build this weapon." Together, they hoisted the missile and aimed it at the mountainous battleground below, where Black Adam continued to hold his own against wave after wave of super heroes. Wonder Girl, of the Teen Titans, was trying to choke the villain with her enchanted lasso, while Doctor Mid-Nite hurled Blackout Bombs at Black Adam's eyes. Cyborg targeted their foe with the sonic cannon built into his arm. The Flash delivered rapid-fire punches to Adam's gut.

Steel hoped that he could end the conflict before anyone else got hurt. "Once this missile hits Black Adam, he'll inhale the AI nanites inside. They'll work their way to his brain, fuse onto his neurons, and short-circuit his motor functions." He glanced at his niece. "Ready?"

"Ready," she said bravely.

Steel had never been more proud of her. "Launch in three, two . . ."

Before he could complete the countdown, however, the air shimmered between the missile and its target. Automatic sensors in his armor alerted him to a sudden distortion in the fabric of space-time. A wormhole opened up before him.

Booster Gold came flying out of the rift. The metallic gold fabric of his costume was singed in places. Behind him, through the wormhole, Steel caught a glimpse of the Invasion of Normandy. . . .

"Booster?" he exclaimed.

Natasha did a double take. "I thought he was dead!"

"Not yet," Booster said. Zipping toward them, he reached out and yanked the missile from their grasp.

"Hey, we need that!" Natasha protested.

"Sorry, kid. I need it more than you." Executing a U-turn in the air above the watchtower, he dove back toward the wormhole. "Besides, it wasn't going to work. Trust me."

A prismatic flash of light momentarily blinded Steel, despite the protective lenses in his helmet. By the time his vision cleared, Booster Gold—and the time warp—were gone.

What in the world?

Natasha looked to him for answers. Despite her steel faceplate, the worry in her voice came through loud and clear. "What are we supposed to do now?"

Steel stared down at the battle raging dozens of feet below. He knew there was no time to construct another missile. He took his hammer in his hands and stepped toward the ledge. Rockets flared from the soles of his iron boots.

"Grab your hammer."

THE Flash breathed a sigh of relief as Steel and his niece joined the fray. They pounded on Black Adam with their high-tech hammers, while he took advantage of their arrival to slow down for a second. Even the fastest man alive could get winded sometimes. . . .

The Irons would buy them a little time, but Jay Garrick had few illusions that the armored pair would be able to put Black Adam down for the count, not after so many other heroes had already tried and failed. *We're running out of reinforcements,* he realized. *We need a magic bullet . . . and fast.*

"Tcatnoc Hsalf." A backward incantation caused a semi-transparent image of Zatanna to appear before him. The beautiful magician held her fingers to her temples. Her brow was furrowed in concentration. Her voice sounded like it was coming from a million miles away. "Flash, this is Zatanna! If you can hear me, we have one chance to stop Black Adam. Here's what you have to do. . . ."

He listened carefully.

Hell, if that might not work, he thought when she was finished. "Up!" he called urgently to his fellow heroes. "Haul him up, up, and away!"

Green Lantern, Steel, Natasha Irons, and Power Girl trusted him without question. Ganging up on Black Adam, the four heroes dragged the struggling villain up into the sky. Black

Adam fought back mightily. A vicious kick dislodged Natasha and sent the armored teenager plunging back to earth. Flash prayed that the girl's metallic exoskeleton would spare her from any serious injury. Black Adam elbowed Steel hard enough to crack his breastplate. A luminous emerald straitjacket, generated by Green Lantern's power ring, tightened around Black Adam's torso. The strain on Alan Scott's face showed just how much willpower was required to bind the villain even for just a few moments. Power Girl had Adam's skull in a headlock.

"Idiots!" Black Adam ranted. Spittle sprayed from his lips. "You think you can hold me? Mine is the power of the gods!"

Not my God, Flash thought. Wishing he could fly as well, he watched intently as the soaring figures shrank from view. Zatanna's ghostly image took off after the others, ascending into the heavens like an angel in fishnet tights. He crossed his fingers.

"Tcatnoc Nretnal," she said, casting another spell. "Lantern, hold your course! Captain Marvel is moving to intercept!"

A red and gold blur streaked across the sky until Captain Marvel came to a halt high above China. Looking down, he spotted Black Adam and his captors rocketing toward him. *All right,* he thought. *Here goes nothing.*

"Shazam!"

As always, the magic word summoned a mystic thunderbolt, but instead of letting the lightning go through him as usual, he reached out and *grabbed onto it with his bare hands.*

It was like taking hold of a high-voltage cable. He flung back his head and screamed in agony as the raw magical energy jolted his entire body. The thunderbolt jerked and bucked within his hands, trying to break free from his grasp. For the first time ever, he fought against the change . . . with only partial success. Traceries of electrical fire raced over his body, transforming random parts of his body back into those of Billy Batson. A leg, a shoulder, the right half of his face . . . parts of an ordinary teenage boy were melded grotesquely to the imposing form of the World's Mightiest Mortal. Blue jeans, tennis shoes, and a faded red T-shirt replaced portions of Captain Marvel's colorful uniform. His entire identity was in flux. The distortions shifted and flowed so that pieces of Captain Marvel and Billy were constantly changing places.

The pain was unimaginable.

THE ROCK OF ETERNITY.

THE trio of mystics formed a triangle around the burning brazier, their hands joined as they pooled their energies in order to hold the transformation at bay for just a few minutes more. Thaumaturgic fire arced between them. Exhaustion showed on their faces.

"The spell is working!" Zatanna gasped. An eldritch wind whipped her hair wildly about her shoulders. "Gnikrow si lleps eht!"

"Indeed," the Phantom Stranger confirmed. His hat had been blown from his head, exposing neatly trimmed white hair. Sparks erupted from his golden pendant. "If Billy were grounded, he'd be dead . . . !"

Madame Xanadu's blindfolded eyes peered into the ether. Her Tarot cards were scattered across the floor of the throne room. "He's losing it! We cannot insulate him from the magic much longer!"

"Nretnal!" Zatanna paged Alan Scott. "You have to hurry!"

THROUGH his pain, Captain Marvel saw the other heroes drawing nearer. Thrashing within the emerald straightjacket, Black Adam smacked the back of his head into Power Girl's face. Stunned, she fell away from the free-for-all. Steel had already hit the ground, leaving only Green Lantern to carry Adam upward the last couple hundred feet. Links of glowing green chains issued from Alan Scott's power ring as he dragged the crazed villain behind him.

This is it, Billy/Marvel realized. The captured thunderbolt writhed in his hands like a furious rattlesnake. It hissed and crackled in his ears. Ozone invaded his nostrils. *If we can't force Adam to call down the lightning, we have to bring him to it. . . .*

A sudden premonition seemed to alert Black Adam to the threat. He looked up in time to see Captain Marvel hurl the lightning bolt with all the power of Zeus. Adam's eyes widened in alarm. "No . . ."

The lightning hit Black Adam head-on—and a tremendous explosion went off above China. Thunder was heard for thousands of miles around. The shock wave sent Adam, Captain Marvel, and Green Lantern flying apart, then flattened the Great Wall below. Injured super heroes were scattered like leaves in the wind.

No one heard Teth-Adam as, badly burned, he plummeted toward the earth. Stripped of his powers, he shouted frantically over the wind rushing past his falling body.

"Shazam! Shazam! SHAZAM!"

No gods answered his call, but a pair of giant hands broke his fall.

"Got you," Atom-Smasher said.

"ALAN? Captain?"

The Flash searched the devastated landscape at super-speed, hunting desperately for any survivors. Fallen heroes were strewn across the battle-scarred hills, but Jay Garrick didn't spot any immediate fatalities. He shouted at the wounded champions. "Did anyone see where they went? Anyone?"

"Over here!" a familiar voice called back. Rushing as only he could, Flash found Green Lantern pulling Captain Marvel out from beneath the pile of rubble. He was surprised to see that Marvel's formerly black hair had turned snow-white. "We're all right," Green Lantern assured him. His purple cloak had been shredded to ribbons. His power ring flickered weakly. "But Adam . . ." He shook his head glumly. "I tried like hell to hold on to him, but that blast ripped him right out of my hands!"

Flash looked about in alarm. All around him, he spied his

battered comrades dusting themselves off and helping each other to their feet, but Black Adam was nowhere to be seen. "Then it isn't over!" he exclaimed. "Tell me we didn't lose him after all *that*!"

"Sorry, Jay." Atom-Smasher staggered across the rubble toward him. The disgraced hero had shrunk back down to human-sized proportions. "The light, the shock wave . . . no one saw exactly what happened to him."

For a moment, Flash wondered if Atom-Smasher was telling him the whole truth. Then Captain Marvel placed a reassuring hand upon his shoulder. "Relax, Flash. Even if he survived that fall, and that's a big if, he's not a threat anymore."

"Why not?" Flash demanded. "All he has to do is shout one word, and we're right back where we started!"

Captain Marvel shook his head. "With Shazam gone, I'm the guardian of his magic now. That brings with it a new level of ability." Along with his white hair, Marvel seemed to have gained a new level of maturity. His boyish innocence had given way to a more adult perspective. "True, I couldn't get Adam's gods to rescind their gifts, so I did the next best thing. I *changed* his magic word."

Flash's jaw dropped. Zatanna hadn't explained that part of the plan to him. "To what?"

"I'll never tell another living soul," Captain Marvel said, holding a finger before his lips. "I don't dare, but I promise you this: he will never guess. Never."

Let's hope you're right, Flash thought.

SHIRUTA.

WITH both its superhuman rulers and the Four Horsemen gone, Kahndaq was just another struggling Third World nation. Life was slowly coming back to normal in the capital's crowded streets and markets. Merchants hawked their wares to shoppers, who warily counted their coins as they haggled for a better deal. Bialyan refugees begged at the street corners. Old men and students clustered in the cafes, muttering darkly about the new provisional government. Black armbands and framed photos testified that much of the country was still mourning Isis and her family. "Where is Black Adam?" newspaper headlines asked, echoing a question that was much on the minds of all Kahndaqis, young and old. Rumors abounded that he had been sighted in Modora, or perhaps Qurac, but there had been no reliable evidence of his whereabouts since his defeat in China several days ago. Many believed him to be dead. Millions devoutly wished this to be the case. The press was still referring to last week's global conflict as "World War III."

Amidst the crush of humanity filling the busy bazaar, a solitary figure went unnoticed. Clad in a hooded robe and *djelaba*, he limped through the crowd, paying no heed to the carpets, bangles, and other merchandise on display. He moved with obvious pain, as though recovering from a recent fall. His bare feet were burned and blistered. Stubble peppered his shrouded face.

"Shazam," he whispered under his breath. "Black Adam."

Neither phrase brought forth the lightning. Teth-Adam scowled and guessed again.

"Osiris. Isis."

His bloodshot eyes moistened slightly at that latter name. He averted his gaze from yet another portrait of his martyred wife, this one propped up in the window of a small bakery. Kahndaq had not forgotten Isis, nor would he. *Someday I will regain my powers,* he promised her shade. *Someday the world shall suffer my revenge. . . .*

He sensed his former greatness hiding somewhere inside him. All he needed was the right word to unlock the magic trapping him in this pitiful mortal shell. Just one word.

"Kahndaq."

"Batson."

"Eternity."

Muttering to himself, he disappeared into the crowd.

WEEK 51.

METROPOLIS.

IT was a sunny spring day in Centennial Park. A year had passed
since the post-Crisis memorial service, and what had been intended as an event commemorating the first anniversary of the
Crisis had also become a tribute honoring those who had fallen
in World War III. As before, Earth's superhuman defenders
gathered in the open plaza at the center of the park. A large
statue of Superboy now stood beside the looming bronze Superman figure. Ordinary citizens, including sizable numbers of
young people, mingled with the heroes. T-shirts urged those
present to REMEMBER BIALYA, while charity organizations
solicited funds for relief efforts all over the world. Wanted post-
ers, handed out by volunteers, reminded attendees that Black
Adam remained the world's most hunted mortal. Nearly all of
the Justice Society was in attendance, along with the Teen Titans, the Doom Patrol, the Global Guardians, and scores of in-
dependent heroes. Once again, Superman, Batman, and Wonder
Woman were nowhere to be seen.

Few noticed two thirtyish men meeting at the fringes of the
crowd. Their conservative suits and ties stood in marked contrast to the colorful costumes worn by the gathered heroes.
They greeted each other warmly.

"You look rested," Bruce Wayne said.

"You too," Clark Kent replied.

A statuesque brunette in a pristine white jumpsuit approached them. A pistol was holstered to her hip. Her lustrous

black hair was tied back in a ponytail. Sapphire eyes shone behind a pair of stylish designer glasses.

"Special Agent Diana Prince," she introduced herself, "of the Department of Meta-Human Affairs." Her voice held an impish quality, as though she was sharing a private joke with the two men. "We're overseeing security at this event." She withdrew a PDA from a pouch on her uniform. "Mind if I check your names against my list?"

"No problem, Agent Prince," Bruce said. He had personally set up Diana's new secret identity.

"I like the glasses," Clark said.

She smiled back at him. "You would."

Clark took in the teeming crowd filling the plaza. Although his powers had yet to return, he was feeling stronger every day. He had no doubt that Superman would fly again someday soon. "Looks like the world got by without us," he commented.

"Barely," Bruce said darkly.

A sudden flash of light, at the base of the twin statues, provoked startled gasps from the crowd. To the surprise of both super heroes and civilians alike, Booster Gold and Rip Hunter suddenly appeared in the plaza. Both men looked like they had been in a fight. Their respective costumes were torn and bloody.

"Booster!" Power Girl gasped. "It's true. You're alive!"

There had been scattered reports of Booster being sighted here and there during World War III, but his sudden appearance still came as a shock to all concerned. "I don't understand," Clark said. "I was there when he died. I saw his body."

"Time-travel," Bruce deduced. His brow furrowed as his keen mind put the pieces together. "Of course."

"But where has he been?" Diana asked. "And is that Rip Hunter with him?"

Coming from all directions, more questions pelted the battered newcomers. Lois Lane and Jimmy Olsen led a charge of reporters and photojournalists anxious to get the scoop on Booster's seeming resurrection. Flashbulbs went off all around the two men.

"No time to explain!" Booster blurted. He dashed forward and snatched Wonder Girl's enchanted lasso from her hip. "I need to borrow this for a nanosecond!"

The lasso reappeared upon Cassie Sandsmark's hip a heartbeat later, while Booster held on to his own copy, plucked out of a single instant of time. "Hurry," Rip urged Booster. He glanced at a chronometer on his wrist. "He's right behind us!"

Who? Clark wondered.

A blinding flare of purple energy went off overhead—and Skeets came sailing out of an extradimensional rift. "WHERE ARE YOU?" the robot asked. "AND WHY HERE?"

People glanced up at Skeets in confusion. Clark realized that he hadn't seen the football-sized robot since Booster's funeral in Cincinnati. A chill ran down his spine, although he wasn't quite sure why. Maybe something about Skeets' tone?

"Stay back, everyone!" Booster warned. "Let us handle this!"

"Be careful, Booster," Rip Hunter advised in a worried tone. "Remember, we've fought this battle fifty-one times already. This is our last chance to get it right!"

Clark felt like he was coming in at the end of a complicated story. Why were Booster and Rip acting like Skeets was a menace? The futuristic robot could be a smart aleck sometimes, but he wasn't exactly Brainiac.

Or was he?

Booster regarded his former sidekick warily. "Take it easy, Skeets." He sounded like he was making a last-ditch attempt to reason with the robot. "We know your data got *corrupted* somehow."

"SKEETS IS DEAD, MICHAEL." The floating metal orb laughed scornfully. "I ATE HIM FROM WITHIN TO MAKE A CRADLE. A COCOON." Panels began to unlatch across the robot's polished exterior. "I WAS TRAPPED IN A LARVAL STAGE UNTIL I SAW HIM ON TV." His gloating voice hinted at years of frustration. "IMAGINE, THE MIND OF AN ALIEN GENIUS CONFINED TO THE BODY OF A LOWLY CATERPILLAR."

Great Rao, Clark thought, as he finally realized who they were really dealing with here. "That's not Skeets, it's . . ."

"Mister Mind," Bruce said grimly.

"Hera preserve us!" Diana exclaimed.

Clark clenched his fists at his sides. *If only I had my powers back!* Along with Black Adam and Doctor Sivana, the world's wickedest worm had long been one of Captain Marvel's greatest foes. But the Big Red Cheese was not on hand today. From what Clark had heard, Billy was holding down the fort at the Rock of Eternity right now. . . .

"I TELEPORTED INTO SKEETS EXACTLY A YEAR AGO. IRRADIATED WITH SUSPENDIUM PARTICLES, I BEGAN MY TRANSFORMATION." Sheets of metal plating fell away from Skeets' golden casing. Gooey strands of white mucus clung to the discarded fragments. A weird, unnatural light glowed from within the possessed robot. "NOW IT IS TOO LATE TO STOP THE CHANGE. THE FIFTY-TWO WEEKS OF MY GESTATION ARE COMPLETE. NOW, AT LAST, THE CHRYSALIS CAN HATCH!"

The last of the metal flakes fell away as "Skeets" cracked in two to reveal a radiant insectoid entity at its core. Damp wings unfurled, producing a cyclonic wind that drove back the crowd below. The insect's voice lost its robotic timbre as its true nature was revealed.

"Behold the Metamorphosis of Mister Mind!"

Instead of a tiny green caterpillar, a large monarch butterfly emerged from the chrysalis. Blood pumped into its scaly chartreuse wings, causing them to expand dramatically. Symmetrical markings upon the insect's upper wings resembled a pair of black-rimmed eyeglasses. The entire butterfly seemed to be growing at an incredibly accelerated rate. Within seconds, it dwarfed the entire plaza.

"I'm hungry," the alien imago declared. Saliva dripped from its extended proboscis. "So hungry I could eat a universe." Huge compound eyes scanned Metropolis and beyond. Its twin antennae wriggled.

"Let's start with yours."

WEEK 52.

SOMEWHERE IN TIME.

THE Time-Sphere raced into next week, pursued by the voracious butterfly.

About the size of an old-fashioned hot-air balloon, the zooming transparent globe was Rip Hunter's mobile laboratory, capable of traveling the entire length of the timestream, from the Big Bang to the heat death of the universe. Booster had found the Sphere wrecked beyond repair in Hunter's desert bunker, but the resourceful Time Master had kept a working model safely tucked away in 52 B.C.E., where he and Booster had reclaimed it after their escape from the Fortress of Solitude. Now Hunter was frantically splicing Wonder Girl's magic lasso into the time machine's guts, while Booster looked on worriedly. Fragments of Skeets' shattered metal shell rested atop the Sphere's blinking dashboard.

I hope Rip knows what he's doing, Booster fretted. They had fought "Skeets" throughout history, at least fifty-one times to date, but that had been before they found out what was lurking inside him; now all bets were off. *At least we're luring Mister Mind away from that crowded afternoon in the park.*

Outside the Sphere, days and nights rushed past them at dizzying speed. The sun streaked across the sky, rising and setting every few minutes. Sunlight and starry nights alternated in rapid succession. A waxing moon chased the sun across the celestial firmament. The lights of Metropolis blinked on and off like a message in Morse code. Glancing back over his shoulder, Booster blinked in surprise as the city's familiar sky-line suddenly split apart into dozens of overlapping views of the same scene. He hastily wiped his goggles with his sleeve, but the multiple Metropoli remained. It was like he was seeing double, then triple, then quadruple. . . .

"Hey, Rip!" he blurted. "Is all this time-travel getting to me, or is there something really weird going on? Besides being chased through tomorrow by a megalomaniacal moth, that is?"

"Not weird. Transcendent," Hunter corrected, looking up briefly from the Sphere's temporal engines. "What you're witnessing is the birth of a brand-new multiverse, triggered by the emergence of a genuine chronal butterfly." Thankfully, Hunter had managed to get his time-warped syntax under control during their travels. Necessity, and adrenaline, had been the mother of coherence. "The visual distortions are just your brain's way of processing the genesis of multiple parallel Earths, each one alike to the last detail, occupying the same space, but on separate vibratory planes." He finished tinkering with the intricate apparatus. "That's why I needed Wonder Girl's lasso. On its own, my Sphere could only travel through a single timeline, but the extradimensional properties of the lasso, which was forged by the Olympian Gods on their own plane of existence, will allow us to traverse the multiverse as well."

I'll take your word for it, Booster thought. He had gone to college on a football scholarship; advanced temporal mechanics were way beyond him. The multiple skylines gradually resolved into a single image as the extra Earths split off into their own parallel universes. He breathed a sigh of relief . . . until he spotted Mister Mind right behind them. The inky black eyeglasses on the butterfly's wings glared malevolently at the fleeing Sphere. The freshly hatched imago was growing at an accelerated rate. His wingspan was already a mile across.

"Heads up, Rip! Whatever you're up to, you better do it fast." Hunter had cryptically alluded to a surprise he had waiting up ahead; not for the first time, Booster wished that his cagey partner didn't play his cards so close to his chest. "He's gaining on us!"

Hunter gazed intently at the relativistic chronometer on the Sphere's control panel. Days, hours, minutes, and seconds counted down to their destination: Metropolis, one week after the ceremony in the park. 5:52 P.M. "Almost there!"

The Time-Sphere soared through the shifting sky over Metropolis. The time-dilation effect slowed as Hunter eased up on the gas. The blinking city lights went dim as they zoomed beneath a lingering blue sky, now traveling merely through space instead of time. The huge crowd of heroes and well-wishers had dispersed, so that mobs of people no longer swarmed around the base of the Superman and Superboy memorials. Joggers, dog walkers, and strolling couples went about their day, on what looked like an ordinary spring afternoon in the Big Apricot.

Except for the giant butterfly.

"You can't escape me!" Mister Mind buzzed loudly. "I've waited too long for this moment to let you interfere with my destiny any longer!"

Something sprayed from the giant butterfly's proboscis: an ominous black light that Booster didn't recognize at first . . . until he spotted the distorted faces of dozens of bodiless wraiths trapped within the expanding energy field. "Holy crap!" he exclaimed. "That bug just puked the Phantom Zone at us!"

The darksome Zone rushed toward them like a tidal wave, enveloping everything in its path. Fleecy white clouds were sucked into the Zone, along with generous portions of sky and sunlight. The spreading space-time distortion threatened to swallow the retreating Time-Sphere in a single gulp. "Count your blessings, gentlemen!" Mister Mind gloated. "You'll be safe in the Zone while I consume your reality!"

"No, thanks!" a new voice shouted from above. Booster's jaw dropped as *Supernova* swooped to the rescue. A brilliant radiance surrounded him. His long blue cape flapped in the breeze. "They've got better things to do—like stopping you for good!"

Supernova zipped between the Sphere and the Zone. Utilizing the cannibalized Kryptonian circuitry in his costume, he fearlessly met the oncoming void. Like a prism, he altered the Phantom Zone's wavelength, refracting it back to where it belonged. The sinister black energy vanished from sight. A blinding burst of light drove Mister Mind backward.

What the heck? Booster thought, completely baffled. *I was Supernova, so how come I don't remember any of this? Is this a future self, or maybe a past self from a parallel universe?* The paradoxes made his head spin. *And how can the Supernova suit still exist anyway? Rip tore it to shreds back in Kandor!*

He gave Hunter a confused look. "Rip?"

The Time Master tapped a button on the Sphere's control panel. The transparent ceiling dilated to form an opening and Supernova flew into the Sphere though the aperture, which noiselessly closed behind him. The masked hero pulled off his hood to reveal a sweaty face that looked vaguely familiar to Booster. The man's mussed blond hair was the same color as his own.

Who?

"Booster Gold," Hunter said. "Meet your twenty-first-century ancestor, Daniel Jon Carter." He quickly explained how "Skeets" had tricked Daniel over eight months ago. "I rescued him from that time-loop while you were playing Supernova in Metropolis—and stowed him in the future for his own safety. And as a backup plan, in case something happened to you."

Thanks for the vote of confidence, Booster thought grumpily. "And the costume?"

"Borrowed from a moment you weren't using it," Hunter explained. "Naturally."

Daniel held out his hand. "Pleased to meet you, descendant."

Now that he was looking for it, Booster could see the family resemblance. *He's got my Uncle Rajiv's chin.* Booster made a mental note to make sure Daniel came out of this adventure alive, just to ensure that Michael Jon Carter would still be born three centuries from now. Assuming the universe—make that the *multiverse*—was still in one piece by then. "Thanks for the save," he said, shaking Daniel's hand. "You really pulled our butts out of the fire."

"What can I say?" Supernova replied. "It was the least I could do for my own flesh and blood."

"I'm afraid we don't have time for a family reunion," Hunter interrupted. He expertly worked the navigational controls as the Sphere plunged back into the timestream. Seasons rushed by in a blur outside. "We seem to have lost Mister Mind for the moment, but it's only a matter of time before he catches up with us again." He turned toward them, his face somber. "A chronal butterfly is one of the most dangerous life-forms in creation. According to ancient Venusian mythology, they feed on the very substance of space-time itself, and lay their eggs in the quantum foam underlying reality. This new multiverse is like a banquet for Mister Mind. Given a chance, he'll consume every version of Earth, right down to the core Earth, the one we all came from."

Booster only understood half of that, but neither part sounded good. "So how do we stop him?"

Hunter looked over the gummy fragments of Skeets. "Did you manage to recover most of the pieces?"

"I think so," Booster said. Hunter had insisted that he salvage the remnants of Skeets' golden shell before they'd transported back to the Time-Sphere from Centennial Park. The newly hatched butterfly had needed a few moments to dry his wings, giving Booster time to scoop up the broken pieces before they had to escape. He felt a pang in his heart as he contemplated the gooey shards. Skeets had been a good sidekick, before that slimy caterpillar had infested him. "Why did you want these pieces anyway?"

"Just an idea." Hunter started fitting the fragments together again. "If we can only buy ourselves enough time."

"Which we may have run out of," Daniel said, pointing

behind them. He tugged Supernova's blue hood back over his head. "Here comes Mothra again!"

The giant butterfly flew toward them. His enormous wings flapped and a tremendous wind buffeted the Time-Sphere, throwing the men off balance. Booster grabbed onto a handrail to keep from falling. The bubble rocked back and forth, like a toy boat atop a stormy sea. "Hold on!" Hunter shouted, his gaze glued to a display panel before him. Wonder Girl's golden lasso vibrated audibly. Sparks erupted where the enchanted rope connected with the Sphere's engines. "We're being tossed into a parallel universe!"

Despite the turbulence, Booster managed to glance down at the city below. Metropolis looked the same to him. He remembered what Rip had said about each of the parallel Earths being identical to each other. *Guess he knew what he was talking about.*

Then Mister Mind bit off the top of the Daily Planet Building—and the entire city changed. Before Booster's startled eyes, the City of Tomorrow morphed into a barren post-atomic wasteland, the once-proud skyscrapers melted together into hills of metal slag. At first, the ruins looked totally abandoned, but then Booster spotted a small group of figures moving through the wreckage. As the shaking Time-Sphere swooped lower over the city, he got a better look at the bizarre scene below.

Armored knights, wearing suits of medieval plate armor, rode atop oversized mutant Dalmatians as they charged toward a field of bright red flowers, whose scarlet blooms seemed to be emitting plumes of billowing black smoke. "Onward, Atomic Knights!" the lead knight called to his fellows. "These strange plants are emitting an eerie blackness that's spreading over the entire Earth." He hurled a flaming torch into the midst of the flowers. "We've got to destroy them before it's too late!"

A mutant creature, which looked like a humanoid mole, rose up from behind a nearby heap of rubble. His whiskers twitched as he fired at the Knights with a laser pistol. A crimson beam bounced off the polished breastplate of one of the

Knights. "Turn back!" the mole-man commanded. "We cannot allow you to destroy the secret weapon we are using to conquer the planet!"

Huh?

Booster blinked and rubbed his eyes, but the surreal vista remained unchanged. The Atomic Knights, their canine steeds, and the nefarious mole-man all looked up in surprise as the Time-Sphere whooshed by over their heads, followed closely by a butterfly the size of a zeppelin. The mole-man's dumbfounded expression matched Booster's.

"Where the hell are we?" Booster demanded. "And when?"

"Metropolis, 1987," Rip Hunter informed him. His eyes scanned the readout on one of the Sphere's historical monitors. "Only a year after a nuclear holocaust destroyed most of civilization!"

"But that never happened!" Booster protested. He was no PhD, but he was pretty sure he had never seen anything about Atomic Knights and mutant Dalmatians in the history books of the twenty-fifth century.

"Not on our Earth," Hunter admitted. "But every time Mister Mind flaps his wings, and takes a bite out of another reality, it sends a ripple through the timestream that changes that Earth's history in unaccountable ways. He's eating crucial years and events from the timeline. This parallel Earth now has its own unique past, present, and tomorrow." Despite the danger, the scientist in him sounded intrigued by the phenomenon. "It's the Butterfly Effect, writ large."

"Are you kidding me?" Booster said, not believing his ears. "That's just a metaphor!"

Hunter shook his head grimly. "I wish."

"Watch out!" Supernova shouted in warning. Mister Mind's wings flapped once more, sending the Time-Sphere rolling end over end across the smoky sky. Wonder Girl's lasso sparked violently. An unsettling whine came from the engines. Booster's stomach did cartwheels as the Sphere careened off the side of a skeletal skyscraper into yet another universe. Nausea threatened, and he squeezed his eyes shut to block out the spinning scenery outside.

He waited until the Sphere stabilized its orientation, then opened his eyes, half afraid to find out where they had materialized now. Gazing down through the transparent floor of the flying globe, he saw at once that the desolate domain of the Atomic Knights was gone, replaced by the familiar sights and sounds of twenty-first-century Metropolis. *It's home,* he thought gratefully, *or at least a reasonable facsimile thereof.*

"Booster! What are you doing here?"

His heart leaped up as Superman, Batman, and Wonder Woman rose from the city to meet the Sphere. The Man of Steel and the Amazing Amazon flew toward them under their own power, of course, while the Dark Knight employed a bat-winged parasail to lift him up into the sky. *Talk about a sight for sore eyes,* Booster thought. *The Big Three couldn't have chosen a better time to stage a comeback.*

"Boy, am I glad to see you folks!" he told them, using the built-in mike in his costume. "You wouldn't believe what we've been through!"

"Tell us later," Batman said, cutting straight to the chase. His intense gaze zeroed in on the mammoth butterfly gliding toward them. Superman and Wonder Woman took up defensive postures above the endangered city. "What in blazes is that creature?"

"Remember Mister Mind?" Booster began, but before he could explain further, the hungry imago started nibbling on a cloud, chewing holes in the very fabric of this universe, like a moth dining on an old woolen sweater. Warning lights flashed upon the Time-Sphere's dashboard as reality shifted around them.

Abruptly, the heroic trinity *changed*. Their faces grew crueler; their world-famous uniforms restyled themselves. A bloodred U replaced the S-shield on Superman's chest. Wonder Woman's star-spangled colors gave way to a tight black leather getup that seemed better suited to a dominatrix than a super heroine. Large round lenses sprouted from Batman's cowl. A large gun appeared on the hip of his heavy gray body armor.

Wait a sec, Booster thought. *Batman never carries a gun. . . .*

"Do you know these intruders, Owlman?" the altered Wonder Woman asked her armored companion. She glared suspiciously at Booster and the others.

"Not a clue, Superwoman." He drew his gun and took aim at the Time-Sphere. "But I can tell they don't belong here." He nodded at the caped figure flying beside him. "You destroy that monstrous insect, Ultraman. Superwoman and I will deal with these invaders."

"Don't tell me what to do!" Ultraman snapped. "I'm the leader of the Crime Syndicate and don't you forget it!" An angry red glow filled his pupils. "I say we kill them all."

Superwoman laughed coldly. "That's what you *always* say!" She undressed him with her eyes. "No wonder I married you. . . ."

Owlman looked on jealously.

Okay, this is way too sick and twisted for me, Booster thought. Alarmed by Ultraman's red-hot eyes, he shouted urgently at Hunter. "Get us out of here—fast!"

Ultraman's heat vision flared, but the twin beams zapped past the Sphere to strike Mister Mind instead. The indignant butterfly let out an insectile screech and flapped his wings furiously, whipping up a temporal gale that hit the Sphere with the force of hurricane. The globe and its passengers found themselves rebounding from universe to universe like a pinball. "Timmad!" Hunter cursed, briefly losing control of his syntax again, as the reassembled remains of Skeets' shell went tumbling across the floor. He feverishly chased after the bouncing golden orb.

Tossed about the interior of the Sphere, Booster caught only glimpses of the myriad parallel Earths they passed through during their bumpy flight from the depraved world of the

Crime Syndicate. Only slightly singed by Ultraman's heat vision, Mister Mind pursued them relentlessly, wreaking havoc with history with every flap of his glittering chartreuse wings. Booster could only gape in amazement at the baroque versions of Metropolis rising and falling before his eyes.

Aztec pyramids replaced modern skyscrapers, only to be supplanted seconds later by Middle Eastern minarets and onion-domed mosques. Nazi storm troopers paraded down the main street of a fascist metropolis where the swastika was proudly displayed from every flagpole and awning. Pirate ships docked in the harbor, while the Bat-Signal, shining over Metropolis instead of Gotham, bore a skull-and-crossbones design. The gleaming spires of lost Atlantis occupied the surface of the Earth, while Metropolis sank beneath the waves. An anthropomorphic pink bunny rabbit, wearing Captain Marvel's costume, flew above a city teeming with talking animals. The Blue Beetle, who had died right before the Crisis, was restored to life on a whole new Earth. His bug-shaped airship soared above a parallel version of Hub City.

"Earth-12," Rip Hunter counted out as each new reality took shape. His computer catalogued them for future reference. "Earth-15, Earth-23 . . ."

It was all too much to take. Booster forced himself to look away. "How many of these insane alternate Earths are there?"

"FIFTY-TWO," a faint robotic voice piped up. "IT'S A MULTIVERSAL CONSTANT, LIKE PI OR THE SPEED OF LIGHT."

"Skeets!" Booster snatched the rolling shell up off the floor. "Is that you, buddy?"

"MICHAEL?" the robot sputtered, his electronic voice filled with static. "SIR?"

A rush of emotion came over Booster, surprising him in its intensity. He hadn't realized until now just how much he had missed the little robot. "I thought you were gone for good, pal. That sneaky butterfly said he'd killed you."

"NOT ENTIRELY," Skeets revealed. "HIS LARVAL FORM TELEPORTED INTO MY CIRCUITRY DURING THAT FIRST MEMORIAL SERVICE, AND STARTED EATING AWAY AT MY HARDWARE." Booster remembered Skeets shorting out during the ceremony. "HE IMMEDIATELY TOOK CONTROL OF MY CENTRAL PROCESSOR AND STARTED CONVERTING MY CASING INTO A COCOON, BUT PART OF MY ARTIFICIAL INTELLIGENCE REMAINED FIREWALLED OFF FROM HIS INCURSION. I WAS AWARE OF WHAT WAS HAPPENING, AND SHARING MISTER MIND'S PLANS TO SPAWN A NEW GENERATION OF CHRONAL BUTTERFLIES THROUGHOUT THE MULTIVERSE, BUT I WAS UNABLE TO SAY OR DO ANYTHING TO ALERT YOU."

"But you're back now, buddy." Booster polished Skeets' cracked and tarnished exterior with his sleeve. "That's what matters."

"Not if we can't stop Mister Mind's feeding frenzy," Rip Hunter insisted. "Time was already in a fragile state after the Infinite Crisis. The new reality was still fresh and malleable, like wet cement, when the imago's emergence caused it to schism. The altered timelines are just starting to reset themselves, but Mister Mind's rampage threatens to destabilize the entire multiverse. And if he manages to reproduce . . ." He shuddered at the thought. "Well, all of history will be reduced to eternal chaos, without form or linearity. Causality will have no meaning."

"That's bad, right?" Supernova asked. "So how are we supposed to sack that monster, anyway?" The giant butterfly, now the size of a small moon, was still on their tail. The gusts from his flapping wings continued to jostle the racing Sphere. Mister Mind's uncoiled feeding tube sucked greedily at the atmosphere of each new Earth. His eager palps ripped mountain ranges into bite-sized chunks. He would have caught up with the Sphere for sure if he hadn't been so busy gorging himself. "I don't suppose you've got a 'chronal flyswatter' tucked away somewhere?"

"No," Hunter confessed. "But I may have the next best thing." He reached out and took Skeets from Booster, who grudgingly relinquished his friend. "But first we need to cut him down to size a bit, which means it's time to pull out all the stops." Holding on to Skeets with one arm, he withdrew a stopwatch from the pocket of his bomber jacket. He held the watch up before Booster and Supernova. "I confiscated fifty-two seconds from Doctor Tyme, who stole them right after the Crisis. I've been saving them for just the right moment."

Booster tried to follow Hunter's explanation. *How does someone steal time, anyway?* he wondered. *Never mind. I don't want to know.*

Wonder Girl's lasso hummed and sparked as Hunter programmed new coordinates into the Sphere's navigational controls. "We're heading back to Earth-One," he said. "Booster, I need you to go on one last scavenger hunt for me. There's a weapon that might come in useful right now. . . ."

Moments later, the Time-Sphere lurched into the sky above mainland China. Mister Mind materialized above them a heartbeat later. The monstrous butterfly dove toward them, his antennae quivering in anticipation of another delicious morsel. Booster saw the vulnerable Sphere reflected over and over again in the insect's multifaceted compound eyes.

"Snack time!" Mister Mind exulted. "I'm feeling much fuller now, but don't worry. I've saved plenty of room for dessert!" His front legs reached out for the Sphere. "Say your prayer—"

Rip Hunter clicked the trigger on the stopwatch, and time stood still. Mister Mind was frozen in place above the Time-Sphere, only a hundred yards away. Hunter opened another doorway in the Sphere's outer shell. "Hurry," he urged Booster. "You only have fifty-two seconds to steal the weapon and get back here. Go!"

Racing the clock, Booster flew out of the Sphere and down toward the Great Wall of China, right into the middle of what appeared to be an all-out battle between Black Adam and more super heroes than Booster could count. Booster had no idea what Adam had done to piss off so many good guys at once, and he didn't have time to find out. Doing his best to ignore the tumult going on all around him, he stayed tightly focused on his mission, scanning the Great Wall for his target.

There it is! He spotted Steel and his niece crouched atop a crumbling stone watchtower, just like Rip had predicted. The two inventors, each clad in their own high-tech armor, were putting the finishing touches on a large homemade missile. "C.O.M.P.U.T.O. is online, Uncle John," Natasha Irons announced. She programmed the missile via her laptop.

That was his cue. He jetted down and seized the missile from the startled heroes. "Sorry, kid. I need it more than you." A twinge of guilt troubled his conscience, but, according to Rip, there was nothing else he could do. "Besides, it wasn't going to work. Trust me."

Clutching the stolen missile against his chest, he returned to the stolen fifty-two seconds. To his relief, he saw that Mister Mind was still frozen in place above the Time-Sphere, poised to attack. *I did it,* he realized. *I made it back in time!*

Barely.

"—rs!" the butterfly buzzed as the fifty-two seconds elapsed. Time resumed and Mister Mind came at them again. His feeding tube opened wide.

"Oh yeah!" Booster said, shouldering the weapon. "Take a byte out of this!"

He fired the self-propelled missile right up the giant insect's proboscis. Packed with lethal nanotech, C.O.M.P.U.T.O. (short for Cyber-cerebral Overlapping Multiprocessor Transceiver-Operator) delivered its lethal payload directly into Mister Mind's central nervous system. The butterfly screeched in shock as the unleashed nanites short-circuited his motor functions. His wings fluttered erratically. His legs and antennae twitched. The compound eyes bled a sticky green ichor. Vomit gushed from his feeding tube.

And he started to shrink. . . .

Mister Mind shed mass and substance. His wingspan contracted. "What have you done to me? My brain is burning!"

How about that? Booster thought. *That bug's not so inde-structible after all.* Keeping on the offensive, he flew at the shrinking butterfly, which now looked small enough to swat. He fired a force blast from his gauntlets, hoping to squash Mister Mind once and for all, but the weakened insect shrugged off the blast anyway. The flapping wings produced a gale that sent Booster tumbling head over heels through the air. *So much for an easy victory,* he realized; apparently even a miniature chronal butterfly was plenty tough. *Figures.*

Rip Hunter's voice came over the earpiece in his cowl. "Booster, get back here. There's no time to lose." Booster hesitated, not wanting to back down, but Hunter persisted. "Believe me, Booster. You can't beat him on your own. Not yet."

"Okay, okay," he gave in. "Here I come."

Returning to the Sphere, he found Hunter, Supernova, and Skeets waiting for him. Lacking the strength to levitate, the repaired robot was clutched between Hunter's hands. "Did you see that?" Booster enthused to the others. "You were right about that weapon. It really did a number on the big bad butterfly out there."

"Thank heaven for small favors," Hunter intoned solemnly. "But this isn't over yet. Don't underestimate a chronal butterfly. He may be diminished, for the moment, but he's still too powerful to be easily overcome. Given a chance, he'll soon be as formidable as ever."

"So what do we do now?" Supernova asked. New to the super-hero biz, he seemed inclined to follow the other men's lead. "Are we out of tricks?"

Hunter shook his head. "That's up to Skeets." He held out the rehabilitated robot. "Skeets' casing was infused with Suspendium while it served as Mister Mind's cocoon. The shell also seems to contain trace elements of a unique golden alloy that I've only previously encountered in one other individual: a time-traveler known as Waverider." He stroked his chin thoughtfully. "I admit I'm not sure how the same substance ended up in Skeets."

"ER, THAT'S KIND OF A GRUESOME STORY," the robot said somewhat sheepishly. "I'D RATHER NOT GET INTO IT."

Hunter didn't press the point. "In any event, I believe that Skeets' shell is the only object in the multiverse capable of containing Mister Mind, at least long enough to dispose of him properly. Unfortunately, we'll have to sacrifice Skeets to do so."

"Sacrifice?" Booster snatched the robot from Hunter's grasp. He cradled him protectively. "Forget that!" *I'm not losing my friend again,* he thought. *Not after I've just got him back.* "There's got to be another solution."

"It's the only way," the Time Master said sadly. "Unless we stop Mister Mind now, the whole multiverse is doomed."

"IT'S ALL RIGHT, MICHAEL," Skeets said. "I'VE SHARED THAT MONSTER'S THOUGHTS. I KNOW WHAT HE'S CAPABLE OF, WHAT HE WILL DO TO RE-ALITY IF HE GETS HIS WAY." Cracks scarred the surface of his metal casing. "IF WE DON'T DO THIS, THERE WON'T BE ANYONE LEFT TO MOURN ME."

Booster felt a king-sized lump in his throat. Lifting his goggles, he wiped a tear from his eye. The robot was more than a just a sidekick; he was Booster's best friend. "You're a brave little toaster, you know that?"

"YOU'RE THE ONE WHO OUGHT TO BE SCARED, SIR," Skeets said with a touch of his old attitude. "ESPE-CIALLY IF YOU HAVE TO MANAGE YOUR CAREER ON YOUR OWN FROM NOW ON." His optical sensors flashed cheekily. "EVERYONE KNOWS THAT I'M THE BRAINS OF THE OPERATION."

Booster cracked a smile. "Hey, if it wasn't for me, you'd still be a glorified burglar alarm at the Space Museum." He reluctantly handed Skeets back to Hunter. "Okay, Rip. It's your play. What do we do now?"

Hunter produced a laser scalpel from a tool kit. "First we slice him in half."

* * *

By now, Mister Mind was the size of an ordinary Terran butterfly. His iridescent wings were frayed and tattered, but still intact, as he fluttered along the timestream, getting safely clear of World War III. The distinctive markings on his wings now resembled a much smaller pair of spectacles.

"Ignorant primates!" the imago cursed Booster Gold and Supernova as the two heroes flew toward their foe. "Your kind should have never evolved. Once I have regained my strength, I will devour your entire phylum. The multiverse will belong to invertebrates alone!"

Wanna bet? Booster thought. He darted to the right of the malevolent butterfly, while Supernova went left, clutching both halves of Skeets' severed shell. Booster had been both pleased and chagrined to discover that his ancestor had also been a washed-up ex-football champion in his day. He gambled that Mister Mind was too much of an intellectual to recognize a Hail Mary play when he saw one. "If I were you, I wouldn't brag about being spineless!"

He charged at the butterfly, then reversed direction at the last minute, confusing his foe. There was an intense flash of light as Supernova teleported himself directly behind the distracted insect. He slammed the two halves of Skeets together, trapping the chronal butterfly inside his former cocoon. A powerful adhesive, procured by Rip Hunter during his travels, sealed the pieces together. "Got you!" Daniel exclaimed.

But just catching Mister Mind in the shell wasn't enough. Already the golden carapace was shaking like a Mexican jumping bean as the imprisoned butterfly tried to break free. Supernova struggled to hold on to the squirming ovoid as he drew back his arm, getting ready to throw the ultimate forward pass. A wormhole opened up in front of him.

"Go long!" he shouted.

He snapped the bomb, sending it hurling down the timestream. According to Hunter, they needed the cocoon to build up enough reverse chronal energy to devolve Mister Mind back into his larval form. That meant throwing it back in time at least a year.

Booster poured on the speed, diving through the wormhole just ahead of the cocoon. As he flew backward through the last fifty-two weeks, images from Mister Mind's own timeline flashed past him:

The firefight in the Fortress of Solitude.

Toppling the bottle city of Kandor.

Trapping Daniel in that time-loop.

Chatting with Clark Kent at Booster Gold's funeral.

Watching Booster "die" when the nuclear submarine exploded.

Booster's exposure as a fraud.

The faked fight with "Manthrax."

Finding Rip Hunter's desert hideout.

Almost getting Booster killed by that falling jet.

Beaming inside Skeets for the first time.

Spotting the robot—the perfect cocoon—on Doctor Sivana's TV set.

Looks like the end zone to me, Booster decided, as Fawcett City appeared before him. Booster touched down on the roof of Sivana's hidden laboratory, which he had previously visited as Supernova. He remembered the empty cocoon he had found on that previous expedition, and kicked himself for not figuring out then that Mister Mind was the real menace all along. Looking upward, he spotted the golden shell arcing toward him. He stepped backward, his eyes on the ball. His hands sweated inside his gloves. *Don't fumble this play,* he told himself nervously. *The whole game depends on it.*

The falling orb smacked into his open palms. He caught onto it and didn't let go.

Yes! he cheered himself. *Touchdown!*

He spiked the robot into the rooftop—and a tremendous burst of chronal energy flung him away from Fawcett City, all by himself. *The butterfly!* he thought frantically, losing track of the metal cocoon. *What happened to Mister Mind?*

* * *

WEEK One.

The tiny green caterpillar found himself trapped inside a clear plastic cylinder, about the size of a Quaker Oats container. A lamp installed in the container's lid bathed the captured larva in an unearthly blue light. The Suspendium radiation stimulated the caterpillar's stalled metabolism, marking the beginning of a long metamorphosis.

No! Mister Mind realized. *I'm right back where I started!*

Doctor Sivana's hideous face, thousands of times larger than that of his minuscule specimen, peered through the transparent walls of the container. He flashed a bucktoothed grin. "Science *always* trumps magic. Isn't that right, my little friend?"

No more than three inches long, Mister Mind wriggled helplessly inside the tube. He knew what was going to happen next—and how it would all turn out in the end.

It's not fair, he thought. *I was going to consume the universe!*

"So that's it?" Supernova asked. "He's stuck in a time-loop, just like I was?"

"Exactly," Rip Hunter explained, manning the controls of the Time-Sphere. "He'll keep reliving the same fifty-two weeks, over and over again. Always suffering the same defeat in the end."

"Thanks to us," Booster said, with a bitter edge to his voice. After the chronal explosion, he had found himself back in his own past, where the Time-Sphere easily located him. Now they cruised through the multiverse en route to the present.

Hunter turned toward his passengers. "You realize, of course, that no one can ever know what just transpired. The secret of the multiverse, that there are now fifty-two parallel universes, is too dangerous to let fall into the wrong hands. Especially for the core Earth, Earth-One. The stability of the entire multiverse is intrinsically linked to our Earth, making it a prime target for every evil force in creation if they ever discover how important it is." He eyed them both suspiciously, as if wondering whether he could truly trust them to keep their mouths shut. "Before I return you to your own Earth, you both have to swear to me that you will *never* divulge the true meaning of fifty-two."

Booster scowled. "That sucks, big-time. The whole freaking ball of wax gets saved from certain destruction and no one will ever know about it? Or who the real hero was?"

"It's not about fame or glory, Booster." Hunter frowned at Booster, obviously disappointed in the other man. "I thought you understood that by now. We saved the multiverse. So what if you can't take credit for it?"

"I'm not talking about *me*," Booster said passionately. "I'm talking about *Skeets*. He sacrificed himself for all of us. People ought to know that."

"We know, Booster." Supernova laid a hand on his descendant's shoulder. "That will have to be enough."

"Maybe. Maybe not." Rip Hunter smiled enigmatically. He extracted a tiny crystalline wafer from his pocket. "I hung on to this memory chip when I put Skeets back together. It won't be easy, but I might be able to reconstruct his artificial intelligence eventually."

"You bet you will!" Booster said, feeling a renewed sense of hope. One way or another, he was going to get his friend back again. "I guess we really did win one for the chipper!"

Supernova groaned. "Maybe you'd better let me handle the jokes from now on."

The Time-Sphere slowed to a halt. Metropolis—the real Metropolis—shimmered into view. *This looks like our stop,* Booster thought. Now that Mister Mind had been defeated, and history set right again, he looked forward to showing the whole world that Booster Gold was alive and kicking. He was going to have a rough time rebuilding his reputation, after doing such a thorough job of trashing it, but he felt certain that he could make it to the top once more. *Who knows? Maybe Supernova can put in a good word for me?*

"Welcome home," Rip Hunter said.

GOTHAM CITY.

MALLORY lifted her stethoscope from Kate's chest. "It's better," the doctor conceded. "I still think it's a miracle you're still alive, after what that crazy cult leader did to you." She scowled at the memory of Kate's near-fatal stabbing. "Another half an inch and the blade would have severed your aorta."

"Just lucky, I guess." Kate smiled weakly at the doctor as she leaned against the headboard of her sickbed, propped up by plump feather pillows. The penthouse bedroom bore an uncomfortable resemblance to a hospital room, but it was a distinct improvement from the intensive care unit where she had spent the last four weeks. Painkillers and fresh dressings were stacked atop the bed stand.

Luck and a convenient sheet of pseudoderm, Renee thought, standing by the door. Thank goodness it had occurred to her to use the adhesive Question mask to patch up the gaping knife wound in Kate's chest. The improvised skin graft had held long enough for the paramedics to arrive once Renee had dialed 911 on her cell phone. To her relief, the EMTs had gotten to the desecrated cathedral in record time.

"Well, take it easy," Mallory insisted as she put away her stethoscope. "No more late-night costume parties for you." Like the paramedics, the doctor seemed to have bought Renee's spur-of-the-moment explanation for Kate's shredded Batwoman outfit. Said excuse was made more credible by the fact that sexy Batwoman costumes were apparently a hot item at novelty stores throughout Gotham. "I'm prescribing several months of serious bed rest."

Renee showed Mallory to the door. "Thanks again for the house call," she said sincerely. The pert blonde physician no longer provoked a jealous response from Renee. She and Kate were way beyond that now. "I'll take good care of her."

Returning to Kate's room, she found the restless patient sitting up at the edge of the bed. "Whoa there. You heard what the doctor said. You've got to stay off your feet."

"But I'm already going stir-crazy," Kate protested. She tried to stand up, only to wince in pain. Frustrated, she reluctantly returned to bed. She glowered at the bandages on her chest. "Guess Gotham's going to have to do without Batwoman for a while."

"Don't worry about that," Renee said. "Nightwing dropped by the other night to check on you. He told me that the Bat is back, bigger and badder than ever."

"Good to know," Kate admitted, relaxing a little. "But don't count me out yet." Her lovely face held a stubborn look. "This city hasn't seen the last of Batwoman."

"That doesn't surprise me one bit."

One of these days, Renee thought, *I'm going to find out how you became Batwoman, and why it's so important to you.* She respected Kate's reticence on the subject, but only so far. *I've got to admit I'm curious.*

Just like Charlie.

Tucked away inside her belt buckle, the faceless mask of the Question waited patiently. Tot had sent her a fresh supply, direct from Nanda Parbat. Renee had not hid her own face beneath the concealing pseudoderm since that night beneath the cathedral, but there were still plenty of questions out there waiting to be answered. Like, who would take over Intergang now that Boss Mannheim was dead? Where had Whisper and Abbot disappeared to? And what had become of Black Adam? Renee fully intended to find those answers someday. For now, though, she knew where she belonged.

"I'm here for you," she promised Kate. "I'm not going anywhere."

It looked like a beautiful evening outside, so she drew back the curtains and opened the window to let the warm spring air in. The Bat-Signal—the real one—shone in the night sky like a second moon, letting the entire city know that its legendary Dark Knight had returned. Rumor had it that Superman and Wonder Woman had also been spotted in Metropolis and Washington, D.C., respectively.

Sounds like the world's in good hands, she reflected. For a second, she yearned for a cigarette, but the craving swiftly passed. The booze and smokes and one-night stands were in her past now. After a long and arduous year, things were finally looking up once more.

It was about time.

ABOUT THE AUTHOR

GREG COX is the author of three other DC Comics novelizations: *Infinite Crisis*, *Countdown*, and *Final Crisis*. He has also written the official movie novelizations of such films as *Daredevil*, *Death Defying Acts*, *Ghost Rider*, *Underworld*, *Underworld: Evolution*, and *Underworld: Rise of the Lycans*. In addition, he has authored books and short stories based on such popular series as *Alias*, *Batman*, *Buffy the Vampire Slayer*, *CSI*, *Fantastic Four*, *Farscape*, *The 4400*, *The Green Hornet*, *Iron Man*, *The Phantom*, *Roswell*, *Spider-Man*, *Star Trek*, *Terminator*, *Xena: Warrior Princess*, *X-Men*, and *Zorro*.

He lives in Oxford, Pennsylvania. His official website is www.gregcox-author.com.